Dogs and GODDESSES

Linda Segall Anable

For Mother Earth, the best planet in the universe...

DOGS AND GODDESSES

1
JANEY

Earbuds jammed four millimeters from her brain, Janey cranked up "The Promised Land" until all ambient noise went away, including the motorcycle speeding down Erwin Street at five in the morning. Rosalita trotted freely beside her; at this hour there were no animal controllers slapping citations on innocent dogs not slavishly chained to their owners.

Bruce Springsteen provided the soundtrack for Janey's life. No matter what her mood, his music profoundly suited it. He provided inspiration, validation and this morning, on their walk to Victory Park, medication. By the time they reached their sanctuary, Jane's gloom had almost lifted.

Her nose twitching at bunny velocity, Rosie inhaled the fragrant premises, clearly enjoying the outing as much as Janey. Both cherished this precious hour in the half-light, where in pools of flashlight, Janey and her beloved terrier played the highly underrated game of fetch. Like Bruce, Rosie was a love with no downside.

Victory Park was a square block, tree-filled oasis in the East San Fernando Valley; freeway close and a five-minute walk from Janey's house. It wasn't exactly a dog park, though it was understood to be among the regulars. The modest fifties' tract homes on its border had been upgraded over the years but there were still warts, like the tiny cottage cluttered with silly Grecian statues and oversized electric gates, and the bungalow painted so garishly yellow it could surely be seen from outer space.

The morning was dense with marine layer fog. Janey switched on her flashlight and lofted the tennis ball. Faster than a speeding Border collie, Rosie charged, leaped and caught it in mid-air. "Great catch," Janey exclaimed as Bruce exhorted her to, "blow away the dreams that break your heart."

As Janey heaved the next pitch she heard a voice yell, "Get the fuck out of here!" It was loud enough to drown out Bruce and she yanked out her earphones. Rosie barked and ran toward the shrieker while Janey followed, praying it wasn't who she dreaded it was—Cleo—the most unpleasant woman in Southern California.

Wrapped in a ratty blanket under an oak tree, Cleo looked as if she'd spent the night in the park. Her insecure Springer Spaniel, Trixie, crouched in fear under her arm.

"What are you doing here?" Janey asked, fearing that Cleo might have become homeless and was living in park, marking the end of all future happy hours.

Throwing off the blanket, Cleo unveiled her lumpy physique and yawned. "Did ya see a really gorgeous guy around here, black hair, stubbly beard? Name of Ricky? He fucked my brains out last night, right here by this tree." She got up and shook the twigs and leaves off her blanket.

"Uh, no," Janey replied, because imagining someone having a romantic encounter with Cleo was inconceivable.

"You probably think I have no sex life but I got one now. Big time." She looked around in dark. "Maybe he went to pee or something."

Janey made a note to watch out for desperate men named Ricky on her way home. "Maybe. C'mon, Rosie."

Rosie was busy nosing around in the garland of beer cans and Burger King debris surrounding Cleo, which Janey knew Cleo had no intention of ever picking up. Later, Janey would add it to the other wrappers, balled up tissue and Popsicle sticks, not to mention dog poop left behind by slobs intent on desecrating Rosie's and her park. Janey couldn't have that.

"We met buying Vaseline at the Sav-On," Cleo went on, like they were having some sort of girlfriend moment, "then we made our own Vas-o-line right here under the old oak tree, if you catch my drift."

Her drift imprinted on Janey a permanent and ghastly association with petroleum jelly.

"Bruce Springsteen can't fuck as good as Ricky," Cleo declared matter-of-factly.

Hearing her personal savior's name taken in vain made Janey's swift departure a lot more urgent. The garbage would have to wait. "Rosie," she commanded, "we have to go."

Janey coaxed Rosie away from the trash-fest as Cleo screamed, "Shout if you see Ricky!"

They hadn't gone twenty feet when another woman's voice, unidentified, called out, "Bean! Blossom! Come!" What were these people doing out so early?

At least it wasn't Cleo's alleged Ricky-person.

A beam from Janey's flashlight revealed a beautiful woman with an exorbitant mane of long red hair, barefoot, wearing a white nightgownish dress, who seemed to float when she moved. She was carrying some red liquid in a large Fiji water bottle. Two Labradors, one black and one white, emerged from the mist and bounded over to Rosie. "They're friendly," the woman said.

"Mine too," Janey replied, though it was obvious that Rosie

and the Labs had already sniffed each other out and become close personal friends.

"I'm Lily," the ethereal woman said and held out her hand, which surprised Janey because it was the protocol of the park that dog names were known but not always people names.

Lily's hand felt unusually warm when Janey clasped it. "I'm Janey," she said then pointed. "And that's Rosalita, a.k.a. Rosie."

"Bean," Lily said of the black Lab, "and Blossom. They're brother and sister through adoption."

"Meaning you didn't mate with a Lab?"

Lily laughed at her joke, a requirement for any future relationship, even a sporadic park relationship. "I just moved here," she volunteered, "from Vermont. One of the things that sold me on the house was this park nearby. It's an energy vortex."

"It is? What does that mean?" Janey felt vaguely uneasy that something might be wrong with her park.

"I believe that special people are attracted here who love the Goddess Mother Earth and are helping to restore her health." Lily touched Janey's arm and her touch felt warmer than before. Perhaps she was running a fever and had left her sickbed in the nightgownish dress. "Like you, Janey. You clean up for her."

"How do you know that?"

"You have too many baggies in your pocket for only one dog."

Janey decided that she liked Lily a great deal, that it was perfectly fine if they shared the park together, even during happy hour. They fell into step together flanked by the dogs. "Well, maybe you're a detective but you look more like Madam Marie."

"Who's that?"

"She gives readings on the Asbury Park boardwalk. Bruce

Springsteen made her famous in the song '4th of July, Asbury Park, Sandy.'" She paused. "Sandy's in brackets."

Lily stared at her. "You must be quite a fan to mention the brackets."

"Oh, it goes way beyond the brackets."

"When I was here a couple of years ago I saw him at the Forum. I'll bet you were there."

"There? I was standing in front of the stage! He sweated on my friend Amy and she wiped some on me. I keep the shirt in storage."

"You know," Lily said, "I got a Pleadian vibe from him. Have you ever considered he might be from another planet? The Pleadians are very musical."

On that note Janey reclassified Lily from 18th century waif to spawn of Shirley MacLaine and Timothy Leary. "No, I can't say that I have."

"He has a beautiful soul," Lily understated. "Lots of Pleadians have come here to help us."

Janey conjured images of alternate New Jerseys somewhere in the galaxy. "Well, he's sure helped me," Janey said. "You couldn't get a better guy to save the world. Though I'd settle for him being my gynecologist."

Lily laughed again and Janey enjoyed it again. "What does your husband think about this?" she asked, adding, "I noticed you have a wedding band."

The complexity of being torn between two lovers—one supernaturally idealized and the other a vestige of a man once known as Wild Billy—was daunting. "Let's put it this way," Janey said. "During the reunion tour he spent three of the most exciting hours of my life at the Staples Center reading the biography of Lyndon Johnson with a pen light."

"Wow," said Lily, because what else could she say? "Why did he even go in the first place?"

"Spite. Irrational jealousy. Last week he recorded the Senate hearings on C-SPAN over my VH1 Springsteen special."

"That's intense."

"Boy howdy. I mean, I love Billy—my husband—but I don't see why you can't have unattainable love and real love simultaneously."

"I know all about unattainable love," Lily said, sounding grave.

"Really? Who's unattainable?"

Lily stopped walking. "He's just someone I know who I can never have. It's agony. I know I should let it go but I can't. He's my whole life." She looked distraught. Obviously had it bad for this guy.

"Sorry to hear that," Janey said, hoping to coax her into confession. It didn't take Madam Marie to figure she was having an affair.

"It's about fifty-one percent wonderful and forty-nine percent painful," Lily replied, "so I guess I'm lucky."

"Is he married?" Janey knew it would slip out. "I apologize if that's too personal."

Lily said nothing for a moment as they resumed walking. "It's not that I don't trust you, Janey. I feel like we're already friends. But I can't talk about this."

Janey got the hint. They rounded the north leg of the well-worn path around the park's perimeter and the sky turned a rich periwinkle blue. Janey noticed Cleo walking in the distance, her blanket dragging behind her, still searching for Ricky. "What brought you to LA?" she asked Lily.

"I do healing work with herbs and massage," Lily said. "I've been working on movie sets for years and I met a lot of people in the film business, who mostly live here. After awhile it made sense to relocate."

"Wow, masseuse to the stars." Virtually any woman with an official career made Janey feel inadequate, but a gorgeous healer who might be having an affair with a celebrity was exceptionally intimidating. "I just take care of my family. And not very well."

"Oh, I'm sure that's not true."

"Well, I haven't killed one yet." They neared Cleo's dump site. "But I am good at picking up garbage. And if I don't pick up that pile over there, I won't be able to go on with my day."

"I'll help you," said Lily.

En route Lily suddenly buckled and sank to her knees, clutching her abdomen.

"What's the matter?" Janey asked, alarmed. "Are you okay?"

"Fine," said Lily. "Go on ahead. I'll be right there." She assumed a squatting position and fanned out her gown. All three dogs sniffed at its hem, trying to nose underneath.

"Are you going to be sick? Want a bag?"

"No, it's just my period. It's very heavy."

"Cramps?"

"Not exactly."

Turning away from Lily, Janey snapped open a big plastic bag and got busy clearing up the landfill. When Lily appeared, looking refreshed, Janey smiled.

"I'll tell you an amazing secret if you really want to know," Lily said, plainly reading her mind.

"Do I?"

"Well, you might think it's a little strange."

"I love strange. Tell me."

"I came here to donate my menstrual blood to Mother Earth and bless this park. It's a way that women can deeply communicate with nature. All our DNA is in our blood and Earth reads that and responds back."

Janey wondered why Lily had waited all this time to move to California. "I was wrong. You shouldn't have told me."

"The blueprint of life is in the blood," Lily went on, growing impassioned. "Blood is creation. Men are afraid of the power of blood and women have been taught to suppress that power but the future of humanity is at stake."

While she spoke Janey noticed that Lily's water bottle was empty and that the dogs were intently sniffing the premises. "That stuff you had in the bottle—it wasn't Hawaiian Punch?"

"No, it was blood and clustered spring water with some flower essences to attract loving vibrations. It's giving Mother Earth back some of the food that she gives us." Lily's hands were poised yogi style, as if she were about to burst into meditation. The dogs looked at her like she was their guru. "The dogs understand."

Janey thought of Bruce's words in the song she'd just heard: *The dogs on Main Street howl... 'cause they understand...* She felt slightly disoriented. "You don't use tampons?"

"Sometimes I do and then soak them in water but I like to use a diaphragm to collect it all."

While she tried not to look appalled, grossed out or horrified, though she was all three, Janey reviewed everything she knew about menstruation. "I think periods are The Curse and that P.M.S. stands for Psychotic Mood Swings."

"Periods aren't a curse, Janey. They're power. We need the return of feminine energy a lot more than we need protection from our menses. Giving our menses back to the soil is magical."

If not the strangest thing Janey had ever heard, it was definitely the strangest thing she'd ever heard at 5:30 A.M. She decided to proceed cautiously with this potential friendship, although overlooking her vampirish obsession with blood, Lily was awfully charming. Janey couldn't wait for Solange to meet her. Solange was deeply in touch with the bizarre.

"Look at it this way." Lily went on. "You already have a relationship with the Goddess. You clean her and make her look more beautiful. She's indebted to you for that."

"That's nice," Janey admitted, "but all I want is for everyone to pick up their own crap."

"If you pour your menses around your property, the Goddess will protect you and things will improve with your husband."

Menstrual cheerleading—even for LA, a freaky concept. "It sounds interesting, Lily, but I gotta tell you, the idea just isn't grabbing me. But we can still be friends, right?"

"Of course." Reaching out her arms, Lily hugged her and Janey felt heat shoot through her like a missile. It was an odd but not unpleasant sensation.

The first ray of sun appeared and Janey's magical landscape reverted back to a public park, the perfect time to make a gracious exit. "I've got to get back and start breakfast," she said. "I can hear my family now, banging their knives and forks on the kitchen table."

"I understand," Lily said and smiled.

"Like the dogs understand?" asked Janey.

"Every important thing I know I've learned from dogs," Lily

said. "They understand life a lot better than we do."

Janey gazed at the trio of dogs nosing the area that Lily had anointed. "Well, they sure enjoy a hearty smell."

Again Lily laughed at her joke and Janey decided that if Lily was a vampire, she was a vampire with a good sense of humor. Janey saw no signs of fangs or adverse reaction to the sun. On the contrary, Lily's ivory complexion seemed to attract its finest rays.

2
SOLANGE

Every mirror in the large communal dressing room at Spanky's Cabaret had some minor to major flaw; not fun-house bad, but warped enough to warrant constant griping by the dancers. But Solange had no complaints tonight. Standing naked at her station beneath the unforgiving fluorescent lights, she admired her reflection for the trillionth time. The cheapest mirror in the world couldn't ruin her look today, not from any angle.

"Wanna change my clothes, my hair, my boobs..." she sang, echoing the Bruce Springsteen lyric Janey had sung to her earlier at the park when Janey first beheld the incredible mounds in person.

There was no denying it—Solange had the finest breasts in the western hemisphere. Dr. Rose had performed a miracle—two miracles, to be precise. He must have been Renoir's love child.

Fudgsicle, her cocoa colored, three-year-old Yorkshire terrier, sat up on his silk pillow and looked at her. He was unusually attuned to her moods and she was clearly in a fine one today.

"What do you think, Fudge? Am I a knockout?"

The Yorkie yapped agreeably. Solange picked him up, kissed his silky brown hair and let him poke his face into her cavernous cleavage. "Look, you fit right in." His hair tickled; she had worried that she would lose sensation after the implants were put in, but her boobies were throbbing with life and eager to be seen.

She moved to a three-way mirror to examine her skin tone, the product of long hours under the ultra-violets at the tanning salon. The color was deliciously tropical and looked thrilling against her nipple-length black hair. She felt like an island girl whose breasts defied gravity.

Before she left the house she had given herself a coffee enema. She was having her period, the murderous second day no less, and every ounce of bloat would be on display. Though the process was gross, coffee enemas flattened her stomach and added a nice buzz to her performance. No magic in how she earned such big tips—she was dedicated to her craft.

Sucking in her stomach she analyzed her side view. No one would guess that she was ragging.

A hand cupped her butt. "Can't stop lookin' at 'em, can you?"

Solange squealed, so engrossed in her examination, she didn't notice that Goldie had sneaked up behind her. "Make some noise next time, would you? You scared the shit out of me." Although there was none left in her to scare out.

"Behold the golden arches," Goldie said. "See? Told ya. You should've listened to me a year ago."

Too old to dance anymore, and since February, part-owner of the club after the accidental botulism poisoning of her eighty-year-old husband left her a rich widow, Goldie appointed herself mother hen and tried to stay vicariously involved in her dancers' personal business. Solange ignored most of Goldie's advice on the principle that she was the CEO of her own life, but at that moment Goldie's encouragement was just what she needed to hear. "Really? Do they look natural?"

"Who wants natural?" Goldie squinted as she viewed the newly expanded orbs from every angle. She cupped her hands under her own pendulous breasts. "Personally, I think these old silicone girls give you a better lift but they'll probably kill me one of these days." She cackled a nicotine chortle.

"Peggi and Roxanne haven't said a word to me since I got here."

Goldie waved her hand dismissively. "They're so jealous they're putting sheets on your deathbed." Shaking her head she added, "The back-stabbing around here is getting pathetic. Sure glad I'm not dancing anymore."

For a brief spell Solange worried that a couple of Peggi and Roxanne's steady customers, the ones who never smiled and wore heavy business suits in August, might be hit men. She wondered how many blow jobs and spankings those nasty girls might barter to have her knocked off. It was time to start saving money for art school so Solange could become a famous painter when she retired.

The sight of Fudgsicle, posed on his pillow in maximum adorableness, inspired her. "I'll paint you, sweetie. We'll be rich."

She opened the lock on her trunk and removed her new costume, a bondage-y leather and red lace number that set her back $700 at Trashy Lingerie; no wonder she couldn't afford art school. She slithered into it. Her breasts looked like two giant scoops of coffee ice cream.

Out came the five-inch spiked heels. They were also pricey, but paid for themselves repeatedly with foot fetishist tips; plus, they could be lethal weapons if her life was in danger. Years of practice and Tina Turner videos had transformed Solange into a stiletto master. If necessary, she could run a marathon in them.

Running backstage in her "Girls Just Wanna Have Fun" cheerleader outfit, Peggi screeched to a halt, as though she had just noticed that Solange's breasts had tripled in volume. "Wow, you got your boobs done."

"Thank you for noticing." She did not seek Peggi's opinion since the subject had been gossiped to death from one end of the club to the other and Solange had heard every snarky comment.

"He needs a flea collar," Peggi said and sauntered off as if she'd inflicted pain. Solange almost felt sorry for her; Peggi's attempts at zingers were so pitiful. But the unspoken breast endorsement felt great.

Demanding a walk, Fudgsicle yapped.

"But I don't have time to take you," Solange whined. "We'll go for a nice walk after my show, okay?"

Inside Fudgsicle was a Great Dane. He started to lift his leg.

"No!" Solange screamed. "We'll go now." She was certain he kept a secret reservoir of urine to use as a power tool. She stepped into her shoes, threw on a robe from her trunk, picked him up and headed to the rear exit.

Once outside, Fudgsicle took his time scanning the parking lot.

"Hurry up!" Solange said in vain. "I'm up next."

When he finally wet a corner of the big metal dumpster, she snatched him and hurried back in. She had barely enough time to dash into the bathroom and hastily change her Tampax. Ten minutes later, bathed in lasers and welcomed with hollers, she took the stage to debut her new number, "Pop It," by Moral Vacuum—a tribute to her proud new breasts.

Routinely combing the underground record stores had paid off; she'd found the perfect song to debut tonight. Her body twisted vine-like around the pole; then, as the band sang, "pop it!" her breasts burst from their leather cage in a neat magic trick.

A ticker tape parade of currency flew onto the stage. Solange enjoyed the pendulum action on her chest as she bent down to collect the bills. It seemed more than the drooling oglers at the rail could stand, so she stopped to go cheeks-to-cheek on a lucky man's face. Just to put them all over the edge.

She caught sight of her most devoted fan, the skinny guy in the back with his comatose stare, and blew him a kiss, which was all he ever required. Solange knew how to connect with every man in the audience, to make him feel that she was there for him only, that when he went to the bathroom she'd miss him. The skinny guy might never even know he needed to pee—he looked that mesmerized. But whenever she tried to solicit a lap dance, he'd leave the premises.

She coiled her body around the pole and worked herself up to a dangerous level of passion; so hot she could no longer bear the smothering heat of her scanty outfit.

"Pop it!" sang Moral Vacuum, and the rest of her drag fell away. The audience whooped; money fluttered. Solange had them by the libido. She ran her fingernails through her heart shaped pussy—when it came to pussies she preferred classic shapes—and turned herself on.

Breathlessly, the crowd awaited relief from its torture, but Solange continued to dance as if all attempts to subdue her fever were futile. From the corner of her eye, she noticed the skinny guy stroking himself under the table. That was a first. It got her so excited, she gave herself an orgasm at the climax of her performance, letting the audience decide if was real or fake.

After her number, Solange disappeared behind the curtain and, moments later, returned in a day-glo, rainbow hued tie-dyed bustier with shreds and rips that offered peeks of her tan skin. Black lights flashed—the room became the late sixties for her signature number, "Light My Fire."

At its crescendo, Solange ripped off her G-string and thrust her butt into the sea of faces. A few unusual hoots stood out amid the sound-wall of adoration. She went on alert, prepared to nail Peggi or Roxanne in some subversive prank until she caught a glimpse of the skinny guy's stricken face. He was looking at her crotch like there was something wrong with it. Solange's hand slid between her thighs and felt the little white string. It was sticking out at least an inch, burning violet under the black lights. Deftly, she shoved it back inside while appearing in the throes of a libidinal surge.

The strobes came up for the finale and she saw the skinny guy staring open-mouthed in silent movie motion. Finally, her song ended. Flaunting a beauty pageant smile, she gathered her cash and hurried off stage.

In less than a minute she returned in a white iridescent bikini and set off to work the crowd, kissing certain men on the cheek, toying with others. Breasts shining like big white headlights, she ambled over to the skinny guy.

"Hey, you're not hiding from me, are you?" She touched his

cheek and he reacted as if he'd felt a bolt of radiation.

"No, I'm not hiding. I'm right here." Clever repartee was obviously not his strong suit.

"Wanna buy me a Diet Coke?" The club was a totally nude establishment; it could not serve alcohol.

"Okay." He waved over a waitress and ordered two Cokes, one regular. That was good; he needed every calorie he could get. Maybe the sugar would help him be more talkative.

She watched his face contort, trying to muster up some conversation. Finally, he mumbled, "You're a good dancer."

"Thanks. I've noticed you watching me."

He looked whiter than a glass of milk. When she reached over to touch his hand, he jammed it into his pocket and pulled out a thick glob of currency. "Might as well take it all," he said, pushing a serious wad of dough in her direction.

"Thanks, honey. What's your name?"

"My name?" He appeared startled. "Marvin."

"Can I interest you in a lap dance, Marvin?" She grazed his cheek with the back of her hand. "No extra charge."

He looked incredulous, as if she had a third eye. The Cokes arrived and he seemed grateful for a new activity, something he could handle. He took a healthy slug. "What do I have to do?"

"Are you a cop?" She didn't think so, but had to ask.

Marvin blanched. No doubt it was the rare person who sized up his puny countenance and thought: officer of the law. "No, no, I do...research."

"That sounds very exciting." She wondered what kind of research could be that lucrative. "Come on, Marvin," she said, taking his hand. "Let me do some research on you."

During the short distance to the private booths, Marvin pulled away. "I have to go," he said. Solange watched him awkwardly weave through patrons and strippers like a fleeing suspect.

***

"I've got a present for you," said Goldie, stopping by Solange's station while she was getting dressed. The smug expression on her face made Solange wary.

"What is it?"

"Ta da!" With a dramatic flourish, Goldie plopped down a box of Instead feminine protection on Solange's countertop. "They're little cups. No strings attached. You put 'em in like a diaphragm—lucky you don't need that stuff. Anyway, you can't see any trace of 'em on stage without an X-ray machine." She tapped the box. "And, I might add, they're off the market. Discontinued. These are contraband."

Her face hot with humiliation, Solange shoved the box aside. "I was in a rush. It must have worked itself out while I was dancing. Go ahead and fine me."

"Hey, don't come down on me, honey. I'm just letting you know that modern technology has come up with a way to show pussy on stage while you're on the rag."

"Thanks," Solange said.

Goldie made a clucking sound and walked away.

No doubt the story was all over the club by now. As Solange stuffed the Instead box in her purse, she saw Fudgsicle gazing up at her, fanning his tail. "This is your fault," she said. "You made me late." The tail went limp. Solange picked him up and held him under her chin. "I'm sorry, sweetie. You didn't know. Mama's just embarrassed, that's all."

When she finished dressing, she did another evaluation in the mirror. Her new tits strained against her tee shirt—flaunting

23

became her. She locked her trunk, attached Fudgie's leash to his rhinestone collar and strode grandly into the club.

A pod of dancers gave her rolling eyeballs and suppressed giggles as she passed. She wished it had to do with her breasts but they were already old news. It was the stupid string they were snickering about. She wished she had the nerve to tell them to go fuck themselves. Instead, she said it under her breath.

Her fearless Yorkie growled at the lookieloos, which gave her a boost. At the door, she saw a smarmy grin on Keith the bouncer that annoyed her. Normally, he had all the charm of a funeral director.

"Have a good evening," he said cheerily, making her want to throw up. Her errant tampon would soon be a legend, part of strip club folklore.

Solange pulled a tampon out of her purse and handed it to him. "Souvenir for ya. Stick it in whatever hole you like."

3
LILY

Bean and Blossom barked as though a battalion of squirrels was at the door, vying to be first one to greet Gary. When Lily opened the door they nearly knocked her down to get to him.

Quickly handing off a huge bouquet of pink lilies, Gary hit the floor and let the dogs cover him with affectionate slobber while he called out their names and howled in a key that exacerbated their inane behavior. There could be no doubt—he spoke Dog.

It was far too wonderful, advanced wonderful, couldn't get any better and he'd only been there fifteen seconds. To keep from becoming overly stimulated, Lily transported herself to a peaceful pond and let a bit of excess joy leach out into the calm water. "What is it about you?" she asked in the most lighthearted tone she could fake. "Are they starstruck or do you smell like liver?"

Gary cleared away the dogs and got up. "Dogs understand me." He looked around briefly. "Welcome to California. Nifty house." He held out his arms for a hug.

Lily seized any opportunity to make body contact with Gary, not only because he felt so good but also to be closer to the sublime vapors pouring from his golden skin. The dogs crowded them, seeking their own intimacy. Clearly, Gary had the most powerful pheromones in Hollywood—and Doggywood.

So monumental was Gary's consecration of her new home, she'd needed acupuncture to balance her meridians. That he drove there himself surely meant that she mattered in his life. She was careful never to be flirtatious, even though she had access to his body—the only woman who did. Lily knew him in ways that no one else could, not even a lover. His body spoke to her. It revealed its emotions.

His seduction of her began seven years ago when she saw his film debut in *The Trial of Doctor Ben*. Her heart scampered down the aisle when he kissed Chloe Hammond in Times Square and mist collected on his long, black eyelashes. When Lily was hired as the on-set masseuse for his next picture, *Battles in Darkness*, filmed in upstate New York, her life peaked.

Her first touch of him, on the upper back, brought her to the brink of tears. Once she'd overcome the swooning, she switched on her finger jets and flooded him with love. The massage, at that time her personal best, led to a professional and personal friendship that filled Lily with prodigious happiness and quiet despair.

"Thank you for the gorgeous flowers," she said when the hug ended. "You look wonderful." And you smell like a heavenly god. "But you're so thin."

With a thumb in his pants, Gary indicated the lost inches. "I'm on the tabloid diet. Juicy scandals three times a day."

Lily didn't mention that she'd read the sordid stories in the checkout line and didn't believe one lying word. "I'll make you some anti-tabloid tea. Can you stay for dinner?"

"Glad you asked. I was going to sit at the table and wait."

Lily jumped up and down inside while her outer facade laughed. She took Gary's hand and led him into the kitchen, an expansive white space with a three-foot wide skylight that provided sunny access to dozens of potted botanicals. The counters were filled with jars of dried herbs and colorful liquids that made the room look like a turn-of-the-century apothecary, save for the six blenders, four Cuisinarts and the trio of stainless steel refrigerators that stored ingredients used to make her customized herbal blends.

"Let's start with a nice calmative drink, then we'll cast out your demons and eat."

Gary shook his head. "The demon part might take awhile."

"Speaking of demons, did your boarder move out?" Lily had vowed never to mention the woman's name.

"Yes, but she left the cat condo and dead plants."

Trish Foley was a high school friend of Gary's from Kankakee, Illinois who had shamelessly used him to gain a foothold in Hollywood. When she lied that she'd been his high school sweetheart, he let her get away with it. He squired her to functions, even let her live in the guest house of his Benedict Canyon home while her career percolated. Apparently that wasn't enough—she wanted him to marry her. He turned her down; she accused him of emotional abuse.

When a picture of Gary and basketball star Wade Collins passionately kissing on a hotel balcony in Rome appeared in *The Star* it was open season on Gary's sex life. Desperate to keep the façade going, Trish tried to claim that Gary had forced her to abort their child. He threatened to sue; she caved in but her career suffered severe karmic damage.

Lily once met Trish at Gary's house when she was there giving him a massage. Her obvious desperation challenged Lily's capacity for empathy though she clearly understood how unrequited love for Gary could drive a woman insane.

"Did you warn me about her?" Gary asked as he watched Lily combine the ingredients for the mystical potion: green tea, clover honey, asafoetida, garlic, olive oil and cayenne. "If not, why didn't you?"

"I'm sorry, Gary. I didn't think it was my place." Lily hoped that in a previous lifetime she'd gone ten rounds with the selfish bitch.

"It's a side of beef for the tabloids now."

With a whir of the blender, the golden liquid swirled to a smooth consistency. Lily poured two tall glasses and handed him one. "This will fix you right up."

"What's in it?"

"Trade secret."

"It's not Dr. Kervorkian punch, is it? Because that would be okay. I just want to know so I can call my sister."

Lily took a substantial swig and held the glass over her heart.

"Did you see that? A bat came out of my nose."

"I did." Gary picked up his glass and clinked it against Lily's. "Cheers." Then he took a slug and stopped breathing for a few seconds. "Jesus H. Goldberg! You didn't tell me it was radioactive! Holy shit!" He stomped his foot on the ground like a horse counting to five.

Lily laughed so hard she came down with hiccups, which made Gary laugh. Like pot-smoking hyenas they giggled, alternating with gulps of their drinks. Then the energy shifted. Gary seemed drained of energy, as if he'd exhausted his monthly allotment of joy.

"Want to talk some more?" Lily asked.

Gary nodded. "Yes, ma'am." He stood up. "But I need to lie on your couch."

They went to the living room. With Gary occupying her overstuffed sofa the world was a better place. She plopped a pillow on the floor and sat next to him.

"Her mother was always so nice to me." He sighed. "I felt obligated to help her."

What an unbearably sweet man, Lily thought as she fought the urge to leap on top of him and smother his pain. "It's just life lessons, Gary. That's why we're on this planet. You only have to worry if you stop learning. No one graduates from Earth school alive."

Gary reached for his empty glass and held his arm up like Frankenstein. "May I have some more brake fluid, please?"

"Coming right up." Lily picked up both glasses and took them to the kitchen. She felt an energy spiral travel up and down her body and knew it came from the recipe she'd channeled for Gary's visit. Pouring another round, she thought the Goddess ought to have a cooking show.

By the time they went into the massage room, Gary seemed well on his way to mellow-dom.

"Wow, this is beautiful," he said. "I'll be spending lots of time in here."

Lily let herself imagine that for a few glorious moments. It was a magnificent room. Orchid colored walls, soft floral sheets on the massage table and fresh-cut flowers echoed the garden outside the French doors. The garden was why she'd bought the house. The day she moved in she'd planted it in a euphoric frenzy. It was where all her blood-fertilized ingredients would grow.

Letting Gary undress, Lily left the room and saw Bean and Blossom standing by the door. She bent down and whispered to them, "Big night, puppies. Really, really big night."

The dogs smiled and wagged their tails. As soon as Lily went back in and closed the door behind her, she saw their noses wedge under the crack and let out big twin exhales.

When Lily reentered, the wind chimes were tinkling though there was no discernible breeze in the room. She poured lavender oil into her palm, rubbed her hands together and drew out the healing energy. When she touched Gary's shoulders, she felt an electric current and for a moment, pulled back. In the dimness, she saw rich blue light seeping from his body.

"I need to touch you," he murmured. "Now."

She knew what he was saying but dared not presume. "Gary..."

"Lily..." He turned over and looked up at her. Their eyes united for a brief eternity as their frequencies combined. Volumes were unspoken. Lily heard the dogs resume their lament but paid no attention. Outside, a mockingbird repeated a long and complex melody.

"Where?" he whispered.

"Outside."

He wrapped his arm around her shoulders and she guided him off the table. There was a quilted blanket folded on a rocking chair; she draped it around him. He was burning.

The dogs howled. Lily went back, opened the door to the treatment room and allowed them in. They were instantly quiet and laid down in the doorway where they had an outside view. They just needed to see her.

Gary opened the blanket and took her into it. They stepped into the garden and walked on a stone path, pausing on a patch of grass next to the irises. Taking Gary's hand, Lily placed it on her heart to let him feel the pounding. She ran her fingers through the coarse, dark hair on his chest then glided her hands down his body, finding the soft thicket below. She traced the high angle of his phallus and held it in her hand.

Gary swallowed hard and Lily saw his eyes were wet. They drifted together in a kiss and their spirits danced on waves of light. No words were spoken. The night air conducted music from their souls.

When their lips finally parted, Lily stretched and rolled her head back. Gary smothered his mouth on her neck and began to remove her light cotton dress. She sensed his exhilaration at the newness of the experience; he kissed and fondled the cloth as it passed his face. When she was naked, he stared, then took her face to his for a kiss.

His need to know her felt overpowering. She telepathed what she was about to do to prepare him and his instant reception produced in her a sweet cramp of pain. Reaching inside she withdrew her diaphragm. In the center was a small pool of blood. He watched as she poured the liquid blessing into the ground and set the receptacle on the grass. She held up her hand to him and he suckled her fingers. She smiled.

Sinking to the grass, she reached out to touch the profusion of auras surrounding him while he covered her with his body. Lily sensed the presence of loving entities lacing the atmosphere with angelic blessings from the Goddess.

When Gary entered her time collapsed. She felt the powerful exchange of knowledge as blood and semen combined in an explosion of information from their merged DNA. In a single moment they knew each other on every level, in all time, throughout eternity.

This must be how the first man and woman made love, Lily thought, taught by instinct, guided by the sacred joining of souls. At the height of their great concerto, the charge of his elixir made her own climax explode with joy that approached divinity.

If she had entered an alternate reality, then she chose to remain there forever.

Gary's eyelids drooped and Lily suggested they go inside. She bundled him in the blanket and led him to her bed, where he flopped down like a child carried home past his bedtime. Then he opened his eyes.

"I love you, Lily." Husband-like he kissed her cheek—then fell instantly asleep.

The words remained suspended in the passion-drenched air.

"I love you, Gary," she whispered. Then she went to the bathroom and let the magical fluid they'd created drip into her watering can. Tiptoeing outside, she poured it onto the exact spot where the miracle occurred.

4
JANEY

Over the din of the vacuum cleaner, louder than Rosie's ferocious barks at the enemy appliance, Janey heard Billy shouting her name. She turned to see him wince in pain, make the channel-changing gesture with his thumb and adjust his position on the couch. Firing off a string of epithets heard by no one, she took the remote control from beneath the coffee table and handed it to him. Next time, she'd tie it around his neck.

Billy deposited the device between his knees in the fold of his Navajo Indian blanket. "Can't you do that some other time?"

"You mean when you're not here?" He'd been parked on the couch for several weeks with a ridiculous back malady that seemed to kick in after work and on weekends but mysteriously abated for bathroom breaks and hobbling outside to smoke a joint. "How about if I come back in October?" The remark set her off on a sweet fantasy. Would anyone die of neglect if she were gone for six months?

"Can't you at least make it quieter?" With another hand signal he motioned her away from his obstructed view of the History Channel.

"Vacuums are noisy, Billy. It's one of those bitter realities that tidy folks have to endure."

"Don't we have a carpet sweeper in the garage?"

"Yeah, we probably have a butter churn in there too, but I don't have a week to go searching for it."

The defiant silence that followed was punctured by the sound of Janey's email chime. Most likely, it was a BOSS post: Babes Organized in Support of Springsteen—her female-only email list where Bruce-obsessed women from twelve different countries gushed X-ratedly over their mutual object of adoration.

"Uh oh," Billy said. "Bruce just took a dump." Unlike many boyfriends and husbands of BOSS women, Billy was not a VTM: Very Tolerant Male.

Hostile fumes stunk up the room. Ever the peacemaker, Rosie approached Billy and licked his hand.

He pushed her away and wiped the saliva on his shabby security blanket. "You know, the house would be a lot cleaner without your goddamn dog."

Janey fought the urge to vacuum him up. Uncontrollable suction, she would tell the court. "Fine, if you want to wallow in dirt, that's one less thing for me to do."

"Good. Leave me alone." He turned the TV volume up high and wedged the remote between his back and the couch.

Janey reached in, boldly fished it out and lowered the sound back to a normal plane.

The barometer of family disputes, Rosie cowered under the coffee table. Janey kneeled and gave her a hug. "It's okay, sweetie," she lied. "We're not arguing."

"What's going on down there?" Eleanor's voice cackled from her bedroom upstairs.

"Nothing, Grandma!" Billy shouted back. "Everything's fine." Janey found it odd that he could sound so cheerful while never breaking his glare.

"I heard yelling!"

"Turn down your hearing aid!"

Janey came to her own rescue. "Hey, Rosie! Wanna go to the park?"

Rosie shot out from under the table and ran in circles, pausing to give Janey ecstatic flea-bites while she attached the leash. Why couldn't cranky humans have temperaments like dogs, so easily converted from despair to nirvana? They ought to be in charge of the world. "Want to run for president?" she asked Rosie.

Rosie barked.

Janey was relieved to find the park deserted since she hadn't stopped to change out of her cleaning clothes. The elastic on her yellow sweat pants was gone at the ankles and her 1984 *Born in the USA* tee shirt was marred by ugly grease marks. Soon she would be faced with the heart-wrenching chore of sending an old tour shirt into the trash, where it would be forced to mingle with real trash.

Growing up, Janey endured the annoying and unoriginal label "Plain Jane," until she heard Bruce Springsteen's first album, *Greetings From Asbury Park*, NJ at age sixteen and changed her name to "Crazy Janey," after the character in "Spirit in the Night." The following year she met William West, a diehard surfer whose nickname was Wet Willy.

Willy was not remotely into Bruce; the wildest music he ever listened to was The Beach Boys—the earlier, less sophisticated records. But he was madly in love with Janey and agreed to become "Wild Billy" of the same song. After all, Janey had noted, "Willy West sounds like the direction your dick is pointing." It was enough rationale for Billy at the time and they married straight out of high school, like working class heroes in a Springsteen song.

Janey fantasized about moving to New Jersey and slaving in a factory, but Billy hated cold winters and did not aspire to blue collar martyrdom. After a honeymoon in Asbury Park, she stayed true to her proletariat ambitions and helped put Billy through UCLA waiting tables at Hamburger Hamlet.

When children failed to materialize right away, Billy went surfing and Janey went to thirty-four Bruce Springsteen concerts, carpooling with fellow devotees to half the cities listed on her tee shirts.

Between the *Born in the USA* and *Tunnel of Love* tours, Janey became pregnant with a girl and yearned for a name from Springsteen songdom. There were so many to choose from but Billy vetoed every candidate. It wasn't that he was fighting for a name he liked; he just objected to the Bruce-related criteria. The baby came and had no name for a long, cold month.

Then Billy lost the bet that he could go a full week without getting stoned, or as it turned out, at least not get caught. The baby was named for "Candy's Room," from *Darkness on the Edge of Town*.

The following year, when Janey was again pregnant with a girl, Billy, too mellow to care, relinquished his vote. The new baby's name came from "Sherry Darling," the lighthearted ditty from *The River*.

Janey had hoped that her girls' special names would ensure that they grew up to be faithful Springsteen devotees but as it turned out, despite all the anguish, neither Candi nor Sherri cared one hemi-powered engine about Bruce Springsteen.

***

Janey let Rosie off the leash and watched as she raced over to Carlos and his pit bull mix, Hercules. Carlos waved and she felt like a trapped bag lady, the bloaty water retention from her period adding to her slovenly image. She walked toward Carlos, wondering if she was stepping on sacred ground consecrated by Lily's menstrual blood. She hadn't dared reveal that she had a working Tampax on when they'd met.

"No school today?" Janey asked. With his thick, dark hair slicked back in a pompadour, Carlos looked like a fifties rock star. Janey felt maternal concern that he spent more time at the park than he did studying.

"I was there for awhile," said Carlos. "I went to history class. Mr. West gave us a lot of homework."

Janey saw an opportunity for some innocent probing. "Do you think he's a good teacher? Be honest."

"Yeah, he's alright."

"He has a back problem, you know. He won't talk about it, but I'm curious...do you think he's straining himself?"

Carlos shrugged. "I shot some hoops with him last week. He seemed okay to me."

"Well," said Janey, biting her lip, "he's very courageous."

***

Janey and Rosie walked in at the same moment Eleanor was coming down the stairs in an ornate, sequined ball gown and a pound of her finest jewelry.

"Keep that dog away from me," Eleanor warned. "This dress cost over a thousand dollars." She stopped to review herself in the mirror and seemed pleased with her ensemble. "What time is it?" she asked Janey.

"It's a little past three."

"Vern is always late. They don't let you sign up if you're not there on time. You drive me."

36

"You can't dance by yourself, Grandma, so you might as well wait," said Janey.

"I don't need him. I can get another partner." She glanced over at Billy. "If he wasn't so lazy, he could be my partner."

Janey made up a list of events that would occur before Billy would become his grandmother's dance partner: cross-country skiing on the 405, elephants in hang gliders, moon plummeting to Earth... "There you go, Billy. A reason to heal."

Billy pasted on a mean smile.

Eleanor looked ready to go several rounds with the lazy slug. "I got no cartilage in my knees," she sneered. "You don't hear me complaining. Take a goddamn aspirin."

Janey enjoyed the sparring but tried not to show it. To keep from smirking, she played Bruce's 1985 stadium tour cover of "War" in her head.

"You wouldn't be dancing if you had a slipped disc, Grandma, I can assure you," Billy said.

"Cut the crap. You're loafing. Get off the damn sofa and take your slipped disc with you."

Billy rose up as if he were going for Eleanor's throat, then fell back. A pathetic groan erupted from some cavernous place inside his chest.

The doorbell rang. Eleanor narrowed her eyes. "That better be him."

Janey opened the door to Eleanor's eighty-year-old prom date Vern, slender and spiffy in a powder blue tuxedo and ruffled shirt. He looked truly delighted and Janey wondered what it was like being designated boy-toy to a 102-year-old partner.

"Where have you been?" Eleanor asked.

Vern grinned. "Shining my shoes for you, my sweet."

"Yeah, well, now we're late."

With a wink at Janey, Vern ushered Eleanor out the door. The ballroom dancing competition would probably last until midnight and Eleanor had the kick-ass stamina of a woman decades younger.

Billy settled back into his nest and in his Pavlovian manner, flipped on the TV.

Janey kneeled down beside him. "Do you really want to watch the Hitler Channel?" she asked coyly, batting her eyelashes like a cheap dancehall girl.

"I was planning to watch the Napoleon documentary."

"The girls aren't home." She tickled his cheek.

"What do you want? I said you could hire gardeners to mow the lawn. I don't feel like getting up."

Janey kissed his pursed lips. "You don't have to get up. Not all of you, anyway." Her hand slipped under the blanket and into his pants. Billy tensed for a moment, then relaxed.

It had been a long time since she'd spontaneously offered her services. As she untied his sweat pants and worked them down to his knees, his penis responded with military posture. Janey moved her fingers across his belly, through his fine, wheat colored pubic hair, and caressed the insides of his thighs.

Billy's groans escalated to incoherent gibberish. That was a good sign. Janey smiled as she took him in her mouth. The noises became more carnal. Clearly, she hadn't lost her touch.

She coaxed Billy to distant boundaries of the pleasure galaxy. The goatish sounds rising from his gut meant he was close. Moving in for the climax, she closed her lips around his yearning cock and sucked hard. Billy screamed and let loose. Janey swallowed the thick hot liquid and held on until his spasms subsided.

"Jesus," he said, when he regained his sense of speech.

"Was that better than Napoleon?"

"It was better than the entire French Revolution."

"Good. Let's fuck." Without question, Billy's most impressive skill was his ability to have sex immediately after ejaculating.

He thought for a moment. "Aren't you still...?"

"It's almost over." Far less appealing was his revulsion about having sex during her period.

She could be sarcastic and ask for a hand job with rubber gloves, but decided to let the matter drop.

Rosie, who had been taught not to interfere during intimate encounters, came by with a fuzzy doll in her mouth and offered it to Billy.

"I thought you got rid of all the toys," he said, annoyance creeping into his après-fellatio good mood.

"It's a stuffed animal. It's harmless."

"Not if I trip and fall on it. She always leaves her shit on the floor. I could end up in traction."

Rosie continued to thrust the doll at Billy, clearly hoping he would fling it across the room.

Janey wrested the toy out of Rosie's mouth and threw it over her head. Rosie went racing after it. "Maybe you should just watch where you're going."

Billy pulled the blanket around him, folded his arms across his chest and descended into fuming.

Mouthing the foulest words she knew, Janey got up. Rosie returned with the doll and Janey grabbed it, using it to lure her out of the room. As the two engaged in a game of tug-of-war, the Battle of Waterloo raged in her living room.

Janey, don't you lose heart, no no no no no... Janey don't you lose heart... The lyrics of her savior played in her head. She would try to remember that.

5
GODDESSES

The dogs stood guard over Gary, whose slumber looked more like hibernation. It was seven A.M. Lily stared at him while she slipped on her dog-walking tee shirt and shorts. She figured she'd gotten around fourteen minutes of sleep, which in her heightened state was about all she could manage.

She decided to let Gary process the events in the uncensored privacy of unconsciousness. In the kitchen she brewed a pot of vanilla coffee and left a note: "Went for a quick walk with the puppies. Back as soon as caninely possible. Coffee is ready. You are wonderful. Love, Lily XOXOX." Then she poured a traveling cup, leashed up the dogs and walked out into the World That Had Changed Forever.

Bean and Blossom seemed satiated with joy as well, prancing through the morning mist like show dogs, looking as if they had finally found a dad.

"You may have witnessed a miracle last night," she confided and on their hopeful look added, "But it's complicated. Let's live in the moment."

As she neared the park she spotted Janey with three other women and their dogs. Two gorgeous women appeared to be lovers and kept trying to fondle each other's breasts while playfully slapping each other's hands away. Based on body language the third woman was a party crasher.

"Hey, it's my new best friend," Janey said and waved Lily over. Janey was wearing a Bruce Springsteen tee shirt.

When Lily unleashed Bean and Blossom, they joined Rosie and a brown Yorkie in a smell-a-thon. The other dog, a frightened looking Springer Spaniel, never strayed from the crasher's side.

"Lily," Janey said, wrapping her arms around the girlfriends, "I'd like you to meet Solange and Joie." She pointed at the Yorkie. "And their son, Fudgsicle."

Lily couldn't take her eyes off the stunning Solange. With her waist-length black hair, olive skin and contest-winner smile, she looked like a Eurasian Tinkerbell. And Joie's blue-gray eyes against coffee-colored skin made her Solange's exotic equal—the pair was a smorgasbord of ethnicity.

"I'm Cleo," said the outsider, stepping in front of Joie and Solange. "Mrs. Springsteen said you were here yesterday morning. Did you see a lost guy walking around?"

"No," said Lily, "I would have remembered that." Aghast at the contamination in Cleo's energy field, Lily pulled herself in.

Scrunching her face like a schoolyard bully, Cleo clapped her hands to her hips and thrust herself at Janey. "You think I made him up, don't you?"

"I didn't say that," Janey said, "I'm sure he's everything you said."

"He's better than everything I said," Cleo countered. "We had supernatural sex."

That she had something so intimate in common with such a foul woman left Lily breathless. She tried not to attach too much meaning to it.

"He could have been a hologram," Janey suggested. "They're all the rage now."

"Holograms don't fuck!" Cleo growled. "You hottie-twatties think it's so fuckin' easy. You look at a dude and he's got a boner."

Joie placed herself between the warring parties and turned her commanding stature toward Cleo. "You need to walk your dog," said Joie, directly in her face.

"Eat shit, pussy-breath." With a yank on the leash, Cleo stomped over to the well-worn path along the park's perimeter, the Spaniel glued to her side.

"She makes her own smog," Janey said.

"I'll bet she's riding the rag," said Joie.

Solange poked her. "Honey, I don't like that term."

Joie acted embarrassed. "Sorry, I meant to say she's having the monthly embrace of her womanhood."

"So am I," said Janey, "but I try to be civil."

"I am too," echoed Solange.

With a shrug Joie added, "Sol and I do everything together."

They all looked to Lily, who broke out in a smile. "Ask Janey. I'm president of this club."

Solange shook her head. "That's so amazing! We're all in sync!"

"We have to stop bleeding like this," said Janey.

"Cleo has got to be on a different cycle," said Joie. "No guy would bang her when she was too wet to plow..."

Solange cringed. "Joie..."

"I mean, while she's woman-stru-a-ting."

"I think Lily should weigh in on this," Janey said. "She's an expert in this field."

"If you have sex with a man while you're bleeding, he becomes a carrier of the Goddess energy," Lily said, "which our planet really, really needs."

"We don't do men," said Joie, "but we have plenty of feminine energy." She grabbed Solange's boob and received an elbow in the ribs.

"You can still donate your menses to the soil," said Lily. "They're a special gift to Mother Earth."

"What?" asked Solange. "Are you serious?"

"I saw her do it yesterday," Janey said. "There was a flash of lightning and a burning bush."

Glad that Janey was talking about it, Lily laughed.

"Awesome," said a wide-eyed Solange, "let's do it right now."

"No!" Joie shrieked. "You wanna get arrested?"

"For being a woman?"

"Jesus, Solange, you are not pulling down your knickers in the park."

Lily became distracted by a black Range Rover that drove halfway onto the sidewalk and parked awkwardly. She panicked when she saw Gary emerge in sunglasses and a Chicago Cubs cap. He looked around, obviously not seeing her, and began walking in the wrong direction. Like rockets, Bean and Blossom dashed over to him, leaped up on his chest and brought him to a halt.

When Lily saw Cleo heading toward Gary, she knew she had to devise a way to rescue him without causing a scene.

"Is that Cleo's boyfriend?" asked Solange, craning for a good look. Cleo had Gary cornered.

Lily's words spewed out like a belch. "Sorry—I gotta go." She took off speedwalking toward Gary. When they made eye contact, his shoulders slumped.

"Excuse us," Lily said to Cleo, who didn't budge, forcing Lily to yank Gary away.

"Lily," Gary said and fell into her, clinging as if she were his missing teddy bear.

His neediness overwhelmed her. "I'm sorry, Gary. It was just a quick trip to the park."

"Don't leave me." He kissed her. It felt desperate.

Google-eyed, mouth ajar, Cleo stared.

***

Janey fell back against the tree to keep from fainting. So that was the guy Lily couldn't talk about—the most famous, most scandalous, most gay superstar in Hollywood, Gary DiCaro? And if Lily had that level of personal magnetism, maybe she could show Janey how to get Bruce Springsteen to come to the park looking for her.

Solange squinted, trying to focus. "I swear to God, that's Gary DiCaro! Isn't it?"

"Sure looks like him," Joie said, stretching her neck for a better view. "I thought he was gay."

"I thought so too," said Solange. "But that doesn't look very gay to me."

***

Lily hustled Gary and the Labs into the Range Rover. She put him in the passenger seat and he immediately dropped his head into her lap. "I had to find you," he said, then explained how he had driven fifteen minutes in an attempt to find the park that was only three blocks away.

"I'm sorry, Gary. I thought you'd be sleeping until we got back."

"I needed to know it wasn't a dream."

Lily pulled the car into her driveway. "I'll make us some breakfast."

"Brake fluid," he moaned into her crotch.

"No brake fluid, I promise. How about eggs fried in motor oil?" She reached for the car door but he swung an arm around her neck and pulled her down for a long, deep kiss that became a tangled orgy when the dogs barged into the front seat and joined them.

Lily screamed and flailed and like a slapstick comedy routine, they all fell out of the car.

Entering the kitchen, Lily sat Gary down at the table and kissed the light veil of warm sweat coating the back of his neck. He arched his head back and their lips met for somewhere between a minute and three hours. Then she poured him a large mug of vanilla coffee.

He stared into it then gazed at her, his face filled with concern. "Anything in here I should know about?"

"Just coffee. I promise." She opened a refrigerator and began selecting breakfast fixings.

"Breakfast can wait. Let's talk." He patted the chair next to him.

She poured herself some coffee and sat down.

"Last night," he said. "That really happened, right?"

Lily nodded.

"I saw colored lights. I haven't seen colored lights since I ate magic mushrooms in Amsterdam fifteen years ago."

"I saw them too. They were all around us. You have an amazing aura." The remembered visual brought on a surge of emotion. She wiped her eyes.

Gary squeezed the back of her head. "Hey, it's okay. I loved it. I just thought maybe it was something in the drink."

"It was an herbal drink. I channeled the recipe."

Gary raised his eyebrows. "You channeled it. From where?"

"The Goddess." His eyebrows continued to dance. "Mother Earth. I asked for something to help you and she responded."

"She talked to you about me?"

"No, it's not like that. I ask for guidance and my intuition tells me her response."

"Did she say it was...safe to be with me? Because in case she didn't, I want you to know that I am normally so paranoid, I take my own lab technician with me on dates."

"I know that, Gary. I wasn't concerned. I just wanted to help you, whatever you needed. I let the universe decide what I should do. Then I don't have to figure out the strategy."

Gary picked up her hand and kissed it. "I envy you your faith. I was born without the spiritual gene."

"Everyone has spirituality."

"Then you're mine."

A whoosh of affirmative energy lit up Lily's body when he said that and Lily felt crazy with emotion.

"This must be what it's like to be born again," said Gary. "I needed that. I've been in need of redemption for a long time." He stroked her hand. "I've got to tell you something."

She braced, didn't know if she could take things getting any more wonderful.

Looking at her the way he did in film close-ups he said, "You're my first. In high school when I dated girls...it was never entirely successful." A deep breath. "Last night was in some other realm. Do you know what I'm saying?"

Moving her eyeballs to keep the watery overflow in check couldn't stop the tears. "I love you, Gary. I loved you before I met you. Don't feel any pressure or obligation. If last night was all we ever have, I'll still be in ecstasy for the rest of my life."

"I love you too, Lily, and I need to be with you. Something changed in me. Even if you don't want me—well that isn't an option. You have to want me."

Lily took a quick excursion to heaven and back—to heaven. "Gary, you've always been number one on my want list."

"Good, then we're together on this."

6
SOLANGE

"Maybe he's one of her massage clients," Solange speculated to Joie as she poured Betty Crocker pancake batter onto the griddle. "And he showed up early but she wasn't there so he drove around and found her at the park and then he started groping and kissing her passionately."

"Not too plausible," said Joie, sitting at the table in their small, sunny kitchen reading a motorcycle magazine. "Maybe he's faking the gay thing to be more famous. Gay's really in."

"Not anymore," said Solange. "It's been so done." Fudgsicle sat at his mama's feet, awaiting a handout or accidental spill. "He's plenty famous," she said. She allowed Fudgsie to lick butter off her fingers then wiped her hands on the long industrial apron she wore over her Bebe suit. "Do you think they're secretly a couple?" She built a five-inch tower of pancakes and presented it to Joie.

Pouring enough syrup on the pancakes to set them afloat, Joie said, "That might explain the hasty getaway, but not the full nelson and lip-lock with the whole park watching."

Solange sat down with a cup of tea and two pieces of whole-wheat toast. "Maybe you could stake out her house in the truck."

"Sure, no one would notice a UPS truck parked in front of their house all day."

"Maybe she works on Scarlett Johansson. I'd bet you'd park your truck there then."

"Yesterday's lunchmeat next to you, honey." Reaching into her pocket, Joie pulled out a little velvet-covered box and slid it in front of Solange. "By the way, I've been meaning to give ya this."

Solange stopped in mid-chew. "What is it?"

"If I wanted you to know right off the bat, I'd just show it to you. Why don't you open it and find out?"

Picking up the box, Solange turned it over a few times. She was afraid to shake it.

"Honey, I gotta get to work. Will you open it already?"

A flip of the lid revealed a two-carat, pear-shaped diamond ring. She gasped. Looked at the huge grin on Joie's face. Put her hand over her heart. "Oh, my God. Joie!"

"Don't worry, I didn't buy it. My great grandma left it to me in her will. And now I've got a use for it. What do you say, honey? Wanna be official domestic partners?"

"I can't believe you're giving this to me."

"Well, you don't get it unless you say yes. Then we can get health benefits and insurance and all that other romantic stuff. What it's all about, right?"

"How about love?" Solange said, fluttering her eyelashes.

"I wouldn't buy insurance for someone I didn't love, would I?"

Solange had never looked at it that way. Even though she made far more money than Joie did, Joie knew what to do with it, which seemed equally important. "Yes! Put it on!"

"Good answer." Joie took the ring out of the box and pushed it onto her finger. It was a little too big. "We'll get it adjusted. Better too big than too small."

"I'm not taking it off. I'll wrap some yarn around the band." She hugged Joie, hoping to quell the unrest in her stomach, which she decided was engagement convulsions.

Joie broke the hold and pretended to be out of breath. "Man, those knockers are dangerous!"

With a giggle Solange lifted her breasts high in the air as she advanced toward the retreating Joie. "That's right. I could smother you with these babies anytime I want, so no parking in front of Lily's house to see what hot tamales are going in there. Got it?"

Joie's hands went up in front of her face. "Yes, my dominatrix. I will obey your every command."

Fudgsicle barked for attention and Solange stopped to pick him up. "Don't worry, Fudgsie. You're still the man of the house."

"Look, he's got a woody," Joie said, pointing.

Sure enough, he did. Nose-to-nose with her virile Yorkie, Solange asked, "Who's Mr. Macho, huh?"

"That would be me," said Joie, bussing her like a suburban hubby heading to work. "See ya later, wife-to-be. Meatloaf tonight, okay?" She cupped her hand over the crotch of her brown UPS Bermuda shorts and bent over to moon Solange before walking out the door.

***

49

Ernie was on duty when Solange and Fudgsicle pulled into the Olive Street gate at Warner Brothers. When the Yorkie stuck his head out the window, Ernie produced a dog biscuit from his pocket. They weren't the most famous celebrities who passed by Ernie's post but they had one of the better perks—Clint Eastwood's former parking space.

Howard Hertzberg was one of the biggest producers in town and a club regular, the kind who came through the private entrance and who often booked Solange for exclusive parties in the back room. For a year now, she had also been his regular Thursday, eleven A.M. studio appointment.

His office was in one of the old buildings that dated back to the days when the actual brothers ruled the kingdom. The floors beneath the carpeted hallways told tales in dialects of creaks and groans, while musty smells in the wood and stucco recalled the ancient glamour of movie stills that lined the walls.

Solange walked the corridors with mogul-like confidence. No one would guess that under her double-breasted gray linen Bebe suit was a hot pink bustier and G-string. Her oversized Prada bag held an ostrich feather boa, whip, dog collar, and for Fudgsicle, bags of rawhide sticks and turkey jerky.

Paulette, Howard's ambitious personal assistant, seemed nervous and edgy when she greeted Fudgsie and Solange.

"Is everything okay?" Solange inquired, always prepared to be a staunch comrade to a sister in need.

"Fine, he's on the phone but it'll only be a minute." She twisted strands of her hair around a pen. "Would you like something to drink?"

"I'd love some iced tea, thanks. And a c-o-o-k-i-e for Fudgsie."

Springing from her desk to the kitchen alcove, Paulette

plucked a can of iced tea from the refrigerator, biscuits from a drawer and poured out a tall glass with ice and a lemon wedge. When Solange reached out to take it, Paulette noticed the ring. "Oh, are you engaged?"

"Yes, since this morning." She gazed at the diamond in the recessed lighting of Howard's outer office. "I can't stop looking at it."

At that moment, Howard appeared—short, mid-forties, in reasonably good shape, but with a hairline vanishing so rapidly, Solange kept track of its retreat from week to week. "Solange," he cooed. "Sorry to keep you waiting."

"She's engaged," Paulette interjected, before Solange could reply.

Howard took the ringed hand. "How exciting for you and..."

"Joie."

"Right. Have you set a date?"

"Why, would you like to come to the wedding?"

"If you invite me, and my schedule permits, I'd love to." He paused. "Does this change anything, you know, professionally speaking?"

"No."

"I'm relieved to hear that. Shall we?"

Solange led Fudgsicle into the office, placed him on a comfortable chair and gave him a rawhide chew. She was surprised when Paulette followed Howard inside and closed the door behind her.

"I transferred the phones," Paulette announced.

"Good." Howard turned to Solange. He appeared transfixed by her new breasts. "May I touch them?" he asked.

"It'll cost you," she replied in the little girl voice that always got him excited.

"How much?"

"Fifty apiece."

"Deal," he whispered and slipped his hands inside her suit jacket. He had too much patchouli oil on. "Magnificent. You're more beautiful than ever." As he kissed her cheek, she noticed Paulette watching them intently.

"I have news for you too, dear," said Howard, as he pulled his polo shirt out of his pants. "Not as exciting as your engagement, of course, but Paulette and I have been seeing each other. For some time, actually. And I've finally persuaded her to become part of our visits."

"Become part how?"

"She goes down on me while you dance."

Solange considered the proposition then shrugged her shoulders. "Okay, but it's extra if I have to watch a live sex act. Five hundred for the hour."

Howard grinned as though he'd mind-melded with Hugh Hefner. "Put the music on." He took his pants off and sprawled expansively on the couch. Sitting primly beside him as if balancing a teacup on her knee, Paulette never took her eyes off Solange.

To match her upbeat mood, Solange had brought some Bob Marley. When she and Joie were in Jamaica smoking *ganja* with the natives, she'd learned some exotic moves and recalled that big breasts swung happily to a reggae beat.

Solange extracted the pink feather boa from her bag and shed her jacket, exposing the tempting mounds of love spilling over the bustier that happily no longer fit. Whipping the boa around her neck, she caught the end between her knees, reached under her skirt and rubbed it against her pussy.

With hand signals, Howard indicated to Paulette that he wanted her to get busy on the boner he'd produced. She seemed uneasy, as if she had never performed oral sex in public, but finally broke down and stroked him. Her technique, Solange imagined, was like an Amish girl on her wedding night.

The costume was designed to come off like the peel of ripened fruit. With a flick of her pinkie the bustier fell away. Down to her G-string, she again toyed with the boa, sliding it under her breasts and between her legs.

Howard yanked Paulette's hair and thrust his erection in her face, caveman behavior so moronic, Solange was inspired to camp up the performance with smoochy facial expressions. Moaning, she sucked her fingers and feigned excitement over Howard trying to get off.

"Slow down, baby," he croaked to Paulette, and with another tug on her hair, lifted her head. With his other hand he took control of his penis, easing it back to second gear, just enough to keep himself stiff. He muted the sound with his remote. "Come and join us."

Solange wanted to clobber him.

"You and Paulette," he urged. "C'mon, she likes you."

Paulette rocked forward, hands to her lips in the prayer position, and looked down at the floor.

Mindful of the poor girl's obvious embarrassment, Solange chose her words carefully. "I'm really flattered, but I don't get it on with other women."

Howard huffed and spat, seeming flabbergasted. "But you'll blow me. What's the difference?"

"You're a guy."

"You said getting engaged wouldn't affect your career."

"I only do men. That's how it's always been."

Paulette looked up, her face a deeper fuchsia than Solange's bustier. "It's okay, Howard. She's engaged. She's just being faithful to her partner."

"Jesus fucking Christ," said Howard, shaking his head. "Now I've heard everything. A hooker with morals."

The words were a slap. "That was mean, Howard."

"What is this, some kinda Clinton bullshit? You're paid for sex. Look it up."

"I'm not a hooker." She tried to set him on fire with her glare as she scampered into her clothes—couldn't get them on fast enough.

"I can make sure you'll never work in this town again," Howard said, his hard-on downgraded to al dente.

Bristling, Paulette moved to another chair and flopped into it, arms folded.

"Yeah, right," said Solange. All the Hollywood moguls combined couldn't stop her. Solange did not have intercourse with men; she gave head, like Monica Lewinsky. Was Monica a hooker? No way. Solange wasn't a man hater, but had never been in love with one either. Men could be good people, generous providers, even close friends. But they did not arouse her sexually. As a turn-on, sucking a dick was like milking a cow—a cash cow.

Howard grabbed his pants and took a wad of bills from his pocket. Counting out five hundreds he handed them to Solange. "Have a nice wedding."

"Thanks," she said, inserting them in her cleavage. She pulled the chew out of Fudgsie's mouth and attached his leash.

Paulette walked them to the door and the two women hugged. "I'm sorry, Solange," said Paulette.

"I am too." Solange referenced Howard with a quick eye gesture. "Call me if you need anything," then waving over her shoulder called out, "Happy trails, Howard."

***

"Don't take that crap, honey," said Joie after Solange recounted the day's events to her over meatloaf and mashed potatoes. "There's plenty more where he came from."

"First the Tampax string, now this...I don't know." For the first time in her life, Solange had begun to think about life after dancing. At twenty-five, with a superb diet and exercise regimen, she figured she had about ten years of peak physicality left.

"Well, I know. We'll get married and start a whole new life. What would you say to the idea of someday getting out of town altogether?"

"Like where?"

Joie helped herself to a third hunk of meatloaf. "Well, I was thinking—and this is part two of the marriage proposal—that when you hang up your pasties—maybe a few years from now—that we might move to Colorado and start a family."

Staring at Joie's forehead, Solange saw herself baking cherry pies in a red checked gingham shirtwaist dress, surrounded by screaming kids all demanding attention, while Joie was out at the barn birthing lambs. "Colorado?"

"There's a cute little town about an hour out of Grand Junction called Paonia, near the San Juan Mountains. My Aunt Marla has a local Starbucks-type place there. She's starting to slow down and I'm sure she would dig it if we moved there someday and bought her out."

The domestic tableau continued with Solange now in a blue checked gingham dress, standing behind the counter pouring a mocha-latte-to-go for a weather-beaten cattle rustler who had to lean forward to read her nametag because it sloped back so far on her enormous breasts.

"It's something for the future, honey. You can't stop dancing yet. We need to save up for a house and a red pickup and a barn. And kids cost a freakin' fortune. Can't swing all that on my salary."

Solange wondered how her breasts would hold up after nursing and how many tips she'd have to save to afford to keep them properly lifted.

Joie belched the way she always did when she talked and ate at the same time. "What do you think about kids?"

"You mean, besides Fudgsie?"

At the mention of his name, Fudgsicle trotted over to Mama and scored a piece of meatloaf.

"Well, if you got pregnant and a puppy popped out of you, I'm sure I would love it with all my heart. But chances are, it would be a human."

"Maybe you'll be the one to get pregnant."

Joie threw her arms out wide. "Or we could take turns. How many couples can do that?"

"No one in Paonia, I'm sure," said Solange, wishing to protect her fantasy children from becoming grist for small-town ridicule. "And it's cold there."

"But I can teach you how to ski."

"I only like water skiing. Mainly I like bathing suits."

A more resonant belch sprang from Joie's throat. "Great meatloaf, honey." She knocked on her chest a few times. "Tell you what. We'll go there on vacation, meet Aunt Marla and you can decide, okay?"

It sounded reasonable in theory, but Solange knew that when Joie made up her mind to do something, there was no escape clause.

7
JANEY

Dinner hour, the time Janey earmarked for family togetherness, had unraveled. Billy had opted to eat all meals on his beloved sofa and complained when Janey refused to bring them in on a tray. She'd also enforced a no-cell-phone rule for Candi and Sherri, which only made them eat faster.

The girls regarded questions about their personal lives as invasions of their privacy and Janey had stopped asking. It wasn't possible to eavesdrop on their cell calls—they'd never use a land line so listening on the extension was out. Janey wondered why they never confided in her; was she a confidable mother? Probably not. So, to pass the time while Billy reclined and Eleanor watched Judge Judy on the kitchen TV, Janey imagined horrible secrets the girls were keeping from her.

Dinner was a prolonged event, as Eleanor's fork moved with the speed of an elderly tortoise. When her morbid fantasies became too disturbing, Janey found comfort, as she always did, in Bruce daydreams. This night, in the midst of an erotic rendezvous on the boardwalk in Asbury Park, the phone rang. Loathe to interrupt stolen moments with her dream lover, Janey let the machine answer.

But when Eleanor heard the voice of Lynn, her PR agent, she pointed at the phone and Janey picked up. "Just a second," said Janey and handed it to Eleanor.

"Oh, really? When?" said Eleanor, sounding blasé, a clue that it was something big. "I'll check my calendar."

"Isn't it interesting how she can hear just fine when she wants to?" Janey whispered to the girls.

They giggled, which earned them a scolding wave of the hand from Eleanor.

"Thanks, dear," said Eleanor. "Tell Johnny I said hello." A pause. "Oh, I forgot." She laughed and gave the phone to Janey to hang up. Then she sat there.

Sherri bounced up and down in her seat. "C'mon, Grandma. What did she say?"

"I didn't get any broccoli," said Eleanor, looking coy.

Janey set the bowl down in front of her, a bit forcefully. "Are we going to play Twenty Questions or are you going to tell us?"

Eleanor paused to help herself to a serving of veggies. "I'm booked on the Johnny Carson Show."

"Jay Leno," Janey said. "Johnny retired a long time ago."

"I wanted to be on with Johnny," said Eleanor, recounting a story so often told, it was firmly established in the family archives, "but they told me I was too young. I was ninety-two. They said I had to be at least a hundred. Now I'm a hundred and two. I don't know what took them so long."

Candi shrugged. "Maybe they lost your phone number."

Sherri jumped up and gave Eleanor a kiss on the cheek. "That's awesome, Grandma. You finally made it!"

"I'll need a new dress," Eleanor said, looking at Janey, her personal shopper. "And shoes."

Janey knew that as Eleanor's needs escalated and preparations became more elaborate, this event would suck up the next three weeks of her life. No one could deny a centenarian diva, especially if she was footing the bill. Janey wondered if the long-expired Valiums in the bottom drawer of her dresser were still safe to take.

Before ballroom dancing, Eleanor had been a mah-jongg aficionado in Tucson, but when she was widowed for the second time at eighty-two, she decided to pursue the passion for dancing that had been long denied her by Billy's grandfather, Joseph Two-Left-Feet West. After he died and left her comfortably widowed, Eleanor hit the floor waltzing, and won ballroom competitions across the country.

The local media in Tucson featured her in newspaper articles. One day, a TV crew came to the gym where she regularly worked out and a career was launched. She did some regional TV commercials, then got really hot after a story in *People*. She acquired an agent of sorts, Lynn, a young woman who made a career of studying centenarians. Lynn made sure Eleanor was featured in every magazine article and TV show dealing with longevity.

When her fame outgrew Tucson, Eleanor moved to the Big Market—Los Angeles—to be "on avail" for movies, television and rest home openings. Living with her grandson afforded Eleanor a full-time cook, driver and secretary, all named Janey. Eleanor made no secret that she believed the honor of being allowed to bask in her celebrity was sufficient reward, but went the extra mile and paid a small monthly stipend which, in her opinion, entitled her to superstar demands.

"I'll take you shopping on Thursday," Janey said.

"Thursday? I can't wait that long. I'm going to be on in three weeks."

Janey felt certain that if Johnny Carson had met Eleanor, he would have retired sooner.

***

In bed that night, Billy's twisting and turning made it impossible for Janey to read the new issue of *Backstreets*, the Springsteen fanzine that arrived in the mail that morning. She gave up. "I have a new friend," she said. "She's a healer. Maybe she could help your back."

"Is she a doctor?"

"No, but she has celebrity clients. I think Gary DiCaro is one of them."

"Everyone in LA has celebrity clients."

"Then go to a doctor."

"I don't want to be in traction."

Janey suppressed a scream. "Traction is for people with broken bones. Not people who go to work and play basketball."

"You don't know how I feel."

"What about a chiropractor?"

"If I wanted someone to jump on my back I'm sure you'd volunteer."

"Why won't you discuss this with me?"

"There's nothing to discuss. It's just pain. I'll feel better when I feel like feeling better."

Once again Janey thought about Lily's assertion that you can infuse men with feminine energy by having sex during menstruation. While Janey didn't fully understand what that energy was, she knew Billy needed it. But she could think of no way to get her blood onto his penis.

She stared at a hot, sweaty picture of Bruce in *Backstreets* and wondered if he ever received feminine energy from his wife—but forced the idea out of her mind because she hated thinking of him having sex under any conditions except with her.

"You make it sound so hopeless. You won't do anything to help yourself and you won't let anyone help you."

Billy settled into a semi-fetal position so close to the edge of the bed, the magnitude of a toilet flush could catapult him to the floor. "I'll be fine."

A song bubbled up and Janey decided to let it come forth: "'You can hide 'neath your covers and study your pain...make crosses from your lovers...'" but stopped abruptly when Billy punched the mattress.

"Don't Bruce me, okay?"

Normally, in their arguments, that was the signal for to Billy to leave the room. But he was ailing, apparently physically incapable of storming out, which forced Janey to be the retreater. She took her *Backstreets* and hopped out of bed, landing hard on her feet to make some useless point. With Rosie at her heels she stomped to the kitchen. The two shared a piece of leftover chicken and Janey read Rosie some letters to the editor.

It was close to midnight when Candi and Sherri came home from "a party at someone's house," as much detail as they typically divulged. Janey scanned Candi's facial décor—harlequin eyes with rhinestone teardrops, clusters of tiny pink stars on her cheeks and lips outlined in burgundy—for signs of smearing. That none of it appeared hastily repaired was a relief. With Candi's unchecked ripeness growing in proportion to the number of men who leered at her, Janey needed to be ever more vigilant.

Somewhere, Janey suspected, there was a missing link in their family tree, a voluptuous gene that somehow bypassed the flat prairie-chested women like her and mutated into Candi's magnificent mountain range. Few people believed Candi's breasts were real and Janey was often criticized for allowing her to get implants.

The girls joined the snack-fest, polishing off the chicken and assorted other goodies in plastic containers. They cringed, as they always did, when Janey took the bones off their plates and crunched them in her mouth. "I need the calcium," she explained.

Candi scraped the last bit of peanut butter from the Skippy jar with a spatula. "Is Grandma ever going to die?"

It was a question Janey often pondered. "Give her fifteen or twenty years." She laughed at her joke, then remembered it might not be a joke.

"Is she rich?" asked Sherri, ripping the top off a pint of Cherry Garcia ice cream.

Candi made a world-weary face. "Don't start spending your inheritance. She'll probably leave everything to the Disabled Ballroom Dancers."

It had never occurred to Janey that Eleanor would not leave her estate to her heirs. After years of being catered to by her grandchildren, surely she was hoarding the loot so she could look down from heaven and smile when they gasped at the grandeur of her bequest.

"Maybe," Janey said, joking to quell her newfound worries, "she'll leave it to some gullible country and they'll put her picture on a stamp."

Candi shook her head. "I think she's going to be frozen, like Ted Williams, then she'll come back and live with Sherri and her kids."

"Why not you and your kids?" asked Sherri.

"I would never put up with her shit."

"Candi…" said Janey.

"Oh, like Dad doesn't say 'shit' every five minutes."

"Dad does a lot of things that you shouldn't do."

"Don't worry, Mom, we're not potheads."

Certain that a chicken bone shard had punctured her digestive tract, Janey coughed. She had long suspected that the girls were aware of Billy's pot habit, but since they had never brought it up, she could pretend they weren't.

"Is that why Grandma's so mad at Daddy?" Sherri asked. "Because he smokes so much weed?"

"He doesn't…" Janey said, with such a lack of conviction, the girls gawked as if she were defending Cheech and Chong, "…but not as much as he used to."

Sherri passed the ice cream to Janey's outstretched hand. "How come you don't smoke weed, Mom?"

"So she can be like Bruce Springsteen," Candi said, before Janey could respond. "He doesn't do drugs and it pisses Daddy off when Mom mentions it."

"Where did you get that idea?" asked Janey.

"From you," Candi replied in her most insouciant manner." I was listening to you guys fight."

"What did I tell you about snooping?"

"Nothing. You never told me anything about snooping." She turned to Sherri. "So Mom goes, 'what're you, trying to smoke all the pot Bruce never smoked?' and Dad goes, 'Yeah,' and

Mom goes, 'Then you should be a vegetarian because Bruce eats meat.'"

"Ohmygod!" Sherri exclaimed with the rapturous glee of a teenager hearing shocking dirt about a schoolmate.

That she was such a poor role model humiliated Janey. She wished her life had more purpose. Before the girls came along she'd meant to go back to school, then Eleanor showed up and Janey fell into her servitude. Janey often wished she could smoke pot—being stoned might make it easier to deal with Eleanor—but when she'd tried pot in high school, it made her low, not high. These days, she had enough lows in her life. Besides, if she smoked, she could no longer hold it against Billy.

When Eleanor first moved in, Billy had treated her like a queen, which took some of the burden off Janey, but after awhile, Eleanor's attitude toward him deteriorated. Her snide comments made it clear she disapproved of his indolence. In the past few months she'd become downright hostile but he never fought back. Janey suspected he was afraid that offending Eleanor would threaten his inheritance. It bothered Janey that Billy seemed an understudy to his own life.

"Hey Mom," whined Sherri, "you ate all the ice cream."

Peering into the empty carton, Janey was embarrassed to find she'd been trance-eating. "I'm sorry. I didn't mean to. There's some Dove Bars on the left side of the freezer, under the bag of Orange Roughy fillets, wrapped in foil, marked 'ground beef.'"

"Really?" asked Candi. "How come?"

"I was hiding them from Grandma."

The girls giggled and went for the freezer.

A subversive thought took hold of Janey—she wondered what would happen if she put a tiny drop of menstrual blood in Billy's beer. It couldn't hurt him and he'd never know. Then again, maybe a drop wasn't enough and she'd have to add more until Billy's beer turned red and he had her committed. She decided not to risk it.

That night, Billy's ferocious snoring made it impossible for Janey to sleep in their bed so she sublet his beloved couch for a few hours. She invited Rosie to snuggle at her feet, but that came at a similar price. At least Rosie's snores were softer.

At six A.M., ignoring her exhaustion, Janey slugged down two cups of coffee and took off with Rosie, hoping Lily might be at the park. Janey wanted to talk to her because any woman who could lure a gay megastar into her arms must surely have valuable insights on men.

In a stroke of good timing Janey spotted Lily jogging with Bean and Blossom around the concourse. Since Janey only jogged when her life was threatened, she waited for Lily to come around to her.

"Hey," Lily called out when she saw Janey.

"Born to run—just as I suspected."

Stopping to wipe perspiration from her face, Lily invited Janey to join her. It seemed the perfect time to begin an exercise regimen—dead tired, out of shape, but yearning for a change. "Sure," Janey said.

Helpfully, Lily slowed down and Janey kicked her feet to start them moving. The dogs trotted alongside.

"I know this is really personal and possibly involves the man you said you couldn't discuss," Janey said, "but we couldn't help but notice that hot scene between you and Gary DiCaro yesterday."

For an instant Lily stumbled. "I've been working on Gary's

movies for years. He's a good friend."

"Really, really good friend?" Janey asked with an Ed Sullivan inflection.

"It's too soon to talk about it," Lily said, stopping to snatch a piece of discarded tissue with her poop bag. "I'm neurotically superstitious. I don't want to jinx it."

Janey was surprised and a little relieved to discover that Lily had insecurities. "That's okay. I can delay gratification. But it's going to be good, isn't it?"

Lily smiled and flipped the bag into the trash. "How's your husband doing?"

"Morose, withdrawn, unresponsive. And those are the good days."

"Male vibrations are very confused right now. They're searching for their true identity." Lily squeezed Janey's upper arm. "Try giving your blood to the Goddess, Janey. Once she knows you intimately, she can help your husband."

In the distance, Janey noticed the dogs squirming on their backs under the pine tree, evidence of a recent squirrel fatality. Or perhaps they were being driven mad by Lily's womanly fumes. "I'm sure it's true for you, Lily, but..."

"It sounds too exotic?"

"Good word. Not the one I would have chosen."

"Janey, you have an important mission."

"Me? Nah. I'm just one of the teeming masses."

"Believe it. The Goddess is trying to reach you."

"I'm sure I'm unlisted."

Lily smiled. "Your blood is the phone number."

8
LILY

At five A.M someone named Rudy called from *The Globe*. "Why you were kissing Gary DiCaro at Victory Park?" His voice barged through the phone and exploded in her ear.

"What?" Lily said, as the shock of the call momentarily canceled her reflexes.

"I got the photos. Give me what I need and let's get this over with," he said. "You want the facts straight or not?"

Appalled by his rudeness and creepy energy, she did what her body told her to do. She hung up. The phone began to ring again and she let the machine get it. It was *The Star*.

How in the world had tabloids learned of a fleeting moment at Victory Park? Someone must have snapped a picture with their cell phone. She recalled the way Cleo had stared slack-jawed when Lily hustled Gary into his car and deemed her a possible suspect; she seemed a bitter, troubled woman. But blaming was pointless, so Lily constructed an energetic security fence around her and Gary and brewed a cup of kava kava to calm her for her morning clients.

As she normally did during business hours, she muted the ringers on her phones but she could feel the calls coming in. By noon, her weary answering machine had logged messages from the entire catalog of supermarket tabloids, plus a couple of haughty sounding stringers from their TV and Internet equivalents. She felt invaded.

The only call she returned was Gary's. "I have to see you," he said. "Bring the dogs."

The mere mention of Gary's name was enough to set off the Labs, who reached maximum excitement on the ride to Gary's ultra-modern cliff-side mansion, though they had never been there before. When Lily pulled into the gated driveway they yelped like banshees.

Gary stepped outside and Lily released the dogs, who charged headlong into Gary and monopolized him for thirty seconds. "Okay," he finally barked, "let me greet your mother." They backed off at once, Gary seized Lily and they kissed until they ran out of saliva.

Inside, Gary gave her a quick lesson in publicity. "You'll need your sense of humor right away," he said as he obliged Blossom's plea for a belly rub. "I'm a media bad boy and now there's a whole new world of bad. Even Trish got sick of my publicity, and she craved it."

"There's nothing bad about you," Lily said.

"I'm glad you think so," Gary said, "but I think Darth Vader has a better reputation."

"Well, they can just talk to me," Lily said, resolving to purge fear from her mind and replace it with instant media savvy. "I'll set them straight."

Gary laughed. "Probably best to avoid that word. Let's just try to keep a low profile, okay?"

"Okay."

"And we've got Francesca, my new bodyguard who knows all the paparazzi tricks. She's moving into the guest house. Ex-cop. You'll love her. She can crush a car."

Lily felt an unexpected pang of jealousy that another woman

was taking care of her man—living with him in a way—then scolded herself, then decided her concern was so petty and unenlightened she actually needed paparazzi hounding her so she would have something legitimate to worry about. "A female bodyguard. That's so progressive."

"She'll take care of things while we're in Australia."

"Australia?" Lily echoed, feeling dizzy.

"Just for a few weeks on the John Lone picture. I know you just moved into a new house and you have clients and dogs and everything, but I want us to be together."

Stunned and shaken she asked, "When?"

"Thursday."

Thursday? That was only a few days away. Lily felt a warm fluttering below her navel and put her hand over her third chakra. Her body was the Goddess incarnate; she always bowed to its higher wisdom. It was giving her the Stop response.

"Are you okay, Lily? Why are you holding your stomach?"

She wrapped him in her arms and kissed him. "I'm fine. I just had to kiss you so badly it was making me queasy." Staying fastened to his face she rescanned her body and made it repeat the warning though it never lied. "I don't think it's a good idea."

"But you've been on every movie with me since we met. We can't be apart now."

"Maybe you need time to make sure I'm not a fluke. It all happened so fast."

"So did the Big Bang." He closed his eyes and exhaled. "Lily, you are not a fluke." His eyes laser-beamed into her. "You know that, don't you?"

Lily nodded.

"So come with me."

She felt despair on the molecular level. "I want to go, Gary. I want to be with you all the time. I even want to go back in time and be with you from birth. But my body is warning me not to go."

"Your body? Which part of your body?"

"Here," she said, touching her solar plexus. "The Goddess-point, the seat of all wisdom."

He stared at her navel. "And what does your bellybutton think will happen if you go to Australia?"

Lily was loathe to reveal the paranoid scenarios playing out in her mind, all of which involved Gary shrugging off this fleeting, heterosexual lark and returning to men. On every film she'd worked on, Gary had acquiesced to the lust of some hot actor or set designer, which tortured the women on the crew and made them wistfully lament his unfortunate sexuality.

Sparing her that heartache had to be the reason for the Goddess' admonition. "If our love is real it'll grow and be even better when you come home," Lily said, the Thing She Had to Believe.

"I'm not sure it could get any better," he said, "but I don't want to argue with your body. In fact my body just told me that if I don't make love to you right now, my dick will fall off."

On the way to Gary's bedroom, Lily tried to be philosophical—if Thursday marked the end of their relationship, she'd still been given a perfect gift, an answered prayer. She wouldn't give in to fear; she'd live this joy through to the fullest, burn it into her heart and make it last forever.

The bedroom was modern, minimalist, with a floor-to-vaulted-ceiling window. An oversized bed dressed in a white down comforter sat upon a black granite pedestal. A snow bank of pillows huddled like fallen clouds.

Moments later they were naked in those clouds. Lily's body hurt with desire.

"I have to taste you," Gary whispered. His lips worked their way down from her neck, hot breath forming erotic islands of warmth on her breasts and belly. When he reached the swelling between her thighs he savored her as if she were a melting ice cream cone.

Dizzying waves of pleasure consumed her. At that moment, given the choice of leaving the bed versus staying put and being put to death, she would happily give up her life. Gary's lips and tongue explored her exquisitely; she momentarily wondered if he had been kidding her, that he'd been with women his entire life. But she knew he hadn't, and the thought that she was his first, that her vaginal lips were the only ones he had ever savored, made her reverent.

She touched his hair and he looked up at her. "My turn," she whispered, and as he rose up to his knees, she slid her face under him and took him in her mouth. Her hands massaged his melon buttocks the way she'd always yearned to—without the veil of therapy. For a few moments she left her body and floated to the ceiling, hopelessly star-struck, watching a pretty red-haired woman making love with the sexiest star in Hollywood. Oh, to be that woman.

Then she realized she was that woman, with his penis in her mouth, and he was calling her name. After awhile, she had to have him inside her, now, now. Before the thought escaped he was there, connecting to her like a shivering hand inside a warm mitten. They were lifted by celestial choruses from across the galaxies blessing their union. She could see them in his eyes.

Her whole being danced in a heightened state of awareness, her climax reverberated in every cell. Gary rode in perfect rhythm on its waves.

A glorious flood of light splashed through the window as he emptied himself inside her. It lit up his face and she saw prisms of light in the beads of sweat trickling down his cheeks and forehead. He gently collapsed on top of her and she held him in place. She would not let him separate from her body. They drifted into a semi-sleep for no particular time—an hour...or a year.

When they awoke, Lily went to the kitchen and discovered sea salt and baking soda, which she poured into Gary's spa-sized marble bathtub. "It removes toxins," she explained as they settled in.

Bean and Blossom stood by, making a game of licking water off Lily and Gary, then resting their chins on the edge of the tub.

"You know, I never think about toxins," Gary said, "and here you are saving me from them." He leaned forward and kissed her. "I like it when you look out for me."

"I like to look out for you. And I like to be with you and look at you and kiss you." She kissed his compelling lips. "And I like to touch you." Reaching for the part of him that was floating under the water she easily coaxed it back to its extended splendor.

Gary slipped back inside her. The water in the tub sloshed quietly back and forth as they rocked, creating a new game for the dogs. They advanced and retreated from the waves, lapping up the overflow that sloshed to the floor.

Much later, when they were temporarily exhausted from lovemaking, Gary made fluffy Swiss cheese omelets and they sat out to eat on the redwood deck overlooking the canyon. Lily wore one of his white tee shirts which, she informed him, she would never, ever return.

The dogs soaked up the setting sun, lulled by the serenity of a perfect day.

"I'm going to be completely honest," Gary declared, as he twisted a string of cheese around his fork, "about everything. To everyone."

"Honesty is always good," said Lily, but as the words left her mouth she felt apprehensive, not wanting to think about some future 'honest' conversation from Australia.

"It's the new Gary," he proclaimed, "Up front, unashamed and free of toxins."

The phone rang, as if someone were calling to test his resolve. "Hello?" It was a guy named Jet, and Gary seemed happy to hear from him.

A jealous rumble interfered with Lily's digestion. The name Jet sounded sexually dangerous, someone a younger John Travolta might play. She imagined the *Saturday Night Fever*-era Travolta on the other end of the line.

Gary held up a finger to indicate he would only be on a minute, then reached over, picked up her foot and rested it on his knee, massaging her toes as he spoke. Jet was inviting him to some big event. "Don't bother," he said with a sly grin in Lily's direction. "I'm pretty sure I'll have a date. Hang on." He looked at her. "Lily, will you go with me to the opening of my friend's play at the Mark Taper Forum?"

Lily nodded rhetorically. She would happily accompany him to a recitation of the New York City phone book.

"She said yes...right...I am totally, completely, in love...Jesus had nothing to do with it...I am too...We'll see you then." He hung up the phone and turned to Lily. "We're not going to hide."

***

The play, a dark comedy starring Goldie Hawn about a woman who adopts her teenage lover, was called *Hopscotch*. Afterwards, Lily and Gary went to a party at Dragonia, the hot new downtown restaurant. Entertainment show anchors were planted at strategic locations to confront the abundant stream of celebrities.

Gary wouldn't submit to Lily's suggestion that he present her as his massage therapist. "Screw the media. When they see how I look at you and can't keep my hands off you they'll be talking anyway, so I might as well be honest. I'm the new Gary, remember?"

Lily silently asked the Goddess for Gary's protection as his love-struck countenance and frequent kisses to her cheek caught the attention of stars and paparazzi alike. And it was soon obvious that Jet, who had a platinum blonde buzz cut, black rimmed glasses and looked nothing like John Travolta, had already launched scuttlebutt about Gary's sudden foray into the straight world.

"You're so clever," said Avery Balin, the character actor, poking Gary in the chest, "cheating on your beard with another beard. So labored." His dismissive glance made Lily feel like a large wart on Gary's chin.

"Thrilled to make you happy," replied Gary. He cupped Lily's face and kissed her amidst fireworks of camera flashes.

Avery averted his gaze the way people do at a car wreck. "There's no need to be desperate," he said. "You're still huge in Europe."

It wasn't hard for Lily to read the noxious energy in the room;

Avery's cynical take on their relationship was clearly the general consensus. Amazingly, Gary didn't seem to be bothered by the elevated brows or salacious smiles and, fortified by his calm demeanor, Lily refrained from judgment and concentrated on projecting love.

Later, as she sat in a stall in the ladies room, she couldn't help but eavesdrop on a loud conversation during which she learned that she was a transvestite. On the trip back to the table, a few gay men watched her with hostile eyes, but they were tame compared to the women whose smiles hid such obvious contempt, Lily wondered if they had condemned her to death in some past life in Salem.

Jet, thankfully, seemed warm and genuine. "I was all prepared to make rude faces at you," he said, "but you're way too hot." He leaned in close. "I'll call you if I ever want to cross the street."

By the time they sat down to dinner, Lily felt like Yoko Ono in a room full of Beatle fans. They were seated next to Jet and his boyfriend Martin, a handsome, long-haired sculptor, plus avant-garde comedian Yolanda Bernstein and her date Laurence Chen Loh, a feng shui master. While they dined on the first course of warm duck salad with shaved truffles, Laurence relayed a consultation he'd had with one of the guests, who wanted him to rearrange the furniture in her daughter's doll house.

"She was appalled when he wouldn't give her reduced doll house rates," Yolanda added.

"I can put her in touch with Feng Shui Barbie," said Jet.

Lily laughed, grateful to be at a table where she and Gary weren't the main topic of conversation.

But before that thought left her mind, Yolanda stuck a fist under her chin and gawked at them. "You two make a blindingly gorgeous couple. Have you noticed that everyone in this room wants to date you?" She batted her eyes. "Including me."

"Really?" said Gary, seeming abruptly sober. "I got the feeling we were at the McCarthy hearings."

"Don't flatter yourself, Gary," Yolanda said, swiping her hand through the air. "On my scale of kinky, you're barely a seven."

For some reason, Lily appreciated that sentiment.

"You know how hard it is to get ink in this town these days?" Yolanda went on in full stand-up mode. "I ran for president of Hadassah and it didn't even make their newsletter."

Their laughter was interrupted by the return of Avery, walking in a pronounced zig-zag motion. He pulled up a chair next to Gary and put his arm around him. "Hi, I'm Gary, but the 'R' is silent," he said in a voice snotty and heavy.

"I am so embarrassed for you, Avery," said Yolanda.

"Suck your dick," Avery sneered.

Yolanda turned to him with a gaze that could wither a watermelon. "You are monumentally pathetic."

"Fuck you, bearded asshole."

Gary got up, snatched Avery's chair and dumped him on the floor. He got up slowly, straightened his leather pants and left without another word.

Everyone who saw it acted like it never happened.

9
SOLANGE

Marvin came to the club every night and showered Solange with impressive sums of money. Though all the girls had their special customers, Marvin outdid them all, which created rampaging jealousy among the dancers.

"You've got that boy wrapped around your Tampax string," Peggi said one night after Solange tallied up a $2000 evening. "You're blowin' him, aren't you?"

"Don't have to," Solange boasted.

Peggi rolled her eyes. "Yeah, well let's say I believe that, which I don't. One of these days he's gonna want a return on his investment."

Later that night in bed with Joie and Fudgsicle, Solange repeated the exchange to Joie. "I don't like the way they talk to you, honey," she said. "I might have to hurt some of them bitches."

Joie's bravado made Solange feel safe. Sometimes, when they made love, Solange would pretend to go on a treasure hunt for the hidden balls she'd accused Joie of having tucked away. Joie always laughed and said she'd never find them but to please keep looking.

For the first time since their engagement, Solange began to visualize the future, wondering what it would be like to actually live in the country. She was sure Colorado was a kinder, gentler place than California, except for those high school shootings and JonBenet Ramsey. She could learn to paint landscapes in Colorado.

And kids...having some around could be like time-tripping back to Venice with Andi Nyler, her first crush...how they'd ride up and down Canal Street together, logging thousands of miles, it seemed. When she was eight and Andi died, her childhood had ended.

"I think living in Colorado might be fun," said Solange.

"Really? I wasn't sure you were digging the idea."

"Well, it was kind of startling at first, but I've been thinking about it. Dancing's not fun the way it used to be. Maybe we could go sooner. I could paint landscapes."

"Honey, landscapes aren't going to pay like your new friend Marvin does."

"How do you know? I could become a famous landscape artist."

"And I could become an astronaut, but let's not count on that either."

"I thought you had faith in me."

"I do, honey. I'm just being realistic."

"Well I put my women-strual blood in the back yard this morning and I asked the Goddess to make me a famous painter."

"Holy shit," said Joie. "You're not getting sucked into that Vampira crap, are you?"

"It was very spiritual, Joie. I think we should combine our blood and offer it together."

Joie put her hands to her throat and made gagging sounds. "No, no, Mr. Bill!"

"Sorry, I think it's a lovely idea." Solange didn't want to sneak off to perform her monthly ceremony but it seemed that she might have to from now on.

"Great. Don't let me stop you. You go commune with fairies and I'll pay the bills."

"I don't want to dance forever, Joie."

"Not forever. Maybe five more years. I've made some good investments and now that Marvin's come along, we can really kick some financial butt."

***

During a "Sadie Hawkins" promotion in which customers got twenty free seconds in the lap dance booth, Solange put on her Mylar string bikini, crooked her finger and led Marvin, who walked as if tethered, to a booth. She swung her leg around his lap and did a few warm-up gyrations, feeling his hard-on swell beneath his pants. The twenty seconds passed in an instant. "More?"

Her obedient lamb nodded, begging for slaughter. He was homely and devoid of charisma, yet there was such innocence in the way he looked at her like an undernourished Basset Hound, she almost wanted to protect him from her ability to get his money.

She licked his ear and considered giving him a free hand job, but sensed he was about to blow; men that needy never held out too long. Before the thought left her mind, he howled like an off-key coyote, then slumped. Solange hopped off his lap to avoid goo seepage onto the Mylar, though in her experience, the Dockers he wore were good at absorbing ejaculation.

The going rate for a lap dance was $100. He gave her a $500 tip.

After the initiation, Marvin became a lap dance-aholic, quickly graduating to table dances which put him in hot-breath proximity of her full, naked magnificence. She knew how much cash each of her moves elicited. Sucking her fingers then making spiral patterns around her nipples—that was an easy $500. Pretty much anything she did with her breasts made him happy and he gradually became less self-conscious about masturbating. Technically, of course, that wasn't allowed, but guards liked money too, and for a mere $50—chump change—they would gladly look the other way.

One evening, the featured attraction was the Blondage Twins, practically the biggest porn stars in the country. Porn stars guaranteed a huge take for the house and for the girls since they came with a built-in fan base that followed them everywhere. After the show, their groupies all wanted dances so they could act out scenes from their favorite films.

The Blondage Twins had a wild act; they liked to push the boundaries as far as possible. Tonight their choreography was loaded with simulated sex, glistening lubricants and nifty props like the two-headed ice dildo, which made their fans hoot like horny seals in an echo chamber.

Solange chose to be inspired by the challenge of performing after the house had been brought down. She slithered on stage in black spandex with an orange flame design and launched into a steamy interpretation of Bruce Springsteen's "I'm On Fire," a track suggested, naturally, by Janey.

As she soared to a state of high internal combustion, money came at her from every direction. She saw Marvin huddled at a table, one hand around a glass of cola, the other underneath and out of sight.

After she pared the final shred of clothing off her body, she exposed the orange flames painted on her butt and around her pussy. She flung herself around one pole, then sprang to the next in a fiery frenzy. On her way to the third pole she failed to see an oil slick left behind by the Blondage Sisters and fell ungracefully on her flaming derriere.

Whoops and hollers changed to a collective groan. The pain was intense but she wouldn't let it show on her face. Then from her seated position she saw Marvin rushing the stage, trying to dive over a throng of much larger men who held him back like a human tidal wave.

The music stopped and the crowd fell silent. Unable to get up, Solange watched the guards try to stop Sir Marvin from rescuing his fallen damsel.

"We'll take it from here, sir," they assured him before hauling him away. Patrons were not allowed on stage, especially when the dancer was completely nude.

Finally, with the assistance of a guard, Solange rose to her feet and smiled bravely amid cheers and whistles as she was escorted off the stage.

When she got to the dressing room, she picked up Fudgsicle and lowered herself onto his pillow. He cleaned her face with kisses and she cried into his soft, brown fur.

Goldie came by. "Do you need medical attention?"

"I'll be fine, but my tush is going to look like a bad tattoo job. I'll have to use industrial strength concealer."

Goldie cackled. "Maybe you should paint a bulls eye on it."

***

As Solange hobbled out of the club with Fudgsie pulling her forward on his leash, she saw Marvin standing by her Mercedes in the parking lot. He was pacing and blowing air like some sort of warped yoga exercise.

"Solange!" he called out when he saw her. "Are you okay?"

She laughed politely. "There's a lot of padding down there. I'll be just fine."

"I think you should see a doctor. Let me take you. I'll pick up the bill."

"That's very thoughtful of you, Marvin. If I need a doctor, I'll let you know."

"Can I drive you home?"

"You're standing next to my car." It occurred to her that he must have been watching her to know which one it was.

"I could drive it and take a cab back to get mine."

His comment set off a tiny alarm. She would never get into a car with anyone she hadn't checked out first. "You're very sweet, Marvin, but I don't have that far to go."

"Will you have dinner with me?"

At that point it became necessary to cut to the chase. "I'm a lesbian and my girlfriend and I are engaged. I only date professionally. And no sex."

Eyes wide and blinking, he was Marvin-in-the-headlights. "Really? I've never…"

"Met a lesbian before? Sure you have." Solange sensed the gears shifting in his brain as he reprogrammed everything he knew about her.

"Would it be possible to take both of you to dinner?"

"We don't do scenes with guys."

"How about just food?"

With Joie in the mix, Solange's fears vanished. "Sure, you can take us to dinner. But I gotta warn ya. Joie's a major eater."

Marvin smiled in a measured way, probably conjuring up a 300-pound bull dyke who could take his scrawny butt down in a heartbeat. Which, of course, she could. "I don't mind," he said. "You pick the restaurant."

"We're free Thursday night." Solange opened the car door and put Fudgsie inside. She sat down, wincing at a stab of pain in her right cheek and hip. "Give me your number. I'll call and tell you where we'll meet you."

Marvin lunged forward as if he wanted to catch her from falling, but held back. "You're in pain."

"I'll be fine." But it was nice that he cared. When she got home, she called her private detective friend Jay and had Marvin checked out. Within ten minutes, Jay discovered that Marvin came from a prominent Ohio family that owned a Midwest motel chain. No blotches on his record. Almost too perfect.

Joie lit up when Solange told her about the dinner. "A loaded guy with intimacy issues. With him as a private you could quit the club."

"And we could make lots of money and then I can quit dancing and become a famous artist."

Joie rubbed her hands together. "Let's make him an offer he can't refuse."

***

The Black Angus Steak House in Panorama City was Joie's favorite restaurant; oversized proportions were her main criteria. For added impact they decided to overdress. Solange wore a liquid-fitting snakeskin print dress, Jimmy Choo patent leather sandals and her hair half down, half Gibson. Joie chose a black tuxedo jacket over a white sports bra and low ride jeans.

When they walked in, Solange spotted Marvin, in jacket, button down shirt and tie, sitting at a table sipping cola.

"Super-dweeb," Joie said as they approached.

"Be nice."

"Nice is my middle name."

For his part, Marvin did just what Solange thought he would when he saw her delicious fiancée—he gulped. "You must be Joie," he said, offering a shaky hand that Solange guessed was probably sweaty as well.

Joie received him in a power grip. "Must be."

His posture sagged and Solange feared he was already

hopelessly intimidated. "You look nice, Marvin," she said.

Her remark returned him to an upright position. "Thank you." They sat down.

Joie beckoned the waiter to kick off the cavalcade of food.

"Amazing, isn't it?" marveled Solange as minutes later, she and Marvin watched Joie polish off a pound and a half of blood-red prime rib with garlic mashed potatoes, coleslaw and three glasses of milk. "Her metabolism is off the charts."

"Lots of people think I throw up," Joie said, "but the last time I threw up was in third grade."

"Do you work out?" Marvin asked.

"She plays racquetball every morning," replied Solange, since Joie's mouth was occupied with beef. "You know Jackson Harmon, from the Lakers?"

Marvin nodded.

"He's the only guy who ever beat her."

Joie poked her fork in the air. "I think I had a sprained elbow that day."

A brief silence as Marvin stared at his plate. Then, "Solange, have you ever thought about leaving the club?"

Solange gave Joie a nudge and forced out a chuckle. "I sure thought about it the other night."

"What if, say you were to leave there, and whatever you were making...let's say I paid you more than that and you would only perform...at my house?"

Solange pretended to lapse into a meditative state in which the suspense built while she contemplated the offer. "You mean like a private dancer?"

"Right," said Marvin, his gaze following the pattern of her dress into her cleavage.

"I think we can work something out. What do you think, Joie?" Aside to Marvin she confided, "She understands business."

Joie chugged down half a glass of milk. "Let's lay our cards on the table, Marv. You with me so far?"

"So far." He swilled some cola and chewed up an ice cube.

"You may not know this, but Sol is an artist in more ways than one. She dances like an angel but she can also paint like..." Joie squinted and looked at Solange. "Who do you paint like, honey?"

Solange couldn't come up with a name. "My style is still in early formation."

"Doesn't matter," Joie said, "she has a real gift. So let's say you put her through art school, and while she's honing her craft, you purchase all her paintings."

"You don't have to keep them," Solange quickly added. "A lot of them will be terrible, you know, while I'm developing."

"That way," Joie pressed on, "she can invest the money legitimately, say, in the stock market. I'll be in charge of that. You get three dances a week." She leaned forward and lowered her voice. "And, as a bonus, you can take her shopping in Beverly Hills."

Solange studied Marvin's reaction for signs that they'd gone too far. But while he still looked nervous, they appeared to be the nerves of a satisfied man.

"I promise to stay within your budget," Solange said with a practiced laugh. "And I looove sales."

Ping pong-like, Marvin stared at them. "It sounds like you rehearsed this."

Solange and Joie's eyes met, betraying nothing.

"Nah," said Joie. "We just think alike. Now, couple more

things. If everything goes well, you get bonuses. Say we want to go to the movies—we see a lot of movies—you can tag along and we'll only charge you a half day's rate."

"Joie is really fun to be with," Solange enthused, "and two hot chicks are better than one."

As he flashed a victory grin, Solange knew she was firmly in command of the Marvin control panel.

"But we don't do scenes with guys," said Joie.

Solange put her hand on Joie's arm. "I told him that already."

"Then I assume she also told you that her body is strictly off-limits. Look yes, touch no."

"I'm not a hooker," Solange said, putting her hands up for emphasis.

"But if ya need one," Joie volunteered, "we can fix you up." Reaching over, she pronged Solange's untouched baked potato and transferred it to her plate. "We want you to think of us for all your manly needs."

10
JANEY

When Billy finally did get up from the couch it was to tell Janey he was going to Hawaii on a surfing trip.

"What about your back?" she asked, because she was too shocked to say anything else.

"It's a little better."

"Better enough to surf?"

"I won't do anything strenuous."

They were in the living room around ten o'clock, sitting on

his precious sofa, credits rolling on *Black Hawk Down*, one of Billy's favorite movies. Eleanor was asleep upstairs and the girls were staying overnight at a friend's house, clues that he'd carefully planned the timing of the announcement. That he was idly stroking Rosie's head told Janey that his thoughts were elsewhere.

"Will you be coming back?"

Billy stretched his arms over his head and folded his hands behind his neck, showing no sign of the shoulder pain he'd complained about earlier in the day. "I'm thinking about a career change. Teaching isn't a challenge anymore. I need to write."

"Are you leaving us, Billy?" His passive-aggressiveness was so extreme, she always had to beat out every detail.

"I'm stressed. I'm not enjoying my life."

"Everyone is stressed. What makes you so special?"

"Vic Wakeman has a surf shop in Maui. He offered me a job."

"Oh," she said with phony relief. "Vic Wakeman. I didn't know he was out of rehab. So you're going to drop out of society and become Moondoggie?"

Rosie leaped up and pawed Janey's shoulder but there was no stopping this argument.

"I told him I'd think about it," said Billy. "I haven't made any definite plans."

"Except the plan to leave home."

"You'll have Bruce all to yourself."

"Can we refrain from sarcasm?"

"I'm serious. I'm just in the way here."

"What if Grandma died and you weren't around?"

"Trust me. Grandma doesn't want me here."

"Are you asking me for a divorce, Billy?"

"If I did, would you beg me to reconsider?"

Her slight hesitation, not more than a heartbeat, divulged more than all the arguments they'd ever had. She saw pain in Billy's eyes and unlike the phony slipped disc crap, it looked real. "I'm not the begging type."

"Not exactly a vote of confidence, is it?"

Janey's head pounded from the pressure of things moving way too fast. "We have to get some perspective, Billy. Maybe a third party, some sort of counseling type."

"I think getting away is the best way to get perspective."

His determination was so unexpected she was unable to conjure a thoughtful rebuttal. "You'll end up being one of those leather-faced, long-haired homeless guys with an old surfboard and a tooth missing."

Billy sighed and got up from the sofa. His back looked straight and resolute. "I'm sorry I could never be your hero," he said as he walked out of the room.

***

In a singular stroke of good fortune, there was no one at the park at 11 P.M., allowing Janey to act out in any way she chose. She banged her fist on the stone bench for awhile but it proved a painful, ineffective therapy. If only she could be a tree. Trees projected wisdom; they had clearly mastered life. Listening to the wind rustle through the enormous oak above her, she speculated on how it might advise her, but scared it might call her an idiot, she decided not to ask.

It was all her fault; she'd allowed Billy to slip away. She wanted to save her marriage, or she felt she should save it, or at least she wanted to want to save it, but for years neither had done the necessary work to keep the romantic pilot light burning. Lovemaking had given way to sex and then masturbatory fucking. Neither seemed willing to come to the rescue until Billy waved the white flag of Hawaii.

Her best friend looked up at her with concern in her eyes and Janey realized how difficult Rosie's life had been lately. "I'm sorry, Rosie," she said. "You're my best sweetie. I promise things will be better," and the song came forth: "'Cause we made a promise, we swore we'd always remember...no retreat, baby, no surrender.'"

That evening, Janey insisted that Billy join them at dinner to explain his imminent departure. To keep him from using his back as an excuse, she pushed the La-Z-Boy recliner up to the kitchen table.

Billy slowly settled into the chair, leaning so far back he couldn't reach his food. Janey had already prepared for that—she handed him a lap tray. While she explained to Eleanor and the girls that Billy was headed for Hawaii, he fiddled with the hand-lever and avoided their stunned faces.

"You can't even wait until the Tonight Show?" wailed Eleanor. "It's only two weeks away."

Lifting his head to speak, Billy winced. "I promise to watch it, Grandma."

"You're no damn good," she said with a scowl.

"I'm sure you're right," Billy replied.

Sherri's bottomless tear ducts exploded. "You can't leave us, Daddy. I won't let you!" She flung herself into Billy's arms, forcing the chair back another notch.

"I can't believe you want to be a beach bum," Candi said. "I'm gonna tell my friends you're going to prison."

"Me too," sobbed Sherri. "For murder, because you're killing our family." She clung to him mightily, like a deep-tissue probe. "What's wrong, Daddy? Why are you doing this?"

Billy held her close. "It has nothing to do with you and Candi. It only has to do with me."

"That's what parents always say when they're going to get divorced. Are you getting divorced?"

"No," said Janey, as if that made it official. "Your dad needs space and apparently there isn't enough of it here."

"Can't you just take Prozac?" Candi asked. "It's a lot cheaper."

Billy gently pushed Sherri off. "I'm not depressed." He reached around and rubbed his lower back.

If Billy wasn't depressed, Janey thought, she hoped she'd never have to witness the real thing.

"Did I hurt your back, Daddy?" Sherri looked stricken.

"I'll be fine."

"This is about Bruce, isn't it?" said Candi, lobbing an accusing gaze from one parent to the other. "How lame can you get? You don't even know the guy."

Sherri glared at Janey. "Mom, you're way too old to be a groupie."

"I don't want you at the Tonight Show," Eleanor declared, pointing a 102-year-old finger at Billy. "If you come I'll make them throw you out. You're no damn good."

After brief eye contact with each member of the family, Billy stared at his buckskin slippers. "I'm sorry," he said in a barely audible voice. "I wish I could explain it to you. I really need to go away for awhile."

Janey sensed the situation had reached the point of diminishing value. "Your dad needs to find his wave," she said to the girls. "We'll be fine."

Sherri ran to her room wailing.

Candi also wept, tears pooling in iridescent swatches on her cheeks, glitter sprinkling her scalloped potatoes.

Eleanor continued to eat.

Billy left the next day.

11
LILY

Lily found sudden notoriety not all it was cracked up to be. She had always appreciated when people responded to her love frequency but her environment had grown hostile. When she left the house she assumed every van she saw was hiding paparazzi, which it frequently was. Bean and Blossom quickly learned to discern photographers' predatory scents but since Lily refused to be held captive in her own home, she made sure to always look presentable and avoid strange facial expressions.

A simple trip to the herb store in North Hollywood became another stop on an unwanted personal appearance tour, where people felt free to launch intimate conversations. The dry cleaners pleaded for an autographed eight-by-ten glossy, guaranteeing it a spot on the celebrity wall between Tito Jackson and Debby Boone. Lily's new cleaning lady Esperanza, who had never spoken English, managed to scrape together enough words to praise her for rescuing Gary from eternal damnation.

Lily was polite if not forthcoming in response to people's liberally offered opinions. After the assorted questions about Gary's sexuality, she was often asked whether she was or planned to be an actress, the logic being that any woman involved with Gary must inevitably follow the same life track as Trish and end up being voted off a reality show.

The day before Gary shipped out—for it felt like he was going off to the front lines, Lily kneaded out a stony kink in the neck of Julie, a forty-year-old casting agent and ascended master of gossip. More than once Lily had advised Julie that talking shop instead of relaxing was counter-productive, but Julie's perpetual gabfest could not be stopped and it became Lily's challenge to overpower it with her calming life force.

When Julie failed to comment on the red-hot story singeing everyone's lips, Lily felt grateful that of all people, Julie had been mindful of her feelings. Then, as she was leaving, Julie said, "I fucked Val Segui once. We were really drunk and I went down on him."

Lily felt Julie's need for approval. "Uh huh," she said though she dreaded hearing the rest.

"He got so huge, I thought, wow, no gay guy can resist me. So I got on top of him and wham, did the air go out of that tire. He could not deal with a vagina." She checked a smile. "I hope you don't get hurt."

"Thanks," Lily said, not wanting to be rude but wishing she could be, just this once.

At five, when Lily went to Trader Joe's, she wore sunglasses, a baseball cap and dark liner altering the shape of her lips; the effect made her look like she had violently kissed a two-by-four.

Her need to see Gary that night verged on desperation. As she drove to his house with the dogs, she felt confident that she had made the right decision, that this test of fire was necessary and inevitable. She chose to have faith that the Goddess would never give her something so beautiful and then take it away.

After Gary forged bravely into her vagina while remaining hard as a Scud missile, she considered phoning Julie with the reassuring details, but only for a moment as she was far too preoccupied savoring their last night for a three-week forever. Afterwards, lying beside him on the bed, she stroked his chest.

Their heat made them kick the covers off. She stared at his penis lying exhausted along his left thigh and dwelled on how much she would miss it. Not to mention its owner.

"C'mere," he said, pulling her closer than conjoined twins. "I feel like you're going to be amputated from me."

Her hands moved randomly over his wondrous physique; she loved how that excited him. "I'll send you my continuous love vibration. You'll feel me every second."

"God, that makes me so hot." He kissed her like a hungry savage. "How many times can I call you a day?"

"Eight?"

"Okay, twelve."

***

In the morning, Francesca showed up to drive them to the airport. In lieu of the car-crushing Amazon woman Lily expected, Francesca looked barely able to crush a soda can. Bike shorts covered her lean thighs and a tee shirt with the logo "Violent Vixens" hugged her thin arms and modest breasts. Around her waist was a plastic belt with a buckle the size of an evening bag. Lily imagined it concealed money, lip gloss and a weapon.

"I'm extremely delighted to meet you," said Francesca, whose potent handshake helped mitigate Lily's fears about her job qualifications. For all she knew Gary might have hired her because she could crack her knuckles or play the harmonica. He was like that.

"Thanks for taking such good care of Gary."

"He's a dream," said Francesca. "But you're the one taking care of him. He's never been so happy."

Lily liked her immediately.

For the drive to the airport, Francesca insisted that the lovebirds sit in the back seat. "My eyes will be on the road," she promised. But due to canine interference, they could do little but remain squashed together, as the panting dogs refused to share Gary's lap. Lily was merely a platform for their hinds to rest on while they kissed Gary's face, exactly the thing Lily had in mind.

"Good thing I'm not insecure about their love," Lily remarked, "but they ought to check for stowaways on the plane."

"I'm really a dog," Gary said. "That's the secret truth about me."

"That must be why I love you."

When she left him at the international terminal, transferred to the custody of Terrell, a private security guard, it felt like a bandage ripped from an open wound. Gary blew one last kiss and disappeared into the crowd.

As the car pulled away, Bean and Blossom stuck their heads out the window and looked back at the airport.

***

The volume of phone calls from Wollongong, Australia went a long way toward suppressing Lily's fears. She bought a headset so they could talk during every non-working hour. Time expanded when they weren't connected, creating anxious spaces to fill.

One night, following a trail of links from an online CNN story about how the media was over-covering the non-story of Gary

DiCaro's enigmatic sexuality, in a weak moment, Lily found herself visiting an open message board.

The first thing that amazed her was that they all claimed to know someone who had witnessed the plastic surgery to replace one of Gary's testicles that a male model had allegedly bitten off at a bathhouse.

As someone with first-hand knowledge that his testicles were authentic, Lily logged on, posing as a "close friend" of Gary's "lady friend" and posted that she knew for a fact the testicle story was false.

"Well, I know it's true," said Garydelicious.

"Are you her?" asked Lovebuns.

Lily's face went flush, fearing there might be a hidden spy-cam in her computer. "No."

"Your username's Gaia and you're in Valley Glen, California. That sounds like her," Lovebuns IMed back.

Her Internet smarts were pitiful—Lily had no idea her location would be posted. She froze at the keyboard.

"How big is he?" asked KinkyLola.

"How big is his uniball?" asked Lovebuns.

"Have you seen him on Santa Monica Boulevard in his limo picking up fifteen-year-old boys?" asked GayGuy69. "I have. I was one of them."

Lily thought she'd hit some new rock bottom and hadn't even known she was in danger. Obviously, facts could only irritate people whose minds were made up. Gary sighed across the continents when she relayed the sordid dialogue on the phone. "If you need to chat, chat with me, okay, honey?"

"I don't know what I was thinking."

"People like to talk about my sex life. It takes their minds off their problems. I just heard that we're the victims of an alien-orchestrated human bonding drama."

Though she knew he was kidding, she thought it best not to mention that such things were actually possible. "Really?"

"It says right here in *Unexplained Phenomena Digest*: 'UFO-logist and psychic Delphina DeKoven explained that allegedly gay superstar Gary DiCaro's conversion to heterosexuality was induced by alien intelligence from Zeta Reticuli, part of an alien/human genetic hybridization breeding program.' Friends of yours?"

"Casual," said Lily.

"Is the mother ship from Close Encounters going to land in my driveway?"

"Maybe," she said. "You're part of the inter-galactic tour of the stars homes."

"That would explain the map of the Milky Way I found with my house circled on it."

Lily giggled. "What makes you think I'm an alien?"

"I never saw anyone make the Northern Lights go on in Southern California. And that flashbulb thing. I thought it was a special effect but I went with it."

He's too good to be true, she thought. "You're too good to be true," she said out loud.

"All the aliens say that. What's your mission, anyway?"

"To be with you, of course."

"Will you take me to your home galaxy?"

"I'm ready to go right now."

"Why do I believe you?"

"Because so many more things are possible than people think and it's wonderful to know that. And even more wonderful to experience."

"Lily, if things get any more wonderful, I'll be in intensive care."

She laughed. When they were about to hang up she said, "I'll visit your dreams tonight."

"Be naked."

She promised she would. Exhilarated, she stood up on the bed and bounced a few times. The Labs got all excited. On the way down from her fourth jump she grew dizzy. Her legs buckled and she fell, splayed like a newborn Bambi, sweating from head to toe.

In an instant the dogs were tongue-wiping her clean. Her next recollection came at two A.M. when Bean's wet nose startled her, but she was even more surprised to find herself covered in the throw from the living room sofa. Blossom's head was on her shoulder and when Lily stirred, Blossom licked her with a vengeance. "Did you bring me this blanket?" she asked Blossom, as Lily was in the same awkward position that she'd landed in and didn't recall getting up. Blossom smothered her with kisses.

Lily's limbs did not want to function; her body felt tense and inflexible. On her first step she became dizzy and to remain upright, rested a hand on Bean's neck. A canine balance beam, he stood perfectly still. She held onto him while she moved toward the kitchen.

The dogs yawned as she put the kettle on for tea. Their look of concern, the never-ending depth of their sacrifice and devotion brought tears to Lily's eyes. Easing into a kitchen chair she reached out and drew their soft heads to her chest. One dog was all the love anyone could handle; two were a hundred times better. Whoever invented dogs, she thought, outdid herself.

There was no sufficient way to reward such loyalty but while she waited for the water to boil she defrosted two marrow bones in the microwave. When she offered them to her love puppies, instead of running off for some vigorous gnawing, they held the bones in their mouths and stared at her with quizzical looks.

"Okay, it's two A.M. So what? Enjoy." But they kept staring.

The kettle whistle made her queasy. She switched it off, sank to the floor and put her head between her legs. The kitchen spun into orbit around her.

Bean and Blossom dropped their bones. They rushed to her and their tongues wiped every inch they could find.

She was unable to talk, had to push the dogs away, crawl to the bathroom and throw up. The Labs' faces were cheek-to-cheek with hers. The thought of how powerful the smell of vomit must be for dogs brought on another round.

A few minutes later she managed to get up and shuffle back to the kitchen for a cup of mint tea. Its perfume restored her equilibrium and she was able to ingest a graham cracker and a spoonful of goat milk yogurt.

It was May second. She was as regular as Greenwich Mean Time and her period was due in two days. But her body told her something very different.

The only time she hadn't used her diaphragm was the first night she was with Gary and bleeding heavily, the night they combined their DNA. It was virtually impossible to be inseminated at the height of a menstrual cycle; only a few weeks had passed—not nearly enough time to detect pregnancy. But when Lily looked up to the sky, she felt confirmation from the unborn world. If she and Gary could create a light show together, their love had the power to break all the rules.

12
THE PARK

When Lily went to the park that afternoon she felt like she was carrying the planet Jupiter in her stomach but no one seemed to notice. The park was the only public place she felt safe these days, and she thanked the Goddess for responding to the essence she'd fed to the soil.

Jupiter flip-flopped when Lily saw Solange and Janey under the Sugar Pine tree. Humbled by the magnitude of news bursting inside her, she was grateful that there was no sign of Cleo to interfere with its delivery.

Fudgsicle confronted Bean and assumed the international play position; tiny punk dogs were forever trying to lure Bean into a fight and he good-naturedly played punching bag while Fudgsicle attacked him. Elsewhere, Rosie and Blossom engaged in a futile race to catch a squirrel as it scampered up a tree.

As she got closer, Lily noticed the bewildered aura swirling Medusa-like around Janey's head. Even her hair seemed confused, as if part of it would rather be home in bed. Janey was on a spiritual journey, even if she was not yet aware of it. "Hey you two," Lily called out.

Janey did her *Home Alone* impersonation. "Wow, it's that chick on YouTube."

"Stop it," Lily said, waving her arms. "No, go ahead. It eases the tension."

"You know," Janey said, "this is the most exciting thing that ever happened to me and it's happening to you. Which says a lot about my life."

"But you must be upset, Lily," said Solange. "Those rags only print lies." Solange reached out for a hug. When their bodies touched, Lily felt an electric shock pass through them. She jumped back. "Wow," said Solange, "what was that?"

"I'm not sure," Lily said but suspected Jupiter had announced his presence.

"You felt like a joy buzzer." Solange grabbed Janey's arm. "Here, you hug her."

When Janey and Lily embraced, another tingling sensation made them shriek. Janey put her hand over her heart. "You must have swallowed an appliance. I'm guessing alarm clock."

Solange held out her arms. "Let's all hug!"

They did. And let out a brief, collective scream.

"What's going on?" asked Solange.

Seized by a wave of fatigue and vertigo, Lily put her hand on Janey's shoulder. "Can we sit down?"

They formed a campfire circle. "I have some big news to share with you," Lily said.

"Uh oh," Janey said. "More big news?"

Solange crossed her heart and zipped her lips. "I'm a phenomenal secret keeper. You wouldn't believe the stuff I know. I wish I could tell you, but unfortunately, I can't."

"Whatever it is," said Janey, "Bruce Springsteen couldn't beat it out of me. Although he's welcome to try."

Lily cupped her hands around her mouth. "I'm doing this in case there are stalkerazzi with telephoto lenses who can lip read." She leaned in. "I think I'm pregnant."

Judging by their unhinged jaws, they were aghast.

"Is that why you're buzzing?" asked Solange.

"Maybe. It's so surreal. I was having my period when it happened."

Janey laughed. "You know that's impossible, right?" She paused. "Except maybe for you."

"Lily has different periods than the rest of us," said Solange. "And she does instant messaging with the Goddess. Is that what happened, Lily?"

"I know it sounds crazy."

"'Nuns run bald through Vatican halls pregnant, pleadin' Immaculate Conception...'" quoted Janey.

Solange looked puzzled. "I don't get that one."

Janey shrugged. "They don't all make sense."

"I can't get over this," said Solange, also upping her hands over her mouth. "Here we are sitting with the woman...who's having Gary DiCaro's baby."

"He's beyond gorgeous," Janey said with a sigh.

Solange nodded. "Even I'm attracted to him."

"I've gotta admit," Janey said nodding at Lily, "I thought he was strictly gay, but if anyone can bring out his recessive gene, it's you."

"We're not into labels," Lily said. "That's my new answer to the question everyone keeps asking me. What do you think?"

"I think it's no one's beeswax," said Solange.

"You'd be amazed," Lily said, "apparently it's everyone's beeswax. Maybe it's best that Gary went to Australia so this can die down. But truthfully, I don't know how any of it happened. I just know I've been in love with Gary forever and I love him so much that maybe I tipped the scales in my favor." She shook her head. "I don't know. Solange, could you ever fall in love with a man?"

"I doubt it," Solange replied, "but I don't believe in labels either. Anything is possible, especially with you. I think it's incredibly romantic."

"Have you done a pregnancy test?" Janey asked.

"No," Lily said. "So far, it's just a feeling."

"I see," Janey said, looking skeptical. "But I'll keep an open mind and pick up a test for you. You don't want some idiot taking a picture of you at the pharmacy buying that. Besides, it'll make me feel young and fertile."

Nodding, Solange said, "Now that you're famous you have to be extra careful."

A surge of love for her new friends made Lily weep unabashed. "I feel so close to you," she said, taking their hands. "Our lives are so connected. That's why we all felt that quivering."

"Be honest," Janey said. "Are you an alien?"

"Sometimes I wonder about that myself."

Janey leaned forward. "Let's hug again."

The women rose to their knees and as they pressed together, strobe-like currents rippled through them.

"I love it," said Solange. "It's so trippy."

"This is going to be one amazing baby," said Janey.

***

The next day, Solange, Joie, Janey and their dogs came over for dinner and a pregnancy test. Lily served a pasta salad of homemade gravlax, capers and tomatoes, an herb salad with feta cheese and olive bread from La Brea Bakery. Joie and Solange brought two expensive bottles of Pinot Noir and Janey brought five assorted pints of Ben & Jerry's.

In the yard the dogs feasted on a huge bag of sirloin scraps and beef bones bequeathed by Mr. Kim, lap dance aficionado, Solange-admirer and meat department manager at the Asian Ranch Market. Lily provided a side dish of ground cabbage, broccoli stalks and carrots seasoned with fish oil and garlic. The dogs slopped and flung the stuff every which way, then set to work scouring every last morsel off their plates, bowls and the patio.

While Joie and Solange cleaned up and Janey wrangled the boy dogs, Blossom and Rosie followed Lily into the bathroom. As females, they seemed very interested in supervising the test. Already, Lily had felt her baby's soul contact her from his holding pattern in the universe. He had a male vibration drenched in Goddess wisdom and Lily loved him with a force matched only by her love for Gary.

"It's a plus," Lily said when she returned with her helpers and as she said it out loud, she was clobbered by the realization that this third party had something do with why she hadn't gone to Australia.

"Just an ordinary plus?" asked Janey. "I kind of expected a fireworks display."

"Right, like the buzzing at the park," Solange said. "Your baby is already putting out amazing energy."

Prying open a pint of Ben & Jerry's, Joie stuck in her spoon and extracted about half of it. "Solange wants to be in your coven," she said during a huge mouthful.

Solange's face reddened; she looked stricken. "Joie, don't be like that," and like a sudden squall she broke out in unearthly sobs.

The outburst seemed so out of proportion, Lily sensed that

Solange had opened a big karmic pocket, something Lily often witnessed when she performed deep-tissue massage. Lily wanted to touch her but Joie loomed in a proprietary manner that suggested she'd better not.

"It's okay, honey," said Joie, gently rubbing Solange's back as her crying diminished. "Do you want to go home and talk about it?"

"No, I want you to apologize."

Joie retracted her hand. "For what?"

"Being rude to Lily."

"No apology required," said Lily as she concentrated on flooding the room with pink, compassionate light. "I've been called 'witchy woman' before."

"You're not a witch," Solange said emphatically.

"What do you think, Janey?"

"Prescription strength loony," said Janey, "but loads of fun."

"Look," said Joie, "Solange is very impressionable. She gets carried away."

Solange made a gagging noise. "Excuse me. Am I still here?"

"Honey, we need to go home and have a family discussion."

"Don't speak for me," Solange snapped. She turned from Joie to Lily. "I gave my period to the Earth Goddess this morning. It was awesome. I think that's what made me cry. And now that you're pregnant and can't give any for awhile, we should all help out."

"I'll see you at home," Joie said, rising then heading for the door.

"Blood has power," Lily whispered to Solange. "Go home and make things better."

***

Janey pondered her own menstrual situation after the door closed on the bickering lovers. "Okay, I'll give one period for you," she told Lily. "One. But if my Petunias die…"

"You're about to have mega-Petunias," said Lily with such assurance, Janey got a sudden cramp and blamed Lily for causing it. "I swear, I think it just started."

"Really? I'll get you a jar and a watering can. My roses are starving."

Janey laughed as hard as she'd laughed years ago when Eleanor's home permanent turned green. Of all the things she thought she'd never do in life, menstruating into the soil was just below joining the circus. "Now?"

"Strike while the blood is flowing."

"You're not going to watch me, are you?"

"Nope. You're on your own. There's a hose and towels out there to clean yourself up."

It was every bit as weird as she'd imagined. She squatted over the jar and saw Rosie's head rotate like someone watching a freak show. "What's so funny? You think this bathroom is private?" Then she felt her flow begin and squeezed a ribbon of blood into the water.

Rosie's nose scrutinized every step of the procedure.

Swishing the blood into the watering can, Janey set off to nourish as many of Lily's plants as possible. As their new godmother she felt responsible for their well-being.

"You did a great job," Lily said when Janey returned to join her for tea at the kitchen table.

"Were you watching?"

"No, but I felt the plants reacting to you. They're ecstatic."

"They say nice things about you too."

They shared a stupid giggle, then Lily grew serious. "I'm worried the baby might be too much for Gary. So much has happened already."

Though Janey wanted to be helpful, Lily's problem was in an echelon unimaginable to her. She tried to imagine herself pregnant with Bruce Springsteen's baby but couldn't wrap her brain around the concept, not even theoretically. "What would you say to me if something this fabulous happened in my life?"

When Lily's grin returned Janey knew it was a great question. "Enjoy it," Lily said. "Expand your capacity for happiness."

"Gee, I'm really wise."

"It's true. You are." Lily reached across the table and held Janey's arms at the elbow. "Janey, would you be my baby's godmother?"

Leveled by the immensity of the proposition, Janey felt colonies of goose bumps breaking out. "But you hardly know me. And mothering isn't my greatest skill, though I don't really have skills."

"You channel Bruce Springsteen, don't you?" Lily put her hands together. "Call it a personal request from the Goddess. What do you say then?"

"I am incredibly honored. Beyond honored. I'm standing 'stonelike at midnight suspended in my masquerade.'" Later she would consider the implications of being godmother to Gary DiCaro's child—when she was alone and free to jump around and act like a moron.

"Thank you, Janey. I feel less anxious now. You're going to be the most wonderful godmother."

Janey hadn't felt so sincerely appreciated in a long time. She almost couldn't take it. "I get to turn the kid on to Bruce, right?"

"Of course. You can even take him to New Jersey."

They did an encore of the stupid giggle.

13
SOLANGE

Marvin's imposing ranch house sat at the foot of a cul-de-sac in the hills of Encino; according to Solange's *feng shui* manual, a negative location. The décor looked like it came from the Spanish Inquisition: oversized pieces with iron legs, heavy fabrics in dark colors, sword and antique gun collections. Above all there was paper. Bookcases were jammed and most of the chairs held piles of yellowing newspapers that nearly reached the ceiling.

Meeting Marvin on his own turf, Fudgsicle seemed reserved; Marvin was clearly not a dog person. But the paper totem poles caught the Yorkie's attention and Solange worried that he might be unable to resist marking one.

"You need smoke alarms," Solange commanded, as it was clearly necessary to assume authority. "It's a major fire hazard in here."

"I have some—I just never put them up." Nervously he began rearranging piles of paper, moving them from one crowded spot to another. "It's just some research material I've been meaning to organize."

"Do you have a ladder? I'll install 'em for you."

An erection formed a tent in Marvin's khaki Dockers. "Really?"

"Sure, I learned tons of handyman stuff from Joie. She

practically lives at Home Depot." A brilliant plan bubbled forth. "Hey, we can kill two birds with one stone. I'll do it naked."

Marvin stumbled running for the ladder.

"Get a screwdriver too. I'll take Fudgsie outside to pee."

In the abbreviated back yard that dropped off into a canyon, Fudgsicle sniffed the foliage with some hesitation. Solange couldn't tell if he was curious or frightened. Watching him wet a Bottlebrush tree, she decided to utilize some of her next period to bless and secure the area for his protection.

When she came back she saw the stepladder set up with an array of tools on its shelf and Marvin revolving in his swivel chair. On the CD player: "Light My Fire," perhaps a sign that he had a sense of humor but he probably just liked the number that had snared him into her web.

Solange dropped a bit of clothing on each step: first the Jimmy Choo pumps, then the frilly Betsey Johnson skirt, sheer white schoolgirl blouse, teddy and finally the garter belt.

Marvin rolled his chair under the ladder and moaned when he looked up at her pink vagina.

"Don't come yet, honey, we haven't screwed yet," said Solange. "I mean, I haven't put your smoke detector up yet."

His grunts spoke of immense pleasure.

"I'm sticking it in now." She picked up the screwdriver and ran it along the crease of her thigh. Had Marvin been more of a cleaniac she might have worked it a little, but no way that nasty thing was touching her snatch.

Marvin fondled himself as she deftly fastened the alarm to a plate on the ceiling.

"I'm done," she declared.

"Come on my head," he said, hand pumping.

"Okay," Solange whispered, "if you really want me to." She kept one foot on the top rung and the other down two steps. With her right hand she went searching for her G-spot and rubbed her fingers over it until the song climaxed and her juices dripped out over the span of five consecutive orgasms. She could have faked it but the demonstration of her technical prowess had gotten her unexpectedly hot.

***

Two days after the incident at Lily's, Solange and Joie had yet to discuss it. Solange suspected that talking wouldn't solve anything and might drive them further apart but she also knew that her newfound power was having an effect. Normally Joie liked to hash things out on the spot, but now that Solange was tight with the Goddess, she thought Joie might be devising a new control strategy.

No doubt Joie was stressing over the situation—she began leaving food on her plate. One morning as she listlessly dragged her spoon through a bowl of soggy Wheaties, she looked up and asked, "Can't you at least admit she's got you under a spell?"

After all the pondering Joie had done, Solange expected more than a feeble question. "I'm not under a spell."

"So why do you buy into all her hocus pocus?"

"Maybe we were friends in a past life."

"Exactly," said Joie, dropping her spoon into the milk. "You're a sucker for that weird shit."

"Wrong. I'm maturing and evolving as an artist. It's not about Lily."

Joie put her bowl on the floor for Fudgsicle. "Since you've become chummy with her you've been going off on crying jags. You're not happy."

Everything Joie said reaffirmed Solange's suspicion that the enlightenment gap between them was widening. But she had no time for an in-depth blow-up. "I'm meeting Marvin at ten. I have to get dressed." She got up.

"Maybe it's Marvin, then. Maybe you miss the club."

"None of the above, Joie. It's all going great."

"It's not. You just don't see it."

Solange left the kitchen. In her bedroom she set her attention on auditioning clothes for her shopping spree at the Continental Art Supply in Reseda. Eventually she settled on an Indian batik wrap-around skirt over a black halter, buckskin sandals and gold hoop earrings. With practiced fingers she braided leather cords and beads into her hair. The effect was bohemian retro. She looked incredibly artsy.

It was vital that she appear professional, which she was, in her mind. Since enrolling in the non-credited summer course at Valley College she'd been dreaming up painting concepts for a major gallery exhibition or at least an important showing at the Fashion Square Mall.

An hour later she was at Marvin's house. "You look like Pocahontas," he said when he answered the door.

"Was Pocahontas artistic? I'm going for artistic."

"Oh." His face turned a maroon hue. "You look very artistic."

Solange accepted his validation, although a man who wore nothing but Dockers and polyester polo shirts was clearly not a fashion savant.

Marvin opened the garage and they walked to his car. She'd planned to let him drive but when she saw the interior of his Lexus, a mobile version of his house crammed with papers and fast food containers, she declared that until it looked presentable, she would be the designated driver—which also entailed a $10/mile surcharge.

Eight miles and $80 later they arrived at the art store where in front of the Liquitex acrylic paint display Solange slipped into an alternate reality.

"Guess they got all the colors," said Marvin with the clueless look of a longshoreman at a Tupperware party.

The display twinkled like a prism. But one color, Phthalo Blue, touched a place so deep in Solange's emotional reservoir she grew lightheaded. Her hand reached out and extracted a tube. Like a joystick to a time machine it thrust her back to 1990; she was riding with Andi Nyler down Canal Street in Venice. Her orange hip hugger shorts and lime green tee shirt clashed exotically with their Schwinn bicycles—hers in hot pink and Andi's in bright, metallic Phthalo Blue.

Andi was her first kiss, before her sexuality had a name. Their Ken and Barbie dolls copulated daily. She ate dinner at Andi's house every Friday night—her mother inevitably made rump roast, an unending source of private giggles.

But mostly they rode, from Venice south to Redondo Beach or north to Will Rogers State Park. Long after Andi's funeral, her shiny blue bike remained on the Nylers' front porch.

"Are you okay?" inquired Marvin. The sound kicked her back to the present. Crumpling to the floor, she squeezed the tube of Phthalo Blue to the brink of detonation and cried twenty years worth of tears all at once.

Marvin went pale and stiff, a man in an invisible straightjacket. His head rotated, perhaps seeking help or to ensure they were not being observed, as the scene resembled a parent in a toy store with a tantrummy child. "What's the matter?" he asked in a sharp whisper.

"My friend Andi died." The words sputtered out between sobs. "She had leukemia. She was my best friend." Holding out the misshapen tube of paint, she added, "This was the color of her bike."

"Please get up," said Marvin.

But she couldn't. Andi's brief life was suddenly all around her, consuming her. She felt her embrace from a magical place she saw vividly, a canvas demanding to be painted. She touched the tube of paint to her lips.

"Need some help?" asked a thin, heavily pierced young man whose nametag read "Juan." He seemed unfazed by the scenario, as though it was a typical exhibit of artistic temperament.

"Her friend died," explained Marvin who, with a determined heave, lifted Solange to her feet.

Juan paused, his eyes roaming the vicinity as if searching for a body. He seemed satisfied that the fatality had not occurred on his watch. "Do you need some art supplies?" he asked with queenly inflection.

Marvin looked at Solange, engulfed in her trance. "She'll take one of each color."

Juan raised his eyebrows ever so slightly.

In the distance Solange saw Andi wave goodbye. She held out the tube of paint in her open hand as a parting gesture.

Marvin took it from her. "This one too."

Solange reoriented herself. "What does Phthalo mean?" she asked Juan.

"It's a transparent pigment with a metallic element."

"Like a bicycle?"

Juan shook his head. "Whatever."

Marvin glared at Juan. "Just give her the works," he told Juan. "Brushes, easel, canvases, turpentine…"

"Right, turpentine." She'd forgotten about turpentine and was impressed that Marvin hadn't. "Do you carry any brands that don't have that bad smell? You know, like lemon or floral scented?"

"This is acrylic paint," Juan explained slowly, as if she had a learning disability. "It's water soluble. Turpenoid, not turpentine, is what you use to thin oil paint." He pointed to a similar paint display nearby. "Oils." Back to where they were standing. "Acrylics."

Solange felt intimidated by Juan's unspoken censure. He would of course claim he'd taught her everything she knew when her first exhibit opened, including a special anecdote about the Phthalo blue paint. She struggled to come up with a question that didn't sound ignorant. "Which kind of paint do you prefer?"

"I just work here."

Marvin took out his American Express Platinum card and flicked it back and forth between his fingers. "She'll take both kinds. We'll have them delivered."

On the way back to the car, Marvin reeled off a string of expletives barely under his breath. Solange decided not to ask him why.

When she got home, Fudgsicle scampered out the door wearing a yellow plastic rain slicker with matching booties. The temperature was at least ninety and he was panting.

"Hello, sweetie boy," she exclaimed as he leaped into her arms. "Look at you! Is it going to rain?"

Joie stood in the doorway wearing Solange's Halloween Elvira costume, which featured yards of black nylon hair and pale stage makeup that clown-whitened her dark complexion. "Fudgsie saw it at Petco and he had to have it. You know what a clothes-dog he is."

"Cute," said Solange, liberating Fudgsie from his fashion prison while she debated whether it was Cadmium Yellow or Yellow Light Hansa.

Lifting her hands in the air and wiggling her inch-long acrylic nails Joie said, "I'm casting a spell."

"Are you going to make it rain?"

Joie brushed Solange's face with a hank of Elvira hair. "We're trying to get you out of your funk."

Solange sighed. "I'm not in a funk."

"Are so," insisted Joie. "And I'm not going to change clothes until you're out of it."

"If you want to be hot and sweaty that's up to you."

Joie remained in the Elvira ensemble when they took their afternoon trip to the park with Fudgsie, although being LA, the only looks she received were of the "nice outfit" variety. At dinner Joie used the fingernails to scoop margarine out of the plastic tub and to spear her turkey burger.

Exhausted from her trauma at the art store, Solange ate heartily, taking pains to appear indifferent, as if Joie were clad in her customary white tee shirt and black denim shorts. She was determined not to get into a drawn-out discussion since Joie liked to dissect ideas and talk about them persistently until they became an abstraction and her opponent succumbed to fatigue.

Rising from her chair, Joie leaned in close to Solange and popped her boobs out of the Elvira dress. "How about some melons for dessert?"

"Burnt Umber," Solange replied.

"What?"

"Your nipples are Burnt Umber." Solange was amazed by her precise color recall and knew in her heart she was gifted. "They're almost the exact same shade as Fudgsie. I never noticed that before."

Joie shoved her breasts back inside the dress. "What's the matter with you?"

"Nothing. I'd just like to be alone for awhile."

Joie bowed in an exaggerated, royal manner, her nylon wig dusting the floor. "Yes, Miss Garbo. Call me when you want me, Miss Garbo." Flinging the hair back she fled the kitchen, leaving behind half a turkey burger.

Solange winced as the bedroom door slammed, then she split the burger remnant with Fudgsie. When she looked up she saw Andi Nyler sitting across from her at the table. Andi smiled warmly, produced a deck of cards from the pocket of her blue jeans and shuffled them like a pro, a skill that had always delighted the eight-year-old Solange.

Andi didn't speak but her thoughts were as obvious as if there were cartoon balloons floating over her head. "Show the light, Solange. Offer your gift."

Nothing about the vision seemed unnatural. Andi's presence exhilarated her and brought an end to her mourning. Her words felt like a call to action, a message from an angel.

14
JANEY

The first thing Eleanor noticed when they settled into the limo was the mini-bar. "I hope the driver doesn't have one of these," she said loud enough for him to hear.

The driver, a portly, gray-haired man, displayed the carriage of a Buckingham Palace guard.

"He's a professional," Janey assured her, hiding her own delight over the mother lode of little bottles, surely a gift from heaven to ease her forthcoming ordeal. "What can I get you, Grandma?"

Doing her best Queen of Sheba, Eleanor studied the sunlight's reflection off her diamond rings. "Scotch on the rocks."

Janey went for the ice bucket. The trip to Burbank was only about fifteen minutes and she wanted to make sure there was time for a second round. She handed Eleanor the Scotch and poured herself a glass of Chablis.

"Can we have a drink?" asked Sherri.

"Not unless you turn twenty-one before we get there," Janey said, offering each girl a can of diet soda.

Candi rubbed the cold can on her chest. "You must save a lot of money on air-conditioning," she called to the driver. A few moments later a blast of cold air made them all shiver.

"Hey, turn it down!" yelled Eleanor. "I don't want to have blue skin on television!"

"Why not? It'll go with your hair," said Candi, inserting the soda can into her cleavage. Exploding from her skimpy tube top like twin mushroom clouds, her young breasts seemed exempt from gravity. Janey wondered how milk from her flat prairie chest had produced Candi's endowment.

Unzipping the tote bag she used to carry her dance shoes, Eleanor began tossing in liquor bottles.

"When we get home we'll all get drunk," Eleanor promised as

the girls giggled.

A few minutes later they pulled into the studio lot where Sherri pointed out Jay Leno's chocolate Bentley parked by the artists' entrance. "He has a bazillion cars. He drives a different one every day and keeps them in an airplane hangar."

Candi yawned. "What a waste of metal."

"Well, your shoe collection is a waste of leather," said Sherri. "At least no animals are killed making cars."

"Unless they're run over," Candi said. "I wish we were in New York on Letterman."

"You're not going to be on anything," warned Eleanor. "Just me. Don't think those big bosoms are going to get you on television. You have to sit in the audience."

"Whatever you say, Grandma."

Janey slurped down the last few drops of wine. "'Come on, come on, let's shake it tonight', whaddya say?"

Eleanor shrugged. "I'll wave to you from the stage."

As they exited the limo Janey snatched the tote bag and struggled to keep the liquor bottles from clanging.

They were met by Monique, a perky young production assistant with a headset and a carpenter's belt holding enough electronics to stock Circuit City. Monique promised to make Eleanor comfortable and attend to all her needs.

"You must have drawn the short straw," Janey said.

Monique led them down narrow, beige hallways to a room with a glittery star on the door bearing Eleanor's name.

"Take our picture," Eleanor commanded.

But Monique suddenly froze mannequin-like, her eyes slightly crossed as she listened to her headset. "Be right back," she chirped and ran off, obviously called away to some show business emergency.

Eleanor grumbled and Sherri, the family photographer, offered to take some pictures.

"Make sure you can see my name on the door."

While they were assembling for group shots, Janey saw Jay Leno in jeans and a blue work shirt approaching them.

Eleanor noticed him too. "Hey, young man!" she shouted. "We need someone to take our picture."

"Oh, sure," he replied. "That's what I'm here for."

"That's Jay Leno, Grandma," Janey said.

"Did you see my star?"

"Yes, we spare no expense," replied Jay. "I'm looking forward to dancing with you."

"Make sure you don't step on my toes."

Jay promised to do his best while Janey conjured up frightening scenarios of potential Eleanor *faux pas* on national television. Good thing she had the little bottles.

"I'm back," said the re-materialized Monique. She took Eleanor's arm. "Let's put your things away, sweetie, then I'll take you to makeup and the pre-interview." She turned to Janey and the girls. "You guys can wait in the green room, okay?"

The trio followed Monique's directions to the green room, which Janey was surprised to discover was not green. Most of the people sitting around did not appear to be celebrities, except for a woman eating lox and bagels from the buffet who looked like Loni Anderson.

"Have something to eat," Janey told the girls. "It's free, as Grandma would say."

The girls helped themselves to finger sandwiches, fruit, cheese and brownies, while Janey's nerves kept her too jangled to think about food. She stared at the coffee urn, then decided not to mix beverages and poured another glass of wine. She joined the girls in a strategic corner with good celebrity view angles. "Is that Loni Anderson?" she whispered.

Not a hint of recognition on their faces.

"She was married to Burt Reynolds; they had a really ugly divorce, remember?"

"Who's Burt Reynolds?" asked Sherri.

Janey aged a few years. "You need to watch more television," she said, peeking to make sure Loni wasn't eavesdropping. "He's practically your dad's favorite actor."

At the mention of her father, Sherri's face sagged and she dropped her finger sandwich on her plate. "I wish Daddy was here. He would totally get off on this."

"He's probably on his lanai with a big fat joint waiting for the show to come on," Candi said.

Janey glared. "Knock it off, Candi."

"You never want us to talk about him," Candi said, her voice reaching sufficient volume to be heard by all. "He's our father and you won't tell us why he left."

"He couldn't compete with Bruce Springsteen," said Sherri. She spat out the sacred name like it was a disease.

In a moment of paranoia, Janey stole a peek at the Loni woman to make sure she wasn't tuning in. Though Loni appeared to be engrossed in conversation, Janey felt certain she had an ear trained on her family conflict. "We'll talk about it at home, okay?"

"But we're sitting here with nothing to do, so let's talk about it. Maybe Dad read your porno emails."

"What? What are you talking about?"

"The BOSS-list. 'Girls, I had a dream last night. I was in the shower with him and we were making out and oh, I wanted him so bad! And he was...engorged! But we couldn't do it because my husband was standing there with an ax.'"

There was no need to check. No one in the green room including Loni Anderson could possibly avoid their discussion. "That wasn't my dream. And who asked you to read my email?"

"It's so embarrassing," said Sherri. "My mother is in a fan club."

Candi snorted. "All they do is talk about his butt."

"I'm warning you," said Janey.

The look on Sherri's face made Janey feel like a fresh Chianti stain on a white carpet. "No wonder Daddy left," Sherri said. "You totally humiliated him." She leaped up and fired a parting shot: "That's why he does drugs—because of you!"

Sherri's attempt to storm out of the green room was thwarted by her headlong crash into Blue Man Group, a trio of royal blue billiard balls in jump suits. They picked her up as if she were a prop from their act and moved her aside.

"Don't see that every day," noted Candi.

***

Like a showbiz veteran Eleanor waltzed onto the *Tonight Show* set, waving to the audience and soaking up the applause. Jay came up and escorted her to the seat of honor as previous guest Orlando Bloom repaired to the couch.

Janey, Candi and Sherri watched from the green room. Janey and Sherri held hands.

"Could I be more nervous?" Janey asked rhetorically.

"Grandma's a pro," Candi said. "She'll kill."

"I hope Daddy watches," said Sherri.

On the TV monitor Jay said, "It's a pleasure to meet you, Eleanor."

The words had barely left his throat when Eleanor cut in, shouting as if she had to reach the TV audience without technical assistance. "I tried to get on with Johnny but they said I was too young. I was only eighty-five but I already had nine first place medals. Now I have fifty-seven."

Jay waited for the audience laughter to die down. "That's remarkable. When did you start dancing?"

"I was eighty-two. My husband died and I needed something to do. I always liked to dance but my husband was a klutz so I was a wallflower for fifty-three years. How long have you been on television?"

"Fifty-three years? That sounds about right."

"I used to watch Johnny. I never heard of you but you seem like a nice young man."

The crowd howled as Jay accepted the compliment.

"Oh, jeez," moaned Janey in the green room.

"Now, you're a hundred and two," continued Jay, "and you're still dancing. Is that the secret to your longevity?"

"I just keep breathing."

"I see. That sounds like excellent advice."

"You know," Eleanor said, placing her hand on Jay's arm, "for the first eighty years of my life no one liked me."

"Really? I can't imagine that."

She paused before firing off her punch line. "But then, after eighty, no matter what you do, they say, 'Oh, isn't that cute?'"

In the green room Candi elbowed Janey. "Hey, Mom, that's your line."

Janey shook her head in amazement. "I never realized she

could hear me."

The finale of Eleanor's guest shot was a dance lesson in which she taught Jay to do the cha-cha. "One, two, one two three," she instructed as she guided him through his paces. After a few bars of the cha-cha mix of "Tea for Two," there was a musical "ta da!" after which the new Fred and Ginger bowed and curtsied for the audience.

"Thank you, Eleanor," said Jay as he kissed her hand and attempted to guide her off the stage.

But Eleanor refused to exit. "You're a nice young man. You didn't step on my toes," she said. "Now I have something to say to my grandson. He's watching in Hawaii." Having trapped Jay she turned to the camera. "Billy, I'm glad you're not here because you're no damn good. You're a bad husband, a dope smoker and you can stay in Hawaii for all I care." Then she smiled and threw a kiss to the audience.

***

On the way home in the limo Janey was elated to discover that the mini-bar had been fully restocked. As she poured herself a Daiquiri she let her brain go off-line. She pictured a miniature bottle warehouse somewhere staffed with tiny bartenders. The scenario, mixed with profound relief that her torment was finally over, made her chuckle.

"What are you laughing at?" inquired Eleanor.

"Nothing, Grandma, I'm just happy." With a finger to her lips to conceal her actions from the driver, Janey added a thimbleful of rum to each of the girls' colas.

The girls mouthed their thanks.

Having vacated the spotlight Eleanor looked a little droopy. "Did you notice that my segment was longer than the others?"

Sherri took the bait. "Oh, much longer, Grandma. You were the star. I'll bet your ratings are awesome."

"It was so rude that they had other guests on the show with you," said Candi.

"How do you find out the ratings?" Eleanor asked.

"Maybe they post it on the Internet," said Candi.

Eleanor beamed.

Relaxing for the first time in weeks Janey leaned back and watched the monotonous parade of commercial establishments roll by. As the limo stopped at a light in front of Petco, she thought she saw Rosie's reflection in the window. It was so startling she instinctively reached out to pet her before realizing she wasn't physically there.

I miss you...I'm lonely, whispered Rosie. It wasn't a voice, but it was louder than a thought.

Staring into her Daiquiri, Janey tried to determine if she was in an altered state or plain old drunk. Her bond with Rosie was perfection, free of struggle, the one person—for Rosie was clearly more than a dog—Janey could depend on. Janey prayed Rosie didn't have serious dog issues. Another disgruntled family member would be unbearable.

Shuddering, Janey poured the rest of the drink down her throat, seeking inebriation to dismiss the notion that her dog was trying to speak and possibly complain to her.

Don't worry, Rosie whispered, *I love you.*

15
THE GODDESSES

"Hi, it's Gepetto," Janey told Lily when she picked up the phone for the third time that morning. "Any minute now my dog is going to turn into a girl. Not that I'd mind having a third child but I don't know how I'd explain it to the neighbors."

Lily had just hung up with Solange, who had breathlessly described visions she'd been having of her late childhood friend, and before that, Gary had called to say he was coming home in two days. Lily invited both of them over in an hour, allowing herself enough time to sit down and have a leisurely anxiety attack.

Forty-seven phone calls and she hadn't so much as hinted at the bombshell she'd soon be dropping in Gary's lap. It was strictly an in-person topic. In her fantasies it was the happiest news he'd ever heard but as the actual moment approached, more sobering scenarios vied with the happily-ever-afters.

The pregnancy had thrown her body into a violently happy state in which she questioned old reliable signals. It was cosmic baby interference, a bursting inside her that knocked out her power source and messed with her basic instincts. Her brain was not her go-to organ; she did not "think things through"—she felt them in the moment. She felt vulnerable to energies she couldn't identify.

Anything could happen.

She felt a burning need for Mother Earth. Returning to the scene of conception, she removed her clothes, dove into the ground and coated herself with grass and soil the way the dogs rolled in formidable scents.

As she let the earth scour her body, Gary's life force rose up to meet her. The grass became his silky hair; gritty dirt the late-day roughness of his beard; the breeze turned into his breath. Climbing inside her, he shouted his presence. She became aroused then had a sudden and spontaneous orgasm, the extreme type that only Gary had ever produced in her.

Bean and Blossom sniffed the area around her as she writhed on the ground, as if someone was next to her, someone like their supreme commander, Gary. But Lily sniffed the space and smelled him as well.

His scent was there. That had to be a good sign. And the dogs looked so happy. He had to be there. She felt ready to tell him at that moment and wished he were physically there already.

Still needing to spend energy, she took the Labs for a well-deserved tour of the local dumpsters as they loved to pig out on garbage smells. To be so accepting, so fascinated with the foul side of life seemed to Lily an enlightened quality, the ultimate in non-judgment, a component of dogs' unconditional love.

Before her guests' arrival, Lily brewed a pot of fresh mint tea and phoned Krispy Kreme for a doughnut delivery, having persuaded herself that the warm glazed crullers relieved morning sickness.

Solange brought lox and a dozen bagels, looking adorably scandalous in her tie-dyed one-shoulder top and shredded cut-off jeans. Janey, in a black Springsteen photo shirt, brought a quart of guacamole with chips. "I made this then I forgot," she explained, "Billy doesn't live with us anymore."

Despite what sounded like a sad refrain, Janey's aura

appeared as a Maypole with colors woven together in a happy pattern. "I feel like you and Billy are going to meet again as different people," Lily said.

"That would be refreshing."

"You'll see. The Goddess will surprise you."

"I'll be her remedial project."

Lily smiled and shook her head.

"I feel very connected to the Goddess," said Solange, unwrapping a pound of Nova, "but it's causing problems with Joie. She's not going to harvest her periods, that's for sure. But when I did, Andi showed up." She examined the lox. "Cadmium Orange. Colors are so mystical. I want my life to be spiritual." With that Solange resumed the crying jag she'd begun a week ago at Lily's house. "Andi was my first love," she sobbed. "I never got over her."

Ordering Solange to sit down and slip off her sandals, Lily sat on the floor and massaged pressure points on her feet. "I wish I could have done this for you last time but I knew Joie would be uncomfortable."

"Uncomfortable?" Solange said, tears subsiding. "She would have slapped you."

"She's a tough broad," said Janey.

Solange threw her head back. "We're supposed to be getting married but I feel like we're growing apart."

Clearly, Solange and Joie were on vastly different journeys and Solange was on a growth spurt that Joie couldn't stop. Lily thought it best not to offer advice, to let it play out. Besides, she was so hungry, Solange's feet were beginning to look appetizing. "Bookmark that spot," Lily said. She got up and extracted three cans of Reddi-wip and a bottle of Chardonnay from another refrigerator. "I'm pregnant. I need a food fix."

They carried the feast outside to the umbrella table, followed by twitter-nosed canines hoping for a misstep that would send it splattering to the pavement.

"Before you got here," Lily said between mouthfuls of doughnut, "I was thinking about how much more in tune with life dogs are than people. If you think about what we teach dogs—sit, stay, roll over—compared to what they teach us—unconditional love, living in the moment, being joyful, it's laughable."

"Well," said Solange, "dog backwards is god. And god backwards is dog. That must mean something."

"Sure," Janey said, "if your dog speaks English."

"Dogs are just waiting for us to get it," said Lily. "I know they have the answers to all our problems."

Fudgsicle leaped up and did a 360. The women laughed.

"What are you trying to tell me, Fudgsie?" Solange asked. Then she looked at Janey.

"Don't ask me. He's obviously a gifted athlete."

"But you know how to communicate with dogs," said Solange.

"No, I don't," Janey argued. "Really. I had a lot to drink that day."

In a gesture that suggested disagreement, Rosie jumped up on Janey.

"See?" said Solange. "Rosie says you do."

"She just wants some Reddi-wip," Janey scoffed.

On that word, all four dogs sat up in formation, tails whipping like Santa Ana winds.

"Coming right up." Lily shook a can and dispensed dollops for each dog to lick off her hand. Then she squirted a foam caterpillar along Janey's index finger. "What's wrong with talking to dogs?"

"Please. I've seen those women on Animal Planet."

"I don't mean pet therapy. I mean listening to what they say. I communicate with nature all the time."

"You know the lingo," Janey said, slurping up the creamy foam. "I can barely communicate with humans."

"Dogs have more interesting things to say," Lily said.

Solange held Fudgsicle up and peered into his eyes. "I would love it if Fudgsie talked to me."

"If I talked to dogs, some of them would tell me about their abusive lives," Janey said. "And then I'd have to beat up their owners. And then I'd go to prison. Besides, I look hideous in a turban."

***

When Solange asked Lily if she thought Andi Nyler was her guardian angel, Janey wondered how she came to be part of this weird cabal.

"I'm sure she's one of many," Lily told Solange. "Maybe she's the ringleader."

"Wow, that makes me happy." Solange paused. "I wonder if she's ever seen my act."

"You know," said Janey, "I wish I had seen your act."

"Really? You want to see it?"

"Are you kidding?" Janey's head bounced like a bobblehead doll. "Next to Bruce, you're the show I crave most."

"I could dance to Bruce," Solange said, "if Lily has any of his CDs."

"I've got *Born to Run*," said Lily.

"I should hope so," said Janey, clutching her heart. "'She's the

One.' Track six."

As Lily went to get the CD, Janey decided that a live strip tease was exactly the diversion she needed and never could have thought of. "I'm so excited, I can't get comfortable," she said when Lily returned with Born to Run and the remote. She auditioned viewing postures on the couch. Lean back? Hunch forward? Hands cupped under chin? "Am I a pervert?"

"Yes," said Lily. "Now move over."

"Remember," Solange called out from the 'backstage' kitchen, "this isn't my normal drag. I have to improvise."

"Darn, I wish I had a pole," Lily said.

Janey shook her head in wonder. "Improv stripping. Can life get any better?"

"Hit it!" yelled Solange and Lily queued up the song. Solange sauntered out with two cans of Reddi-wip that in her hands looked like fat aluminum penises.

With her killer graces...And her secret places...That no boy can fill...With her hands on her hips...Oh and that smile on her lips...Because she knows that it kills me...

Solange bent over and in a smooth motion gradually spread her legs until her hair brushed the floor. It looked like if she wanted to, she could give herself head. Like some X-rated Cirque du Soleil, she performed a series of rubber-boned leg lifts, pelvic thrusts and undulations. Throwing a kiss to the audience, she arched her back and fell to her knees. Her hand slipped inside her shorts, exploring. She moaned. Then in one fluid move she withdrew her hand, peeled off her top and flung it at Janey.

"Woo!" Janey cried as she caught it and assumed position number two: hunched forward.

The sculpted breasts were exposed. They were exquisite;

Janey and Lily traded open-mouthed glances. Solange hugged and kissed them—they were huge and she could.

With her long hair falling...And her eyes that shine like a midnight sun...Oh she's the one...She's the one...

Showing the grace of a gazelle, Solange stepped out of her shorts, kicked them aside and hooked her fingers into her G-string panties, which made Janey recall the day she'd tried to wear a thong and spent the day fishing it out of her butt. As she moved closer to the imaginary rail, Solange worked her panties down until only her high-heeled sandals remained. She picked up the Reddi-wip cans and shook them up.

The only things that moved with the shaking cans were boobs and that long, dark hair. Flipping off the red plastic tops, Solange pushed the nozzles with her fingers, forming concentric circles around her breasts and two white soufflés on her nipples.

With her soft French cream...Standing in the doorway like a dream...

Janey felt like a lecherous sailor on leave as Solange danced just out of her and Lily's grasp. As Bruce kept repeating: Oh she's the one...she's the one...she turned her back to them and sank to her knees. Arms draped across their thighs she thrust her cloud-covered chest into the air before them. "Go ahead," said Solange, "I won't tell anyone."

Lily took the right hill, Janey the left and together they lapped up the whipped topping.

There followed about twelve seconds of silence.

"If I become a lesbian," Janey finally said, "you think it would improve my chances with Bruce?"

"You never know," said Solange.

Lily gave Solange's sticky, still-naked body a full-court hug.

"You are a gifted artist."

They kept hugging and Janey thought that this must be what it was like in the clothing-optional free love scene of the late sixties. She'd been too young for that—had to watch it on TV.

"First we were blood sisters," said Solange, "now we're Reddi-wip sisters."

To celebrate, they leashed up the dogs and headed for the park. Lily made iced green teas to drink en route. When they arrived they found Joie hanging out with Carlos and Hercules. Joie accepted a quick kiss from Solange but ignored Janey and Lily. "How was the séance?" she asked Solange.

Solange's eyes narrowed. "It wasn't a séance."

"What was it?"

For a few panicky moments Janey worried that Joie had been spying on them and was trying to bust Solange and make her confess.

"Just a little food orgy," Solange replied. She sounded utterly nonchalant even when she said the word 'orgy.'

"No one invited me," Joie snapped. She had on her UPS uniform.

"You were working," said Solange.

"Well, thank God it didn't interfere with your work," Joie said in a parting shot to Solange before she turned and walked off with Carlos.

The Reddi-wip sisters had no time to discuss the incident as Joie's vacancy was filled by Cleo, seemingly materialized from the ether.

"Hey Voodoo," she said to Lily, "how's your boyfriend?"

Janey stepped in front of Lily, prepared to take Cleo down if she got out of line.

"It's Trixie's birthday a week from Saturday." Cleo handed the three women photocopied hand-scrawled invitations. "You can bring Mr. Superstar if ya want. That's still going on, right? Because if it isn't, you gotta introduce him to me. I love gay guys."

"Sorry," said Lily. "He's out of town."

"Oh, that's too bad." Cleo's mouth turned down in an exaggerated pout. "He's gonna miss a great party. Bring presents." She waddled away with her dutiful shadow-dog.

The sisters held a brief conference on the feasibility of avoiding the soiree, but decided that non-attendance would cause even more unpleasant confrontations in the future.

"I'll pick up some gifts at Petco," said Janey.

16
LILY

Mystically, Lily's perpetual morning sickness cleared up the day of Gary's return, only to be replaced by nipples that felt like gas burners. It even hurt to wear her summer pajamas. Fortunately, she had non-stop appointments to keep her focused in the moment. She treated each patient with a dose of her heightened energy, channeling love through her fingers into their needy bodies.

She'd even made a breakthrough with her 300 lb. stockbroker, Harvey Wayne, with whom she bartered therapy for help with her portfolio. In his latissimus dorsi she found the 'issue in the tissue,' allowing Harvey to finally release the pain he'd been carrying since age five, of his mother's suicide. Harvey was so emotionally spent after the catharsis, Lily made him a cup of hot chocolate and invited him to lie on her couch and watch TV until he was ready to leave.

In the brief intervals between patients, she endured the Gary countdown in measurements used by particle physicists while she revisited all the welcome-home-I'm-pregnant scenarios and consciously sent the hormonally-induced negative versions into her Bermuda Triangle of Unwanted Thoughts.

The Labs helped by firing off a symphony of noxious emissions each time her mind veered to the negative side. Lily appreciated the dogs' benevolent aversion therapy and served them fennel tea blended with beef broth to combat the odor. But all meditations, energy exercises and frantic calls to the Goddess failed to quell her anxiety. The only thing she could do was to indulge her raging physicality. So outside she went to do some bumping and grinding of her own.

Bean and Blossom sniffed and pawed Lily's tee shirt, shorts and panties she tossed aside and when she sang, they watched her like she was a rock video. "Oh, with his hands on my hips... oh, and that smile on his lips, because he knows that it kills me... Ohhhh, he's the one..."

They thumped their tails to her performance. How wonderful, Lily marveled, that dogs can smile but not laugh, because in her painfully sensitive state she did not wish to be ridiculed. With the afternoon winds kicking up on her bare skin, she felt a surge of gratitude for dogs, high fences and the lack of children in her neighbor's tree house.

By the time she came inside she had freed herself of all thoughts except how much her nipples hurt and how Gary would be soothing them with his soft touch in less than two hours.

At 5:25 P.M., awash in vanilla and lavender she sensed the plane landing. She'd assumed she could just pick him up at the gate, until he'd explained that meeting him at the airport wasn't like meeting a 'normal' guy. "Francesca and I have a system."

Obviously, everyone needed a system for dealing with the inhumanity of airports, including big celebrities, but Lily wished she could be an integral part of it. She spent the last hour before he arrived in fervent prayer just to maintain a shaky hold on terra firma.

When Gary's Range Rover pulled into the driveway, the dogs went so batty Lily feared they might have a stroke. As Gary got out of the car she flung open the front door and they charged. Gary dropped into a gymnastic roll and was instantly covered in Labs but Lily saw an arm shoot out from under Blossom and wave.

Lily tried to budge the dogs but couldn't deter them from their mission of Licking a Man to Death. Shoving her head into the fray, she succeeded in making contact with Gary's silky lips. "Welcome home, sweetie."

"You too," he said and they tried to kiss but couldn't compete with the two super-sized tongues. "Inside," Gary ordered.

The Labs obeyed their commanding officer; three weeks away did nothing to diminish their cultish devotion.

The lovers rolled on the blacktop like it was the crashing wave in *From Here to Eternity*. On a respiratory break, Lily caught sight of Francesca smiling down at them.

"Hi," Francesca said, blowing an orb of pink bubblegum.

Gary's hand reached out to her. "Help us up."

Once vertical, Lily invited Francesca in for a cup of tea and tried not to look elated when she declined. As Gary gave his bodyguard a hug and noisy smooch on the cheek, Lily's mind projected irrational images of them making kung-fu love in a tree. As her Goddess-point was preoccupied with the new life in its midst, Lily felt lost, cut off from her wellspring of wisdom. Yet she realized the risk of indulging in bizarre, estrogen-driven thoughts and emotions for the next seven months. She needed to become enduringly rational in the next five minutes.

The challenge left her weak, with a bursting bladder. After sitting Gary down with a glass of clustered water and a dozen kisses she went off to pee and rehearse. When she returned, Blossom had carted all the toys from the front door and had laid them at his feet.

Gary stared at the bounty. "Is it my birthday?"

"They want you to have their toys," Lily said, touched by the gesture. She sensed that by way of their gifts, they were preparing Gary for the daddy news. She reached out and gave them a two-armed sandwich hug. "My sweet babies."

Gary petted all three on their heads.

"Are you ready?" Lily asked.

"You bet. For what?"

"Hold on to the dogs," she whispered and closed her eyes. "We're infanticipating."

Gary frowned and blinked as he worked out the definition of the clever term she'd discovered online. "That's not something you would joke about, is it?"

Lily shook her head.

Gary went limp, slid off the chair and landed in the pile of toys. Blossom picked up a rattling bunny and circled him Indian war-dance style. Bean barked.

"I didn't plan this. It happened our first night when I had my period, which is technically impossible." She spoke softly. "It's a miracle."

He clamped his hands over his ears. "Head, please do not explode."

Unsure if that was a positive or negative reaction, Lily allowed him a few seconds of contemplation, then she began to panic. "Honey, I need feedback."

He pulled her into him and held her fiercely. "It's the best news in the history of news."

"Thank you, thank you," Lily said, to Gary, her body, the Goddess and friends across the universe.

"You're the miracle." He kissed her over and over until she felt secure. Then he pulled back and grinned. "Roberta's going to love this."

"Roberta who?"

"Roberta Landers. She wants me on one of her specials. We go back a long way."

"You mean on television?"

"I'm afraid so. A Roberta Landers Special."

Lily swore she felt the baby kick, but it was probably just her apprehension colliding with her Goddess-point.

17
SOLANGE

Solange attended two and a half art classes before she realized her instructor didn't understand her and she quit in frustration. With Joie's permission, she fashioned her own Technicolor beaux arts emporium in the former dining room, painting canvas after canvas, often directly over a previous work. She experimented in a variety of genres, but her subject remained constant—Solange.

Not that she stared into a mirror all day in some vain attempt to idealize herself; her quest was to free the Goddess within—a striptease of her soul. She fed her Muse with Alanis Morrisette CDs, imported Italian espresso, ripe bananas and marijuana—the same formula she'd used at Spanky's Club, with espresso replacing the cocaine.

The quality of her work would be decided sometime in the future. Solange preferred that no one view her paintings until she deemed them fit for public consumption. Occasionally she let Joie see one but only to appease her curiosity and let her feel involved.

Joie knew nothing about art but said all the paintings were great and pronounced Solange "Picasso's love child." But she said it in an unconvincing way that made Solange feel patronized. It was pretty clear that Joie didn't believe in her talent and thought Solange could only make money taking off her clothes. For the first time, it occurred to Solange that she was living with her pimp.

"I'll pay you five hundred Monopoly dollars if you'll let me give you an eight minute orgasm," Joie announced one night as they were watching Court TV. She walked her fingers over Solange's body in the standard route she used to reach the place of worship.

"How about a rain check?" Solange asked, intercepting Joie's hand at the bellybutton. "I don't think I could appreciate it right now."

Joie leaned over and took out a pad of paper and a pen off her nightstand. "For the record," she said, "and I know how you like to keep track of these things, the last time we had sex was April." She wrote out an IOU and handed it to Solange. "I'd like to get it in writing, okay?"

After Solange scribbled her signature, she rolled on her side and snuggled up with Fudgsie. "You can keep the TV on," she said, ending the discussion. "It won't bother me."

***

As their sex life diminished, Joie started inviting herself on Solange's visits to Marvin's, rationalizing that Marvin had both a pool and a pool table, plus a 60-inch high def TV, which Joie said made watching sports on their puny 28-inch Sony pathetic. While Solange danced for Marvin, Joie channel-surfed in his bedroom; his privacy issues demanded it and Solange didn't want her there anyway. Joie also tagged along on the shopping sprees, managing to finesse her work schedule to accommodate trips to the mall.

"Let's all go to Psychogarden," Joie said one afternoon after Solange's performance. They were sitting in the kitchen with Marvin feasting on Crystal Light and pistachio nuts.

Another fetish club, Taboo-Ray, was where Solange and Joie first met but they hadn't been to one in years, mostly because Joie found them irritating. "You're kidding, right?"

"No, in fact Marv and I were talking about it while you were in the shower. He digs the idea, right, Marv?"

Marvin's shrug told Solange that Joie had done some strong-arming. "Might be interesting," he said.

"There's a lot of body contact," said Solange. "And everyone's on drugs. People come right up and touch you—you become part of their fetishes. And FYI, Marvin, you don't have a fetish. You're totally Victoria's Secret."

"Maybe he never thought about it," Joie said.

Solange narrowed her eyes. "Why do you want to go?"

"Like I told Marvin—it's good to try new things, not be so stuck in a rut."

"You don't sound sincere."

"I'm more sincere than a psychic in Sedona."

"Do I have to wear a costume?" Marvin asked as he struggled to open a stubborn nut with an Exacto knife.

"Nah," said Joie, "you can be a lookie-loo." Joie took Marvin's knife and pried open the nut. "I promise I'll protect you. They wanna touch you because they're high and it's a fetish club. But if you do this..." She demonstrated a "hold it right there" gesture, "...they smile and back off."

Marvin shook his head. "I don't do drugs."

"Me neither," said Joie. "I swear to God, I'd hallucinate if I took a Tylenol. We'll go straight. Maybe a beer or two, tops."

"You're not doing this for me, are you?" Solange asked.

Joie cracked two pistachios with her teeth. "It's for all of us, Sol. I admit it—I'm a fuddy duddy. I need to be more adventurous. And Marv just needs to get out—how better than being seen with us?"

Whatever scheme Joie was cooking up seemed to involve Marvin as an insurance policy. But Solange knew the club scene and Joie didn't; Solange felt secure there. Besides, colorful laser lights and kinky costumes could be a creative stimulus. More than anything, she wished to be a slave to her art—maybe her Muse was lurking at Psychogarden. "All right," she said with studied indifference, "we'll go."

The following Saturday night Solange put on her Hooker

Heidi outfit: blue and white checked micro-mini-pinafore over a white blouse with short puffed sleeves, white anklets and black patent leather Mary Janes. She tied her hair in high pigtails with white satin ribbons. Underneath she wore a G-string.

As Peter-with-tits, Joie wore blue suede leiderhosen that showed off her legs far better than UPS shorts, suspenders slung over a white tank top and combat boots.

Joie drove Solange's Mercedes when they picked up Marvin, whose kinky touch was a Mighty Ducks cap to complement his regulation polo shirt and Dockers. When he squeezed in front next to Solange, Joie pulled the cap down over his eyes. "Very fetishy, Marv."

His eyes walked all over Solange. "That's a nice dress," he said. For the first time she noticed he was wearing cologne—Brut, the most irritating fragrance on planet Earth.

"Thanks. You look kind of...cowboy," Solange lied, because he looked like a dork and in the eyes of a bondage queen, helpless bait.

"So, Marv, what's your craziest fantasy?" asked Joie. "Handcuffs, harems, corsets, boots, spikes..."

His eyes remained fixated. "I like what Solange is wearing."

"Super," said Joie. "We're not into whips and chains either. We prefer adorable characters of classic fiction." She rested her hand on her lover's bare knee and Marvin's gaze adjusted accordingly.

"I don't feel like Heidi," said Solange. "I feel like Alice in Wonderland."

As they pulled into the Psychogarden parking lot, Joie said, "Marv, sudden thought. I know you're not into scene wear, but really, it's only a state of mind. We can all act out a fantasy together. That'll make it more fun, right Sol?"

"I'd rather not."

"Nothing elaborate—I was thinking it would make an interesting dynamic if you and Marv are lovers and I'm the jilted dyke who wants you back." She smiled. "Just want to get the most bang for my fetish buck."

"I'm not into scenes," said Solange, then noticed that Marvin's chest had expanded. It appeared he'd received an identity transplant; an inkling of smile crossed his face.

Solange knew this would not go well.

For those on the sexual fringes, Psychogarden was the Disneyland of fetish clubs—a melting pot—and the three dance floors, two bars, game rooms and performance areas were always packed.

Hands reached out to pet and caress the trio as it snaked through the dancing masses. Solange ran interference for Marvin, who kept his head down and cap brim low.

At the performance area a huge, hairless black man wrapped in chains, naked but for a red velvet penis sock, roamed the stage like a panther. He was selecting candidates to suck the fat toes of Kimba, a six-foot, 250-pound platinum blonde dominatrix sitting spread-eagled in a chair. As their reward, the toe-suckers received verbal condemnation from Kimba and floggings with her suede pussy whip.

Joie raised her hand to volunteer for abuse. Solange tried to stop her but Joie bounded onto the stage and down on all fours, opened her mouth to receive Kimba's foot. An Olympic hygiene freak, Joie had to be gagging; that she was doing this to impress Solange made it all the more sickening.

"Suck my toes, bitch!" Kimba screamed over the pounding

techno-music. "Make my toes come!" She cracked the whip on Joie's butt. "Harder, bitch!"

Instead of the requisite look of masochistic pleasure, Joie's face filled with pain; her eyes froze on Solange, pleading. Seeing Joie so desperate and vulnerable made Solange well up, which provided Marvin an opportunity to slip a sympathetic arm around her waist.

At that moment Solange wished that Andi would appear so the two could fly away on their bicycles over the mass of writhing bodies like the kids in *ET*, but it seemed pretty unlikely that Andi would do a guest shot at a fetish club.

Seconds later Joie was booted off stage, a concrete smile locked on her face. She snatched Solange away from Marvin. He relinquished her without a struggle; even when playing a role he was devoid of aggression. "I'm sorry I haven't given you enough freedom, Sol," Joie shouted into her ear. "You know I'd do anything for you. Geez, I sucked someone's feet!" Joie nuzzled her neck.

"I need to get a drink," Solange said, wiggling out of Joie's arm-cage. "Why don't you guys go play pool or something?"

Before Joie could respond, Solange slipped away, losing herself in the milieu of Fisters, Spankers and Navel Worshippers. Stopping to gaze into the needle blizzard of multi-colored laser lights, she waited for a bolt of artistic inspiration. Two lovers of uncertain gender in biker jackets and leather shorts with mesh seats broke her reverie as they begged to be her slaves. They pouted in tandem when she declined.

Solange pushed her way to the bar and ordered a glass of lemonade. Next to her a Chubby Chaser poked playfully at his Size Queen with a rhinestone studded dildo.

The coldness of the drink made Solange realize how hot and sweaty she was but she couldn't check her underarms for fear of attracting a pit fetishist. She needed a place that was cool and unpopulated.

Walking through a dark hallway near the rear exit she spotted two men tangled up with each other in a chair, passionately kissing. The glass nearly broke in her hand as she stared in horror—one of the men was Gary DiCaro.

For a moment Solange swallowed her heart, then she calmly looked again to make sure she knew what she was seeing. Black hair, blue eyes, a glimmer of the crooked smile—the smile that might soon appear on the baby he and Lily had made.

She wanted to run but couldn't take her eyes off the shocking scene. As if branded by her burning stare Gary turned, looked at her and sent a shiver through her bloodstream. Bearing witness to this encounter, she realized, was the true reason she was at the fetish club—not for art and not because Joie needed a venue for her grandstand play.

On the way home Joie spoke—exclusively to Marvin—in the phony-cheerful manner she used when something was bothering her. "Marv," Joie said, tugging the bill of his Mighty Ducks cap, "what's next? Guess humiliating myself in front of perverts doesn't prove I'm a gamer. The little princess snobbed out on our scene."

Marvin squirmed like a man in mohair jockey shorts. "I don't want to be the middle man."

"But she's not listening."

He turned to Solange. "Are you listening?"

"Yes, I'm listening." But only vaguely. On instant replay she continued to watch Gary DiCaro kissing that guy.

Joie nudged Marvin. "Houston, we have a problem. Ground control to Major Solange."

Solange found her voice and it was loud. "I don't feel like talking about our relationship in front of Marvin and I don't like how you've been trying to get him on Team Joie." She turned to Marvin. "Nothing personal—she just shouldn't be butting into our business arrangement."

"Now you're getting him involved," said Joie. "Marv and I are friends. Is that against the rules?"

"Yes."

"Now who's controlling?"

Both lapsed into silence that lasted long after they dropped Marvin off. Around two A.M., as they flanked the east and west coasts of the bed, Joie resumed the discussion.

"Honey, I'm worried about us. Lesbians can't seem to stay together anymore. Lucinda and Joni, Cloud and Thunder, Carolyn and Marilyn—and they rhymed, for God's sake." She touched Solange's cheek. "I don't want us to be on that list."

Solange felt no ill will toward Joie. She didn't fault her for her earnest but misguided efforts to win her back. But at that moment she felt herself fall out of love. Joie had become her roommate, not her lover, not the woman she wanted to marry. Gay women called it lesbian bed death.

"Joie," she said quietly, "I need my freedom."

18
JANEY

Janey awoke from the recurring dream in which her seats at

the Springsteen concert were behind the monolith from 2001: A Space Odyssey. The giant obelisk increased in size and blockage with each installment of the nightmare.

When a day started out this badly, by the laws of equilibrium it usually turned around at some point, but to open the cupboard and find herself out of coffee seemed an irreversibly bad omen.

She was forced to drink some of Eleanor's Lipton tea. In the fifties Arthur Godfrey's endorsement had made Eleanor a steadfast Liptonite and she frequently maintained that as living proof of its health benefits, the Lipton people were foolish not to build an ad campaign around her.

Janey brewed a pot then poured some into her traveling mug. A little health boost might not be bad. Maybe she wouldn't live to 102 but she was determined to be at Bruce's final concert—with an unobstructed view.

Along with her poop baggies she stuck a small bottle of watered down menstrual blood in her fanny pack. Since last month's donation, Billy had fled to Hawaii, Solange and Joie had split up and Lily discovered she'd conceived during her period. Which of those were positive or negative developments remained to be seen but she was secretly hooked on the drama. She even wondered what would happen if she took a harvest to New Jersey in hopes of triggering a Bruce encounter.

On their way to the park, while Janey listened to "Tougher Than the Rest," Rosie stopped to explore the expanse of dirt and weed clumps that passed for a run-down house's front yard. The place also needed paint, a new roof and the removal of a rusty '84 Buick that to Janey's knowledge, had been parked in its driveway since 1992.

A shrill voice cried out, "Get offa there!"

Janey pulled off her earbuds and saw a haggard looking woman in a housecoat halfway out the screen door, Janey's first ever look at the home's occupant. "What?"

"Get your damn dog off my lawn!"

Unable to curb her tongue Janey blurted, "That's a lawn?"

"Go away!" the woman screamed. "Keep moving!"

Janey yanked Rosie's leash and they hustled off. A mere block later, a girl about eight years old, walking with an older woman, tossed a wad of tissue in Janey's path. Janey snapped open a baggie, scooped it up and caught up with the young offender. "Excuse me," she said politely, "did you drop something?" And held out the plastic covered evidence.

The little girl lied with conviction. "No."

"Do you really think your snotty Kleenex looks better on the sidewalk than in the trash?"

The woman's mouth dropped like a marionette on a string. "Don't swear at my daughter, you stupid cunt."

Janey was not too insulted to appreciate a good bit of irony. As the obnoxious duo departed she put a lilt in her voice and called out, "Every litter bit helps."

The back-to-back ugly incidents upset Janey and it occurred to her that her menstrual blood might be toxic, that even as she carried it around it could be sending out hormonal bat signals to deranged women. "C'mon, Rosie," she said, pulling her along, "we gotta get rid of this stuff."

Kids were playing soccer when Janey and Rosie arrived at the park; they were too preoccupied to notice Janey pull the red liquid from her fanny pack. At the stone bench where she'd had her moment of contemplation, she looked up to the gray sky. "Hey, Goddess, here's some breakfast for ya." And poured it in a circle around the bench. She imagined the Goddess wrinkling her ethereal nose: What's this stuff?

Rosie sniffed the bloody trail as if it was the path to the Dog Treat Emporium. When she reached the end she went around again, assumed play posture, then retraced her steps. Her actions looked a little neurotic and Janey wondered what they meant.

On the way home Janey listened to *Summertime Bruce*, one of her favorite bootlegs, and as he always did, Bruce lifted her out of the muck. She no longer worried that she had bad blood. But upon opening the front door, Eleanor clobbered her with stunning news. "Sherri ran off to live with that no good, dope smoking, so-called father of hers."

"What?" Janey bolted up the stairs, two at a time, praying that Sherri was merely in the shower, or hiding in her closet, or under the bed or having sex with some high school classmate— anywhere but Hawaii.

She found Candi sprawled out on her bed in the girls' room reading *Vanity Fair*. When she saw Janey she picked an envelope off her nightstand and held it out. "She left you a note."

Janey's hands trembled as she took it, then noticed that it was five pages long, single spaced.

"It's basically her opinion of everything you've ever done and said since she learned how to talk," said Candi. "I tried to read it but there were too many typos."

"Did you know she was leaving?"

"She talked about it but I didn't think she would do it."

"Why didn't you tell me?"

"I thought you'd be mad. It was all secret phone calls and emails and then he sent her a plane ticket. She said she'd get him to come home."

"I can't believe this could happen right under my nose."

"A lot of things happen under your nose that you don't know about."

Having no time to ponder that ominous insight, Janey said, "Give me every single phone number you have in Hawaii. And you're grounded for not telling me."

"Number four on the speed dial," said Candi, handing her a cell phone.

There was no time to be flabbergasted. Janey punched four and got voicemail: "Aloha! Billy and Sherri are unable to come to the phone right now but if you leave a message, we'll call you back at low tide. Mahalo!"

"Sherri, this is your mother." She sighed deeply. "I'm not angry. I know your intentions are good but I wish you would have talked to me before you went running off..."

"But if I did, you wouldn't have let me go," said Sherri, picking up.

Hearing her live voice, Janey heaved with relief and urged herself to remain calm and non-judgmental. "How are you honey? Did you have a nice flight?"

"Slept right through it. Daddy looks good. I'm making him a tofu omelet for breakfast. Don't worry. I promise we'll be home before school starts. I gotta go. I don't want him to know I'm on with you." She hung up.

Janey wished she could crawl through the line and abduct her. She clicked off the phone and tossed it back to Candi.

"How's our little surfer girl?" asked Candi without looking up from her magazine.

"It's just a brave front." Then a new fear surfaced. "You're not planning to run off somewhere, are you?"

"Nope, I finally have my own room. 'Candy's Room,' remember? I shouldn't have to share."

"Y'know, Taco Bell is hiring. Save up for a condo."

"I'll just wait for Grandma's room."

***

Janey was actually grateful for Trixie's birthday party—it would take her mind off Sherri for an afternoon. She invited Eleanor and Candi but Eleanor declined, saying she hadn't walked on grass in twenty years for fear of tripping on a rodent. Candi admitted that with the exception of Rosie she wasn't into dogs. But both were stationed at the kitchen table to get an eyeful of Solange, Janey's date for the party. Lily would be coming later, after she helped Gary prepare for their upcoming Roberta Landers interview.

Solange looked fetching when she showed up in a paint-stained denim romper, cutoffs and flip flops with daisies between her toes. Fudgsicle wore two silver clips that kept the hair out of his eyes. The two women shared comfort in a warm, breasty hug.

"Come in for a second and meet what's left of my family." Janey led Solange into the kitchen and made the introductions.

Never one to have qualms, Eleanor gawked openly. "Are those bosoms real?"

Solange laughed. "You are so cute. They're actually twin pieces of sculpture by Dr. Harry Rose of Beverly Hills." She gave them a prideful uplift. "Can you tell?"

"They're whoppers, all right," Eleanor said with a nod. She nudged Candi. "Go stand next to her."

Breasts encased in a tight camisole, Candi got up and stood

boob-to-implant with Solange.

"Hers are real," Eleanor noted.

"I feel like Kansas standing next to Colorado and Wyoming," Janey said.

"Did you see me on the Tonight Show?" Eleanor asked Solange, eyelashes fluttering.

"I did. You were fabulous."

Eleanor puffed up until she looked five feet tall. "They look good," she told Solange.

"Want to touch 'em?"

Eleanor's hand reached out for a quick melon-test. "I forgot what bosoms feel like. All the air's drained out of mine."

"I can give you Dr. Rose's number."

"Don't give her any ideas," Janey said, pulling Solange away. "She's already got one 'oldest living' title."

Rounding up the dogs and gifts, Janey and Solange set out for the park. "Joie moved out," Solange announced. "I got up this morning and she was gone."

"Did she leave a note?"

Solange shook her head. "Nothing."

"Must be something about us that makes them want to leave home. For me it's either my cooking or my winning personality." Janey hoped Solange might have laughed but she seemed too agitated.

"I thought Joie and I were gonna make it. But it must be even worse when it's your daughter."

"Kids come with a lifetime of anxiety. They're fearless, you know, so you have to do all their worrying for them."

Solange stopped abruptly and clenched Janey's arm. "Janey, I have to tell you something. I've been freaking out for two days.

You didn't notice because I'm acting."

"What? Tell me."

"I'm just going to blurt this out. A few nights ago I saw Gary DiCaro at a fetish club making out with a guy."

Janey felt like an Edvard Munch painting. "Are you sure? Isn't it really dark in those places?"

"It's a continuous light show. I got a really good look at him."

"Shit. This has been a very bad news day."

"I didn't tell Lily but you know she'll psych it out."

"I knew it," Janey said. "Sexuality doesn't change. Lily's just a lark to him. She said those stories weren't true but my hairdresser's ex-husband was an intern at the hospital when Gary got that testicle implant."

"The nurse from my breast surgery knows someone who was there, too. Lily might not even know which one's fake. Surgeons are so amazing these days."

"I really love Lily," Janey said, "but my bloodletting experiment is over. I'm going back to Goddess Stay-Free."

"I'm so bummed," Solange said.

"No one can escape problems, Solange, not even Lily."

In an unnerving segue, Bean and Blossom bounded into view followed by Lily, looking ridiculously happy in an oversized white tee shirt that probably belonged to Gary. "Hey youse," she called out.

"We were just procrastinating," Janey felt compelled to explain. "It's so uncool to be the first one at a dog party."

While the four dogs and their people walked en masse to the park, Solange steered the conversation to what Lily was going to wear on the Roberta Landers interview.

"I don't know. Will you help me?" Lily asked.

Solange spun in the air, nearly landing on Fudgsicle. "Are you serious? I'd love to be your dresser!"

"Will I look pregnant on TV?" Lily asked.

"Absolutely not," said Solange.

"I look more pregnant than you," Janey added.

"Check this out." Lily lifted up the shirt to expose a small bump.

"Wow," said Solange, rubbing it like a magic lamp.

"Some of it is Krispy Kremes," Lily said, then gave them a giggling, detailed account of her mood swings, constipation and nausea that in light of the revelation about Gary, made Janey feel pretty queasy herself.

"So," Janey said, hoping to pry information in a clever and innocent way, "what do big movie stars do at night?"

"Mostly we just hang out. Gary's been to some screenings. I don't go because I have to pee every five minutes. It's too embarrassing."

Solange and Janey's eyes met briefly on the depressing confirmation that Gary had been going out without Lily. Janey hoped she could hold it together when she inevitably met the scumbag superstar.

When they arrived at Trixie's party, Cleo greeted them with, "Oh, the hotties are here." Janey could barely imagine a sillier remark, but it made her feel good to be a hottie in anyone's eyes.

Oscar the Dachshund's person, Jack, smoked a pipe as he tended a small barbecue grill jammed with wieners. Other park regulars set out buns, salad, condiments and potato chips on an aluminum table covered with a red and white checked tablecloth. An ice-filled cooler brimmed over with soft drinks and beer.

The women deposited their gifts in a cardboard carton

guarded by Margaret, who carried her white Pomeranian, William, in a blanket. She smiled in an official way. Despite the casual occasion, Margaret wore her regulation Chanel suit, clunky gold jewelry, high-altitude power hair and always held William in the burping position. His legs had never been seen in public.

"Does anyone know what Margaret does for a living?" Janey asked when they walked away.

Solange pursed her lips. "I think she works at the cosmetics counter at Bloomie's. Or maybe that's what she looks like she does."

"Why don't you ask her?" said Lily.

Janey shook her head. "We're sure to be disappointed."

At that innocuous moment, a day that had been deteriorating like an ice cube in the microwave took an astonishing turn.

A young man walking briskly with a Golden Retriever at his side approached them. He was about twenty-five, slender, with dark curly hair, in a gray tee shirt and black jeans. When he smiled, he exposed a slight gap in his front teeth and an under bite. Janey could draw but one conclusion—it was Bruce—time-traveling from 1975.

"Hi. Is this the party?" he asked.

She didn't want to faint at his feet so she tried to steady herself by focusing on the oak tree behind him but she was unable to look past his ravishing face. "Yup," Janey burbled, "'Way down beneath the neon lights.'" She wanted to sing the line before that, "Cause there's a party, honey," but felt it was too soon to call him 'honey.'

The young man grinned and broke into song. "'When I'm out in the street, oh oh, oh, oh, oh...'"

Then Janey did faint, but remained standing. She became aware of Solange and Lily slowly backing away, leaving her alone with him, smiling.

"Hi, I'm Davy."

At the mention of his name, Janey suffered a temporary loss of bladder control but got it back in the nick of time. "Hazy Davy?"

"You got it." He tousled his dog's head. "And this is Clarence Big Man Clemons the Third."

Janey leaned down to pet him. "I can tell you play a mean sax." She offered her hand to Davy. "I'm Janey. Crazy Janey."

Davy enclosed her hands in his, which were small, round, Bruce-like. "Sweet. We're in the same song."

At that moment Janey fell deeply in love.

***

Cleo demanded everyone's full attention as she opened Trixie's gifts but after the third Kong, the pretty blue and white marbled model from Janey, it appeared she could no longer be gracious. "Trixie ain't into Kong, in case you hadn't noticed." She swung the rubber toy by its thick rope and hurled it fifty feet. Six dogs ran after it. "She likes squeaky toys."

"Sorry," Janey said. "I'd be happy to exchange it." She was sitting on the grass next to Davy and felt magnanimous.

"Yeah, well, you can't exchange it now. It's got dog slobber all over it."

Hercules retrieved the Kong and paraded it across the park, followed by the runners-up.

Janey felt vaguely guilty that she'd never paid attention to Trixie's toy preferences but quickly got over it.

The next gift was Lily's organic dog biscuits, which got a

weak thumbs-up from Cleo, while the lavender shampoo and conditioner set from Solange aroused suspicion. "Ya think she smells?" Cleo asked, not in a kidding way.

"All girls want to smell nice," said Solange.

Cleo snorted. "Okay, time for birthday cake." She pointed to Davy. "Would you hand me those pink boxes over there, muffin?"

Janey recoiled at the term of endearment, praying it had no romantic connotations.

Davy did as instructed. Cleo ripped open the boxes, unveiling two chocolate cakes with "Happy Birthday Trixie" written on them. "One for humans and one for dogs."

Janey leaped up. "Wait! Is that carob?"

"Hell no," said Cleo. "It's chocolate."

"Chocolate is toxic to dogs," Janey said.

"It's just the frosting," Cleo whined. "The inside is white flavor. Trixie loves chocolate."

"Please don't give her chocolate," said Lily.

"I second that," Janey said, fully intending to seize the nearest cell phone and call the SPCA if Cleo went ahead.

Cleo picked up a cake and scraped the frosting off with the back of her hand. She deposited the chocolate globs into a paper cup half-filled with soda, then palmed a handful of naked cake and offered it to the birthday girl. "Here ya go, Trixie."

Trixie made quick work of it.

Cleo set the rest of the mutilated concoction on the ground for the dogs. "Come and get it," she called out, sparking a dog stampede.

Davy and the women watched the dogs devour the birthday feast and lick the grass where it had lain. Clarence appeared to be getting the lion's share. Janey noticed that Rosie deferred to Clarence's dominance and hoped that they were finding each other irresistible.

"He loves junk food," Davy said sheepishly.

"He's the Big Man." Then Janey finally asked the question that had been plaguing her. "How do you know Cleo?"

"We go to the same vet."

Holding back shouts of relief, Janey searched for something clever to say that would catapult their relationship to a new stage, but could only manage a few relieved peeps. They stood and watched the dogs, who, revved up on sugar, broke into madhouse play. Fudgsicle ran laps around Clarence while Rosie, bowing to competition from the yappy runt, grabbed the discarded Kong and tried to lure Trixie into a round of tug-of-war. But instead of snatching the toy, Trixie began to bark and snap. Rosie growled and barked back. It sounded portentous, not her typical play-bark. As Janey moved to break it up, the witch-form of Cleo streaked into the fray screaming, "Get away from her!" In the next instant Cleo's wooden-soled sandal found its target in Rosie's ribs, causing the terrier to go airborne and land with a thud.

19
THE GODDESSES

As Janey's new friend Davy gently placed Rosie on a homemade stretcher, Lily asked the Goddess Mother Earth to send golden energy into Rosie's body. Lily kept her hands poised over the injured dog, forming a protective healing canopy as they slowly walked to Lily's Subaru Outback.

Solange and Fudgsicle sat in back with Janey while Lily held Rosie in the front. The Labs took their usual spot in the rear. Davy drove. For awhile there was no conversation but much was said in silence. Janey's grief pervaded the atmosphere—she sat hunched over, hands pressed between her knees. In an effort to deflect thoughts of dread from Janey's mind, Lily steered the conversation to the intriguing young man. "What do you do, Davy?" she asked.

"I make furniture."

"Awesome," said Solange. "I knew you were an artist. I am too. But I'm aspiring."

Davy's sylvan essence knocked Lily out. "Would you make me a cradle?" she asked him. "I don't even need to see your work. I can tell you have a love affair with wood."

"Sweet. I'd love to make a cradle." Lily saw him look in the rear view mirror at Janey. "Maybe when Rosie gets better you can all come by and visit my studio."

Janey swallowed her lips and nodded slightly.

***

At the hospital Rosie was rushed into surgery to repair a ruptured spleen and broken ribs. Seeing Janey pasted against the treatment room doors broke Lily's heart.

The rest of the dogs, captive in their chamber of horrors, cowered in a corner and trembled as the occasional howl or shriek rang out from behind swinging doors. Fudgsicle hid beneath the security blanket of Bean's body.

Lily rubbed Janey's back and eased her away whenever vet personnel and animal traffic needed to pass. "How about if we all go to my house for a prayer circle?"

"I can't leave Rosie," Janey said. "You all go ahead."

With that, the darling young carpenter came up and took Janey by the shoulders. "Janey, let me tell you something. By the time Rosie meets the morning light...you'll hold her in your arms..."

Janey looked up at him, her face in contortions.

"Say it with me, Janey... 'Doctor come cut loose her mama's reins...'"

Miraculous. He knew how to speak to her in Bruce Code.

"'Hold on tight, stay up all night...'" Davy continued and Janey murmured along like responsive reading in church. Janey crumpled into him and Lily thanked the Goddess for sending them such a precious angel.

***

Rosalita watched the doctors working on her body with fascination; she had never seen anything so incredible. She hovered over the operating table, seeing things happen to her own body that she couldn't feel. Her sense of self expanded and she became aware that she had plugged into human consciousness.

Without warning she took off flying—at unheard of speeds—along with countless other dogs made of smell and light. They told her not to be afraid, to just go along with them and enjoy herself. In no time they arrived at a place that had no ground, no trees and no food, only dogs.

Rosalita found herself in a Presence of such unimaginable proportions it could not even be smelled, only sensed. Though she was not occupying her physical body she quaked with a wobbly combination of fear and anticipation. Information came at her like a rainstorm, each drop turning into a scent that carried bits of knowledge.

This is Dogstar where the communal dog soul lives. The thought was imparted to her by the Overdog, the mutual soul of Dog. Rosalita could not see or smell Her, but she knew that she had being singled out to receive Her teachings.

You are a dog with human understanding. Your lady person has been chosen to teach others but you must help her. Dogs love humans more than they love themselves. The unconditional love of dogs can save humans.

The Overdog surrounded Rosalita with all the dog love in creation. The power of so many dogs embracing her seemed more than she could handle but since she wasn't in her body it all came rushing in and made her feel as big as the world.

Many humans are blind, not just in their eyes but in their hearts. All dogs are Guide Dogs. Humans have been training dogs. Now dogs must train humans.

Rosalita wondered why, since dogs had always given humans unconditional love.

Humans have lost their way. Showing isn't enough. Dogs must learn to communicate in human ways.

But how? Rosalita wondered.

Use your intent. Teach humans to the capacity they can understand.

Rosalita promised to do her best to teach humans about unconditional dog love. Fervently wishing that she could contact her lady, Rosalita found herself in the doctor's place where her lady was sitting with their human and dog friends. But Rosalita could not reach her. Her lady was crying because Rosalita was sick and injured.

I'm here with you, Rosalita told her lady, but her message would not go through. So Rosalita concentrated on her lady's arm and licked it with her energy tongue. When the lady rubbed the very same spot as if she had felt it, Rosalita became excited.

Rosalita also noticed that Bean and Blossom had picked up her scent-form and welcomed her presence. Rosalita brought them awareness of the Overdog and the dogs realized that their lady persons were deeply attuned to Her. It was very, very exciting and on the Imaginary Plane where dogs hang out and have adventures, they played celebratory games and rejoiced.

Fudgsicle, on the other hand, smelled of apprehension and clung to the physical dimension with all his might. He didn't acknowledge Rosalita at all. Like most little dogs he served as a pampered ornament, though Rosalita could tell how much he longed to be his lady's guardian. But because of his size he lived in fear.

Just when she was imagining living on Dogstar forever, Rosalita violently popped back into her body. She had been placed inside a cage and all around her cats and dogs were wailing. Dogstar had vanished and she'd lost her energy link to the Labs. All she felt was pain.

***

Though he was holy in her eyes, Janey didn't pray to Bruce Springsteen, though his music frequently moved her to prayerfulness. But to be sitting in a meditation circle beside his vintage clone had to have some religious significance. In the way Bruce's music helped her through hard times, Davy provided a down comforter for her fear.

Lily put on some music with flutes and wind chimes and suggested that they all send Rosalita white healing energy and love. Janey visualized a river of high-octane dog fuel charging up

Rosie's tank.

Instinctively they all held hands. Lily took Janey's left and Davy the right and their passion crackled through Janey's body. Lily's hands felt warm enough to give off steam.

Janey wasn't sure if Rosie was contacting her or not. It was hard to decipher all the energy fueling the prayer circle. In moments Janey wasn't praying for Rosie she was asking Lily's Goddess to be there for Lily when the sad truth came out about Gary. And she also wondered what bodily substance might have brought her this young Bruce-like person at such an intense moment.

As if he'd heard the question, Davy broke into song—Rosie's song. "'Rosalita jump a little lighter...Señorita, come sit by my fire...'" He paused, smiled. "I just got the feeling she wanted me to do that so you'll know she's okay."

"Thank you," Janey said, tearing up. He could even sing.

"I feel her too," Solange said. "She is absolutely pulling through this."

Like campfire marshmallows the four met in a spontaneous squeeze. Visible waves of heat rose from their bodies. Davy's warmth melted Janey.

"Look," Lily said. "We're creating light." In the same moment Lily's cell phone rang. A few words later Lily wore a big smile when she handed it to Janey, who could no longer deny that a day filled with tragedy contained an equal amount of joy.

***

Davy insisted on walking Janey home. "How many times have you seen Bruce?" he asked as they rounded her corner.

"Eighty-seven."

"Wow, I'm only at eighteen. More if you count the times I

went in my mom's stomach."

The cold, wet rag of age slapped Janey in the face. "When was that?"

"Um, I think it was the 'Born in the USA' tour." He cringed as if expecting her to blanche at how young he was, which is precisely what she did behind her plastered-on smile.

"Is your mom still a fan?" she asked, continuing the smile.

"Completely and totally obsessed. You should meet her."

Bruce would record a polka album before that ever happened. Not only would meeting Davy's mother force Janey to confront the age chasm she kept trying to overlook, but she had no yearning to meet a woman who had savagely one-upped her by producing a living replica of The Man Himself.

"So you and your mom," Janey said, then broke into verse, "'like the same music,' you 'like the same bands,' you 'like the same clothes?'"

Davy laughed. "Well, not the same clothes."

Boy, he was cute. Probably dangerous. For her anyway.

She vowed to put a rubber band on her wrist and whenever she had a romantic thought about Davy, snap it hard until she was fully deprogrammed.

When they reached her house, she held out her hand and said, "Hey, thanks. It felt weird walking without Rosie, but being with you and Clarence helped a lot."

Davy touched her palm to his mouth in a kiss. "May we come sit by the fire with the señorita when she comes home?"

He was coming on strong.

***

Solange and Lily were laughing about whether the heat display had come from all of them or just Janey and Davy when they noticed Bean and Blossom spinning in circles at the front door and barking in high-pitched tones.

"Oh, I almost forgot," said Lily, "Gary's here."

Most the blood and all of the sanity drained from Solange's head as Lily danced to the door and opened it. When Solange saw Gary's smiling face her stomach heaved.

Lily attached to her lover like a mussel clinging to a rock. While their kisses looked convincing, they churned up creepy images Solange wished to erase. "Gary," Lily said when they unhinged, "this is Solange."

Shaking her hand Gary flashed The Grin, displaying not a hint of recognition. She looked for betrayal in his eyes but saw warmth and friendliness. It gave her new appreciation for the art of acting.

The dogs went wild in his presence, as though he'd been basted with chicken fat. Blossom ran around the house grasping any item she could fit in her mouth: throw pillows, a banana, an Emmylou Harris CD, and laid them at his feet. Bean cried and rubbed his head against Gary's pant leg. The yapping Fudgsicle did figure eights around his loafers.

"I think my dog wants your autograph," Solange told him.

"Really?" Gary picked up the Yorkie and went nose-to-nose with him. "Or do you just want to meet Benji?"

Fudgsie licked Gary's face. As they all chuckled over how endearing that was, Solange decided Lily and Gary were the most gorgeous couple she had ever seen and looking at them made her heart splinter.

"Now that I've won your dog over," Gary said with a bonus beam of his perfect teeth, "would you like to join us for dinner?"

"Oh no, I couldn't." One glass of wine and she'd be blurting out things she'd regret for the rest of her life.

"Of course you can," said Lily. "Bean and Blossom will look after Fudgsicle."

***

Gary chose Talesai, an upscale Thai restaurant in Studio City, because it had great food and discreet personnel. On the ride over, Gary lamented that eating in restaurants had become almost intolerable. He'd always enjoyed talking to fans, but not since they'd developed "so many loud opinions." Solange had a number of her own opinions which she decided to keep to herself.

Gary and Lily chose a table facing the wall, across from Solange. They began with the house specialty, morsels of spicy seafood in a coconut broth baked in tiny covered clay pots that were opened at the table. Every time Solange mentioned an item that sounded good, Gary ordered it.

Solange asked a few innocent questions about Francesca that mostly Lily answered. The description made Francesca sound like the woman in the spandex policewoman's outfit at Psychogarden. Hopefully Solange would meet her soon and discreetly ferret out the details of Gary's secret life.

It was impossible not to look at him, so while Lily recounted the horrific dog drama at Trixie's birthday party, Solange avoided thinking about his infidelities by imagining him as the devoted husband he'd played in *Phoebe's Roses*.

Gary seemed genuinely interested in the story—his face reeked of sincerity. But Solange knew plenty of men who had outrageous, extracurricular sex lives and then, after making sure the riding crops and dog collars left no telltale marks, went home and played with their children.

By her second Thai beer Solange decided to quit obsessing on Lily and Gary because their relationship was none of her business. In a grander sense it was karma, something that was created in the infinite past.

She hoped she'd made good sound plans for herself in the infinite past.

A sudden cramp, the climactic moment of P.M.S, signaled the start of her period. There had been much uproar since she last gave blood to the Earth Goddess—Andi had come back and Joie had gone. Still, she yearned to do it again, to plunge deeper into life for herself and for her art.

She became aware of Lily speaking to her. "I'm so glad you're going to help me pick out a TV outfit," Lily said, shaking her head. "I'm not good with clothes."

Gary gave Lily a nudge-nudge elbow. "She's much better without clothes."

"Don't worry," said Solange, then brazenly added, "I saw some wild outfits at Psychogarden last week. You could totally blow their minds and wear latex." She studied Gary's reaction; he laughed with Lily and took a swig of beer. Inconclusive.

The wisecrack made her feel nauseous; she could have blown her friendship with Lily wide open. Excusing herself, she went to the ladies room to deal with her period. She took out one of the contraband Instead cups she kept in her purse.

As she slipped it in, she closed her eyes and asked the Goddess to keep her friend safe and protected. A profound sadness came over her followed by another unexpected chapter of her crying jag. Hormonal crying was one thing; this felt much bigger yet still unrelated to anything specific in her life. She hoped that when the lake of tears dried up its meaning would be revealed.

As she sobbed quietly into a wad of paper towels she heard someone jiggle the doorknob. "Just a second," she called out in a fake cheerful voice.

Scrunching up her face, she managed to stop the waterworks, but on her eyelid movie screen a new show began to play: Andi, riding her Phthalo Blue bicycle up a steep hill, pedaling hard. When she reached the top she sailed down the other side, arms held high, waving free.

"See ya soon," she said.

20
LILY

On the morning of the Roberta Landers interview, Lily awoke with a giant zit on her nose. After working on it for an hour with steam, lemon juice, garlic, aloe, tea tree oil, Milk of Magnesia and toothpaste, she succeeded in doubling its circumference. She figured her endocrine glands had served up the blemish to provide an excuse to avoid the interview, but bailing out wasn't an option. She called Solange.

"Visene," said Solange. "I swear by it."

As there was no Visene in Lily's skin care arsenal, Solange said she'd be right over to deflate the pimple and give a final review to the ensemble they'd chosen for the interview. She arrived in attire made entirely of tropical print scarves fashioned into a bandana top and wrap skirt with a matching kerchief for Fudgsicle.

"You should get a Girl Scout badge for knots like that," Lily said, marveling at her talent.

"It's simple. Want me to show you?"

"Maybe another time. Right now I have to divert attention from the active volcano on my nose. I think I should wear a hat with a veil."

"You're going to wear Lily pink. It's settled." She sat Lily down at her kitchen table and from a secret pocket in one of her scarves extracted a bottle of Visene and a dozen Q-Tips. "Now, let's eradicate that sucker."

With pressing and dabbing so astonishing Lily assumed Divine Intervention was involved, the unsightly blemish became sightly in less than two minutes. There simply were not enough ways to thank Solange. Then she thought of one. "Come with me today," she said. "It'll be fun. You can talk fashion with Roberta. And I need you to be there."

"You do? Is that allowed?"

"Of course. Gary has people. You're my people."

***

Solange had been in celebrity homes before but only on a professional basis. As she drove Lily over to Gary's house in her freshly detailed Mercedes she knew this would be quite different.

"Are you worried about the personal questions?" Solange asked on the way down Benedict Canyon Road.

"It can't be worse than what's in the media and on the Internet. Did you know that I tried to rape Elton John when he went into rehab in 1997?"

Solange laughed. "You never told me that."

"Oh, yeah, and I had to use force. Apparently my master plan is to rape every gay celebrity in Hollywood and bring him home to straighthood. That's what it says on all the 'Hate-Lily' sites."

"What?"

"Yup, the world hates me, especially religious radicals, gay Gary fans and women. Until recently I was doing a daily search to see how many new sites popped up but it was making me nuts. After today I'm sure the number will spike."

"It's hard to be gay, Lily."

"I've been so clueless." Lily shook her head. "I keep thinking they can't be serious. I've never been around attitudes like that. Why do people care so much?"

"Sex is a big deal."

"But sex is a magic carpet ride to spiritual dimensions—when there's love. I don't get how love inspires hate."

"Lily, you have fairy dust in your head."

When they turned onto the long driveway, Solange saw Gary outside directing them to a parking space reserved with an orange cone. In a less desirable spot—ABC-TV trucks. "How cute is that?" Lily observed with goo-goo eyes.

Solange had to admit—Gary was pretty darn loveable. While he held onto Lily, he greeted Solange with a kiss on the cheek and urged her to make herself at home.

Lily excused herself to go to the bathroom.

"Please help Lily stay relaxed," Gary said as he led Solange inside. "This is very scary for her."

It was the perfect opportunity to confront him. But just as she summoned her nerve, the backlit silhouette of the great television icon appeared in the doorway. A halo-crown of Dioxazine Purple light shined all around her; Solange couldn't determine if it was her aura or her stature. As Roberta stepped into the living room, her perfectly tailored teal blue linen suit made Solange feel self-conscious in her silly scarf outfit. Though the crew wore shorts and ultra-casual clothes, Solange wished she had worn something more Roberta-like.

"Roberta," Gary said, waving Solange over from where she was lurking, "I want you to meet Lily's friend Solange."

Roberta Landers clasped both of her hands and spoke to her. "Solange. Lovely name and a charming ensemble." After that Solange felt much better about her wardrobe.

While the preparations droned on, Solange watched the ebullient Gary, in a gray Henley shirt and black jeans, schmooze everyone in sight. He amused the crew by juggling oranges which he promised to do on the air if the interview got boring. "But that's unlikely," he said.

All the while, he kept an eye on Lily, mouthing words of affection, looking madly in love. The Goddess had obviously gone wild doling out the charisma the day he was born.

Scooting beside Lily on a chaise lounge, Solange whispered, "I'm going to go out and ahem, feed Gary's plants. Will you be okay?"

For the first time all day Lily looked excited. "Really? That's fantastic. Thank you."

"You're sure it's not going to stir things up too much?"

"No, it will help me connect. I've never planted my blood here. Yours will be the first!"

"I'm honored." Solange pressed Lily's hand and sauntered over to the catering area where she poured some Evian water into a paper cup and headed for the bathroom.

Until Lily entered her life, Solange had never appreciated her heavy periods but she now gave thanks for the abundant flow that turned the Evian water bright red. With her hand cupped over the rim lest someone ask for a sip of "punch," she exited the bathroom and slipped out the patio doors.

Strolling past the spa and pool area, she came to a gazebo where a patch of swaying lavender beckoned her. Having never been beckoned by a plant, she kneeled down and poured out the red liquid. "Goddess, please protect Lily and her baby from suffering. If Gary is being unfaithful, make him tell her. And also tell me why I feel such a strong connection to him. If it's not sex, which it isn't, what is it?"

Back inside, sitting ten feet from Lily, Solange felt more nervous than she'd ever been on stage. She put her hands in the prayer position and blew an air kiss. "You look beautiful," she whispered.

The look Solange had created for Lily had won kudos from Roberta's producer and makeup artist: the soft pink, gauzy sleeveless dress, white lace shawl and fresh pink lily behind her ear. Lily had thought the flower too self-involved but she'd let Solange overrule her.

When the cameras finally rolled, Roberta got right to the point. "Gary, the last time we got together, I asked you about rumors that you were gay and you said, 'Sexuality is a private matter and I'm a private guy.' Then actress Trish Foley moved into your house and you were seen in public as a couple. She moved out after intimate photos of you and basketball legend Wade Collins appeared in an Italian magazine. After that, you neither confirmed nor denied that you were gay. Now you're in a declared heterosexual relationship with your massage therapist, Lily Bennett. Can you explain all this?"

Gary laughed. "Sure, but you'll probably be even more confused." He took Lily's hand. "The truth is, I've been gay all my life. I never broadcast it but it's been no secret in Hollywood.

Friends like Lily have always supported me and no one ever stopped me from doing the work I've wanted to do. So I thought fine, people can think what they like—if they absolutely must contemplate my sex life."

"You say 'friends like Lily.' What changed?"

"We just fell in love."

"Just like that?"

"Just like that. I went to her house one night and somehow I left the Earth's gravitational pull. Came back madly in love."

It was so romantic Solange couldn't stifle a sigh.

"And the same for you?" Roberta asked Lily.

"No," Lily said, "I've always been in love with him."

"How do you feel now that he returns that love?"

"Way overly lucky and incredibly happy."

"So you're just a regular pair of lovebirds?" Roberta asked.

"We are," Gary said, "and it really bothers me when they attack Lily. I'm used to reading bad fiction about me but I'll take on anyone who does it to her."

Solange wished that the scene she saw at Psychogarden had been bad fiction.

"Can you be a gay man in a sexual relationship with a woman? Doesn't that mean you're bisexual?"

It looked like Gary pondered the question though he must have thought about it a lot. "It would be so easy to say yes, I've been suppressing heterosexual feelings all these years then boing, I met Lily and they came flooding out, but that's not the case. I never thought I'd be with a woman. I've never had sexual feelings for any woman until now."

"Including Trish Foley?" Roberta asked.

His sigh filled the room. "I don't mean this as a slam but yes, including Trish Foley."

"What is it about Lily that makes her different?"

"She's smart, gorgeous and she gets fan mail from Pluto, but there are plenty of smart, gorgeous women in the world and they don't interest me. You need to ask her dogs. They're the only ones who understand her. I'm just a satellite in her orbit."

Lily closed her eyes and Solange saw her exhale love-breath into the air.

"Are you still attracted to men?"

On the monitor, the camera showed a close-up of Gary's response. "Not at the moment."

As he lied to millions of people, Solange could not fathom how sincere he looked.

"But possibly in the future?"

"No one can predict the future, Roberta, but I think I can safely predict that Lily and our baby and I will be together forever."

A moment of dead air elapsed as Roberta blanched; she looked like she'd been hit in the face with a pie—a juicy news-breaking pie. "Gary, was that an announcement?"

He nodded. "Well, Lily knows of course, but yes, we've been breeding."

"My goodness. When is the baby due?"

Lily massaged her belly. "Late January."

"Will you marry?"

Pointing his index finger in the air Gary said, "I knew you were going to bring that up. Hold on a second." From under his chair he pulled out a ring box and flipped it open. Perched inside was a drop-dead three-carat Marquis diamond ring in an exquisite platinum setting. He turned to Lily and cleared his throat. "Lily, I love you as much as the law allows. Will you marry me? Before you answer, be aware that millions are recording your reply."

It looked like Lily might swoon right out of camera range. "Of course I'll marry you, Gary." Her hand trembled as he put the ring on her finger. The camera moved in for a sparkly close-up.

After their scorching kiss of affirmation, Gary beamed. "I think we've made some news here. I predict monster ratings."

"What a gorgeous ring," Roberta said. She took Lily's hand and paused for a long second. "You've almost thrown me off stride tonight, Gary DiCaro, but we must press on."

"I love to make you happy, Roberta." Gary's high wattage grin competed with the lights while Solange shook her head in wonder at the master manipulator. How much publicity did one person need?

Roberta smiled graciously. "Now you know this will fuel those groups who say that you are either a traitor to the gay community or proof that homosexuals can be converted."

"I'm sure it will," Gary said with a nod, "but I will continue to support the gay community whether they want me or not. As for the religious groups who claim they can 'cure' gays—it's bullshit—they are doing a great deal of harm." He paused. "You don't have to bleep the whole word, do you?"

"We can leave part of it in," said Roberta.

"Great. Take out the 'bull.'" He paused another beat. "I wasn't cured because there was nothing wrong with me. I just fell in love with a woman."

Roberta sighed and shook her head. "Lily. Your life has been turned upside down. You're in love with one of the biggest stars in Hollywood, carrying his baby and soon you'll be married. Yet he openly admits that he's gay. How do you come to terms with that?"

"I don't think sexuality is the main priority when you love someone. When hearts make a connection you celebrate. I've loved Gary for so long I think I've loved enough for both of us and he finally got sucked in."

"Do you ever worry that he might go back to men?"

"Anyone who is in a relationship might wonder if their partner could be unfaithful." She looked at Gary. "I've known Gary almost seven years. He has always been my friend and I trust him completely."

Head lowered, Solange recalled the soap operas she used to watch in which the heroine declared it was the happiest day of her life—right before the ax fell.

Gary leaned in to kiss Lily's cheek. "I'm totally committed to this woman but the fact that she's a woman is secondary to who she is."

Solange felt slightly nauseous. It was partly due to Gary's duplicity, but there was another reason, the discovery of a common electrical field that somehow linked her with Lily. She felt as if she could jump into Lily's body and say hello to the baby.

Turning back to Gary, Roberta asked, "Now that you're going to be a father...had you ever thought about having children?"

"I have thought about it, Roberta. I love children. In fact, I once considered becoming a surrogate or donor or whatever the term is for guys like David Crosby. I was all ready to do it but the couple broke up."

"What kind of a dad do you think you'll be?"

"I'm sure it'll be my greatest role of all time."

"Gary is the most loving man I've ever known," said Lily. "He'll be an amazing father."

As Solange stared at the impossibly happy lovers, the nature of her physical connection with Lily's pregnancy came into focus. Like an overlay on the happy tableau, she saw herself in Lily's place with a baby in her arms. Not Lily's baby, but her own.

21
SOLANGE

When Solange got home that night, exhausted from her day among the rich and celebrated, she plunged into a steamy bathtub for an hour trying to make sense of her thoughts and feelings. Where had the incongruous baby idea come from? Ever since Joie conjured up that freaky Waltons-in-Colorado scenario, bearing children had seemed about as appealing as working on a chain gang.

Though Lily was her spiritual role model she didn't want to be her. For a brief guilty moment she considered Joie's contention that Lily was a sorceress who had taken control of Solange's mind. But in her heart she knew that Lily was pure goodness whose only bad influence was the man she'd hooked up with. Understandable, since Solange felt a bizarre attraction to him as well. None of it could possibly be healthy. In a worried frenzy she scrubbed her body raw.

After the bath she drank a half-gallon of ice tea and sought refuge in her studio. Her latest canvasses had taken on a Maxfield Parrish quality, filled with golds, yellows and copious amounts of her signature color, Phthalo Blue. As she stared without inspiration at a half-finished painting of a girl lying in a bed of flowers, she decided to sit in the dark and readjust her inner vision. Curtains closed, she shut out the lights and opened her eyes.

She stared into the blackness, a canvas awaiting an image. The smell of paint aroused her subconscious and in the dark with eyes wide open she felt she could see through seductive illusions and get to the truth.

Abstract images came up, lit from a subconscious source of light; they looked like the black magic crayon drawings she'd made as a child. Colorful scrawls began to twist and form into shapes. Her body reacted, throbbing, shaking, making its needs abundantly clear as it screamed in the darkness: I want a baby.

The scribbles formed strands of DNA—she knew in her heart they came from the blood she'd fed to the soil. And at that very moment her baby request was probably being beamed to an unborn soul somewhere in the cosmos. She had never stopped to consider that her body, the one used solely for exhibition until now, could actually grow life.

In ecstasy she leaped up, switched on the lights, stripped off her clothes and tossed them on the floor in a makeshift art installation. Moving to her bedroom she gazed at her nakedness in the full-length mirror, appraising herself like a member of her audience. Her weight had remained constant, plus a pound for the implants, at 115. Being pregnant would be so radical.

She caressed herself the way a perfect lover would—slowly, pausing at every curve, in no hurry to reach the harbor. Her opened palm skimmed across the carefully manicured, heart shaped thicket of black hair, then a finger wandered into her moist opening, lightly kissing its wet surface. She touched the last remains of her period, brought her fingers to her lips and suckled. Then she offered her hand to Fudgsicle, the only man she'd ever really loved.

Lying back on the bed she spread her legs wide and imagined they were shackled there with iron chains. Her hand returned to her clitoris; she was her own prisoner now. She massaged it, cooing with pleasure, holding out for greater heights. Finally, she let her fingers plunge into her waiting vagina and touch the magical spot that sent a rush of liquid streaming into her hand. Dizzy from the intense sensation, she moaned, then cried out.

Her water had broken. A new self was born.

***

The last person Solange expected to see when she and Fudgsicle arrived at Marvin's door the following afternoon was Joie. But when she did see her standing there in short shorts and a sports bra, it seemed so obvious.

"Hi kid, hi Fudge," said Joie in a chipmunky voice. "You're right on time." Joie bent down and gave Fudgsicle a kiss on the head.

"What are you doing here?"

Joie shrugged. "Everybody's gotta live somewhere." She took Solange's arm and led her inside. "You look fabulous."

Solange was dressed in a robin's egg blue Capraro suit—one of Roberta Landers' favorite designers. Fastened on her lapel, a delicate jeweled flower. On her feet, Manolo Blahnick bone sandals and a topaz ankle bracelet. Underneath she wore a black lace bustier and crotchless panties from Trashy Lingerie. The Roberta look empowered her.

She stared inside. If not for Marvin sitting on the couch watching a Dodger game, she'd have thought she'd come to the wrong house. No paper totem poles, no chairs full of books, no clutter of any kind. The house was as put together as she was. There were even plants—actual living things—scattered here and there.

"How did this happen? I was just here a few days ago."

"You know me, I work fast," said Joie. "We must've schlepped a million cartons to storage. Looks bitchin', don't it?"

Solange had to admit it did.

Marvin put the game on mute. He was wearing a sweater. Joie liked frigid air-conditioning; finally she had someone who would put up with it. "How was the Roberta Landers interview?"

"It was very interesting," Solange said, not wishing to share details.

"Your friend better be careful," said Marvin. "Most of those faggots have AIDS."

The terminology bothered her but she remained cool. "I hate that word, Marvin. Joie and I are lesbians—do you call us dykes when we're not around?"

"Women are different."

"That's a double standard. Lesbians are okay but gay men aren't?"

"Good thing you're not gay, Marv," Joie said, "because then you'd be Marvin Gay."

Marvin seemed unamused by Joie's remark and folded his arms across his scrawny chest. "She should just watch out, that's all."

Beneath Solange's power suit Marvin's words provoked a sea of perspiration. The possibility that Gary could have passed along a deadly virus to Lily and their baby haunted her, made her reconsider failing to speak up.

"Are you ready?" she asked Marvin. She wanted to get this visit over with.

"That's my signal," Joie said with a quick pirouette in the air. "Break a leg!" She danced off.

Marvin unbuckled his pants.

Turning her back to him, Solange hiked up her skirt and stuck her butt in the air as she perused the CD library. She heard him lapse into his distinctive grunting.

To her brief surprise, which turned to annoyance, the CDs had been rearranged in alphabetical order. Joie's obsessive handiwork had put an end to her I Ching-like system of selecting music. In a state of high irritation Solange plucked out Dire Straits' "Money for Nothing."

Marvin's dick was soon pulsating to the infectious beat of Mark Knopfler's guitar licks. As Solange moved closer to him, she removed her jacket and massaged her breasts, a glom away from Marvin's pumping hand.

Money for nothing...chicks for free...

She was being paid to take off her clothes. A lot of money. Teachers earned much less for educating children. Underpaid firemen saved lives. It seemed ridiculous that the accident of her beauty merited large sums of money.

Idly, she inserted her finger into her vagina through the crotchless panties and imagined how much the narrow opening would have to expand to allow a human being to emerge. Of course, other women did it—why not her? Surely it would bounce back to its normal size, and if it didn't she could get into fists.

Lost in thought, Solange paid no attention to Marvin's fading erection. "Hey," he shouted over the music. "Did you forget I was here?"

He had never reprimanded her before. Perhaps in addition to remodeling, Joie had given him assertiveness training. "How could I forget you, honey?" She snapped off her panties and held them to her face, her hot breath heating the nylon. "Is something wrong with Mr. Wiggly?" she pouted as she approached, wrapping the warm, moist panties around his flaccidity and kneading until the dough grew stiff.

She let the panties soak up his ejaculation and left them there as a souvenir. They were finished as work clothes.

Offering no post-climactic comments, Marvin used the lacy undies to wipe himself, zipped up and turned the game back on.

Solange went outside with Fudgsicle but as soon as she opened the back door Joie appeared like a nosy genie. "Hey," Joie said, "sounds like you put on a great show."

"I can't believe you moved in with Marvin."

Joie laughed. "He's been very cooperative. Of course I'm still grieving over our separation and I cry myself to sleep every night but aside from that, living with Marv isn't too bad."

"This is the most manipulative thing you've ever done."

"Really? Is it working?"

"I don't like being trapped."

"Freedom is a two-way street, Sol. You've got our house. Don't I have the right to live where I want?"

"Like you really want to live here."

Joie picked up a stick and played tug-of-war with Fudgsie. "I do want to live here, Sol. I've learned a lot about Marv. He's lonely."

"You had to move in to figure that out?"

"It's more than that. He's estranged from his parents and his sisters. He thinks of us as his family."

The reference to "us" made Solange want to scream. "Marvin is not my family. If you want to be his family, go ahead and marry the guy."

"You sound a little hostile, Sol. Maybe you need to meditate or something."

Solange wanted to strangle Joie, but instead stormed back inside and tripped over a brand new welcome mat.

Marvin muted the game. "Is everything okay?"

"Look, Marvin, Joie and I aren't a couple anymore and I'm not comfortable dancing when she's in the other room. Is there something we can do about that?"

"Well, she lives here now..."

"But it's your house and you own it. Do you want her running your life?"

"I don't know what I can do." He seemed perfectly content with the new situation.

Solange made sure he heard her exasperated sigh. "She could go to the movies or to the pool hall. It affects my dancing when she's here. You saw it today. My vagina was all tightened up."

Marvin looked away. When he spoke his words tumbled out and his face turned Alizarin Crimson. "Why don't you two make up and we can all live here together?"

"Sorry, Marvin," she said, shrinking from his whacked-out Ozzie and Harriet and Harriet notion, "I don't think that's going to happen."

His eyes roamed the floor. "If you want her to move out...just tell me."

She wasn't about to be the heartless bitch who wouldn't let junior keep the homeless puppy. "No, she doesn't have to move out." *I'm about to quit this gig anyway.*

"You're not mad at me, are you?"

"You didn't do anything wrong, Marvin. This is between me and Joie." She picked up her Manolos and slipped them on. "I have to get going." And sped out the door as quickly as her four-inch spikes could carry her.

When she got to the car, Joie was leaning against it holding Fudgsicle. "Don't forget your dog."

22
JANEY

Janey blew $100 at Petco on Rosie's homecoming gifts, wrapping them before helping Rosie open them. With the various drugs Rosie was on, Janey could only imagine the effort it took for her to express appreciation, but Rosie put each present in her mouth, then carefully handed it back to Janey as if to say, "No, you deserve this more."

Three times a day Janey blended the prescribed steamed chicken and oatmeal in the Cuisinart and fed it to her. While Rosie slept she kept a close vigil, in case she awoke in distress. The look of gratitude in Rosie's eyes was more than enough thanks. "Bruce was thinking of you when he wrote 'Tougher Than the Rest,'" Janey told her.

No matter what Janey said, Rosie would cock her head and let the thought drop into her brain. Once she grasped it, she would return her head to its upright position, proving that she understood every word. Janey hoped that someday she might be half as bright.

After some brief moments of anguish, Janey chose to turn down an invitation from Lily to join the Reddi-wip Sisters at Gary's house for the Roberta Landers interview. Though it would have been fun to meet Roberta Landers and strong-arm her to get Bruce on her next special, she owed it to Rosie to be by her side. Besides, Janey was not ready to meet Gary DiCaro with non-accusing eyes.

Candi and Eleanor did not adhere to the notion that due to her infirmity, Rosie was now to be treated as royalty. To Eleanor she was still "the dog" and to Candi, who normally regarded her as a piece of animated furniture, she continued to be "Mom's dog." But Rosie did receive an animated email get well card signed, "Sherri & Daddy."

While Janey yearned for Davy to phone, there seemed no way he could come by without being seen by Candi or Eleanor. When he finally called on Rosie's second day back, Janey's defenses vanished when he uttered the provocative words, "Can I come over?" Then she worried she'd said yes before he had completed the sentence.

She practiced downplaying his next-day arrival, settling on the honest explanation that a young man would be stopping by to visit Rosie, an announcement made with the utmost breeziness while she burned the breakfast toast.

"How young?" Candi asked, her face painted like an Egyptian princess with thick kohl eye shadow over a yellowish foundation. Barely covering her breasts was a white bikini top of such flimsy material, a change in humidity could render it transparent.

Janey pretended to think about it. "Around thirty," she lied by half a decade.

"Is he cute?"

"He's way too old for you."

"He must be really cute if you're wearing makeup."

Janey realized she'd made a telltale error. "I was a little blotchy this morning, that's all."

Candi's eyebrows and breasts rose simultaneously. "Wow, you are so nervous. I should hang around and meet this guy."

With forced nonchalance that nearly fractured her throat, Janey said, "Sure, be my guest."

"No, I'm going to Melissa's pool. Maybe next time, if he comes over again."

"You got it." Janey turned her back on the women for a moment and kissed her hand. Reverse psychology—what a concept.

"What does he do for a living?" Eleanor asked.

"He's a carpenter."

Eleanor pointed her butter knife in Janey's direction. "Have him fix the leaky faucet in my bathroom."

"He's not a plumber and he's only coming over to..." Her voice was growing defensive. "I'll have him take a look at it."

Seeming satisfied, Eleanor nodded and turned to Candi. "Do you need money?"

"What's the catch?" Candi asked. Her meticulously arched eyebrows met in a flat unibrow.

"Get me my pocketbook. I'll give you twenty bucks if you put on some clothes."

Candi leaped from the table and raced upstairs. Thirty seconds later she reappeared in shorts and an undershirt carrying Eleanor's Eisenhower-era black patent leather handbag. She watched Eleanor remove a coin purse, snap it open and extract a twenty. Candi bestowed an air kiss near her cheek before bounding out the door.

Janey wondered if Eleanor's unheard-of generosity signified the onset of some horrible senior ailment.

"You owe me," Eleanor said, clicking the purse shut.

"For what?"

"That was for the faucet."

***

Just before she opened the door Janey experienced a few butterflies left over from her high school prom. Davy stood there grinning while a stray sunbeam bounced off his lower teeth. "Hey, little darlin'," he said.

"Hi," said Janey, coy as a four-year-old meeting Santa.

Pausing from Judge Judy reruns on her old VCR, Eleanor swiveled her head to view him. "Are you the plumber?"

Off his quizzical look, Janey gave Davy an imperceptible nod. "Yes, and I am so honored to meet you." He gave a little Sir Walter Raleigh bow.

Janey could almost see the thought balloon over Eleanor's head: why can't everyone treat me like this?

"Come sit down," Eleanor said, tapping the chair beside her. "I'll show you my press clippings."

"I will," Davy replied, "as soon as I say hello to the señorita." He kneeled down beside Rosie, who sat in repose on Billy's sofa, and stroked her head.

As Rosie licked his hand and gazed into his brown eyes, Janey realized she had competition.

"'I ain't here on business, I'm only here for fun,'" Davy quoted from Rosie's song and Janey knew that for the foreseeable future she'd be praying for him to turn to her and continue the lyric:

"the only lover I'm ever gonna need's your soft, sweet little girl's tongue."

Without any sign of boredom even after Volume Three, Davy granted Eleanor's request that he view her press clippings. Afterwards Eleanor took him on a guided tour of her dance trophies, from the plastic cups to the ones that Janey someday planned have melted down and made into costume jewelry.

"Looks like you have a lot of first places." Davy was acting so obsequious, Janey opened a window to let out the hot air.

"They're all first places," Eleanor scolded. "You're not paying attention."

"I'm sorry, Eleanor."

Eleanor turned and led the way downstairs as fast as she could go, up to a quarter mile per hour. Forced into close proximity behind her, Janey and Davy held their feet poised in the air, waiting to take each step together. The nearness, the soft brushing of arms and shoulders, made Janey want to do an about face and yank him into her bedroom.

Horrifying. Improper.

Maybe next time.

At the bottom of the stairs Davy turned to Eleanor and asked, "Would you show me some of your award winning moves?"

"I don't dance alone. I have to have a partner."

Davy offered his arm. "I'm a partner. You're not paying attention."

It might have been the first time since the *Tonight Show* that Eleanor's face cracked a smile. Janey scrambled to the CD player in the living room and cued up one of Eleanor's favorites, the snappy: *Enjoy Yourself: The Hits of Guy Lombardo*.

"Seems Like Old Times" began to play. Eleanor offered her

hand and Davy led her onto the Oriental rug where he proved he could Fox Trot with the best of her ancient colleagues.

Sitting with Rosie, Janey watched the couple drift into "Red Sails in the Sunset" then went into the kitchen to make lemonade. Perhaps if she phoned Lily she could learn what secret ingredient to add to make herself twenty years younger.

Rosie followed Janey and watched her perform kitchen duties as Rosie always did, with the concentration of a brain surgeon. Fascination with every detail of life—guru lesson one from Swami Rosalita.

But in mid-surgery Rosie turned, looked up at the kitchen phone and barked once. Moments later, it rang. A shiver rippled through Janey's body that replayed when she picked it up and heard Sherri's voice on the line.

"Oh my God," Janey moaned.

Sherri sounded better than the acoustic version of "Thunder Road." "Greetings from Haiku," she whispered.

"I can hardly hear you, honey."

"I'm talking low 'cause Daddy's in the other room."

Janey pictured Billy smoking a giant hookah made of bamboo and puka shells. "Is everything all right?"

"I just called to see how Rosie's doing."

When Sherri mentioned Rosie's name Janey noticed Rosie's ears perk up though she couldn't possibly have heard it. It spooked her. "She's doing great. She misses you and wants you to come home."

"Well, tell her I miss her too."

"Rosie also said, 'I hope she's not smoking pot.'"

"I'm not." She said it in a flat, unconvincing tone.

"What do you do all day?"

"I go to the surf shop with Daddy, hang out with the island bros, boogey board."

"Is Daddy earning a living? Are you getting enough to eat?"

"Yeah, we've got money. I have to go now."

Janey tried to rid herself of the notion that they were selling joints at the surf shop. "Come home, Sherri."

That Rosie had foreshadowed the call, like Babe Ruth promising a homer, stunned Janey and she had trouble replacing the phone in its cradle.

"I plucked chickens at her age," said Eleanor, then excused herself to take a nap. "Don't worry about the faucet," she told Davy. "You can fix it the next time."

"Sure thing," Davy said.

"That was my daughter," Janey mentioned as a reality check. "She's fifteen."

"Cool," Davy replied.

"She's the younger one," Janey pressed on.

"Even more cool." He appeared unflapped.

Their aloneness begged for function. "Want to copy some bootlegs?" Janey asked.

"Thanks but my mom sends me everything."

"Does she have his old answering machine song?"

"She has everything. She's a completist."

A completist with a look-alike son, Janey thought enviously. "Where does your mom live?" She hoped he would name a foreign country.

"Rockford, Illinois. That's where I grew up."

"That's a very Springsteenian town."

"It is. It could move to New Jersey and fit right in."

His sensibility meshed so well with hers she felt as if he were about to admit that he was actually her son, the one she'd had during the drug-induced memory lapse in college. Then she remembered that to the best of her knowledge she neither did drugs nor went to college.

Aware she was on the fast lane to depravity, Janey regretted not following through with the rubber band aversion therapy. She snapped her fingers sharply against her wrist.

Davy noticed. "What are you doing?"

"Oh, just a pressure point."

"Would you and the señorita like to see my studio?"

No one had ever used any semblance of the etchings come-on with her before and it gave her a rush. "Well, if Clarence promises not to get rambunctious..."

"He'll be a gentleman and I'll try to be," said Davy.

As fireworks went off in her genitalia, Janey turned to Rosie, who was sitting on her favorite ottoman. "Would you like to go over and visit Clarence?" Janey asked.

Climb in back, heaven's waiting on down the tracks...

No matter how eager Janey was to be alone with Davy, she had to stop and wonder how Rosie managed to send her thought-lyrics from "Thunder Road." But only for an instant.

They drove over in Davy's Volkswagen Jetta, that like her Saturn, had an interior layer of dog hair Janey found charming. When they pulled up to the nondescript warehouse in an industrial zone off Van Nuys Boulevard, Davy said, "It's not much from the outside." He ran around to let Janey and Rosie out of the car.

Clarence bounded out when Davy opened his front door, gave Rosie a nuzzle and rolled over in submission. It seemed that Rosie, in addition to being the smartest dog who ever lived, was also a femme fatale.

Janey was instantly smitten by the smell of wood and camphor upon entering Davy's studio and was staggered by the craftsmanship in the works of art he made. Nature-inspired organic lines and rich surfaces polished to glass-like perfection—Davy's furniture looked like it could take flight. In no time he'd be famous and wealthy and would vaguely remember her.

"Your work is poetry," she said. "It's beyond lyrics. But then, Bruce never wrote a song about a chair."

Davy pointed to a mahogany rocking chair shaped like a swan. "How about 'I'm a Rocker?'"

While Janey wondered how he could possibly know that cute whimsical talk got her sexually aroused, he took her hand and led her to a huge bed with a carved headboard that looked ideal for clutching. He glided her to a landing upon it and began to move his fingers across her face. She felt like a piece of lucky timber he was examining for a new project. The hands she'd admired at the park felt like a silk scarf brushing across her skin.

"What do you use on your hands?" she asked, detecting yet another layer of intoxicating scent.

He held them out to her. "Hoof ointment."

"Really. You must have nice hooves."

"I do. Want to see 'em?"

Janey nodded.

Davy slipped off his worn Nikes and crew socks, leaned back and deposited his feet in her lap. He wiggled his toes. They were curvy and artistic and the two little ones looked like hazelnuts.

She longed to put them, infant-like, in her mouth but held back. Lightly, she traced his lovely arches.

"Smoothest hooves I've ever felt."

"Want to know my beauty secret?"

"Sure, I love beauty secrets."

Davy hopped up and returned with a large jar of Wyoming Hoof Manicure Cream. "Says here on the label it contains sunflower seed oil, jojoba oil and peach kernels to nourish dry, brittle hooves. Yeah!" He handed her the jar, kneeled on the floor and removed her sandals.

Hopefully, the Cheeky Pink nail enamel she'd applied that morning would draw attention away from her bunions. "I've never had an equestrian pedicure," she admitted. In a moment of dread she worried that her misshapen feet would repulse him but he went ahead, dipped his fingers in the balm and rubbed some into her left foot.

Janey had no idea that her feet were a hotbed of G-spots. Everywhere he touched felt like an E-ticket ride at Hedonism-land. She fell back slowly and when her head met the mattress Davy swung her legs around to position her vertically. By the time her feet had absorbed the hoof cream she was inebriated. He'd massaged the inhibition out of her.

He removed his tee shirt and jeans so deftly they might have been fall-away clothes. His lean, muscular, fat-free physique was like the body of a man in his twenties. Her vagina contracted when she recalled that he was, in fact, a man in his twenties.

Davy straddled her and put her arches against his cheeks like parentheses, then lowered himself to give her a noisy kiss. "Music?"

"Of course," she said in a voice already hoarse with anticipation of too much pleasure. She watched his adorable tush move to the CD player, so round it could be a visual aid in geometry class. Decades would pass before it would succumb to gravity.

"I have the perfect song in mind," he said.

Janey enjoyed the next few seconds scanning hundreds of potential song candidates in her head, but didn't dare dream Davy would play the most woman-melting, obsessively devotional song in Bruce's musical pantheon: "Drive All Night."

I swear I'd drive all night again...Just to buy you some shoes...And to taste your tender charms...

Shoes. Hoof cream. High pressure bliss.

Davy and his perfect anatomy returned to her side. Starting at her shoulders his hand glided over her breasts, stomach and down her legs, returning to slide under the dress and reach into her panties. She moaned. He pulled them off and pushed up her dress. His lips grazed her abdomen and lavished feathery kisses on the way down to the promised land between her legs. Over and over he kissed its slick, wet folds, letting his tongue become soft, then hard, in unfathomable compliance with her unspoken desires.

She pushed forward to let his mouth savor her juices. Her arms reached over her head and seized the headboard. Sounds came forth from her that surely mocked the mating call of wild pelicans.

Davy lifted the dress off her body and closed his mouth around each of her nipples. Then his tongue drew a slow, painstaking line from her feet to her lips.

Janey gripped harder and her legs opened for business. His entry was smooth and unforced and his mouth approached hers for another kiss, but before bestowing it he looked into her eyes and said, "You're beautiful."

It was the most fantastic, unbelievable thing anyone had ever said to her.

When she freed her hands from the rail he clasped her wrists and held her arms down on the bed. It was a gesture she could never imagine Billy performing—he never wanted to keep her in place that badly.

She knew Davy had the stamina to fuck her until tomorrow but she could not deny the orgasm that was about to consume her. Letting herself go she rode wave after wave after wave.

The intensity of emotion produced a torrent of tears that embarrassed her; women her age do not cry in the presence of much younger men who might be confused or uncomfortable with mature hormones. But Davy seemed touched by it and held her close, staying inside, smoothing her hair.

His lovemaking left Billy in the dust, even compared to their pre-marital, wall-to-wall fucking days. Looking into Davy's sweet face she truly believed that he would gladly drive all night.

Just to buy her some hoof ointment.

23
GODDESSES

"We never should have done it," Gary kept saying in the aftermath of the Roberta Landers Special. No one, apparently, believed their story. The hope that the interview would have normalized them in the public view proved wildly naive. Instead, Gary's bad boy image took on a layer of self-delusion, Lily was spoken of with New Age disdain and together they were thrust into the berth formerly occupied by Britney Spears and Kevin Federline.

From a sociological viewpoint, the accumulation of myths about her—like the *Enquirer* story that following her secret coronation by a fringe Wicca cult, she pricked the fingers of twelve lesbians and drank their blood—would be fascinating if they concerned someone else.

As much as she wished to dismiss her public image as a fascinating sitcom and wallow in her private life paradise, she and Gary had a mission to accomplish. She told herself that obstacles in the form of negative publicity proved they were on the right course.

The couple mostly hung out at Gary's and took Francesca with them everywhere they went. Gary didn't enjoy becoming inaccessible, but it was impossible to determine which people were friendly and supportive and which wanted to spout the latest homophobic slur.

Around Gary's property they put in remedial landscaping to thwart telephoto shots from the relentless paparazzi, but once away from the demilitarized zone they were fair game, especially for the highly coveted shot of Lily's bulging profile. They laughed that the money the baby had already earned in media profits could finance his college tuition many times over.

One Saturday afternoon as they were lying in a bed strewn with half-read scripts, Gary massaged her belly and said, "I was thinking we could move to Santa Barbara and raise llamas." A second later a homemade cherry bomb shattered the kitchen window.

Lily half-swallowed her scream. The other half came out. Gary wrapped himself around her like a straightjacket.

She encased her womb in light while her heart banged out an S.O.S. to the universe. "It's okay," she whispered. "It's a prank, it's a prank." She had no idea how she knew that, but she did.

Within seconds Francesca called to say she'd already called armed security after she'd heard commotion in the dense brush on the slope behind Gary's house. "Two guys laughing and hollering," she said. "I think one of 'em fell."

Francesca proved right; the young, drunken perpetrators were caught first by gravity, then the police in the pit of the steep ravine. One suffered a broken leg. They proudly identified themselves as anti-fag terrorists intent on sending all perverts to hell. Not exactly suicide bombers, but quite willing to be caught and treated harshly for the sake of their cause.

The incident got volumes of coverage. Showbiz pundits marveled at Gary's ingenious ability to remain subject du jour when he hadn't even murdered anyone.

The level of hate trying to invade their lives left Lily breathless. "We have to make more love so we can fight back," Lily said one night as they relaxed in Gary's bathtub. "We can't let the haters win."

"I'm all for that," Gary said, "but I think we should move to your place."

"My place?"

"That's where your energy vortex is, right? The one I fell into? So tell your gods and goddesses to protect us and Francesca can come around for safekeeping."

Lily smiled. "How did you get so wise?"

"From you."

One day and a few suitcases later, Gary moved into Lily's middle class house in the Valley, with its sheltering ambience and giant refrigerators filled with exotic panaceas. "Now that's a refrigerator," he'd say when he opened one in search of a snack, even though he couldn't identify most of the contents. Lily made room for his favorites: chocolate covered biscotti, Creamsicles and frozen Vienna wafers. He also drank copious amounts of buttermilk, the thought of which had always made Lily gag until one day she had a yen to taste it. From then on she drank a quart a day.

It didn't seem to bother Gary that his living quarters had been drastically reduced. "It's not a house, it's a manger," he liked to say. Lily felt the same way and regarded their new alarm system as an unnecessary evil, though she allowed its installation. In addition, they each got a walkie-talkie line to Francesca.

Despite the suspension of her blood contributions, Lily felt safer in her own house where her DNA was pervasive in the soil, plants and flowers. The paparazzi, of course, moved right along with them but even they seemed more polite in Lily's neighborhood, sometimes greeting them quite sincerely while they snapped photos.

It charmed and amused Lily that the focus of Gary's life was her belly—the new center of the universe. He spent hours staring at it, riding its movements, rhapsodizing over the slightest gyration even when Lily knew it was merely indigestion. If she let him, she suspected his hand would be permanently affixed on the budding life for the duration of their pregnancy.

"Let's be John and Yoko and stay in bed for a week," he suggested one lazy morning.

"But John and Yoko invited the press over," she said. "We don't want to do that."

"Not that John and Yoko—John and Yoko Fleckenstein, the Canadians. It's so cold they just stay in bed all the time and make love." He kissed her ear and she squirmed.

"Oh, well that's different." It so happened she had an irresistible desire to taste him, so she slid out of his grasp and burrowed under the covers.

Feeling him rise in the cup of her hand, she brushed her fingertips over his belly and down his inner thighs until she felt goose bumps pop up there that she found exceedingly cute.

She threw off the blanket and looked at his lovely penis in full extension, begging for her attention. Her fingers combed the jet black hair around it.

"I love torture," Gary croaked.

"I love you," Lily replied, and lowered her lips onto the smooth head.

Gary moaned as she held him, allowing him to thrust into her as her hands roamed his body, tracing patterns in the goose bumps. His cries increased until minutes later he climaxed with a great animal howl that sent warm liquid into her mouth.

It tasted sublime; she craved every drop of him. After a brief recovery period, Gary resumed the vigilant monitoring of her stomach and asked, "You think that stuff's good for the baby?"

"Are you kidding? That stuff *is* the baby."

Gary shook his head. "I'm having way too much fun."

"Are we too lucky, Gary?"

"Hell, yes. We're living on top of Lucky Mountain."

"Don't you think it's incredibly unfair that there's so much suffering in the world and we have all this?"

"Someone's got to have it or we're all doomed. As long as we're not jerks and give back, we're contributing to the world's happiness, right?" He lifted his finger off her belly to point at her. "You taught me that."

"You're right," Lily said. "It's all about bringing everyone into abundance. That's my purpose. I have so much; I want to contribute as much joy as possible and help move the world toward peace."

"I'll do it with you," Gary said. "John and Yoko Fleckenstein are all about saving the world. You're the healer, so you figure out how to do it and I'll put my life and money behind it. Deal?"

"Deal," said Lily, stupefied, awed that she was in love with a true bodhisattva. "We have a huge mission to accomplish together. That's why all this happened."

With the timing of veteran actors, Bean and Blossom came over and licked their masters' faces in unison.

"This was all the dogs' idea," Gary said. "All good ideas come from dogs."

"It's true. If we all lived by their values our lives would be so much better."

"Then let's do that." Gary said. "The world according to dogs. That's the world I want my kid to live in."

"And what form does this world take?"

"Well, it's a beautiful place with lots of dogs, lots of fun and unconditional love. Where everyone can lick their balls. Or a friend's."

Lily poked him. "It sounds wonderful."

"Hire your friends," Gary said. "The dog women."

***

On that exhilarating notion, Lily asked Janey and Solange to meet her at the park that afternoon, which coincided with Rosie's triumphant return.

The women joined in an electrically charged hug. "Wow," said Lily, acknowledging their wild chemistry.

"We've still got the sizzle," said Solange.

"It's got to be a plus to be radioactive in this day and age," Janey said.

Lily bent down to kiss the terrier while the Labs gave Rosie a thorough sniff-down. "Rosie, you look better than ever. How are you feeling?"

"Way better, thanks," Janey replied, then added, "That was just me pretending to speak for Rosie."

"Whatever you say," said Solange.

Lily felt a blast of static interference and noticed that Solange and Janey had just noticed Cleo's prying laser gaze about fifty feet away.

"I hate when she watches us," said Solange.

"Might as well give her something to watch," Lily said. She put her arms around Solange and Janey and sensually massaged them.

"Do you think she's taking our picture?" Janey asked. "I'm sick of Eleanor getting all the publicity in my family."

"I don't care," said Lily. "I used to act neutral when I was out in public but now I'm trying to have fun and project love to those spying lenses out there. It's better than being hostile."

Solange clapped her hands. "Let's do the 'Charlie's Angels' poster."

They struck a pose aiming "weapons."

"How would you angels like a real assignment?" Lily asked.

"What?" asked Solange.

Lily held her arms out wide. "Saving the world."

***

Janey always thought that saving the world seemed like a great idea if you didn't have to save all of it. Many people, she believed, would be better off in some other world. "What did you have in mind?" she asked Lily.

"Help people become happy."

"Springsteen," Janey said. "Front row. Physical contact. Lots of sweat."

"That takes care of you," Lily said, "but what if we could find a way to help people like Cleo?"

"How about a do-it-yourself lobotomy?"

"Gary had an idea," Lily said. "Actually, he said it's the dogs' idea. Something that promotes peace and unconditional love, so humans can learn to live more like dogs. Whatever it turns out to be, he'll finance it. I think the three of us could come up with something amazing. It's our mission together."

The idea sounded wildly idealistic. Janey envisioned Lily on the front lines of the peace movement, conveniently distracted while Gary searched for trouble on Santa Monica Blvd.

"Do you mean like a school?" Solange wondered.

"Yes, but not a traditional school. More like a retreat where dogs teach people how to live—a physical and spiritual empire of joy."

Solange gasped. "Wow..."

"An empire?" Janey considered the implications. "Would that make us empresses?"

"But of course," said Lily. "Not that we aren't already."

A world under Janey's domination seemed awfully appealing. "Rosie and I could put litterers under house arrest. We could even clean up New Jersey—Bruce would have to take notice of that."

"How could he not?" said Lily, giggling.

"What would I be in the empire?" Solange asked. "The only job I've ever had is stripping."

Lily rubbed a circle in Solange's back. "Which makes you the expert on all things physical, right?"

It seemed the best response Solange could have imagined. Janey felt certain Solange's tap was about to burst and sure enough, precipitation rushed forth. "You're so amazing, Lily," Solange said. Her hands covered her face. "I worship you."

Janey fished around in her fanny pack for some Kleenex that she'd begun keeping on hand for Solange's serial bawling jags. As Janey handed her a wad she despaired that if Lily's grand dream depended on Lily and Gary's continued connubial bliss, it was probably doomed from the start. Which was more than a little disappointing.

"It'll be a role model for the world," Lily said, arms encircling Solange, "a place where people and dogs and nature are all equal."

Pawing the back of Janey's foot, Rosie got her attention. Janey looked down to see her hairy genius staring at her with fervid eyes. In the space above Rosie's head, an imaginary movie presented that very place, filled with people, dogs and children. Despite Janey's doubts, Rosie was clearly encouraging her to believe in it. "The Promised Land?" she asked Lily.

"Exactly," Lily replied.

After reining in the last of her sobs, a stricken look came over Solange. "Lily, I have to tell you something."

Janey's blood rushed to her feet, her legs wobbly enough to be toppled by a sparrow's sneeze. Solange was about to blow everything. Rotating her eyeballs, Janey tried to get Solange's attention but failed.

"What?" asked Lily.

"When I was watching you guys at the Roberta Landers

interview...this might sound really crazy but I can't help it. And I know I just said I worship you, but I swear I'm not trying to imitate you. Do you believe me?"

"Of course," said Lily. "What is it?"

"I saw myself having a baby. My own baby."

The relief Janey felt that Solange hadn't uttered the fatal blurtation was so profound, her mouth hung open as she awaited her next coherent thought.

"Solange, that's fantastic!" Lily said. "If you hurry our babies will be siblings!"

"I knew you'd understand, Lily. My body is craving a baby. It's all I think about. Babies and Andi."

"Maybe Andi's going to be your baby," Lily said.

In a peculiar display, the daylight intensified around Solange's head. It remained that way even after Janey blinked a few times.

"Of course," Solange said. "Of course!"

"Excuse me, I'm having a spooky spasm," said Janey. "I'd better go home."

Solange grabbed her arm. "Wait, Janey, this is amazing. It's groundbreaking. Don't you see?"

"You're asking the wrong person. Then again, you're glowing and it's daytime."

"We're becoming multi-dimensional," Lily said.

"Is that good?" Janey asked. "I have enough trouble with the dimension I'm in now."

"It's evolution," Lily explained. "It's where humanity is headed. And it fits in perfectly with our project because the dogs are already there."

As Janey considered her approaching mutation she noticed Fudgsicle and the Labs walking toward Rosie with sticks in their mouths. Rosie accepted each stick in turn and added it to a carefully laid out design that looked like spokes of a bicycle wheel. "What...is...that?" Janey asked, stupefied.

Lily and Solange stared at it as well.

Standing over the object d'art, the dogs wagged their tails, hung their tongues at jaunty angles and smiled.

Solange gasped. "It's dog art." She looked to Lily. "Is that what it is?"

"I don't know what it is," Lily said. "But it sure looks like they're trying to tell us something."

Impulsively, Janey bent down to touch the stick formation then drew her hand back. "I'm scared if I touch it I'll spontaneously combust."

Rosie pawed at Janey, then at the stick design.

"Okay," said Janey, determined to remain rational. "They made a circle of sticks. It's not Stonehenge."

"It's Bonehenge," said Lily.

24
SOLANGE

Solange spent the night trying to bring Andi back to life on canvas. Her brushes flew on an internal power she set loose to recreate Andi's spirit. Fueled by a pot of espresso and Thin Mint Girl Scout cookies she worked until four A.M., completing three impressionistic snapshots of the girl who might soon be her daughter. Baring her visions felt like seeing Jesus' face in her bathroom window or tears streaming from the eyes of the Madonna.

She knew the paintings were the best she'd ever done. Her other works, while decent enough for a modern living room, lacked relevance. But these freshly minted portraits of her precious Andi meant something. They meant everything.

Fudgsicle stayed up with her all night watching her work. At some point when she wasn't paying attention he'd dipped four paws into a pool of Phthalo Blue paint and tracked it all over the floor. Since she'd barely set her palette down for even a moment, she was convinced it was his way of expressing his deep connection to his future sister.

She picked him up and hugged him; blue paint blotches tattooed her shirt. She didn't care about the floor. Someday she would break it up and sell it for a million dollars. "From now on," she declared, "this color is 'Andi Blue.'"

During the few hours she slept she dreamed about Andi. They were at a carnival on a Ferris wheel packed with happy people. But the Ferris wheel began to spin faster and faster until all the people flew off and only she and Andi were left.

She awoke frightened but quickly recovered when she gazed at her night's work and saw Andi safely committed to canvas. Over a bowl of soy granola she worked up the courage to phone Joie's art gallery owner friend, Daphne Isenberg, hoping Daphne could see her before she had to be at Marvin's.

"I can't wait to meet you," Daphne said, sounding more excited than Solange would have expected. She asked Solange to come to the gallery in the Sherman Oaks Fashion Square when it opened at ten.

There was no time to take slides of the Andi paintings. Without a digital camera or a portfolio she had to think outside the paint box. Let ordinary artists bring in fancy presentations;

she would bring in the real deal—actual paintings hot off her easel.

She wrapped them in a lovely quilt handmade by Joie's grandmother that Joie had serendipitously left behind, and placed the package on a portable luggage carrier. At five minutes to ten she strode confidently into the mall wearing a black Armani pantsuit and subtle makeup that wouldn't compete with her canvases. Her hair was pulled back into a loose ponytail held in place by a diamond clip.

"You're even more beautiful than Joie described," Daphne said, holding open the door for her arrival.

Solange shook Daphne's unmanicured hand and sized her up. She looked about fifty, slightly overweight with short silver hair; cakey, too-dark foundation and a deadly shade of port wine lip gloss that she began to suck off. In the handshake that lasted about a second too long, Solange saw casting couch fantasies in her eyes.

Gazing at the display of paintings Solange felt the need to lower her voice, as if she had entered the Louvre. Clearly, there were highly talented artists out there but she remained undaunted. No other painter but she could burrow into her soul to extract Andi's beauty.

"So, what do we have here?" asked Daphne, indicating the quilted package.

Solange began the unwrapping. "I know this is a little unorthodox but I just painted these last night and I wanted you to be the first to see them."

"Lovely." Daphne began to blink rapidly but Solange couldn't determine if that was a good or bad sign. Maybe she had some mascara in her eye. As Solange whisked off the quilt—with measured flourish to not appear grand—Daphne put her fingers to her chin and made little humming noises.

"Her name is Andi," Solange said, her maternal pride already showing. "She died almost twenty years ago. These are from memory."

"Oh, how sad," said Daphne, flipping through the other two canvases then letting them fall back into place. "Well!" She seemed to be searching for the right terminology. "You've certainly captured her spirit."

"Really?" Solange felt her skin redden.

"But I don't think they're right for us," Daphne went on. "We cater to a more mainstream clientele."

As she was used to doing on stage when a drunk called her vulgar names, Solange held on to her composure. "What is it about my paintings that isn't mainstream?"

Daphne appeared to be weighing her words again; she obviously didn't want to sound offensive and lose any future chance of seduction. "Well, they have a certain elemental naiveté and primitive, impressionistic zeal but given the raw and inconsistent painterly effects, the unsure brushwork and discordant passages, the uneasy tension between the opposing hues and thematic visual overload, the result is a vague sense of inadequate artistic heft."

Solange knew bullshit when she heard it. "So they suck, right?"

Daphne reached out and squeezed her shoulder. "Not at all, Solange. In fact, I'd like to see more of your work, the ones you didn't paint in a Pollockian frenzy." She laughed at her lame art humor. "Perhaps we could set up a private consultation...in your studio."

"How about in your dreams?" said Solange, throwing the quilt over the Andi portraits. "But thanks for the review."

The despair that consumed Solange on her way home from the art gallery evaporated when she went into her back yard and discovered a mysterious curlicue etching. At first she thought it might have been done by squirrels or alien beings, but the dirt on Fudgsie's paws and the tiny blue flecks in the design was proof positive that her darling Yorkie was a genius, an extension of her own artistic soul.

She scooped him up and peered into his gifted burnt sienna eyes. "Let Dykey Isenberg try to get this into her gallery," she boasted. "Cows will play chess before that happens." Then she reconsidered because the way things were going, chess-playing cows didn't seem all that peculiar. "Okay, even if cows played chess and baked oatmeal cookies, that bitch is history."

She went inside and opened a bag of Beggin' Strips. "My little Leonardo DaFudgsicle," she said as he gobbled them up.

Solange wanted to phone Lily to share the excitement, but since Gary had moved in with her, there was a good chance he might answer the phone. She still felt weird around Gary and even on the phone there was no telling what she might say. Instead, she called Janey.

"Take a picture," Janey suggested. "I haven't gotten over the sticks yet."

"Our dogs are artists. It must be what Lily said about becoming multi-dimensional. I'm thrilled that Andi will be born into a world of culture."

"The world is terminally insane, Solange. I'm not even sure Bruce could save it. Are you sure you want to bring up a child in this place?"

"Of course. Andi is going to change the world. And so will Lily's baby."

"Well, you two have your chakras in retrograde."

"Janey, remember when you thought that giving blood made bad things happen? Well, what about Davy and our future happiness empire?"

There was a pause on the line. "Davy is good—I'll give you that—but what happens when Lily finds out that Gary's been playing with boys? That'll be the end of financing for Happyland."

"Maybe he told her and it's okay with her," Solange said without a hint of conviction.

"That's not what he said on Roberta Landers," Janey reminded her. "He's a faithful heterosexual now."

The idea troubled Solange but if her dog could become an artist then anything was possible. "I trust Lily," said Solange, "and I trust the Goddess. We're going to be a happiness empire. And just to show you how much faith I have, I'm going over to Marvin's right now to quit my job."

***

The return of clutter to Marvin's living room alerted Solange that Joie had vacated the premises.

Fudgsicle seemed very excited, running around scoping out the mess with his busy nose.

"Joie moved to Colorado," Marvin said in response to her unspoken question. "I told her you were uncomfortable with her staying here."

Solange leaped into a vat of guilt. Had she realized she'd be breaking things off with Marvin so soon, she would have encouraged him to let Joie stay there indefinitely. Laying the bad news on him now was sure to make her look like a heartless bitch. Hopefully the six paintings she had for him in her car would be a sufficient consolation prize.

"Oh," she said. "That was fast."

"She left yesterday," Marvin said, shoulders slumped.

"Are you okay with that? It seems like you enjoyed having her here."

He looked down. "She has family in Colorado."

"I'm sorry I made a fuss about her being here, Marvin. I was wrong to do that."

"Too late now."

She knew he hadn't said that to make her feel worse but she did. "I'm so sorry," she repeated, trying to inject atoning balm into her voice. "But I have a surprise for you. Six, actually. Want to help me bring them in?"

"Bring what in?"

"Paintings, of course." She struck a 'ta da!' pose, arms extended. "It's showtime!"

Marvin seemed perplexed as they walked to the car. "I didn't think you actually painted."

"Are you serious? I wouldn't let you buy me all that paint and not use it." She pointed to Fudgsicle, who was lifting his leg on a nearby bush. "Even Fudgsie is a painter. See those specks of blue on his feet? He's been doing his own artwork."

"Are these your paintings or the dog's?"

It was perhaps the first joke Marvin had ever cracked with her. "You decide after you see them."

He carried in all six paintings. None were of Andi. Solange had decided not to part with those and regretted ever thinking that Daphne's art gallery was Andi-worthy. The canvases she was giving Marvin were from her brief Van Gogh sunflower period: thickly applied strokes of yellows, greens and black.

Once inside, Solange propped the paintings up against the sofa and a couple of chairs. They brought desperately needed color into Marvin's dreary living room.

"They're nice," he said. "I don't know much about art, but I like them."

His words made her beam. "You know more than a lot of people," she said, struck by the irony that he was far more discerning than that pompous battle-ax at the gallery. "They're all yours."

"Thanks. I'm sure I'll find places to hang them." He moved two paintings that were blocking the couch and sat down.

Solange saw his hand reach for his belt buckle; the crucial moment had arrived. "Wait, Marvin, we need to talk." Moving more artwork aside, she sat down beside him. She was wearing bike shorts and a loose tee shirt, a get-up selected for its lack of turn-on power. This was a business meeting.

"About what?"

"I've made a big decision. I'm going to stop dancing and have a baby."

Staring at her midsection, Marvin sputtered. "How could you be...I thought you were a lesbo."

"I'm not pregnant yet Marvin, I'm just planning to be. Now, I'm going to be honest with you." She took a deep breath. "Remember in the art store when I fainted?"

He nodded but just barely.

"And I told you about my friend Andi? Well, ever since then she's been appearing to me in visions, saying she's going to see me. And I finally figured out that she has chosen me to be her mother when she reincarnates. I don't expect you to understand but I hope you'll be happy for me."

Solange had never seen anyone look more bewildered. "You're not pregnant?" he asked in a hope-tinged voice .

"Not yet, but that's the next step."

"Who's going to be the father?"

"I have to go to the sperm bank and look through the catalogues. I want Andi to help me pick out the right donor."

Marvin's voice grew stronger. "What about me?"

It was a moment Solange should have anticipated but couldn't have, because the idea of having Marvin's baby was so distasteful it had never occurred to her even as a bad dream. "It's nice of you to offer, Marvin, but I want the donor to be anonymous. This is going to be my baby and if there's ever a father it's going to be a wonderful woman I meet someday, not a man."

"But kids need fathers. It's not fair to deprive them if you don't have to."

"Andi only needs me. She hasn't said anything about a father."

"Maybe she's saying it through me."

The remark gave her a chill. Could Marvin possibly be a spokesman for Andi? She prayed that her daughter would jump out of the air and advise her. But following a long pause and the sound of Marvin's fidgeting hands, Andi refused to materialize and Solange had to decide for herself.

"Don't take offense, Marvin, but I'm sure you'd want to be there all the time, like Beaver Cleaver's dad, and I don't want that. I'll never be able to meet a woman with some guy hanging around."

"Arrangements can be made. We have an arrangement, don't we? There can be rules and restrictions. It can all be drawn up by an attorney. By the way, how do you expect to support this kid if you're not dancing anymore? Kids are expensive."

At least she was ready for that one. "I'm going into business with Lily and my friend Janey. We're going to become a physical and spiritual happiness empire."

He looked dubious to the extreme. "What if it doesn't work out? Lots of businesses fail. Especially empires."

"This one will work out."

"Suppose I offered you a million dollars?"

Solange's lungs cleared of oxygen. "Are you supposing or offering?"

"I'm offering. Would that be a consideration?"

"I didn't know you had that kind of money."

"There's a lot of things you don't know."

Looking out the window found no Andi holding up a sign. Then Fudgsicle jumped into her lap and licked her elbow. Did that mean something? It seemed that just when she needed it, the universe was on a coffee break.

"I'll throw in a college education," Marvin continued. "That's worth another three hundred grand."

Solange hadn't thought much past birth. Andi had been smart in school and had she lived would have surely gone to college. "Of course I would consider that."

Marvin's face turned all grin. She hadn't realized he had such nice white teeth. Finally, a positive sign. Teeth could make or break a face. She wondered if he had ever worn braces. She didn't want Andi to have to wear them but they did make nice invisible ones.

"I'll call my lawyer," he said.

She noticed the beginnings of an erection. "Wait a second. We haven't agreed to anything. I mean, it's a great offer but I still have to think about it. And there are a lot of conditions that you might not like."

"Name them."

"Well, first of all, you would not be the 'father.' You would only be the donor. Like I said, I hope to meet someone and share my life and child with her, but if I don't I'll be a single mother. You would be a sort of uncle. And there would be restrictions on how much time you could spend with her. And she can never be around strippers. I'll be honest with her about my past, but she's going to have a very wholesome life. Girl Scouts, charm school, Broadway. And of course, if I decide to do this I'll get pregnant in a doctor's office, not the traditional way. My body is off limits. You can't be my Lamaze partner or be in the delivery room or take pictures or anything like that. That all has to be in the agreement."

Instead of looking fazed, Marvin looked like he'd just hit the jackpot. "Okay."

Blown away she asked, "So what's in it for you?"

He addressed his feet. "You mean everything to me. I wouldn't care if I never saw the baby as long as I could still see you." He looked up. "Can I call my lawyer now?"

"Let me call my own lawyer first." In her mind she ran through a list of attorneys who frequented Spanky's club. Plenty to choose from.

Marvin held out his hand. "How about a handshake? It's not binding, but it's a show of good faith."

A handshake seemed innocent enough. "Okay."

They shook hands.

"Just so you know," she cautioned, "and this might be the only personal thing I ever tell you, I'll be ovulating in seventeen days."

25
JANEY

Janey spent way too much time ruminating over whether she and Davy were actually dating or just fucking. They had never been out in public together except to rent a DVD, which was technically an errand and didn't count. And DVD watching was something she could do with Rosie so it didn't qualify as a date either. There was but one conclusion: she was a sex object. She felt proud.

All movie viewing and copulating took place at Davy's studio. Every time Janey saw him she expected him to call off the relationship, having realized she was old and unattractive. She imagined him shaking his head after she left his place for the last time muttering, "What was I thinking?"

If only she could stick him in a bag with some avocados and bananas and let him ripen a few years. But, while she waited for him to come to his senses, they had sex incessantly. This was, of course, no problem for Davy but Janey considered it an athletic feat equal to climbing K2 or lifting a Buick off someone's foot. As a bonus she'd lost five pounds; fucking Davy was clearly the greatest exercise regimen of all time.

"I hope you're using protection," Candi said one Saturday morning as a bleary-eyed Janey tried to jump-start her body with a pot of reheated coffee. "It would be so gross to have a new sibling at my age."

"Would you mind keeping your voice down?" Janey snapped

in a harsh whisper. "Grandma might hear you."

"She's watching *Judy*," said Candi. "She couldn't hear you on her best day."

In the living room Judge Judy was blasting some poor schnook for his thoughtless transgression, one of more than a hundred episodes Janey had painstakingly recorded for Eleanor to watch at her leisure. Eleanor had even memorized some of the judge's most vitriolic condemnations which she enjoyed shouting along with the TV.

Candi sat down and put her hand over her mother's. "So when do I get to meet your young caveman?"

"We're just friends," Janey said.

"He must be really hot," Candi said, smiling. "Is that why he never comes over?"

"He's been here. You were out."

"I haven't told Sherri yet. It would totally flip her out. On the other hand, it might get Daddy to come home."

Obviously, Davy was a dangerous pastime that could not end well. The wise, mature thing would be to end it tonight after she went to his studio for a get-together with some of his artist friends—their first official socializing. But after deep analysis she decided she wasn't in a wise and mature mood.

"Have you heard from her?" Janey asked.

"We text. I sent her some underwear."

"What? She left without underwear?" An even scarier thought popped up—that Billy might try to enroll Sherri in school in Hawaii; Janey would use military force before that happened. "Don't send anything else. If she wants something, she'll have to come home and get it."

"She wants money."

"Fine. She comes home, I've got cash."

"How much?"

"Somewhere between a dollar fifty and ten million."

"How much do I get?"

"For what?"

"Keeping your affair with the caveman a secret."

"I don't respond to blackmail. You'll have to look to your conscience."

Candi pasted a smug grin on her face. "I will if you will."

Later that evening, after Janey had ransacked her closet in search of an outfit that made her look unintentionally young, finally choosing a long floral print skirt with a trounced hem and a snug tee shirt, she saw Rosie body-blocking the front door. As Rosie's behavior had become so literal since her injury, Janey interpreted it to mean she shouldn't go.

"She's just trying to make you feel guilty," Candi said. "That's what dogs do." She was standing behind Janey as if she was giving her the bum's rush.

"What's going on? Are you trying to get me to leave?"

"No. Melissa's coming over. We're just gonna hang out." Her painted harlequin teardrops made her look more sincere than she probably was. She reached into her purse and handed Janey her lavender rhinestone cell phone. "Take this. We'll watch Rosie and call you if anything happens."

Thoughtfulness and generosity were not among Candi's signature traits but her words sounded oddly genuine. "How does it work?"

"It's on vibrate. If you feel it buzz, flip it open and say hello. When you're done, just shut it." She clipped it onto Janey's skirt.

"It doesn't match my outfit," Janey complained.

"Lavender goes with everything."

"Call me later, okay? I've never gotten a cell call before."

"Sure, Mom. Have fun."

Janey stared at Candi's unusually cheerful face. "You're not up to something, are you?"

"No, I mean it. Do what makes you happy. If you're getting it from some young dude, go for it."

Janey kissed Candi on the head. "We're just friends." She went over to Eleanor, who was lying on Billy's couch watching Thelma and Louise. "I'm going out, Grandma."

"With the plumber?"

"Yes. I'll see you later."

"Why can't he pick you up?"

"He will. Next time."

"Tell him I'll dance with him."

At the front door Janey studied Rosie for further direction. "Are you okay, girl?"

A gentle paw couldn't mean no, so Janey decided to pack up her guilt and go. "I promise to be home by ten." A kiss to her dog's warm head felt reassuring.

A few minutes later, she walked stealthily up to Davy's place. Hip hop leaked from its cracks, which made her feel older than Eleanor. She'd expected to hear Bruce, had no idea how to navigate in this ungodly musical territory. Resisting the urge to turn back, she eased her way through the door a few millimeters at a time.

She tripped when it swung open and revealed Davy making a smiley face. His kiss erased her lipstick and lathered her tongue. "You look juicy," he said, adding slurpy sound effects.

As her eyes roamed the room she saw that few of the revelers looked old enough to vote. Many were probably Candi and Sherri's friends. When the kids learned that a mother had crashed their party, the girls would surely be shunned and ridiculed. Janey envisioned future therapy bills. While she contemplated the high-water mark of insanity she had attained, she saw a shapely woman carrying a meat and cheese deli platter hot-stepping toward her in high-heeled mules.

The woman wore an off-the-shoulder peasant blouse and toreador pants. Her hair was white-blonde and billowy. Her teeth were blazing white, probably veneers. She looked thirty-five but was probably, hopefully, much older. "You must be Janey," she enthused.

Janey knew who she must be as well.

"Janey," Davy beamed, "Meet Wendy...my mom."

After handing off the platter to Davy, Wendy hugged her. "I couldn't wait to meet you, Janey."

Janey wondered how Davy could have neglected to mention that his mom's name was Wendy. "Nice to meet you..." She was unable to pronounce the word. *Wendy let me in, I wanna be your friend....* Though 'Janey' was a character in far more Springsteen songs, she was either suffering: *Janey don't you lose heart... Janey sleeps in sheets damp and wet... or crazy: Janey's fingers were in the cake... Janey needs a shooter....*

But Wendy...Wendy was the object of affection in the greatest rock and roll song of all time. It was Wendy, not Janey whom he loved with all the madness in his soul. Compared to Wendy, Janey was seriously troubled.

Rosie was right—she should have stayed home.

As Davy winked and went off to mingle with his peers, Janey was left with Wendy, who appeared to be on the verge of a seizure. "I have to talk to you, Janey."

"About what?"

"Bruce."

"What about him?" Every nerve ending on Janey's body was rattling.

"I lurk on the BOSS-list. I never post."

Another unpleasant surprise. "Really? Why not?" She didn't really care but it slipped out.

Wendy pulled her aside though there was nowhere to talk privately. "My Bruce story is too personal to share on the list," she confided. "It would hurt my family. That's why I don't post."

It sounded foreboding. "Maybe you shouldn't tell me."

But Janey was dragged into a corner and wedged between an armoire and planks of wood. "I have to tell someone. I can't stand it any longer." Wendy carefully enunciated: "Bruce...is Davy's father."

Lightheaded, Janey steadied herself on the armoire to keep from flopping to the floor and wondered how and why she'd let Wendy in to be her friend. She glanced at Davy; he smiled and blew her a kiss. Wendy's face remained straight as Patti Scialfa's hair. "Does Davy know?"

As Wendy shook her head Janey tried to peer into her severely twisted mind. It couldn't be true, because if it was true, Wendy would either be Mrs. Springsteen or living in a style befitting one whose loins had brought forth a replica of her personal savior. And she would certainly be posting on BOSS—sharing her ultimate Bruce encounter again and again in such hyperbolic detail, every computer on the list would crash.

"I never told him," Wendy said, "or my husband...or Bruce."

"But you're telling me?"

"I've read all your posts. I know I can trust you."

Janey doubted that her body of email on the list, which included detailed descriptions of at least a dozen X-rated Bruce dreams, could inspire trust in anyone. Yet she had to ask the obvious follow-up question: "Does your husband have an under bite?"

With an inch-long red acrylic nail Wendy smiled and tapped her bottom teeth. "I did. I wore braces as a kid. But Davy has Bruce's nose."

For a moment Janey wished the story were true, because that would mean that she, Janey West, had had sexual intercourse with Bruce's protoplasm once removed. "Okay," she said, willing to 'let her in' just a little, "tell me the details, but stop if I put my hand up, okay?"

"Four Seasons in Beverly Hills," Wendy overlapped before Janey finished speaking, "'Born in the USA' tour, 1984. I didn't know he was staying there, but I could feel him, you know?"

Nodding, Janey dove into her archives. The 1984 LA dates for the 'BITUSA' tour were in late October. That would make Davy around twenty-three. A queasy rumble raced through her intestines as she realized he might be even younger than she feared. It was imperative she find out his birth date.

"Two days before," Wendy continued, "I'd had a past life regression from this amazing shaman, Reverend Pringle. He told me that Bruce and I were married in seventeen forty-one. He was an African princess and I was a Christian missionary and there was a huge scandal. I mean, the idea of interracial marriage in the eighteenth century. I'm sure they're still talking about it."

Regardless of how resoundingly Janey discounted Wendy's

story, the notion of Bruce Springsteen as an African princess was somehow disturbing.

Wendy reached into her peasant blouse, pulled out a harmonica and handed it to her. "I brought this to show you. He gave it to me on September thirtieth, ninety-nine at the United Center in Chicago. I was in the front row. And the way he stared when he handed it to me...like, 'I remember you, Thomas Craig, I remember you.' That was my name when we were married."

Cradling the harmonica as if it were a baby sparrow, Janey longed to put it to her lips, caress her body with it, but she worried about where it had already been.

"When I saw him at the Four Seasons, I told him the story and he said he felt like we were still married and let's go up to his room. So we did and that's how we made Davy."

There was no way to ease away quietly as Janey was still trapped in the corner. The story was nuttier than a ton of peanut brittle and Wendy was clearly unstable. Even if she had run into Bruce at the Four Seasons, once she launched into that past life crap, he would have put his hands up like he did when the girls kept climbing on stage to kiss him in the "Rosalita" video, said "Whoa!" and run for his life.

On that thought, a strange buzzing engulfed her and she panicked, afraid it was that electric-sparky thing that happened when she was with Lily and Solange. She could not tolerate being connected to Wendy in that way. After several more buzzings she realized it was the cell phone.

"Mom," said Candi on the other end. "Grandma fell."

***

Davy left the party immediately with Janey. When they got to the house, Eleanor was lying on her bedroom floor with Candi and Rosie at her side. Janey crashed into the fray. "Grandma! Are you okay?"

"Can't dance." She seemed in obvious pain but would never admit it. Can't make it to 102 if you're a weakling.

Davy kneeled down and clasped Eleanor's hand. "You'll be back on your feet in no time."

"At my age, that's all I got left."

"What happened?" Janey asked Candi, noting the smeary streaks of aqua, orange and gold on her face.

"I heard Grandma cry out so I went in and saw her on the floor. Then I called you, then I called 911."

"I'm surprised you could hear me," Eleanor said. "They were making so much damn noise, I couldn't hear the TV. I got up to tell them to pipe down and I slipped on the magazine."

Janey noticed the copy of Ballroom Dancing Times on the floor and a guilty look on Candi's face. "What kind of noise? Where's Melissa?"

"They were having sex," Eleanor announced.

Janey marched into Candi's room and Candi followed the trail of angry-mother fumes. "Melissa wasn't here," Candi admitted. "It was Lyle."

The rumpled bed and telltale beer bottles on the floor told Janey everything she didn't want to know. "Who the hell is Lyle?"

"My new boyfriend."

Which would be the subject of a volatile discussion in the near future. "You could have done a better job of hiding the evidence."

Candi folded her arms across her chest. "I thought it was more important to call 911."

Sirens heralded the ambulance and Davy raced down to let

the paramedics in. They sped upstairs and a young man about Davy's age took Eleanor's blood pressure. "How old is she?" he asked Janey.

Eleanor waved her free hand. "Why do you want to know?"

"Well," said the paramedic, "your vital signs are better than mine."

"She's a hundred and two," Janey said.

"Whoa!" said Davy. "Are you shittin' me? Oops, I mean, are you serious? I thought you were about eighty."

As the paramedics lifted Eleanor onto a stretcher she fluttered her eyes at her young paramour. "Take us to Vegas. We're getting married."

***

On the way to the hospital in Janey's car, conversation was at a premium. Janey's mind throbbed with distressing thoughts: Eleanor's fall, Candi's lack of virginity, whether it would comfort her to get a phony past life reading in which she and Bruce were Tristan and Isolde; she didn't want to talk about any of it.

The only significant dialogue involved the inevitable, formal introduction of Candi and Davy.

"Candi, this is Davy," Janey said after they had driven several miles.

"Hi," she said in a tone flatter than Janey's chest.

"Nice to meet you, Candi." After attempts to make eye contact with her failed, he gave Janey a shrug.

He's so damn nice, Janey thought, how could Bruce not be his father?

At the hospital doctors confirmed what Janey suspected— Eleanor had suffered a broken hip. "She's quite old to be undergoing major surgery," a young doctor with a gelled, slicked-back hairdo informed her.

"Are you recommending that we shoot her?" She stared down the smug pessimist until his shoulders sank. "Talk to her. You might learn something about longevity."

Davy put an arm around Janey. "He's just saying..."

"I heard what he said. He thinks she can't survive." She wriggled out of Davy's hold. "She's survived a lot worse," she told the surgeon, "so go in and fix her." Pointing to the waiting area she said, "I'll be over there."

In the corridor Candi talked on her cell phone.

Davy sat down beside Janey. "Do you want me to stay?"

"Up to you. I'm going to be very boring for the next few hours." She fished car keys out of her purse and put them in his hand. "Here, take my car. Maybe Candi wants to go home. But don't get any ideas. She's in enough trouble."

"What are you talking about?"

"Davy, I'm at the age where women become very irrational, so don't count on me to make sense. I'm sorry, but you'll have to deal with that."

A spear of fluorescent light reflected off Davy's pearly grin. "Janey, I like you because you're funny and pretty. Age has nothing to do with it."

"What about because we both like Bruce?"

"Millions of chicks dig Bruce."

God, how she loved being called a chick. "Davy?"

"Yes, Janey?"

"When's your birthday?"

"September fourth."

"Which makes you..."

"A Virgo."

"I mean your age."

He hesitated. "Twenty-three."

Janey choked on her next breath. The dates fit. Before she had a chance to judge herself she was kissing Son of Bruce right there in the waiting room, where people were anxious and upset. Wendy could not have behaved less appropriately. When their lips unlocked, she saw Candi standing in front of her, an expressionless gaze pointed her way.

"I called Daddy and Sherri," Candi said. "They're coming home tomorrow."

26
GODDESSES

The way to determine if Marvin would be a suitable sperm donor for Andi, Solange decided, was to express her inner vision through the immediacy of pastels. Late into the night she sat in bed with a spiral-bound tablet of art paper and made quick, impressionistic sketches of the second coming or third or whatever coming she was on, of Andi.

A tiny heat ball, Fudgsicle's body snuggled next to her, fueling her maternal instincts.

Instead of morphing her features with Marvin's to see what the baby might look like, she set her mind aside and let her soul draw the pictures. She intended the images as a vehicle for Andi's essence to speak for itself, but after the first dozen faces stared unhappily back at her she concluded that while the merger of her egg with Marvin's seed might produce a life form, it would not be Andi.

She turned on the TV to let her mind unscramble and get rid of the Marvin idea. Five minutes into *The View* and her resolve was firm that Marvin would not purchase paternity at any price. Feeling noble, she surfed over to *Rumor-ama*, the new gossip show on the E! Channel.

"Tonight," announced guest host Carmen Electra, "we have the full poop—can you say that on TV?—about Gary DiCaro. Is he gay, straight, bi or something completely new?"

The shot widened to show Carmen's guest panel. "Joining me in our hot, scandalous discussion are Roy Cardoza, editor of *Gaydar* magazine; Satinique, star of the WB comedy *Erotica Neurotica*; Lance Lutz, author of *Been There, Done Him*, the unauthorized, self-published biography of Gary DiCaro and later, a very special surprise guest, so stay tuned!" The in-house audience hooted and whooped.

Solange sat straight up and dropped her drawing pad.

"Let's start with you, Lance," said Carmen, addressing a swishy young man in a bright pink suit with a faux leopard collar. "You know everything there is to know about Gary DiCaro. Is this gay-to-straight thing for real?"

"As real as Satinique's tits!"

Satinique, whose breasts looked like they could put an eye out at fifty yards, got up and pretended to smack Lance. "You are so bad!"

Lance pushed her out of the way. "Those bazoombas are blocking my shot."

Slapping her hands on her hips, Satinique bent over and stuck her tongue out at Lance before sitting down.

"Like you said, Carmen," Lance continued, "I'm a Gary DiCaro scholar. I know his life better than my own, even though I live in a dense fog." He laughed alone at his joke. "But I'll tell you this—stick him in a bathhouse and he'll make Richard Simmons look like Warren Beatty."

"Did you bone him?" Roy asked.

"You'll have to read my book to find out."

In his traffic cone orange shirt, chartreuse tie and slicked back hair, Roy looked like a Shark from a *West Side Story* road company. "I read your book," he said, "and you never mentioned it."

Lance batted his eyelashes. "Wait until my next book."

"Isn't his girlfriend like a witch or something?" asked Carmen.

Roy nodded. "I heard she got pregnant by slipping the poor boy some Ecstasy. Someone did that to me at a Bar Mitzvah and I banged ten pounds of chopped liver."

"You're so full of bleeeep," said Satinique, her expletive deleted. "You're just jealous that he's playing for our team now. I think his girlfriend's hot and he gets it up for her big time."

"Well!" said Carmen. "There's only one way to get to the bottom of this. Please welcome our surprise guest, the one and only person who can deny or verify all these scrumptiously juicy stories...his own bad self, Gary DiCaro!"

Solange's temperature dropped twenty degrees as Gary sauntered onto the set with an effeminate flourish. He wagged his butt at the audience, spanked himself, then leaped into Lance's open arms for a noisy lip lock.

The audience shrieked.

Solange froze, unable to breathe or even blink.

"It's all true! Every nasty detail!" Gary bellowed, egging on the crowd with hand gestures.

It wasn't Gary's voice. And he was at least three inches

shorter than Carmen Electra.

He sat down to wild applause, got up, took another bow, did a pelvic thrust and sat down again.

A wave of nausea sent Solange to the bathroom where she threw up before she could reach the toilet. Every cell of her body throbbed to its own painful beat.

Fudgsicle came in and sniffed the vomit. "No! Go away!" she scolded, shoving him aside. Unfurling a roll of toilet paper she stared at the mess—a self-portrait of her state of mind—before mopping it up.

When she returned to the bedroom "Gary" was admitting that his real name was Gilbert, that he, contrary to what other panelists had claimed, was the universe's number one Gary DiCaro fan since only he had gone to the devotional extreme of tweaking his appearance via plastic surgery to convert what was once a mere resemblance into a can't-tell-'em-apart-without-a-program clone.

 How could it not have occurred to her that the man at the fetish club had a fucking Gary DiCaro fetish?

Solange turned off the TV and cried herself into a headache. On top of the pain she so richly deserved, she felt some relief that Gary was not cheating on Lily and that their baby would be born to fine, conventional parents.

Baby. Gary. Her stomach heaved from the impact of an even more thunderous revelation. She turned off the lights and opened her eyes in the darkness.

The image formed quickly. Like a round of fireworks returning to Earth, bits of colors coalesced into a portrait etched in the blackness: Solange and Gary sitting on the Nylers' porch smiling... Andi riding her Phthalo Blue bicycle up and down

Canal Street, waving back at them.

In the next two minutes, she leashed up Fudgsie and went running into the night.

***

Lily tried to think of something she enjoyed more than Gary singing to the dogs but she couldn't. Accompanied by his guitar, with Lily snuggled up next to him on the bed, he entertained Bean and Blossom with his soulful rendition of Al Green's "Let's Stay Together."

As he sang, Blossom ran back and forth amassing a new collection of gifts at his feet: a baseball cap, Lily's slippers, a package of Dentyne gum, Ray-ban sunglasses and a box of Kleenex. Lily assumed Blossom was fulfilling her role as president of the Gary DiCaro fan club.

"I-I-I-I'm so in love with you...anything you want me to... is alright with me-e-e-e-e...Cause you make me feel so brand new...I wanna spend my life with you..."

While his sister honored their idol with gifts, Bean sat and listened, ears lifted for full musical impact. He wore a sprightly smile, tongue hanging off to one side.

"Let's...let's stay together...lovin' you whether... whether... times are good or bad, happy or sad..."

When he finished, Lily swiveled to give him a kiss, which made the dogs whimper and paw at the bed.

Lily nudged Gary. "They want an encore."

Gary sighed, acting bothered. "Never enough!" Leaning over, he stuck his face in Bean and Blossom's. "How much did you pay to get in here, huh?"

They licked him in tandem.

"Some fans are insatiable," Lily said.

"Well," said Gary, "when you put it that way..." He strummed his guitar.

Lily bent down to get an aside from Blossom. "She wants to hear 'Blowin' in the Wind.'"

"Did I say I was taking requests?" he asked before singing the first few bars.

The dogs barked and raced to the front door.

Gary stopped playing. "What...last call for alcohol?"

"Dangerous predators," Lily surmised.

The dogs kept barking.

Lily got up.

"Wait, I'll get it," Gary said.

Lily followed Gary to the door. She heard some familiar yapping. "That's Fudgsicle." But when she looked through the beveled glass window she couldn't see anyone.

When Gary opened the door, Lily saw Solange in a heap on the front step, head buried in her arms. Tangled up in his leash beside her, Fudgsicle got a smell-down from the Labs.

Looking up with red puffy eyes Solange said, "I'm so sorry."

"What happened? Is someone hurt?" Lily asked.

Solange waved her hands, indicating no. She seemed unable to form words, could only sputter.

Gary helped her up. They walked her inside and sat her down. Solange bent forward and her hair brushed the carpet. "Something...to tell you."

"Okay, stay here and relax. Better not talk when you're so tense," said Lily. "I'll make you some tea. Want Gary to sing for you?"

The hair nodded. "Heard you through the window."

"No wonder you didn't come in," said Gary. "But your dog

finds my pitch irresistible."

In the kitchen Lily revisited her concern that something had been troubling Solange. Occasionally she'd noticed looks passing between her and Janey at the park and thought they might be keeping a secret. It had to be big—big enough to make the baby perform a Tae Bo maneuver punctuated by an anxiety pang. But he settled down when Gary began to sing "I Can't Give You Anything But Love."

By the time Lily brought in a pot of Passionflower and Skullcap tea, Solange appeared calmer. The Labs laid across Gary's feet while Fudgsicle nestled in Solange's lap. She stroked his head to the music. "I'm ready now," she said.

Bracing for a hurricane, Lily held Gary's arm as they sat on the couch opposite Solange, who leaned forward in the overstuffed chintz chair. Gary massaged Lily's knee.

"About a month ago," Solange began, "Joie and Marvin and I went to a fetish club. I think I told you."

"Hooker Heidi," said Gary. "I remember."

"Right. I didn't want to go, but...Joie had some scheme to get me back. Anyway, it was horrible and I didn't want to be there so while they were playing pool I wandered off and saw these two guys kissing."

She paused and Lily waited for the punch line. "And?"

"And I was absolutely positive that one of them was Gary."

Gary's eyebrows lifted half an inch.

"He looked at me," said Solange. "This odd feeling passed between us. I totally freaked. I didn't want to believe it, but there he was. Of course, I should have figured it out." She knocked her forehead. "I'm in a fetish club! Hello! I've seen plenty of star fetishes but he was such a dead ringer it didn't even occur to me.

I was so upset. I thought about telling you, really, but I couldn't."

"So you told Janey," Lily said.

Solange nodded. "We discussed it. There were good reasons to tell you and good reasons not to." She looked at Gary. "Then at the Roberta Landers interview, I felt this strange closeness to you, even though I was furious."

"That would explain the scowls," Gary said, nodding.

Solange covered her face with her hands. "I'm so sorry."

"How did you find out it wasn't Gary?" Lily asked.

"I just saw the fetish guy on *Rumor-ama*. He's some deranged fan with major plastic surgery. The audience thought it was Gary but when he spoke, his voice was completely different. And he was a lot shorter."

"Everyone thinks I'm a midget," said Gary. So it was just another twisted offshoot of the Gary drama. "Thank you, Solange," Lily said with great relief. "I wish you would have told me right away but I understand."

"That was part one," Solange said, her breathing noticeably labored. "When I went outside during the interview I gave some blood to Gary's lavender and asked the Goddess what our connection was. Me to him I mean."

"Did she tell you?" Lily asked.

"Andi told me."

Gary frowned. "Who's Andi?"

"Tell you in a minute," said Lily.

Dropping to the floor, Solange kneeled in front of Lily and Gary as if they were twin deities. "I love you both," she said. "You're amazing people, so whatever your reaction is I'll understand and I'll still love and respect you as much as I do now."

"Spit it out," Gary said. "You're among friends."

Solange swallowed twice. "Andi wants Gary to be her father."

A moment of silence, then chords from a thousand harps began to play in Lily's head. "What a beautiful idea."

While watery rivulets streamed down both sides of Solange's nose, her face beamed with elation.

"Really? You think so?"

"Of course. It's why we're together."

The women mashed together in maternal bondage. Lily felt Gary shaking her arm. "Wait a second. Who's Andi?"

Lily took Gary's hand and sent a surge of love to every cell in his body. "She's Solange's friend who died when they were children. But she's coming back and Solange is going to be her mother. And it looks like she wants you to be her father."

The way Gary squinted and twisted his head, Lily might as well have been speaking in Farsi.

"Gary," Solange said, still on her knees, "this is totally your choice. But it could be worked out legally so your identity would never be discovered. And I promise you—no way is this about money. Marvin already offered me a million dollars to be the donor."

Lily's mouth dropped open. "He did?"

"Plus more for college. But I turned him down."

"You need sperm?" Gary said casually. "Sure, I got loads of the stuff."

"He has amazing genes," Lily said.

"Tell me about it," said Solange.

As Lily thanked Gary with a kiss she fell profoundly in love with this new edition of him, adding it to the enormous pile of daily fallings-in-love she'd accumulated over the past seven years. "I love you, Gary."

"Glad to help." He strummed a chord on the guitar.

"Our baby is going to have a sister or brother!"

"Sister," Solange corrected. "Andi wants to finish her girl life."

Lily embraced Solange. "This is beyond wonderful. This is the true merging of our lives."

"I know I can never repay you for this incredible gift so I promise to be the best mother in the world and make both of you proud."

"You're already a wonderful mother," said Lily.

"Just one thing," said Gary. "This has to remain secret for at least the next twenty years. Your baby will not have a pleasant childhood if the media finds out, and Lily and I will be forced to bring up our child in Antarctica."

"I swear," said Solange crossing her heart, "no one will ever find out."

27
GODDESSES

"What's that?" asked Marvin when Solange and Fudgsicle appeared at his door with a large, gift-wrapped box.

"If I wanted you to see what it was I wouldn't have wrapped it, would I?" She handed it to him.

Marvin appeared to be excited, or as excited as Marvin ever got. He took the box. "Should I open it?"

"No, throw it in the street. Of course open it." As they followed him inside, Solange realized it was likely the last time they would ever be there.

234

Stacks of hazardous clutter had to be cleared from the coffee table to make room for the box. Marvin peeled off the paper as if unwrapping a hand grenade. Inside the box were three dozen chocolate chip cookies. His eyes widened and Solange saw a slight rise in his pants. Perhaps the consolation prize wasn't such a good idea. "Did you make these?" he asked.

"Yup. And they're not chocolate chip either. They're chocolate chunk. I made the chunks with a Hershey bar and a mallet. Go ahead, try one."

The first bite brought a pleased, almost happy look to his face. "That's the best cookie I ever tasted."

Solange knew she'd better get down to business or the letdown might be too severe, especially on a sugar rush. "Marvin, we need to talk."

"What about?"

"Here's the deal," said Solange. "Your offer was super generous and I'm really touched that you want to help me but I have to do what's best for me and Andi. Not that Andi doesn't like you—she just has someone else in mind."

"But Andi's a...ghost."

"She's as real as you are only she's in the waiting area." She touched his arm. "Please be happy for me. You know, one day you'll meet the right girl and you'll be an amazing father."

Marvin threw down the remains of the cookie, obviously not sharing her joy. "Who's the guy?"

"He's Mr. Anonymous. No one is ever going to know who the donor is."

"But if you're sure it's not me, then you must have found someone who's worth giving up a million dollars."

"Don't jump to conclusions, okay?" Panic spread through her

like a Hollywood rumor. She wished she had never told Marvin about Andi. "I have to let Andi make the decision. That's how it works."

Judging by the incessant bounce of his right knee, Marvin wasn't buying it. "You never said that. You found another rich guy, didn't you? How much is he paying you?"

"I'm not going to sit here and be grilled, Marvin. I told you the truth and you can believe me or not. Andi will choose her father and I will raise her. Money isn't the only factor."

"We shook hands. We had a deal."

"I never said it was final. That's why it was only a handshake." Rising to leave she said, "I'm sorry, Marvin. I really am. You don't deserve to be hurt." She noticed Fudgsicle rolling in a spot on the carpet. "C'mon, Fudgsie."

The Yorkie came running. Solange grabbed him and headed for the door.

Marvin snatched the cookie box and tried to hand it back to her. "Not hungry."

She refused to accept it. "No, please keep them. They're really good." She walked out.

***

Lily stayed up most of the night pondering an idea so exhilarating it required that she remain conscious of her breathing to avoid passing out.

She gazed at her beloved sleeping beside her. Like a brilliant cinematographer, moonlight streamed in and lit his dreamy features. A purplish gleam traced the waves in his black hair, the same midnight shade as Solange's; their child would possess exceptional good looks. Lily felt her own baby responding to his future sibling; his movements felt joyful and eager.

She would not let Solange conceive her baby in a sterile medical room; it was vital that her baby's sibling be created in the same way as her own, surrounded by love and beauty. Though there might be personal issues involved for Solange, Lily felt confident that she would accept and transcend them, especially with Lily there to make sure it would be the most glorious experience of her life.

With her head nestled in the arc of Gary's neck she synchronized her breathing to his and concentrated on transferring her plan. A joyous shiver flushed through her as she felt his unconscious acknowledgment. She believed it was humanity's great fortune that Gary be a father and the more offspring the better. His children were destined to transform the world.

When morning came, Gary rushed off to a breakfast meeting with a new writer-director team touted as the next Coen Brothers while Lily's day involved non-stop clients. Before he left, Gary kissed her and said, "Got something to discuss with you later."

"Me too," she told him and wondered what could be on his mind. Hopefully it wasn't the same thing. She wanted him to accept her idea, not come up with it himself.

All day long Lily felt like she was moving on a carpet of glue. Each client needed to talk more than the last and it threw her schedule off. Normally, she enjoyed delving into their life dramas but today it felt like work.

After a crave-relieving lunch of soy wieners dipped in honey, washed down with two glasses of chocolate Ovaltine, she met Solange at the park. Solange's hot pink tank top—more like a bosom wrangler—couldn't brighten her downcast expression.

She squeezed Lily, then addressed her belly. "Hello Andi's brother!"

"You seem pretty sure about that."

"I am. You're having a boy and I'm having Andi. Her parents wanted her to be a boy. That's why she had a blue bike and 'y' instead of 'i' on her name when she was born. She changed it because she wanted to be a girl."

"I believe you. Now tell me what's wrong."

They linked arms and started walking. "I called a bunch of sperm banks—excuse me—cryo-banks today. They all said that donors have to come in a bazillion times in person, no exceptions. It's a major ordeal."

"I didn't realize that. You can't just bring it in one of those coolers like they do with kidneys?"

Solange shook her head. "Against policy. I couldn't make Gary do that. Someone would see him and go directly on *Rumor-ama*. But I still won't accept Marvin's offer. I think Andi and I should choose an anonymous donor."

That Solange was literally setting up Lily's plan reaffirmed its rightness. "What if there was an alternative?"

"What kind of alternative?"

"What if you could get pregnant the same way I did?"

Solange's mouth flung open so wide, Lily noticed she still had her lower wisdom teeth. "Are you serious? You would let me... sleep with your fiancé?"

Lily beamed. "Of course I would. You're the mother-to-be of my son's sister. I want her to be created under the most loving circumstances imaginable."

"I absolutely cannot believe this, Lily."

"I understand if you have concerns about the sexual part, but really, it isn't about sex at all."

"Hey, I've seen plenty of dicks in my time. To me they're just live dildos." She cupped her hand over her mouth. "I didn't mean that. It wouldn't be in this case! It would be...wow, think of it. How often do lesbians and gay men have actual sex together?"

"Mostly never."

"Exactly. But Gary is in a whole new category now, isn't he?" She chuckled. "Then again, who needs categories?"

"Right. Love is love."

"I love you Lily."

"I love you too. Now, when is your next ovulation?"

Solange looked down. "Today," she whispered.

Today? The urgency put Lily's nervous system on hyper-alert. A great deal of planning and negotiating was necessary for Solange to become pregnant...today. If not today there would be an agonizing, four-week delay during which Gary could change his mind and all sorts of obstacles might arise. "Today? Are you ready?"

"If Gary was here I'd do it right now in the park. God, I'm jumping out of my skin! Will you be there?"

"Of course. And I'll do everything possible to make it happen tonight because," she said with a laugh, "I don't want this to become a regular thing."

"You mean you won't be disappointed if I don't go straight?"

Lily held her shoulders. "I'm counting on you to remain a lesbian."

They giggled as if they were auditioning for a laugh track. Then one of Solange's episodic monsoons broke out and she threw her arms around Lily. "I don't deserve you," she sobbed.

"Oh, stop it. I didn't do anything."

"You're making my dream come true."

Tears trailed down Lily's neck. "This means we're on, right?"

"We are so on, I'm going to go home and douche." Solange snorted to end the weeping and blew her nose in a piece of the lifetime supply of Kleenex Janey had provided her. "I wish I knew what these crying binges mean. They don't seem to be connected to anything."

"Whatever it is, just flush it out."

"I guess. So what did Gary say about...the baby idea?"

"I haven't told him yet."

Solange's euphoria immediately collapsed until Lily assured her that Gary would not oppose the plan. Walking back with the Labs, Lily felt so optimistic she began to sing "Havin' My Baby," then laughed because she couldn't stand that song.

At home she set to work making spinach lasagna—Gary's favorite dish. While she grated up three different kinds of cheeses the Labs laid side by side on their backs, eight legs vertical in the air. It was so cute she bent down to kiss them and rub their bellies, then nearly got upended when they heard Gary arriving and sprang to their feet. Bean scampered to the door while Blossom nosed frantically in Lily's tote bag. She extracted her cell phone and presented it to her hero when he came in.

"Thank you, Blossom. That's very Lassie of you." He took the phone and put it to his ear. "Hello, Blossom? Are you trying to tell me something?"

Blossom pawed at Gary's leg, yapped once and thumped her tail. Bean did the same.

"They want to talk to us," said Lily, amazed but not entirely. "They know the phone is a communication device."

Gary addressed the dogs. "No overseas calls."

"I really believe that a portion of our souls are invested in the dogs," Lily said. "They reflect the best part of us."

"Is that why I like to sniff your crotch?"

Lily snickered before a moment of silence. Unspoken business hung in the air.

"So?" Gary said.

"So?"

He took her in his arms and dipped her carefully. "Want to fly to Vegas and get married tonight?" Out of the blue it came, like a comet.

She had no time to process the equation: Solange's conception or a wedding? "But I made spinach lasagna."

Could she have said anything more ridiculous?

"We'll have it tomorrow night."

"Does it have to be tonight?"

"Short answer, yes. Long answer, yes it has to be tonight. I chartered a plane. Francesca is available to doggysit. What's the matter? Don't you want to marry me?"

There was no choice but to trust the universe. "Of course I want to marry you. It's what I most wanted to do in the history of life. Is it okay if I invite Solange?"

"Sure—gotta have a bridesmaid." He pulled her back up and touched her face. "I just want us to be official before the baby— no media. Afterwards, we'll have a big, over-produced party. Anywhere in the world. On Mars if you want."

Lily threw her arms around him and kissed his fabulous neck. Mars sounded like a great idea because it would take another planet to contain all the love she felt for him.

28
JANEY

Fanned on the couch in her robe at 10 A.M. as the urge to dress had yet to seize her, Janey could mount but a feeble protest against driving to the airport to pick up Billy and Sherri. "What's wrong with a cab?" she asked Candi.

"It costs sixty dollars plus tip." Seemingly overnight Candi had donned the mantle of a responsible adult.

"What about the Van Nuys shuttle?"

"It's a bus."

"And your point is...?"

"My point is, you don't want to face Daddy so you're stalling. But there's a sick old woman in the hospital who ought to see her grandson and you owe it to her to take him there before it's too late."

It was a fascinating gestalt: Janey's petulance forcing Candi's maturity. A comforting sign for the future, Janey realized, when at the New Jersey Home for Elderly Springsteen Fans, Candi could help pump her fist in the air when they played "Badlands."

"We'll leave in a half hour. But don't blame me if there's a jackknifed semi on the 405."

Folding her arms on the shelf of her chest Candi sighed with profound exasperation.

In the bathroom, as Janey attempted to paint on a cheerful, I-hardly-noticed-you-were-gone face, she felt the painful surge of her period commencing. "Nice friggin' timing," she muttered, then, like some hoary B-movie device, Lily's voice played in her head. Give it to the Goddess, give it to the Goddess. A voice she would hear until menopause.

To her surprise, she didn't feel all that ridiculous collecting the blood in Billy's Coors Light mug. While Candi was on the phone she found safe passage to the back yard where, as Rosie watched with keen interest, she spilled the bloody water onto her petunias, marigolds and around the Eucalyptus tree. "'Dreams will not be thwarted...'" she sang to the Goddess, whom, she hoped, was Bruce-lyric savvy. "'Faith will be rewarded...'"

Listening to herself, her plea sounded hollow and pathetic. She was no blue collar Springsteen heroine; she had not a single dream to thwart. Though her name was Janey, Bruce would never be inspired to write her song. She wasn't exotic like Solange, spiritual and mystical like Lily or even terminally delusional like Wendy. She feared she was merely taking up valuable space in an overly populated world.

"I'm 'itchin' for something to start,'" she announced to the blood-fed foliage, then looked up where presumably, the Goddess was eavesdropping. "I'm ready."

Diving into the spot by the Eucalyptus tree where Janey had poured her blood-water, Rosie coated herself with its scent.

"You're weird, Rosie," said Janey.

Rosie continued to swivel vigorously in the magic spot, then sprang to her feet and assumed play posture.

"Very, very weird." Janey slipped back in the house to get dressed. In the bedroom mirror she saw that in spite of the usual water retention, her black tee shirt and jeans showed off the five pounds she'd dropped on her new Copulation Diet.

"You look pretty thin," Candi said as they got in the car. "Must be all that sex you're having."

"Must be," Janey said, bucking the instinct to defend herself. "Did you talk to Grandma today?"

"She said it hurts like hell but she gets to boss the doctors and nurses around. Are you going to tell Daddy about your teen lover or wait till he shows up at the door?"

Amazingly, that very debate was taking place in Janey's mind, where nosy daughters were not invited. "I think it's best if we go straight to the hospital after we pick them up. Does that work for you?"

"He looks a little like Bruce Springsteen. A much, much younger version, of course. Did you notice that?"

"No, never noticed."

***

On the road, just to spite her, traffic on the 405 was light. Janey figured there must be a high-speed chase nearby; those morons always found open roads. They got to the airport with oodles of time to greet the flight even though it was arriving at the most distant gate from the terminal.

"So," said Candi on their leisurely journey to Siberia, "do you think they'll get into a fist fight over you?"

How many times could she keep asking the same question? As many times as Janey would not answer it. "Do you remember where we parked?"

For a few paces Candi stomped her feet. "It won't do you any good to avoid the subject, Mom. You know Grandma will tell Dad as soon as she sees him. I can help you figure out a plan. I'm good at lying and deception."

"What does that mean?"

"It means I know how to play all the angles. But not with you, of course."

Janey made a mental note to revise her worry list. They passed a bar. "I think I'll have a cocktail."

The sublime distraction of a pouty, underage girl in a snug tee shirt and hip-riding shorts seemed to soothe the male bar patrons entrapped at LAX. Janey ordered a Long Island iced tea and a diet Coke for Candi.

"Mom," Candi said, "isn't that a little over the top?"

"It's iced tea."

Candi shook her head slowly as the bartender constructed Janey's drink. "This is going to be so hideous."

At the gate ten minutes later, Janey was in such good spirits she didn't mind learning that the plane, due to a mysterious, unexplained, but benign problem—the airport personnel assured them—would have to sit on the runway for the next twenty minutes. Adding to her fortune were two young men around Davy's age who came by to chat up Candi, giving Janey the chance for a brief shut-eye excursion.

She harked back to the LA Sports Arena, April 23, 1988, when Bruce led the crowd in singing "Happy Birthday" to Roy Orbison. Reliving the moment Janey hummed the song...until someone turned around in front of her holding a harmonica—it was Wendy, barging in on her memory.

"Mom, they're here," Candi announced, disrupting the time-travel but at least making Wendy disappear.

Janey opened her eyes and from the stream of passengers in leis and seashells, Sherri emerged. When she saw Janey she screamed and ran headlong into her arms. It felt better than a goose down comforter.

"Mommy!" Sherri shouted into her ear, sounding like she was five on the playground swings.

Abandoning control, Janey wept. Through soggy corneas she saw Billy walking tentatively toward her. He looked drawn, heavier, paler, like he had been in fast food prison instead of the tropics. He wore a Hawaiian shirt and a baseball cap. He smiled in a measured way.

"Hi," he said when their eyes met.

"Hi yourself," she replied, still holding Sherri.

Billy seemed anxious, which Janey assumed was due to being prohibited from smoking a joint on the plane. She released Sherri to Candi and the sisters glommed together.

"How's Grandma?" Billy asked.

"You can see for yourself."

***

"Who are you?" Eleanor shouted when Billy appeared in her hospital room doorway.

Billy crept over to the bed looking frightened, as if Eleanor actually had lost her memory. Sherri jumped in front of him, prompting Eleanor to raise her arms and gather her close. "Where've you been?" she asked.

"I went to Hawaii to bring Daddy home," Sherri said. "Remember?"

"Of course I remember. There's been an empty chair at the kitchen table for a long time."

"Two empty chairs," said Sherri.

Eleanor shook her head. "Empty chair and empty couch."

Venturing up to the boundary of Eleanor's face, Billy pecked her on the cheek. "How are you feeling, Grandma?"

"Like I'm a hundred and two with a broken hip." She gave him the once over. "You look terrible."

Janey saw Billy's shoulders retreat and she felt a twinge

of compassion for him. Eleanor's disdain seemed so uncompromising, so focused.

"It was a long plane ride," he said in a voice already sounding defeated. "We came right over to see you."

"Then I'll get to the point. Come here so I don't have to shout."

A huddle formed around Eleanor's bed.

"No more dancing," Eleanor began. "I was hoping to go on tour with the plumber but I can't do it. Tell him I wanted him to be my last partner."

That set Sherri blubbering. Janey put an arm around her and wondered how anyone so fragile found the initiative to run off to Hawaii on her own.

"Don't write me off yet," said Eleanor. "This isn't my deathbed. It's too damn uncomfortable. I'll come home, watch some Judy and take it from there."

Sherri's sobbing grew louder, forcing Eleanor to shout over her. "Billy..."

"Yes, Grandma?"

"Talk to your wife. Tell her all your secrets and everything else she needs to know." She glared at him so pointedly he inched a few steps backwards.

"Okay. I promise, Grandma."

A quick glance at Billy's broken-down demeanor made Janey wonder what in the world Eleanor meant.

"Girls?" Eleanor continued.

Sherri sucked up her tears while Candi dropped to her knees and rested her breasts on the mattress.

"Listen to your mother. She's smarter than you think." She nudged Candi. "Bazooms aren't everything. Your mother doesn't have any and the plumber doesn't give a damn."

Searching for a trap door to plunge down, Janey saw only unbroken linoleum.

"Who's the plumber?" Billy asked.

"He's Grandma's young hottie boyfriend," Candi said with a straight face.

"Hey, way to go, Grandma," Sherri said in a way that convinced Janey that Candi hadn't blabbed about Davy. Another stunning sign of Candi's maturity.

Eleanor reached out and took Janey's hand. "Now you. The one who takes care of me without complaining, but maybe I don't hear you." She brought the hand to her lips. "You're a good woman, like a real daughter to me."

Janey soaked up her fifteen seconds of *Queen for a Day*.

"Just so you won't be surprised, I left everything to you. Everything. It's too damn hard to give some to this one, some to that one. To hell with that. I trust you. Keep it all. You deserve it. And get some toys for the dog."

Without looking at him, Janey felt the impact of Billy's shell-shock and prepared for the thud of his body crashing to the floor. Somehow he managed to remain upright.

"He'll be a good husband now," Eleanor said, smiling. "Won't you, Billy?"

The words mumbled out. "Yes, Grandma."

***

Such deathly quiet prevailed on the ride home that when Billy cleared his throat it sounded like machine gun fire. The reunited family entered the house in a single file procession.

Rosie met them at the door. At first she looked as tentative as a concierge at a staid hotel but when Billy actually bent down to pet her, she let loose and ran all over the house like a crazed puppy. Janey thought it noble and forgiving that she greeted Billy at all. If their places were switched she would have bitten his ankle.

Clearly anticipating imminent parental fireworks, the girls found urgent reasons to bid hasty goodbyes and depart to friends' safe houses.

Billy zipped open a carry-on bag and extracted a fuzzy toy. Wordlessly he handed it to Rosie. It squeaked when she received it. Janey swore she'd made it say "thank you."

"That was nice. Thanks," Janey said.

Billy nodded and smiled imperceptibly then reverted to his familiar, checked-out-of-life countenance.

"Would you like to rest?" she asked.

"No."

"Talk?"

"Okay."

They jockeyed for a conducive seating arrangement like self-conscious lonely-hearts on a blind date. As Billy regarded the couch that had been his escapist retreat, Janey saw wistful longing in his eyes. But perhaps in a new sense of fortitude he chose the high-backed armchair. In deference, Janey settled on Rosie's favorite ottoman.

Having been displaced, Rosie eyeballed the couch herself, but Janey's cocked eyebrow convinced her to keep off. With a sigh Rosie laid down next to the ottoman, watchful eyes tilted up at them.

A monument to despair, the couch remained conspicuously un-sat upon.

Nodding at Rosie Billy asked, "How's she doing?"

"Much better, thanks. We almost lost her."

He reached over and patted Rosie on the head. She rolled over in submission and locked eyes with him, a gesture that brought Janey to the brink of her emotional capacity.

"She forgives you," Janey said.

Billy scratched Rosie's belly. "Well, that's one down."

"So, are you staying or going back to Hawaii?"

"School starts soon. I've decided I prefer teaching to surfing. And I'm going to do some writing."

Janey held back a dozen snide remarks about why he looked so chubby and pale if he'd been surfing all this time unless he'd been channel surfing and too stoned to move. "Grandma said you had something to tell me."

With a wince Billy adjusted to straight military bearing in the chair. "I guess since it's her dying wish…"

"She's not dying, Billy. She'll probably outlive all of us. Just tell me what I'm supposed to know."

"Okay." His voice dropped to a level detectable only by sonar, forcing Janey to lean in, which made him lean back further until he merged with the chair. "It's been going on for a really long time. Not the incident, but my feelings."

"I have no idea what you're talking about."

As if sensing his need for support, Rosie got up and sat beside him. "I've always felt you didn't love me. I'm just a poor substitute for Bruce."

Janey failed to keep her eyes from rolling. "Billy…"

"You never stop to consider that he farts and belches like every other guy in the world. If Bruce jumped off the Empire State Building you'd follow him down."

Billy's tirade was older than Eleanor but delivered with such invective, it was obviously leading to something.

"You can't make someone love you. They either do or they don't. And a long time ago I realized you don't."

"Amazing that you have such total insight."

"There was this student teacher assigned to my class..."

Wham! The rubber dart hit her in the forehead and she began to see where he was going.

"She liked me. We talked about history. One day she invited me over to her place and we listened to music and talked all night and then..." Billy exhaled so forcefully, Janey smelled barbecue potato chips on his breath.

"When was this?"

"Last February. It started on Valentine's Day and it only lasted a few weeks. But I felt really guilty and for some reason I told Grandma."

"You did?" Janey said, astonished that Eleanor had kept this to herself.

"She came at me like Judge Judy. That's when she started hating me."

"So you went into seclusion on the couch?"

He nodded. "I did hurt my back but it wasn't as bad as I made it out to be. After awhile I couldn't take it anymore so I decided to go to Hawaii."

A second blast of barbecue breath exploded in her face. "I wonder why Grandma never told me."

"She thought it was my job to tell you but I couldn't. Joyce Brothers says it's better to keep an affair to yourself."

As his expression yielded to the serenity of a man who had finally unburdened himself, Janey felt anaesthetized. It would take a long time to process his bombshell. "I appreciate you telling me," she said while the 400-pound gorilla of her own affair blinked like a cheap motel sign. She understood the appeal of withdrawing to the couch with a phony back ailment.

"Who's this plumber Grandma was talking about?"

For the first time Janey felt cheap and disgusting; it all came on at once. "Oh, someone I met in the park. We kind of hit it off. He's...a Bruce fan. And his mom is much, much worse than I am. Really. She makes me seem indifferent."

"His mom? How old is this guy?"

"Young."

"Was there something wrong with our plumbing?"

"He's not a plumber. That's just what Grandma calls him. Actually he's a carpenter. He's been very nice to Grandma—they danced—I think she has a crush on him."

"What about you? Do you have a crush on him?"

"Kind of. It's nothing deep. Mostly just..."

"Sex?"

"Well...yes, and music."

"How old is he?"

"I don't know for sure. I think around twenty five."

"Twenty-five!"

"How old is the student teacher?"

Billy put up his hand. "Okay, okay."

They stared at each other for a few moments. Slides from the past played on her memory screen: their wedding on the beach, the births of Candi and Sherri, rooting for Eleanor at her first ballroom dancing competition. She couldn't keep the images from flickering then dying like spent light bulbs.

"It's not a relationship," Janey said. She quickly turned to Rosie, who got up, walked over to Billy and curled up at his feet.

"It's just a fling."

Billy's judgmental eyes gazed back at her.

"I didn't know you were coming back, Billy."

Billy's body sagged and his stiff upper lip began to spasm. He got up, took two steps and flopped down on the couch.

29
GODDESSES

Six months ago Solange figured that by this time she'd be married to Joie, not flying off to Las Vegas on a private jet to witness the wedding of her new friend to a movie megastar. With the prospect of—if all went well—her first time sexual intercourse with a man, she had to conclude that her life had taken some intriguing turns of late.

She had hoped that all the plans would be in place before departure, with Gary a willing and able participant in the baby-making project. She worried that he'd say no and it would ruin Lily's honeymoon. She also worried he'd say yes and wouldn't be able to get it up—maybe he could only have heterosexual sex with his amazing, mystical wife. But she held on to Lily's fervent belief that their mutual intention would make it happen in a natural, organic way.

At least Gary hadn't objected to her tagging along; in fact, he loved the idea, which made Solange hurry over before he could reconsider. While Lily was getting ready, Gary took her aside and asked if she would help with a few of the details. "Want to pick out her dress?" he asked. "I've got a woman coming by with some selections."

"I'm all over it," she told Gary. She wanted to add that it was an awesome gesture and to apologize once again for having doubted him, but didn't want to appear to be buttering him up for the Big Favor.

Gary had apparently thought of everything. The minute their chartered Lear jet touched down, a limo was waiting to take them to the Bellagio Hotel. Terrell, security guard and makeshift wedding coordinator, whisked them up to their suite before any bleary-eyed gamblers could identify the man in the baseball cap with the mirrored aviator sunglasses. At Solange's suggestion Lily had her hair stuffed inside a cloche.

The impossible opulence of the huge penthouse gave Solange a fleeting dizzy spell. Everything looked like it was dipped in gold leaf. Upholstery seemed too luxurious to sit upon. And hanging on the wall, near the bathroom of all places, was a small Matisse—an interior of clashing reds and purples. She sucked in her breath and put her face as close to it as she dared. "You're awesome," she whispered. "Will you marry me?"

A Matisse surely boded well for the evening to proceed on a rapturous course even when Solange took Lily to the bathroom to vomit, as the plane ride had triggered a bout of motion sickness.

"Looking forward to this?" Lily asked between heaves.

Solange held back Lily's hair to keep it out of the toilet. "Of course. I'll throw up for Andi anytime."

When they emerged, Terrell said that Gary had gone to a secret location to prepare for the ceremony. Then he excused himself to take care of some last minute matters.

Lily looked puzzled. "Gary told me we were going to the drive-through chapel."

"Oh, right," said Solange. "You're going to have a McWedding." She directed Lily's attention to a rack of clothing covered with a lace tablecloth. "Check these out." Beneath the cloth, a dozen gowns awaited her evaluation. "Do these look like drive-through dresses?"

"Oh, my God," Lily gasped.

"Largest selection of maternity wedding dresses in the state of Nevada."

"I can't believe this," Lily said, gliding her fingers over them as if they were made of spun gold.

"Your guy is off the charts, Lily. He's funny, smart and an amazing specimen of physical gorgeousity."

"I'm way too lucky," said Lily.

"Stop it. Enjoy your good fortune while you have it. The world could end tomorrow."

"Not a chance," Lily said, patting her tummy. "This guy is on a mission to save it. So is Andi."

"Glad to hear it," Solange said, leading Lily over to a brocade armchair. "Now sit down and let's pick out a wedding dress."

Solange opened the fashion show with a long-sleeved beige lace tunic with matching bellbottom pants. Lily touched the delicate fabric. "Beautiful."

"Too trendy. We want timeless." Solange hung it at the back of the rack and displayed the next gown, a lavender silk trapeze with an empire waist, garnished in ruffles and flounces.

"It's a little busy," Lily said.

"Off the island. Adieu!"

The next three candidates clashed with Lily's hair. Solange thought they might have to go with the bellbottoms until she saw something previously hidden that made her swoon. With the dexterity of a pickpocket she freed a diaphanous ivory gown from its hangar and draped it over her arms. The fabric seemed to be made from visible atmosphere. "This," she said in a hush, "is what the Goddess wears."

Lily's face grew wondrous. "Help me get into it." She peeled off her tee shirt and drawstring pants.

The sight of Lily's body heightened Solange's emotions. "You look awesome, Lily. I can't wait to be pregnant." She touched the protruding belly. "Hi, Andi's brother." Drops trickled down her cheeks and she quickly wiped them, afraid of damaging the dress. "This is going to be a wonderful night."

***

Aghast, Lily studied herself in the full-length bathroom mirror. "Holy cow, I need a body stocking for this. You can see my nipples through the fabric."

"I can call the concierge," said Solange, "but this is Vegas. Nipples are everywhere. And trust me—yours are spectacular."

It seemed very exhibitionist but after all, the wedding party consisted of Gary, Solange and maybe a Vegas minister who'd no doubt seen a nipple or two. "Okay, and what are you going to wear?"

From her super-sized Prada tote bag Solange extracted a small, plastic Ziploc bag containing a swatch of shiny material. Twenty seconds later it was applied to her body—a clingy, metallic micro-mini-dress that displayed out-of-control cleavage. "What do you think?" she asked.

"You know, if you get pregnant, you might seriously miss that body for the next nine months."

Solange fetched a digital camera from her bag and handed it to Lily. "I'll have three hundred pictures to remember me by."

A dozen shots into their photo-fest, Terrell came in carrying a tray with half a cantaloupe in a dish.

"Perfect timing," said Solange. She took the tray and handed it to Lily. "This is for you."

"Am I supposed to eat it?" Lily asked, staring.

"Well, if you have another idea, I'm sure we can work it in later, but yes, you must eat it right now."

"Because..."

"Because an hour from now it will make your pussy taste like ambrosia, which should be just about right."

Lily looked embarrassed and Terrell's dark skin took on a reddish cast.

Popping into the bathroom, Solange fetched two bath sheets and draped them around Lily. "Don't spill." She turned to Terrell. "We'll be ready in five minutes."

Five minutes later, when Terrell held out his arm to walk Lily down the aisle, she didn't know which way to go.

"This way," said Solange, rolling the dress rack away to reveal a door. Behind it, a white carpet strewn with pink rose petals led to a canopy covered in blooms. Solange plucked a bouquet of pink lilies from a silver bucket and handed it to the bride.

The room was a fairy tale heaven of lilies. They overflowed containers, wove through draperies, hung in sprays from the ceiling. While Lily tried to take it all in, Sarah Vaughn sang "Someone to Watch Over Me."

But the flowers paled in comparison to the sight beneath the canopy—Gary, impossibly masculine in pale pink tails, smiling his heart out. He could not be real; this was surely the finale of her dream—when the fantasy man was sucked back into the pages of the romance novel and she awakened.

The baby kicked like he wanted out. Lily's bladder felt the pressure but she resolved to maintain control. Silently she promised him he'd be at the next ceremony.

Terrell glided her toward Reverend Richards, whom she later learned was on a sixty minute loan from Cupid's Arrow Wedding Chapel. It amused Lily when his eyes kept darting over to the shiny, metallic Solange, who, like a shapely mirrored ball, reflected everyone's happiness.

"Welcome," the minister began. "We are gathered here this evening to join together Lily Marie Bennett and Gary Giovanni DiCaro in marriage."

When Gary took her hand she surrendered to him the entirety of her life and felt sparks pass between them.

Reverend Richards nodded to Gary. "Gary has prepared his personal marriage vows. Gary?"

Producing an index card from his inside pocket Gary addressed Lily. "I can't take credit for this. You always tell me that I speak dog. Well, this came directly from Bean and Blossom. They dictated it to me."

A pang of love pierced Lily's heart.

"Precious Lily, I am in awe of your beauty, the sounds you make, the way you taste and of course, the way you smell. I want to chase you and lick you and roll over for you every day of my life. You are my goddess and I am your faithful dog, worshipping at your feet. I promise you a lifetime of joyous frolic and unconditional love forever and ever."

Solange's dam of tears broke but she waved her hands in a "Go on, don't mind me" gesture and managed to plug it up with a mighty sniff.

Reverend Richards turned to Lily. "Lily, I know you didn't

expect this and didn't prepare anything to say, but would you like to speak from your heart?"

The baby kicked again, in some international baby code she wished she understood. "Gary, my heart is at maximum love capacity. I don't know how it can fit in my body. You've made dreams come true I didn't know I had."

As Gary clasped her hand, vapors of light particles sprayed from their bodies. No one spoke. The light twinkled for a few moments, then slowly vanished. Lily hoped the magic hadn't spooked Reverend Richards.

"Wow," said Solange, "I knew that would happen."

Terrell looked around. Reverend Richards looked up.

"It's just a little light show," said Gary. "My wife-to-be is from a galaxy far, far away. We're going to the Big Dipper for our honeymoon."

The minister smiled tentatively and made a few awkward attempts to speak. "Do you, uh...have...rings?"

When Terrell produced a pair of gold bands, Lily was astonished at how Gary had planned the event clear down to her ring size. Terrell handed a ring to Gary and as he slipped it on Lily's yearning finger it produced a shimmering halo of golden light.

"With this ring, I marry you," said Gary.

Lily slid Gary's ring on and it gave off a similar glow. "With this ring, I marry you."

Again Reverend Richards looked up but apparently saw only ceiling. He crossed himself. So did Terrell.

"It's not magic," Lily said, sensing the need to explain. "Sometimes when I'm very excited like I am now, my frequency shifts on the cellular level. I guess it's showing."

Reverend Richards' face froze in the wary mask of one who is accosted by a deranged person. With a mild squeak in his voice he declared them husband and wife.

There was eternity in Gary's kiss...and a short outbreak of disembodied barking. Lily broke away. "Are the dogs here?" she asked.

Gary's eyes darted. "Not that I know of."

Possibly for safety precautions, Terrell and the minister stepped back.

Cocking her head like Blossom, Lily listened to another round of barks. "Those are definitely our dogs."

"I'd know Fudgsie's bark anywhere," said Solange.

Lily's eyes welled up. "They're trying to be with us. Dogs are multi-dimensional. Someday we will be too." She turned to Solange and held her close. "This is the best dream I ever had."

"Just getting started," said Solange.

Gary shook hands with the professionally smiling Reverend Richards and handed him an envelope. "Reverend, thank you for joining us in wedlock. We know you have to go now." He thanked Terrell and guided the two men out the door.

The room rattled when the newlyweds exchanged a mighty kiss of wedlock. Lily's plan hung like wedding rice in suspended animation. She focused on Gary's third eye and projected it to him.

"Something you need to tell me?" he asked.

"I adore you," she said. "I adore you." She kissed him with all her life. "I am the luckiest woman in the history of women." Then paused. "But tonight...I want to share you. We need to make a baby for Solange."

A few feet away Solange put praying hands to her lips, closed her eyes and bowed her head.

Gary looked at Lily, then at Solange. His eyelashes fluttered. "Would that be my first honey-do?"

Lily smiled and slowly nodded.

"Wait'll the guys at the office hear about this."

***

Solange was glad she'd brought the musk and vanilla candles to enhance the sexual climate in the room, not that it needed help. The passion pouring out of Lily and Gary seemed potent enough to blow out every light on the Strip and make all of Las Vegas perspire.

There was no discussion about procedure. The trio tumbled back onto the sumptuous bed and let physical communication take over. At first they couldn't stop hugging, clinging to each other like rotating magnets. While Lily and Gary kissed, Solange caressed them. The intimate privilege she'd been given made her heart race, even more so when she thought about Andi's return, minutes from now, in this very bed. She tried to move aside to allow the consummation of their marriage.

But Lily would not let her go. She held Solange's hand firmly while inviting Gary with her eyes. Gary slipped off his shirt, tossed it aside and unbuckled his pants. It didn't seem to register that Solange was in bed with him; his fixation on Lily was so intense, Solange imagined she could hang from the ceiling without him glancing up. While he removed his pants, Solange popped off her dress.

As men's bodies go, Gary's was quite impressive. It was muscular but didn't appear labored and was further defined by a restrained pattern of chest hair. His smooth, graceful hand glided over Lily's gown. "Beautiful dress. Beautiful wife." He bent down to kiss her, slipped the dress off her shoulders and carefully rolled it down off her body.

As gingerly as she could, Solange snatched the gown and flung it over a chair. All the while her hand remained clasped to Lily's. She marveled again at Lily's pregnancy, couldn't wait for her own body to swell and stretch and pulsate with life. As Gary's mouth savored Lily's pale skin on his way to ambrosia, Solange smiled—the cantaloupe so perfectly timed. When he finally tasted her, Lily moaned and pulled Solange toward her face.

Just once Solange kissed her, and wiped tiny droplets of sweat off Lily's forehead. Gary was clearly an inspired lover; astonishing, considering his limited experience. He used his tongue expertly, but mostly his lips. They knew exactly what to do.

Solange found herself growing extremely excited; in her most insane dream she had never conjured a scenario where she was in heat over a penis. Of course, this was no ordinary penis; it belonged to the father of her child. Her fingers meandered inside of her and came out dripping.

Gary grazed his lips across Lily's bush of hair then he rose up and slowly pushed inside her. Reaching over, Solange stroked his back. His groans rose in volume. In all the times Solange had seen live sex, it was the first time she had ever become emotionally involved.

As Lily reached orgasm she cried out.

Solange laid down next to her and opened her legs.

Easing out of Lily, Gary formed a tent over Solange. She took hold of his penis and eased it in.

As Gary emptied himself into her, Lily clenched Solange's hand. The moment his warm liquid made contact, she wailed and climaxed. Gary collapsed atop her pillow breasts, expelled a gallon of air and rolled off, wedging between the two women.

No one spoke for at least a minute. Then Solange said, "I'm pregnant. He hit my G-spot. The Gary spot." She turned to him. "You're a fertility god."

"I do what I can," Gary said.

Solange and Lily found this almost unbearably funny. They laughed until they realized that a bathroom break had turned into an emergency.

"What a wedding night," Lily said when they resumed group snuggling on the bed.

"Andi is so happy," Solange said. She began to cry.

Gary rested his hand on her tummy. "She's a good girl."

The newlyweds fell asleep quickly, Gary providing a warm cocoon to nestle his bride. But sleep was not on Solange's agenda this evening. She remained awake most of the night daydreaming about Andi, reliving the wondrous conception while she savored her first few hours of motherhood.

30
JANEY & GODDESSES

Following his return Billy's mood had shifted from slothful depression to smoldering resentment. He indulged in daily whinings: the thermostat is set too low; can't find the microwave popcorn; goddam bugs ruining the tomatoes; then, once he returned to work, he became downright irritable. Janey found herself longing for the silent Summer of Sofa.

Outraged at being cut from her will, he did not visit Eleanor.

"Screw her," he'd say when Janey asked him to go with her to the hospital. But the situation had obvious benefits for Janey. Davy had taken to seeing Eleanor on a regular basis and the hospital provided a legitimate, if not romantic environment for them to rendezvous.

With Billy around, Janey hadn't felt comfortable going to Davy's. The guilt she had brushed aside while Billy was in Hawaii surfaced like a geyser when he came home, an ever-present cold shower that thwarted her sexual urges, even for Davy. There were a few stolen kisses outside of Eleanor's room, some mild groping in the parking lot but none of the delicious fucking of yore.

She dwelled on Davy's paternity issue until she needed a prescription for the anxiety. As outer-orbital as Wendy was, she could have been with any number of men that night, including the entire E Street Band. Janey chose to believe that Wendy had had marital relations with her husband when she got home and pretended he was Bruce.

It seemed in Eleanor's mind, Davy and Janey were merely friends; Janey assumed that since reality threatened Eleanor's own fantasies about Davy, she was in denial about their sexual relationship.

One Tuesday afternoon while Billy was busy in the classroom, Janey and Davy drove to the hospital to bring Eleanor home. When they appeared in the doorway of her room she was already ensconced in her new wheelchair, raring to go. "You're late!" she bellowed.

Janey looked at her watch. They were exactly on time.

Rushing to her side Davy gave Eleanor a kiss on the cheek. "Sorry, Eleanor. But look what I have for you." He held up an intricately carved oak tray. "See? It has a cup holder for your tea so it won't spill." He gently placed it on her lap. "You can use it in your wheelchair like this," then unfolding the legs: "or if you're in bed, you can open it up like this."

Judging by Eleanor's expression it also doubled as an engagement ring. "That was very thoughtful of you," she said, beaming like a love-struck coquette.

"He made it himself," Janey said.

With hand to her cheek Eleanor said, "Oh, my. You know, you should think about going into the wood business. Why be a plumber when you have such talent?"

Eleanor's buoyant mood increased on the way home. "Turn on the music!" she shouted as Davy wheeled her into the house. Since the injury she looked thirty years younger, which made Janey wonder if her hospital bed was still available.

After parking Eleanor in the living room, Davy put on some Benny Goodman swing music that inspired her right index finger to draw sprightly circles in the air. With a cool cat walk he sidled up to her, reached for her hands and led her in the forearm bebop.

"I knew we would dance again," Eleanor said, beaming.

Rosie sat on her ottoman watching the dancers with a big smile on her face. Every time Janey looked at her she pictured thought balloons over her head containing dog messages that Janey didn't understand.

Their knowledge of each other's vernacular seemed pitifully lopsided. While Rosie knew hundreds of words and phrases and correctly interpreting the subtlest nuances of Janey's body language, Janey could barely comprehend tail wagging. If Janey said something new, with a tilt of her head Rosie had it mastered. Janey felt Rosie's need for deeper levels of communication.

She sat down next to Rosie and gave her a hug. "I'm sorry, girl. "Pure unfiltered love poured from the terrier's body. "I'm working on it."

Rosie swiped her tongue across Janey's face. Janey certainly understood that.

Following "Moonglow" and "Goody Goody", Davy dropped to his knees and into a fainting backbend, like Bruce often did after an especially aerobic number.

Eleanor ate it up. She seemed to be having one hell of a time until she abruptly waved Janey over. "I have to go to the bathroom," she whispered.

"Excuse us," Janey said and took hold of Eleanor's wheelchair. We're going to powder our noses."

Davy lifted his head and "came to." "Okay, while you ladies are in the lava-toree, I'm-a gonna go in the kitchen and make-a you some fantastic pasta you gonna love." He made the Italian kissing gesture with his fingers.

"I could eat him up," said Eleanor.

"Actually," Janey said to Davy, "that's not such a good idea. The girls will be home soon and so will Billy."

Eleanor shrugged. "Who cares?"

"Right, who cares?" echoed Davy. "I think it's time that Billy and I met, brother to brother."

Reconsidering, Janey decided that such an encounter might be stimulating for all concerned. A future with Davy, aside from the stares, the *Harold and Maude* jokes, irrational fears of him running off with one of her daughters, would be impossible unless she knew for absolutely-positively-DNA sure that Davy was not the Son of Bruce. Because if he was, if he actually was, then she could possibly, possibly become Bruce's first...daughter-in-law...

It became the most insane and thrilling thought in her head, one she'd obsess on until its resolution. "Brother to brother—good idea," she said.

"Sweet!" Davy hustled off to the kitchen while Janey drove Eleanor into the bathroom to try out her new handrail and elevated toilet seat.

"Billy bought it for you," she said, hoping to score the beleaguered grandson some Boy Scout points.

Mumbling some vague approval or disapproval—Janey couldn't tell which—Eleanor lifted herself out of the wheelchair and eased onto the toilet. "You can go now," she told Janey. "I'll flush when I'm ready."

Back in the kitchen, Davy was deep into sauce preparation. He swung around to engage Janey in a deep throaty kiss that made her realize how much she missed fucking him.

"Are we ever going to make love again?" he asked, reading her mind.

"I want to but it's more complicated now."

He reached under her tee shirt and cupped his artistic hand over her right breast. "I'm so hard, I could drill a hole in the wall." He placed her hand on the evidence.

They kissed and groped like horny centipedes.

"Maybe we can go to your place after Billy gets home. Leave something here, like your wallet, then when he throws you out, I'll rush out to return it to you."

A loud thump startled them. "Hey!" she heard Eleanor yell. Janey sprinted to the bathroom, opened the door and stepped on a soap dish.

"Were you planning to leave me here all day? You made me break the door."

Janey picked up the plexiglass missile and assessed the damage. "It's just a little gash."

"The plumber can fix that." She let Janey help her back into the wheelchair then motioned for her to come closer. "Listen," she whispered, "if you want to have sex with him, go ahead. He's too young for me."

"You mean Davy?"

"Well, I don't mean your no-good husband. You owe him one. Payback."

While Janey tried to determine Eleanor's ulterior motive, she heard Billy and Sherri arrive. Her heart thumped fast enough to knock paint chips off the door.

"Get me out of here," said Eleanor. "This is going to be good."

They entered a still-life in the living room: Billy and Sherri caught unawares facing Davy, who had bounced in from the kitchen wearing a red plastic apron. He extended his hand. "Hi! You must be Billy."

Robotically, Billy shook hands with him. "And you are?"

"David. Nice to meet you."

Janey white-knuckled the wheelchair handles till her blood stopped flowing.

Billy looked like he'd just spotted termites. He turned to Janey. "What's he doing here?"

"He's making dinner," volunteered Eleanor.

"He wanted to meet you," Janey said.

The termites multiplied. "Well," Billy sneered, "that makes one of us."

"The way I see it," said Davy, flashing his under bite, "things are going to come to a head sooner or later, so why not just cut the bullshit?"

"Why don't you get the fuck out of here?"

"Don't talk like that!" Eleanor shouted. "Be nice or go to your room."

"This is my house. I'll go to whatever room I want."

"I'd like to talk this out," Davy said.

"Get out of my house, punk."

"Don't listen to him," said Eleanor.

Davy visibly gave in. "Okay, I'm going." He took off the apron, handed it to Janey and moved toward the door.

"Wait, you forgot your wallet!" said Janey, then realized she had jumped the gun. "I mean, can't we all get along?"

"Let him go, Mom," said Sherri. "I can't believe you've been hanging around with this creep. What is he—your boyfriend?"

"No, he's my boyfriend," said Eleanor.

Billy looked Davy up and down. "How old are you?"

"Twenty-three."

"Show me your driver's license."

Wanting to make the embarrassment go away, Janey closed her eyes. "Trust me, Billy. He's twenty-three."

Davy produced his wallet and displayed his license. "Sorry, officer. I guess I'm a little under the speed limit."

In the derisive, self-satisfied way he did at reality TV, Billy laughed. "You're twenty-one," he said. "Not twenty-three."

Eleanor waved her hand. "Twenty-one, forty-one. Same thing."

Rapidly Janey moved through shock (twenty-one?), guilt (she was officially a pervert), relief (Bruce hadn't slept with Whacked-out Wendy) and grave disappointment (she could never be part of a hush-hush Springsteen clan). Wendy had lied—she was psychotic; she could be forgiven. But Davy had also lied. "You told me you were twenty-three."

His response could barely be heard. "Sorry."

"You should have told me. I can handle the truth." Now there was a lie.

"I'm sorry, Janey. I was afraid you'd think I was too young for you."

Sherri laughed. "Duh!"

After a few seconds of turgid silence the phone rang. Janey snatched it on the first jangle. It was girlfriend intervention: Lily and Solange asking her to come by to hear some big news. Janey didn't know if she could handle any more news but she sure wanted to get out of the house.

When she hung up she saw Davy halfway out the door. "I wish you happiness, Janey." He slipped out.

She followed him outside. "Hey," she called to the back of his head. "Is this it?"

He turned around. "It? You mean 'Good luck, goodbye, Bobby Jean?'"

"Yeah."

"That's your call. I don't have a husband."

In the late afternoon light he looked seventeen. "Can we be friends?"

"We're already friends. That'll never change."

Janey held out her hand. "'...ain't nobody nowhere no how gonna ever understand me the way you did...'"

Davy kissed it. "I wish I had known you when you were sixteen..."

"My girls are too young for you."

He laughed. "I never even..."

"Just a pre-emptive strike."

***

As soon as Janey and Rosie arrived at Lily's, Janey received a hug assault from Lily and Solange. They both looked high. Lily was wearing the same nightgownish dress she'd worn at the park the day they met.

Rosie made a beeline for Gary DiCaro, who was relaxing on the sofa like some regular guy, and covered him with such excessive slobbering Janey felt embarrassed. She wondered if the Big Secret had been divulged. If so, Gary didn't look the least bit guilty.

Even if he was a heartless cad Janey was excited to meet him as he was an exceptionally dreamy heartless cad.

He stood up and Lily made the introduction.

"Janey, this is Gary. My husband."

"Hi," he said, extending his hand.

"Husband?" Janey looked at Solange, who gave her thumbs up. The Gary issue had obviously been resolved. That left her with high school jealousy—she hadn't been invited to the wedding.

"That guy at the club—it wasn't him!" said Solange, explaining in a breathless torrent how she'd been duped by an impersonator at the fetish club. She wrapped her arms around Gary. "He's for real!"

"We have a lot tell you," Lily said, leading her to the flowered chintz chair. "Sit down and have some tea. It'll calm you down after you faint." She began pouring.

Janey's nervous laugh was encased in panic; with Lily and

Solange, there was no telling what she was in for—perhaps some naked tribal ritual. She took a healthy swig of tea, then worried what was in it.

"Now," said Lily, "you must swear on your eternal life that you'll never reveal what we're about to tell you."

"Or we'll have to kill you," Gary said with a grin that could thaw ice cubes.

Flopping onto the arm of Janey's chair, Solange hugged her. "This is so beyond exclusive it's ridiculous."

Janey crossed her heart and zipped her lips. "I'm 'open to pain and crossed by the rain.'"

Without missing a beat, Gary sang the next line: "'...and I walked on a crooked crutch...'"

For the second time that summer Janey fell unexpectedly in love.

"Gary wanted us to be married before the baby came so we ran off to Vegas last night on the spur of the moment," Lily said. She gazed at Gary. "I thought it was going to be a drive-through ceremony but he turned it into a fairy tale."

"Don't worry, I have pictures," said Solange.

"I wasn't there," Janey said, her face turned down. How could Solange have been invited and not her?

"Janey," Lily said, leaning into her, "you're going to be the matron of honor at our big wedding, the one with everyone we know. This time there were special circumstances—Solange will tell you."

Sliding into Janey's chair, Solange half-sat in her lap. "Janey, remember after the Roberta Landers interview I told you I felt this strange connection to Gary, even though I thought he was an asshole?"

Recalling the feverish phone call in which Solange told her she'd bloodied Gary's lavender in an effort to discover their deep karmic bond, Janey nodded.

"The other night I found out. Gary's who Andi has chosen to be her father." She exhaled in Janey's face. "Isn't that awesome?"

No one, including Gary DiCaro, blinked, so Janey blinked for all of them. Meeting someone this famous was stimulating enough without the disturbing detail that he was also a member of their flourishing cult.

"So I went charging over here, begging them to forgive me and unbelievably, they did. And then, the most miraculous thing... Gary agreed to donate his sperm!"

Janey glanced over at Gary, who made a silly face. "That's fantastic, Solange."

"But then," Solange continued, her adoring gaze falling on Lily, "this amazing, most generous goddess in history over here had a better idea." Her hooded eyes looked down. "And that's how I ended up at the wedding...and the wedding night."

Gary shook his head. "I am one lucky son of a bitch."

Staring at the serene looking menage á trois, Janey's eyes sprung from their cages. "Okay, you're scaring me now." Was no one's sexual identity safe anymore?

"It was beautiful," Solange enthused. "Not sexual at all."

"Hey," said Gary.

"I mean it went way beyond sex. Gary and Lily were like a honeybee and a flower. They looked so gorgeous making love it made me cry. And every time they touched, the mystical lights were shining. Even during the ceremony they were glowing like candles."

Next to Janey's sexual fantasies about Bruce, visuals of the ravishing trio in bed putting on a psychedelic sex show was the most erotic image she could imagine. She began to wish they really were planning a naked tribal ritual. "When will you know the results?"

"It's only been forty-three hours but I know it worked. We all felt it. The Goddess wouldn't lie about this."

While fervently hoping that was true and wondering what would happen if it wasn't and Gary had to be loaned out monthly, she gave Solange a congratulatory squeeze. "I'm so happy for you, honey."

Solange reached over to stroke Lily's arm. "Can you imagine a woman sharing her husband on their wedding night?"

"Well," said Janey, "this is California."

On that innocuous cue, the dogs leaped up and like a wagon train, began to encircle their people. After a couple of rounds, Rosie broke out of the formation and fetched a fuzzy toy, which prompted the other dogs to fetch toys and any other objects they could fit in their mouths, and place them at Gary's feet.

"Maybe they're going to roast me in a bonfire," Gary speculated as he observed the ceremony.

"It's a wreath," said Lily. "They're honoring him because he's the fertility god."

"Looks like another Bonehenge," said Solange.

The dogs stationed themselves north, south, east and west of Gary. Janey sensed Rosie calling her. It felt like a warning.

A bang on the door made them all jump.

The dogs barked in a high octave. Rosie's voice grew unusually amplified and the other dogs seemed to be mimicking her, sounding more like a flock of angry crows than barking dogs.

"Quiet," Lily shouted to the dogs, who kept on barking.

"Stay there," said Gary. "I'll get it." He got up and looked through the beveled glass. "Who is it?"

A muffled voice seeped through the door. "Let me talk to Solange."

Solange folded up. She spoke to the floor. "It's Marvin. Tell him I'm not here."

"She's not here," Gary said.

"I saw her through the window."

Solange rose and walked to the door. "I'll call you later, okay?"

"It's important," Marvin said.

The dogs continued to yelp, making it hard to hear anything. Janey leaped into their midst and wrapped her arms around all four at once. The howls simmered down to a mournful whine.

"I'd better talk to him," said Solange.

Gary held her arm. "Wait, is he dangerous?"

"He's a wimp." She opened the door a crack.

"It's the faggot movie star," Janey heard Marvin say and she gagged with shock. "He's the father."

Solange's voice grew firm. "You'd better go, Marvin."

"He's got the money. He can afford it."

"You're crazy. I told you it was an anonymous donor."

"Bullshit! You just kissed him and your friend called him the fertility god."

Lily went pale. "He's been watching us through the window."

"Close the door, Solange," Janey commanded. "I'm calling the police."

But Marvin would not let Solange shut him out.

Gary leaped up to help. "She told you to leave, buddy."

At the same moment, the tip of a gun barrel snaked through

the crack followed by an unearthly blast. Gary fell backwards to the floor.

Solange screamed. And screamed. And screamed.

Lily pitched herself over Gary while Janey charged forward, yanking Solange away while she tried to slam the door with her foot.

But Marvin had already pushed his way inside. "You never loved me!" he blared, waving the gun like a depraved orchestra conductor.

The dogs formed a cacophonous howling platoon.

Solange yelled, "Put the gun down! Put the gun down!"

Marvin pointed it at his array of targets: Lily, Gary, Solange, Janey, the dogs.

"I can help you," Janey said to Marvin. "Don't shoot anyone. I'll help you." It wasn't a lie because it would surely help Marvin to put the gun down.

Instead, he swallowed three inches of gun barrel and pulled the trigger. The room shook as if it were a movie set.

The dogs screamed.

Though it was not technically possible, Solange shrieked louder than before, flailing her arms, abdicating all control of her body.

Janey took hold of her and guided her to the couch. "Lie down. Don't talk. Don't move. I'll take care of everything."

"It's my fault. I killed Gary."

"Quiet. You didn't do anything." Janey arranged Solange's arms and legs in a semblance of relaxation—they bent and folded like pipe cleaners. Solange never took her eyes off the ceiling.

The dogs formed a warm compress around Gary, licking him, crying.

All emotion siphoned out of Janey's body and disappeared into the seat cushion of the flowered chintz chair. It would be safe there until she needed it again.

To remain composed, Janey became the lead in a horrible crime movie. She went to the phone and called 911. "Two people shot on Allott Street in Valley Glen." *The address... no idea... can't ask Lily... little table by the front door... gas bill.* "Sixty-seven-forty-two. Jane West. Seven-eight-two-four-six-five-nine. Thank you."

When she returned to the scene on the floor she saw that the dogs had created a garland of alms around Gary with the gifts they had earlier offered him. She briefly pondered their meaning and wondered if the dogs had known, if they were clairvoyant. They stood beside Gary as Lily breathed desperate air into his lungs and they licked the blood puddles on the floor.

Janey rushed to the bathroom and pulled all towels and washcloths off the shelves. She grabbed a chair cushion to place under Gary's head.

"He's still breathing," Lily said. "He's alive. He's breathing."

Blood stains expanded on Gary's chest. Lily put her hand over the erupting gash and Janey, inclined to recoil from the horror of a paper cut, could not wrest her eyes from the glistening blood gushing through Lily's fingers. Surely Lily was bringing him back to life and in a moment the wound would heal, reversing the violent mistake that had just occurred.

Janey noticed Gary's eyes open and his lips move.

Leaning into him Lily said, "I love you, Gary, I love you. Don't talk."

Bean and Blossom licked the blood running down Gary's arm. A faint smile struggled on his face. "Dogs'll take care of me..."

"I'll take care of you," Lily said. "I'll take care of you."

"Kiss," Gary whispered.

Lily touched her lips to his. As the contact was made, Janey saw a ghostly blue mist rise up around them and illuminate the air. It felt like the caress of billions of delicate light-fingers.

The lovers melted together, persuading Janey that they had permanently fused into one. She hoped that was so, that Lily's spirit could be Gary's life support. But his eyes drifted shut and his body relaxed into a peaceful looking calm.

Janey watched Lily's nightgownish dress soak up the blood. Like a piece of used gauze Lily peeled it off and applied it to the red hole where Gary's life had escaped. She spread her bareness over him like a protective skin while Bean and Blossom coated themselves in the fluid that continued to siphon away.

"He's not dead...there is no death..." Lily repeated, mantra-like. In serpentine motion, she squirmed over the surface of his body then looked up at Janey. "There is no death, Janey."

Lily's eyes pleaded for confirmation and Janey felt helpless to provide it. Sending up a help flare, she felt Rosie delicately pawing at her ankle.

Everything dies, baby that's a fact...but maybe everything that dies some day comes back... As if under dog hypnosis, Janey repeated the telepathed lyrics to Lily.

Lily brightened. "Bruce said that, right?"

Janey nodded.

"Then I know it's true. Bruce is true."

"He's the truest," Janey said over the catch in her throat. With a shiver of awareness Janey realized that Rosie had been her conduit for Bruce's lyrics from the beginning.

I was his dog in another life, Rosie imparted to her—a

tantalizing bit of information that Janey needed to file away for a future conversation—one of many future conversations they would have—because at that moment, an invasion of police, paramedics and uniformed officials came barging into Lily's house. Horrified by Lily's state of undress, Janey threw a crocheted afghan over her and gently tried to pull her away from Gary, but Lily let out a scream so commanding, so raw, that everyone was compelled to stop and pay rapt attention for its excruciating duration.

After the scream, Lily collapsed. Janey gathered her up and held her while her body reeled from its brutal release. Elsewhere the worker bees went about various tasks of examining the dead; there were many things happening at once. The name of the murder victim had obviously been disclosed or leaked, as more officials continued to arrive.

On the sofa, Solange remained in her mannequin posture, mouth open in a way that on stage might have looked provocative. But when a young officer bent over to flag her attention, she leaped into his arms as though he were her rescuer. Janey watched him walk her and Fudgsicle outside and prayed she wasn't confessing to the murder.

Limp and supple in Janey's arms, Lily reacted to nothing. Once so light-emitting and thermally strong, she felt as cold as her dead husband. The entirety of Janey's maternal instincts rushed forth to shield Lily from all intruders, though Janey knew she could not avoid speaking to the police.

Officer Diamond, who seemed kind, told Janey that Lily could be questioned later, and in a less emotionally charged environment. Janey thanked him, then after responding to a raft of horrible questions she answered in a detached daze, was advised she would be interviewed yet again at a later date. When the officer finally excused her, Janey guided Lily to the bathroom and ran water into the tub. The dogs led the way.

Shrugging off the afghan, her body streaked with blood, Lily stepped into the shallow water and flopped back against the porcelain. "I'm sorry," she said.

Janey wiped the hair off Lily's forehead. "What are you talking about, honey? You have nothing to be sorry about."

"Everything I ever told you—it was all wrong. My beliefs are wrong. They killed Gary. And I'm more dead than he is." Her voice sounded chillingly matter-of-fact.

Help me, Rosie, Janey implored. The thought of Lily abandoning her faith was intolerable, more than Janey's capacity to keep things together could withstand.

*Everything dies, baby that's a fact...but maybe everything that dies some day comes back...*Rosie communicated once again.

In these crucial moments Janey knew she had to summon enough faith for herself and Lily.

The water in the tub encroached on Lily's protruding abdomen; Janey stared into the eye of life—Lily's swollen bellybutton—until the water rose and washed over it.

From some unknown source a hot gust of wind toppled a small framed picture of Gary on the vanity. Lily didn't budge; Janey felt spooked, which was no longer unusual. A flash of light, like passing headlights reflected in a mirror, washed over Lily. She cried out, her hands cupped between her legs, lost in what appeared to be the ecstatic throes of a sudden and prolonged orgasm, moaning with what sounded like uninhibited, delirious joy.

Stunned, Janey tried to make sense of what she was witnessing. She decided to believe the most obvious explanation—that from wherever he was, Gary was still capable of making passionate love to Lily. That seemed unbearably hopeful.

But there was an alternate interpretation. Perhaps Lily was losing the baby, not having some uncanny orgasm. Perhaps the Goddess was protecting her from dying of heartbreak with a shot of endorphins.

Janey fled to the living room to get help. As she passed the flower chintz chair, it coughed up her emotions. The impact made her fall to the floor.

Rosie brought her a fuzzy toy.

31
JANEY & LILY

Following Officer Diamond, Janey led Lily and the leashed-up dogs out the back and around the house to avoid going through the crime scene formerly known as Lily's living room. Lily asked no questions and followed as obediently as the dogs. When they rounded the front of the house, which was wrapped in bright yellow tape, a young woman sprinted over. Face swollen, with bloodshot eyes, she extended two shaky arms. "Lily..." she said and threw her arms around her.

There was no reciprocal embrace.

"I'm Francesca," the woman said over Lily's shoulder, "Gary's bodyguard."

Janey nodded, her urgent look telling Francesca everything

she needed to know about Lily's condition.

"They had pagers," Francesca said in a cracked whisper. "I was three blocks away."

"It happened so fast," Janey said.

"Who was he?"

"Long story." Janey stroked the back of Lily's head and spoke to Francesca. "Lily and I are having a sleep-over at my house. Would you like to join us?"

Francesca nodded.

"I'll drive," said Francesca, who clearly needed a function.

Janey loaded the dogs in the back of Francesca's car while Francesca helped Lily into the front passenger seat.

"Oh," said Lily, holding up a baseball cap she'd lifted off the floor mat. "Gary thought he lost his Cubs hat but it was in your car all this time." Her voice sounded as if it had a built-in echo. She put the hat on and pulled it down over her eyes.

In the back seat with the dogs, head resting on her knees, Janey sobbed quietly during the half-mile ride home. She hoped the girls were asleep and felt somewhat relieved when Billy's car wasn't in the driveway; at least she didn't have to explain all this just yet. But where was he? It seemed like decades ago that he was fuming over Davy.

*Stranded in the park and forced to confess...*Rosie parlayed to her unspoken question.

What?

It's alright, it's alright, it's alright, yeah... Rosie assured her.

Those beautiful words comforted Janey and she knew that if things ever got back to normal she would spend most of her time exchanging telepathic Springsteen lyrics with her amazing dog, who continued to reveal new layers of brilliance, wisdom and, lately, supernaturality.

Dashing inside her house ahead of Francesca and Lily, Janey saw the girls in their sleep shirts watching Janey's favorite movie, *Dr. Strangelove.*

"Mom!" Sherri shrieked. "Where have you been? Where's Daddy?"

"Daddy's fine," Janey said, based solely on Rosie's affirmation. "I have to tell you something. Lily and her dogs and a friend are outside. When they come in please don't react. There was a terrible tragedy. Gary DiCaro was murdered." She hugged them both fiercely. "Please stay calm and act normal. Lily is still in shock."

Visibly stunned, the girls stood nervously when on Janey's nod, Francesca let the dogs in and followed Lily into the house. "I've heard a lot about you," Lily said like a recording.

"Same here," Sherri replied.

"We're having a slumber party," Janey said, because she didn't know what else to call the reason why they were there.

"I didn't bring my pajamas," Lily said.

"I have some you can wear," said Candi.

A sweet bit of kindness at a timely moment. "Thank you, sweetie," Janey said and gave her a love-squeeze. "That would be very nice. You all go upstairs and try on jammies and I'll make popcorn and lemonade."

As they went off to the pajama audition, Janey wondered what type of activities were appropriate for a post-murder-suicide sleepover. Actual slumber was probably low on the agenda but bedding needed tending to. She decided that Lily and Francesca would sleep in her bed, Janey would remain awake and if Billy came home he could repair to the old security sofa.

In the kitchen, she fired up the big aluminum kettle and poured in a cup of Newman's Own popcorn. The popping kernels banged like gunshots and only the sight of Rosie's brown eyes and touch of her soft fur kept Janey from exploding along with them.

Unnerving thoughts of Solange addled her. "Is Solange okay?" Janey asked Rosie.

*In the darkness on the edge of town...*conveyed Rosie, a notion that seemed fraught with danger.

"Tell her to call," Janey said.

***

Lily decided to try sending herself, cell by cell, to join Gary. She wasn't sure how to find him but she'd never get there in a physical body. Life was eternal and this way they could be united as a family, the way it was meant to be.

She was ready to go; the hard part would be keeping the baby safe.

It was a confusing situation that required multi-dimensional skill but she had no contact with the Goddess and couldn't remember what the problem was because her brain had blown a fuse. Her heart kept beating though she tried to shut it down. Nothing was inside it anymore—the beating served only to move blood to the baby.

The baby was strong—he was the only thing keeping her from severing all contact with her physical shell. Not even born and he was already fighting for control.

Another force was keeping her on Earth—Janey—holding on to her like a child with a kite. Her son's godmother, Janey was now immediate family and would make sure her baby survived if Lily left the physical plane. After Lily learned how to be conscious in both worlds at once she would come back.

Lily wanted to tell Janey how good the popcorn was and how much she loved her but she couldn't think of any words. Perhaps was already time traveling. If she was, she hoped she would soon find the portal that would take her to Gary. Meantime, she faded into a protective chamber that shut out the ferocious onslaught of thought, feeling and memory banging at its walls; it would remain her cramped haven from reality until further notice.

***

After fifteen excruciating minutes of the quietest, most somber slumber party of all time, Sherri and Candi excused themselves and went off to sleep in their own room. Alone with Lily and Francesca, who sat side by side on her bed: Francesca quietly working through a box of tissues, Lily staring into nowhere, Janey began to suffocate in unexpressed grief.

Faith will be rewarded...Rosie relayed to her, which seemed almost too hopeful to be true. Faith will be rewarded...Rosie repeated.

"Would anyone like some Ben & Jerry's?" Janey asked.

"I'll share some with Lily," Francesca said.

Lily's fingers made twitchy motions and Janey sensed Lily's critical need for protein. When Janey returned with a big bowl of Chunky Monkey she saw the Labs bestowing a harvest upon Lily: Rosie gave her a makeup bag, Blossom a scarf hanging from the coat rack and Bean a hand towel from the downstairs powder room.

Lily handled each gift and placed it next to her on the bed. Three vigorous dog tongues went to work on her face and arms; that Lily could resist them even a little frightened Janey deeply.

The dogs went back for a second round of treasures: a bottle of water from Bean, a paperback novel from Blossom and a pen from Rosie. Janey looked for any measure of healing—a flicker of Lily-light, a glowing coal in her dying furnace, but Lily seemed lost and disconnected. The ice cream remained in her lap.

Picking up the bowl, Francesca took a quick bite. "This is delicious. You've got to try it." She fed a spoonful to Lily, who accepted it like a baby. Francesca continued to feed her until it was gone.

"Well," Janey said, encouraged by one small victory, "maybe we should all get some sleep."

"Thank you, Janey," Francesca said, reaching out.

Janey went to hug Francesca but once in her arms the bodyguard slipped from her grasp like a bar of soap and sprawled out next to Lily. They both looked comatose.

Janey sensed the atmosphere thickening and the air turning soupy; she got up to open a window. The dogs were acting decidedly weird, looking around, wagging, showing flashy, knowing smiles.

Hovering above Lily and Francesca, Janey saw a pack of flying dogs—flying dogs—soaring into, over and through each other. A veritable canine traffic jam.

Bean, Blossom and Rosie were clearly enjoying the spectacle, which suggested to Janey that she had acquired dog vision. She couldn't determine if Lily and Francesca were truly asleep or in a dog-induced trance. Or if she was.

We have come to teach humans about humanity, the dogs informed her.

It was such hopeful and unexpected news, Janey decided to accept and even cherish the fact that she had lost her mind. Orbiting around her, the swirl of flying dogs gave her the sensation of an anti-gravity amusement park ride, then they atomized like TV static.

But just as she was struggling to push her reality boundary to allow flying dogs, the apparition of Gary DiCaro made her grow faint and grab hold of her heart. Somehow he had semi-materialized alongside Lily, cradling her as if she were a newborn. "Hi," he said.

This appeared to be an extremely wonderful if thoroughly shocking development. "Are you real?" she asked and thought: if he said no, could she believe him?

"It's good to see you, Janey."

"And it's great to see you," she replied. And hesitated before adding, "Am I seeing you?"

"Yes. The dogs have slowed down my frequency so you can see me. They're doing this, not me."

"Those flying dogs—are they friends of yours? Or are they a new manifestation of my madness?"

"You're not crazy, Janey. I need your help. Lily is trying to eject from her body."

Janey didn't know what that meant but it sure seemed accurate. Whether Gary was real or Memorex was irrelevant; Janey would do anything to save her friend. "What should I do?"

"Bring her back."

"How?"

"The dogs will guide you," Gary said. "Just listen and do what they suggest."

Peering into Rosie's eyes, Janey had the odd knowing that her dog was directly wired to all life on earth.

"I have to go," said Gary.

"Lily adores you," Janey blurted out. "And you were a

fabulous actor."

"I love Lily through all eternity."

"I believe you. I hope this isn't a dream so I can tell her you said that."

"Dreams are real," said Gary.

Janey had not expected to feel happy this evening but she did. "What else can I tell her? And will you come back and visit her when she's awake?"

"The baby," he said as his image began to fade. "He has my soul."

"What do you mean?"

Maybe everything that dies someday comes back...Rosie chimed in as Gary melted away.

"Wait," Janey called out to the darkened space he had just occupied. "I don't understand." She continued to stare, waiting for him to return and answer a barrage of questions. But a powerful wave of fatigue knocked her from behind and she landed unconscious at the foot of the bed.

32
JANEY

It was still dark when a wet terrier nose dampened Janey's ear and made her spring like a popover, somehow not disturbing Lily and Francesca asleep beside her. A leash dangled from Rosie's mouth. "Are you serious?" Janey whispered while she obediently got up. No sense arguing with a dog whose wisdom exceeded her own.

Janey felt vaguely hung over, a sense of spotty recall as though she'd been to a party but couldn't remember who'd brought her home. The night's horror came to mind vividly; nature lacked an antidote for witnessing a murder. But everything after that was murky.

Sleeping head-to-head in fetal positions, each with an arm gracefully aloft, Lily and Francesca resembled the open wings of a butterfly. Bean and Blossom's chins pressed into the mattress where Lily slept, as if they feared she might lift off if left unanchored.

Janey wrote a note saying she'd gone out with Rosie, would be back soon, and left it in the upstairs bathroom where it was bound to be seen. She poured a mug of leftover coffee and headed out the door after her intrepid scout.

Rosie went straight to Janey's unspoken destination— Solange's house. On the porch, a mangy neighborhood cat ate the last of the bowl of kibble Solange always kept filled. Janey knocked in vain. "Where is she?" she asked Rosie.

But when you get to the porch they're gone on the wind... One of Janey's favorite lines from "Thunder Road."

Janey thought it sadly ironic that the most fun game she'd ever played with Rosie—a game that left fetch in the dust—involved finding clues in Bruce Springsteen lyrics that would lead to her missing friend. "Gone on the wind" sounded ominous.

Both Solange and Lily were out of contact, untethered from reality. And since she had always been the sane one of the three—although she had surrendered supervision to her dog— she felt compelled to rescue them. She scribbled an order for Solange to go directly to Janey's house and left it jammed in the door, shot a desperate look down the street. Deserted. Silent.

While Rosie navigated in the darkness of so many Springsteen songs, Janey sang passages from "Badlands" to keep her anxiety tolerable. As they approached the pine tree, Rosie stopped and pawed the back of Janey's shoe.

Someone was groaning. The voice sounded nothing like Solange. Janey tensed.

"Janey?"

"Billy?" He was lying under the tree, wrapped in the Navajo Indian blanket that had swaddled him on the sofa for half the summer. He wiped his eyes on the sleeve of his UCLA sweatshirt. "What are you doing here?" she asked.

"Were you looking for me?"

"The girls are terrified. We were all worried."

Rosie head-butted Billy's shoulder and he responded to her request for petting. "I'm sorry. It got too late to call."

She had no energy for confrontation. Falling into him, she burrowed beneath the fuzzy blanket, seeking consolation against his chest. "I witnessed a murder-suicide," she mumbled.

"What?"

"Gary DiCaro is dead. And the man who murdered him shot himself."

Billy tensed and shuddered. "What? You saw that?"

She nodded, her cheek brushing soft cotton jersey.

He clutched her. "Thank God you're all right."

Billy's shirt was quickly drenched in a liberation of tears. "I'm not all right."

"I'm so sorry Janey," he said, "I'm sorry..."

"Billy..." Their bodies smashed together in delirious submission. Frantically, his hands reached for every inch of her at once.

"I love you Janey. I never stopped. I've been so...fucked up."
He kissed her lips, up and down her arms, across her neck,
under her chin, scarcely pausing for breath. "Something snapped
last night, Janey. I need you. Come back to me."

"I need you too, Billy." A sharp cramp punctuated her words;
her period was commencing. She had the sense it had been
pooling inside her, awaiting Billy to unleash it.

He seduced her with a force just short of rape, making short
work of her jeans and tee shirt, unhooking her bra with two-
fingered dexterity and sliding off her panties like they were
greased. If he noticed the red stain in the crotch, it didn't stop
him from closing his mouth over the lips of her vagina, drinking
in its blood and juices. His tongue traveled deep inside her;
farther it seemed, than his penis ever had. Surely he was aware
of her condition by now but he forged on, undaunted or perhaps
inspired by contact with her secretions.

His tongue reached her magic spot and sent her on an
orgasmic joy ride that reverberated in at least five encores. He
threw off his clothes and plunged inside her, making love with a
youthful endurance she thought no longer possible. The banshee
cry of his climax warned any wolves in the neighborhood that he
was, and always would be, The Man.

Afterwards they dissolved into a puddle. Light began to creep
in—enough for Billy to see the red blotches between Janey's
legs. Gently, he brushed his fingers through the sticky color and
brought it to his lips.

*May I feel your blood mix with mine...*Rosie cited and Janey
felt an exquisite stab of pain. Billy kissed her and his fingers
searched for more red that he painted on his face. Before her
eyes he had transformed into a fearless Indian warrior. "Okay?"

he whispered. "Okay?"

"Okay."

33
SOLANGE

Solange had been to countless motels in her life, but she had never checked into one by herself. The Valium she'd taken at the police station kept her hand steady as she signed "Rita Barthalomew," the name of the third grade teacher who'd been a childhood crush. She paid for two nights in cash.

Sprawled on a lumpy bed in a bland, plain-wrap room overlooking Ventura Boulevard, she donned the most cheerful voice she could fake and called Joie's mother, Fern, to get Joie's number in Paonia. Fern sounded delighted to hear from her and made it clear she had hoped Solange and Joie would get back together. Then she started gabbing about the shocking Hollywood murder; fortunately, she sounded unaware of any connection between Solange and Gary, or that her own daughter had recently lived with Gary's killer.

As if she'd been expecting the call, Joie picked up the phone on the first ring. "I'm leaving right now," she told Solange. "I'll be there in thirteen hours."

Solange popped another Valium and slept in fitful spells for a few troubled hours, ordered a pizza, watched a marathon of tawdry talk shows, went for a walk with Fudgsicle, cried for most of an hour, took another Valium, showered and waited. Twelve-and-a-half hours later, Joie arrived.

"I'm so glad you're all right," she said, crushing Solange to her chest.

"Thank you for coming."

"I'm always here for you, honey. I got here so fast, I only stopped once to pee." She ran in place. "Stay right there!" And danced into the bathroom.

Solange picked up Fudgsicle and nestled him between her breasts. "Happy to see Aunt Joie?" she asked.

Fudgsicle growled and his body began to hum like an engine. Startled, she set him back down on the bed and noticed a bright halo surrounding him—the same kind of iridescent light she'd seen around Lily and Gary in Las Vegas. She lifted him up again and touched him to her cheek. The buzzing resumed.

"Man, I peed a quart," Joie said when she returned from the bathroom.

"Shhhhh." Solange held Fudgsicle up against the drab green curtains and watched his colors shift from pink to gold, purple and white. "Do you see that?"

"What?"

"Fudgsie's aura. It keeps changing colors, like those light pillars at LAX."

Joie looked around. "I think we both could use some rest."

"No, no, he's trying to tell me something."

When Joie reached out to pet him he acted aloof, as if she were a stranger. "What's the matter, buddy?" She tousled his ears. "Don't you remember me?"

Fudgsicle growled again.

"He's traumatized. We both are."

"Of course. You've both been through a major ordeal. But I'm here now and I'll make everything all right."

Her trembling dog cradled on her chest, Solange sat on the

bed and hung her head. "I'll never be all right."

Joie slid in beside her and pulled her close. "Sol, I've thought about this situation non-stop since you called. I don't think this had anything to do with you. Marvin was very angry, very disturbed. He hated gay guys. I think he was molested by a priest when he was a kid. He never said, but I had my suspicions. Bottom line, he was dangerously homophobic and he acted out."

"That's not what happened, Joie. It was my fault." Solange felt dizzy and laid back on the bed. Joie did the same. Fudgsicle burrowed in Solange's cleavage and purred.

"You're wrong about that, Sol. Trust me." She moved a strand of Solange's hair and kissed her on the cheek.

Now or never, Solange decided. "The reason Marvin killed Gary is because he wanted to be the father of my baby and I turned him down."

Vaulting as if she'd sat on a tack Joie shouted, "What baby?"

"This one," said Solange, pointing to her belly. "Gary's baby."

"What?"

"It's a long story. I already told the police."

"Well, I've been driving for the past thirteen hours, so I didn't have a chance to hear it."

Solange wished she had taped the endless questions she had answered at the police station. "About two months ago I started having visions of Andi Nyler and she told me she was coming back. She wants to be reborn as my daughter."

"Jesus!" Joie blanched. "You told that to the cops?"

"They asked for the whole story so I told them."

She watched Joie blink, clear her throat and collect herself. "Okay, go ahead."

"When we were at the fetish club...I saw two guys kissing and

I thought one of them was Gary. I didn't tell Lily because I didn't want to hurt her. Then I told Marvin about Andi and he offered me a million dollars and a college education if I would let him be the father."

"What?" Joie got up and paced. "What?" Back and forth, back and forth. "What?" It began to make Solange nauseous.

"I told him I'd think about it and then I was watching *Rumor-ama* and this Gary clone was on it—he was the guy I actually saw at the fetish club. I totally freaked."

Joie rubbed her forehead with both hands. "This is one weird friggin' story."

"It made me realize that Andi wanted Gary to be her father. And he agreed. But Marvin was following me and when he found out Gary's the father he went nuts."

"Are you telling me you're pregnant?"

"Yes."

"And Gary DiCaro gave you his sperm?"

"Yes."

"And Lily said okay to that?"

"She made it happen."

"Unbelievable!" Joie clapped her hands to the sides of her head. "Were you all planning to live together in some hippie commune?"

"No, I'm going to raise my baby on my own."

A hopeful look replaced Joie's anger. "Well, maybe you don't have to. Maybe this is some really crazy answer to our prayers. Remember, Sol, how we talked about having kids?"

Solange thought it must be a very twisted God who would contrive such a dark turn of events to make Joie's dreams come true. "I want the baby to grow up in a safe place," she said, trying to re-envision a blissful life in the rural hinterlands of Paonia. "I can't stay here. I can't live here anymore."

"I'm ready to hit the road right now," said Joie, looking energized. "We can send for your stuff later." She patted Solange on the shoulder. "I've still got plenty of clout at UPS."

It was way too sudden but Solange was no longer at the helm of her life. "I have to be here for the police."

That gave Joie momentary pause. "Okay, here's the plan. We'll hole up at the house for awhile. And then, when you get the all-clear from the cops, we're on the road."

"I don't want to go to the house. There might be reporters there."

Joie continued her pacing. "No problem. I'll go over and secure the premises. You rest. I'll be right back." She was out the door before Solange could say goodbye.

Alone, with a new future to consider, Solange felt a gushing sadness from a dark place in her soul, the source of all those uncontrollable crying spells. So huge was the tragedy, she realized she'd been reacting to it months before it occurred. She sobbed an intense finale, and when she was finished, surrendered to an instant and profound sleep.

Hours later, she awakened in a claustrophobic panic, certain the room had shrunk, that noxious fumes were permeating the atmosphere and that the ghosts of a thousand murderers had trampled her as she'd lain there, calling her name, inviting her to join them.

Then she saw Fudgsicle, a nightlight shining in the gloom. She reached for him and brushed his fur against her cheek. He hummed like a tuning fork. She let him wiggle into her cleavage and felt restored by his soothing vibrations until a sharp knock at the door made her get up.

In the hallway Joie held up a bowl of dog food. "Got meat?"

Fudgsicle grumbled.

"Ya didn't feed him," said Joie, waving the bowl under the Yorkie's nose. "That's why he was shaking. I checked the house— no reporters. And about what you told me—the baby—I'm sorry if I overreacted."

Solange nodded.

"Do you mind if I ask you something?"

"Depends."

"About getting pregnant...when you said that Lily made it happen...what did that mean exactly?"

It was bound to come up, sooner or later. "It means I had sex with Gary."

Seared by the truth, Joie howled, "Fuuuuck!"

"The father of my baby is dead," Solange reminded her. "He was murdered. Why don't you yell 'fuck' about that?"

"Look, I cried for the guy, okay? I cried all the way from Utah to Nevada. I cried for poor fuckin' Marv too." She spat out a bucket of air. "I'm just a little shocked, that's all. How could she let you bang her husband?"

"Because she's a beautiful person and it was a beautiful experience. Maybe that's hard for you to understand."

"As a matter of fact it is hard to understand. But how was it? Are you straight now?" she asked, lips straight as a coin slot.

"I don't want to talk about this, Joie. You are not honoring my feelings at all."

"Oh, excuse me. What about my feelings? Look what's happened since you hooked up with that one-woman freak show. Two people are dead!"

Solange felt the need to scream and did, loud enough to pin Joie to the wall. "Shut up! Just shut up! I never should have called you. You'll never understand me."

"You got that right," Joie snapped. "Sure glad I dropped everything and drove thirteen hours for this shit." She tossed her car keys and snatched them in the air. "Goodbye, Solange." And she was out the door.

The next morning, Solange had convinced herself that Paonia was an unsuitable place for Andi and Fudgsicle—she'd never liked cold weather anyway. But she couldn't go back. She could never go back. Everything she touched had turned to death and heartache. She packed up the few things she'd brought to the motel, tossed them into her car, secured Fudgsie in his seat harness and headed south.

34
GODDESSES

At six A.M., prior to the morning stampede at the park, Rosie nudged Janey and Billy, who were wrapped together under the pine tree. Janey woke up from an overpowering dream that evaporated in the alarm she felt over falling asleep. She hadn't found Solange. If Candi and Sherri were awake they were surely frantic. And she'd left two women suffering at a catastrophic level asleep in her bedroom.

"We've got to go," she told Billy. "Did the girls call?"

Billy glanced at his phone, shook his head. He pulled her close; his touch felt insanely masculine. "Don't worry. I'm here."

She couldn't take her eyes off him; it was as if a sandcastle had blown away to reveal a fortress. A fortress whose face was streaked with her blood.

"Stay right there," she told him and went to the drinking fountain to wet some Kleenex. "Not that you don't look cute as Geronimo." As she wiped off the red marks she thought: Lily was right. I sent out my blood and Billy came back to me. She felt a surge of hope.

They got up to leave. The air was cool and Billy held the blanket around them. His touch felt sublime; she felt safe and protected until spotting in the distance a sudden, dreadful intrusion: Cleo, heading toward them, Trixie marching in her shadow.

"Hey, Bruce freak," Cleo called out.

Horrified, Janey took a reflexive jump to shield Rosie but her brave terrier seemed quite calm in the presence of her human attacker. Trixie inched forward and the two dogs met in a sniff-fest. "What?" Janey said in a way she hoped reeked with go-away inflection.

Cleo bellied up to her. "You took my note, didn't you?"

"What note?" As if an earthly reason existed to covet a personal item of Cleo's.

"The one that Ricky left that morning you and your dog accosted me," Cleo growled.

Janey couldn't think of a reply that didn't include the words "ten-foot pole." She shrugged, hands extended.

"He said he had to catch a plane. He was going out of town and would see me in a week, under the tree, seven o'clock. He was going to take me to dinner at fucking Todai. All you can eat sushi. I fucking love sushi."

"I never saw any note," Janey said.

"Bullshit, garbage freak. You threw it away."

Janey did recall picking up trash with Lily that morning. "You should have put it in a safe place."

"I never saw the fucking thing, okay? Ricky thought I stood him up. He never got my phone number. I haven't seen him in four fucking months. And now he's getting fucking married!"

Somewhere, a lucky guy named Ricky had been saved from a lifetime of misery by Janey's act of tidiness. "That's too bad, Cleo," she said and when they hurried away, Janey didn't know whether to laugh or cry but somehow she felt encouraged.

***

Before Billy could get the key in the door, Sherri's arms looped around his and Janey's necks and clanged their heads together. "I was so worried," she said. "But you're together."

"I'm sorry honey," Janey said. "Are you okay?"

Sherri nodded.

"Are they sleeping?" Janey asked, pointing upstairs.

"I don't know. I've been waiting for you. I'm making breakfast. Candi and Grandma are with Lily and Francesca."

"Grandma?"

"She felt left out so Candi brought her in. I heard her telling them about the *Tonight Show*, but I think they're too sad to talk about it."

As Sherri spoke, Janey became momentarily unhinged, convinced she'd just seen a dog fly into the living room and out the front window, leaving a glittery vapor trail. She chalked it up to stress. "I'd better go up there."

Sherri restrained Billy in a Daddy-hold. "Daddy, will you help me with breakfast?"

Father and daughter repaired to the kitchen while Janey went upstairs to find her bedroom transformed into a girly sweat lodge. Lily and Francesca were in her bed. Francesca had an arm around Lily, who stared intently at nothing in particular. Candi was draped across the foot of the bed, head propped up by her elbow, remnants of Boy George makeup staining her face.

Sprung from her wheelchair, Eleanor reclined on the chaise lounge by the window, a tragic silent movie actress. "Where were you?" she asked, left eyebrow slanted higher than the right.

Truth was out of the question; Janey was not capable of explaining anything that had happened in the past twelve hours, let alone her actions. "I was out with Rosie."

"You have guests. You shouldn't be out with the dog."

"You're right, Grandma," Janey said, trying but failing to separate Lily's gaze from the old braided rug next to the bed. A quiet descended; Janey sensed the room had been hushed prior to her intrusion. So dim was Lily's light, it made everything seem darker. Janey slipped onto the bed beside Lily and enfolded her. "How are you, sweetie?" she said, praying for the familiar heat to return, but Lily felt cool and weightless.

"I'm looking for Gary," said Lily; it sounded less like an announcement than the state of her existence.

Janey felt a chill. "Gary will always be with you, sweetie, but we need you here. You have a baby to grow. You know he loves you through all eternity."

Unexpectedly, Candi broke down sobbing, something she never did for any reason, though this was surely a time beyond reason. "Mom, I have something to tell you." She looked up at Janey. "I'm so sorry," she wept.

Breathlessly Janey waited for Candi's confession but the sound of Sherri and Billy's feet lumbering up the stairs made her clam up and left Janey in a chokehold of suspense, compounded by the ominous certainty that a meteor was about to strike.

"Breakfast is ready," Sherri announced, marching in with bowls of steaming oatmeal on a tray, Billy following with cream, butter and sugar. When Billy reacted to Janey's panicked expression, she head-signaled him toward Candi, who sat curled up on the bed, hugging her knees, looking down. After dumping the trays on the bed, Billy and Sherri quickly sat down together on the beanbag chair from Candi's room.

"I guess I should tell you all," Candi said, then paused a brief eternity before blurting, "I'm pregnant. I was going to get an abortion and not tell anyone."

Meteor. Impact.

"Oh my God," Sherri squealed. "Why didn't you tell me?"

Candi's many-ringed hand went up, pleading for silence. "But what happened tonight...to Lily..." she continued, "it made me change my mind. I feel like her baby and my baby made friends."

Weakened, Janey fell back into Eleanor's wheelchair but managed to keep her arms open for Candi to rush into. Candi clung to her mightily.

"You were having sex with that hoodlum when I fell," Eleanor said, speaking from the stage in life when it is no longer possible to be fazed.

Rosie sought Janey's attention and Janey gratefully yielded to her. *Janey had a baby...it wasn't any sin...* They were crucial lines from the song "Spare Parts." Timely guidance, penned by her savior, dispensed through her dog, sparked by her intimate relationship to the Goddess—proof enough for Janey of the profound meaning in this latest development. If Candi, her unspiritual daughter, could sense two unborn souls reaching out to each other, there could be no coincidence that the Reddi-wip Sisters were all expecting babies—in one way or another.

"It's okay, honey," Janey said. "You did the right thing."

35
GODDESSES

The following day, Janey's house became an auxiliary command post for a murder-suicide investigation and Janey became *über*-caretaker. But overseeing everyone was the angel Francesca: Director of Operations, task coordinator and liaison to the screaming Outside World. Francesca dealt firmly with the media and seemed to have a close personal relationship with every police officer in the San Fernando Valley. "I loved Gary," she told Janey. "I'll do whatever I can for as long as you need me."

She arranged to have Lily's ob-gyn make a house call. The doctor found nothing physically wrong with Lily or the baby. After the visit Janey and Francesca moved Lily into the living room where she could be constantly watched over, but despite the new environment and increased attention, Lily continued to study the walls with Stepford-wife vacancy.

Billy helped by debuting an actual skill he'd learned in Hawaii—cooking. In the afternoon, with the girls' help as sous chefs, he grilled fifteen pounds of Jerk Chicken. The dish moved Janey to tears—not because of its fiery ingredients, but because her reclaimed, sensitive and generous husband had created it.

"I love you," Janey said to the neckband of his apron as he pulled another batch off the fire. It was the same apron Davy had worn forty-eight extremely long hours ago.

"Ancient recipe from the Big Island," Billy said and they kissed, right in front of Sherri.

"Oh, my God," said Sherri, "I've never seen you do that."

"Want to see it again?" Billy asked.

***

Solange couldn't wait to get off the 405 with its perpetual rush hour that heightened her anxiety even on a good day, which this clearly wasn't. She'd driven just fifteen miles when she was spirited off the freeway at Venice Blvd. The pull grew stronger as she turned right on Lincoln, then up Flower Avenue.

The once uniformly white cottages had evolved to earthy pastels since she'd last seen them. Andi's house had fresh-looking mauve paint with dark green shutters. But a few doors down, Solange's house hadn't changed at all; its shabbiness in light of the surrounding upgrades made her forlorn. She parked between two hybrid cars.

Freed from his seat harness, Fudgsicle ran directly to Andi's front porch, scratched on the door and wiggled his tail. "That's right, smartie-pie," Solange said, knocked out by his intelligence. "It's Andi's house." She swiped him up and walked down to her old house. In the weedy front yard, Fudgsie marked the prickly ivy bush that used to scratch her skin. She wondered if his urine had any kind of mystical powers, an easier question to deal with than how her loving intentions managed to cause the deaths of two people in an instant.

As if it could supply the answers Solange studied the house and moved a few steps up the driveway. She yearned to peek into her bedroom through the side window but fearing she might be taken for a trespasser, reconsidered and turned back.

As she bent down to retrieve Fudgsicle, he was nowhere in sight.

Briefly paralyzed, her voice finally burst forth. "Fudgsie!" "Fudgsicle!" He had never run off, not even to chase a squirrel. She had no contingency procedure. When he didn't respond to her calls she threw up on the Azalea bush, incapable of handling this much stress.

But there was no option but to handle it. After ten minutes of frantic searching, retracing her steps, trespassing anywhere and everywhere she could, she thought she might soon keel over and die on the spot.

"How could this happen?" she shouted to her old neighborhood sky, then looked down the street and saw a bicycle in the distance. As it grew closer, it looked like a Phthalo Blue-colored bicycle ridden by a young girl. Solange had no time to process that because in the next moment she saw Fudgsicle sitting in the middle of the street, directly in the bicycle's path.

He was glowing.

Solange screamed and ran to him.

The girl screeched to a stop inches from the Yorkie's tiny body and kicked down her foot brake as Solange snatched him up and pressed him to her chest.

"Is that a real dog?" asked the girl, whose resemblance to Andi made the encounter even more unsettling.

"Are you a real girl?" Solange asked her.

The girl laughed and rode off toward the beach.

36
GODDESSES

It confused Lily when Candi said their babies were friends. She thought about Solange's baby, who was also Gary's creation and her own baby's sister. They were already family. They should be together. She needed to find Gary and bring him back.

Someone was touching her with warm hands; it was Janey, filled with beautiful light, grounding her signal. But it wasn't right without Solange. "Solange will be here soon," Janey said and Lily was amazed because she didn't remember speaking, had lost most of her words.

Lily could feel the Goddess spirit alive in Janey but not in herself. She needed Gary and it was up to Lily to bring him back. If she were multi-dimensional like the dogs she could divide her consciousness and search for him while she waited for Solange, but she wasn't in any dimension; she was in the crawlspace between life and death and Janey was keeping her alive. "I love you Janey." They were the first words she'd said in awhile.

Exploding in brightness Janey said, "I love you too, sweetie. I'll do anything for you. Just name it."

That felt good, a sweet tug from Earth. "I need to see Solange before I go."

"No, you're not going anywhere!" Francesca cried out and through dulled vision, Lily saw Francesca's sad, wet face and felt a powerful, trembling hand take her arm. "I'm so sorry, Lily. I should have been there. I should have saved him." Francesca's shuddering and weeping pulled Lily down, made it harder to disconnect from her body.

"I'll find him," Lily assured Francesca and felt herself being squeezed very hard, hard enough to burn up more cells and help her find release. Watching Janey beam love on everyone, Lily knew Janey was meant to be her son's godmother; she was free to go.

Then all of a sudden Solange showed up.

Lily couldn't determine if she had walked in or dropped from the ceiling, but though Lily's earthly senses were disintegrating, when Solange arrived she felt a spectacular wallop inside her: their babies, calling out to each other, more exuberant than a New Year's celebration.

***

The bang of the door knocker came at a moment when Janey was positive the room had reached maximum sorrow. Seeing Solange and Fudgsicle, accompanied by super-charged Billy who had bounded downstairs to answer the door, was better than a rescue from the cavalry. Janey had to close her eyes hard for a few seconds to take it in.

"Where've you been?" Eleanor asked in her I'm-old-I-can-be-blunt way.

Using Fudgsicle as a chin rest, looking painfully sad, Solange said, "It's kind of a long story."

"Would you rather tell us later?" Janey asked.

"Yes." Solange put Fudgsicle down on the bed where he received a group smell from the other dogs and gave off a faint illumination. Janey wondered if anyone else noticed.

"Does your dog have batteries?" Eleanor asked.

"He's been doing that all day," said Solange.

Sherri moved in for a closer look. "That is totally amazing."

"He's transforming energy," Janey said in a casually savvy way while marveling that until that moment she had no idea what transforming energy meant. "Right, Lily?"

Lily remained a reclining mannequin and Fudgsicle decided to climb aboard her lap and knead her, aglow all the while. She stroked his head but only her hand seemed involved. If Lily couldn't respond to a glowing dog...that was painfully worrisome.

"See how he's glowing?" Janey said, smoothing Lily's hair. "He's talking to you in your special language."

Gingerly, Solange sat down on the bed next to Lily and moved closer to her. "I was going to go away forever. I felt like I broke the world. Fudgsicle made me come back." Delicately she laid her hand on Lily's shining tummy. "Our babies are siblings. Even if you blame me for everything I can't interfere with that."

In the quiet that followed Janey could hear Fudgsicle's miniature feet pawing Lily, who resumed petting him, which brought forth more light. The dogs swathed Lily and licked her with powerful affection, the way they had when Gary lay dying on her floor. But it seemed to make little impression.

Solange began to rub Lily's feet and Sherri leaped up to provide a bottle of hand lotion.

Janey thought it the ideal time for Rosie to jump in and give her the perfect Bruce lyric that would explain everything and tell her what to do but she got the impression that Rosie felt it was time for Janey to stand on her own, to take action, to shed her transient identity and reveal herself as...the dog whisperer. It was easily the most bizarre impulse she'd ever had, but she wanted to embrace it.

Janey sensed words coming to her, but before she could utter them she took a few bounces on the diving board, gathering courage from the dogs, who cheered her on in their panting vernacular. "Lily, your baby needs you," Janey commanded. "Return to Earth right this second! If you don't, Francesca will use force!"

It wasn't very spiritual but it got Lily's attention.

And Francesca's, who sat bolt upright.

"What?" said Lily, the way people answer the phone in the middle of the night.

"Look," Janey said. "Your baby is putting on a show."

The light in Lily's tummy bounced all over the place.

"I've got to go," Lily said, barely a whisper. "I have to find Gary."

"No," Janey admonished. "You have to stay here and take care of your baby."

In a small voice Lily said, "I'm already gone."

"Should we get her to a doctor?" Billy asked.

"This is up to me and Rosie," Janey said, making the momentous decision to assume full responsibility for Lily and her baby. After all, she was the baby's godmother. She saw Rosie's tail whipping up a storm and her eyes burning with approval.

Woman and canine locked psyches on the channel they shared, where Bruce Springsteen lyrics traveled, where knowledge between species was traded. And the message came through: Janey's *sensei* wanted her to sing.

She was a terrible singer; Billy customarily made the sign of the cross when he was in range of her warbling, but this was a holy command. Besides, Billy's steady, adoring gaze bespoke unabashed love and a range of acceptance so wide, she was even permitted to sing.

"Okay," Janey told Rosie and without warning, burst into "Badlands." "'I believe in the love that you gave me...I believe in the faith that can save me...I believe in the hope and I pray that someday it will raise me...above these Badlands...'" She imagined Bruce alongside her, lips to lips on the same mike, for Bruce's energy could raise anyone up, even his imagined energy.

Her head bobbing like a junkie, Lily seemed to be fading. But the light coming from her belly grew stronger.

"Lily, it's Gary!" said Francesca. "He's sending you a signal."

Thunderstruck, Janey stopped singing. "That's right," she said. "It is him. I've never been so sure of anything in my life." Memory-flashes of Gary fired off in her brain; she felt his presence as intensely as a bear hug. He was inside Lily, manufacturing light.

Solange laid her head on Lily's stomach.

In flickering signs of life—fluttering eyes, a lick of her lips—Lily seemed to finally be becoming aware of the miraculous reality playing out in her body.

Solange placed Lily's hand on her glowing pregnancy.

Lily moved her hands over her womb and made sounds like the ones she'd made in her bathtub. Janey paused in mid-breath, wondering what intimate experience she might next be sharing with her entire family. But gauging their reaction, they seemed entranced, as though a religious ceremony had taken a supernatural turn.

"Janey," Lily called out.

"What, sweetie? I'm here."

Lily's fingers busily moved over her mid-section. "Gary is making that light."

"Yes, he is."

"He's here."

"He's very here."

Eleanor narrowed her eyes at Billy. "Did you put something funny in the oatmeal?"

The good-natured smile and head shake Billy gave Eleanor was a moment of domestic reconciliation that sent love tingles up Janey's spine.

A hint of color returned to Lily's complexion. "Do you remember when your babies' souls entered your body?" she asked Janey.

"All I remember is heartburn."

"I felt him come into me, Janey. When I was in the bathtub. That's when it happened."

"Oh, so that's what that was." In the midst of her profound astonishment, Janey wondered why, when Candi and Sherri's souls entered her body, she hadn't experienced an earth-shaking orgasm.

"I was looking for Gary but he's here," Lily said. "His new life is in me."

"You mean he's already reincarnated?" Francesca asked. "Is that possible?"

"Gary is magic," Lily said. "He would never leave us." Lily reached for Francesca and Janey's hands and placed them on her stomach where a wild party had just broken out. "Feel that? He's giving us high fives."

"I do," Janey said. "And you know what? He's still the most charismatic star in Hollywood."

Seeing the smile on Lily's face, a blissful virus that quickly infected everyone in the room, Janey felt like giving a high five to everyone in the universe.

37
GODDESSES

On what would have been Gary DiCaro's fortieth birthday, Roberta Landers came to Dog House—the Santa Barbara mountain retreat run by Janey, Solange and Lily—to tape a TV special. Just open, Dog House already had a two-year waiting list for seekers of spiritual advancement.

Janey enjoyed daily spells of astonishment over the transformation of her formerly uneventful life. Once she'd thought of herself as an empty sweat suit, her mind a parking lot for problems and despair. These days her mind was a cosmic superhighway jammed with messages of hope and inspiration by and for humans and dogs. Beyond Springsteen lyrics—the language she had learned through Rosie to translate dog communiqués—she had become a true interspecies mediator. It was a fun job. Dogs had fascinating thoughts. They weren't thoughts, exactly, which was why she needed Rosie, a dog who bridged the species gap as she did. She was a true bona fide goddess. Within every goddess, there is Dog.

***

While the three women sat with Roberta in whimsical benches that Davy had built in the hanging gardens, a migrating blanket of babies crawled over them. The gardens themselves had become a major tourist attraction—after visitors learned that the plants' robust health was due to female menses, many women who were able accepted an invitation to donate. Dog House was a spiritual and terrestrial nursery—everything and everyone grew here.

Adding to today's tableau: artfully posed smiling dogs, because as Rosie always reminded Janey, smiling causes happiness. And this was an abundantly happy gathering indeed. Little red-haired Giorgio sat on Lily's knee; Janey found it amusing that the toddler with Gary's soul looked exactly like his mother. And it had been solemnly agreed among those who were in Janey's bedroom when his soul's identity was revealed, that they would keep the knowledge secret even from Giorgio until such time, they were convinced, he might figure it out for himself.

Cuddling Fudgsicle in her lap, Roberta began the interview. "Janey, in your upcoming book, *God Spelled Backwards*, you say that you merge with dog consciousness. Explain that."

"It's hard to describe," Janey said, "because dogs don't use words. I just have a vacant space in my brain that dogs figured out how to exploit."

"And dogs speak through Bruce Springsteen lyrics?"

"That's just how Rosie speaks to me because that's the easiest way for her to get my attention. We all get messages constantly, from all kinds of sources. If you can let your mind step aside for a moment, you'll hear them. Springsteen lyrics speak to me. It's a language, a shortcut. But everyone gets communication from the universe. You just have to be receptive."

Roberta reached over and tousled Fudgsicle's head with her fingers. "So what is it you want to tell people?"

Speaking in her diminutive Yorkie voice while her year-old granddaughter Bobbi Jean giggled and cooed, Janey said on Fudgsicle's behalf, "Find the joy in every moment and love unconditionally, especially yourself."

"That's it?"

"That's it," Janey said. "Dogs have shown us how to live and love for countless eons but we just don't get it, so now they're actually speaking to us."

"Why dogs?" Roberta asked.

"C'mon, Roberta, what other species will put up with us? They're praying that one day we'll finally catch up with them."

"Dogs are love amplifiers," Lily said, hugging Blossom with one arm while in her lap, Giorgio clapped Bean on the nose with his chubby palm. "They intensify the love you feel and that love infuses the world. Making more love is the only way to create peace on earth."

"Are dogs superior to humans?"

"All life is equal," Solange said. "We're a huge bunch of energy that's all connected. But life would be better if humans adopted dog values."

Roberta winked. "Will we all have to drink out of the toilet now?"

"The dogs want us to stop messing up their water dish," Janey said with perfect comic timing, having heard that remark numerous times.

"And sniffing each others' rear ends?"

"Not for humans," said Solange. She picked up Fudgsicle and held his backside to the camera. "Dogs have special glands here. They get all kinds of information about each other from smelling. It's like their MySpace page."

"I'm wearing perfume," Roberta said to the dogs. "I hope you approve."

"The dogs smell beyond your perfume," Lily said, "to many

layers of your aroma field."

Moving into Roberta's aura for a polite whiff, Solange declared, "You smell awesome."

In a spontaneous smell-a-thon, everyone, dogs included, paused to take in the prevailing aromas. Janey always found it thrilling to connect feelings with fragrances. She detected some anxiety around Roberta but the dogs were busy neutralizing it.

"It's all about intent," Lily said. "The dogs teach us how to alter our environmental conditions, and how to develop our scent consciousness. Like if you have toxins around you and you want things to be pure, you can transform them to newborn baby smells. Babies have no toxins; they smell like purity and innocence."

"I thought dogs like to roll in things that smell terrible," said Roberta.

"Oh, they do," Janey said, "to mask their odor for hunting purposes, but we're starting to learn things about their world—the world of smell—and it's a big learning curve so it'll take awhile. But it's so amazing that we want to share it with everyone."

"They showing us how to develop our smell perceptions," Lily said. "We may not have their capacity for odor but smell has its own language and that's one thing they're teaching us."

"How?" asked Roberta. "Do they hold classes?"

"In a way," Janey said. "They show us things. Dogs can teach us a lot more than we can teach dogs. Sit, fetch, roll over—not exactly particle physics."

Roberta leaned over and addressed Rosie. "What can you tell me?"

"She's suggesting more fiber and exercise," Janey said. "And keep an eye on that mole on your upper back. Just a precaution for now."

Looking startled, Roberta adjusted herself on the bench. "My goodness. You could be right about that, Rosie."

"Count on it," Solange said. "Rosie's a medical intuitive."

"You might want to add beans and lentils to your diet," said Lily.

"So is Lily," Janey said.

"Thank you both." Roberta spread her arms, indicating the verdant landscape. "Now, let's talk about these lush surroundings. Fertilized with...your own menstrual blood." She shook her head in apparent amazement.

"Ours and also our guests," Janey said. "Some women plan their vacations here around their periods."

Roberta continued her slow head shaking. "It sounds bizarre but I must admit I've never seen plants and foliage as vibrant and healthy looking as these. It's absolutely breathtaking."

Janey reached out and squeezed Roberta's arm. "Thank you for the testimonial, Roberta, and we'd like to encourage women everywhere to put their menses into Mother Earth wherever they are. Earth will respond. Your plants will thrive." Janey looked over at Billy standing with the crew—smolderingly handsome, bursting with testosterone. They had a few moments of telepathic sex. "You'll become magnetic."

Lily laughed and rocked Giorgio. "This is so much fun. I used to be the weird one."

***

As she walked arm in arm with Solange Roberta said, "Three years ago, you were a stripper. Now you're a businesswoman, a painter whose work is called 'metaphysical folk art' and the mother of Gary DiCaro's daughter, Andi. I know you're proudest of the last title."

Holding one-year-old Andi on her arm, in pink, paint-spattered overalls hung low over a white tee shirt stretched across majestic breasts that baby-feeding had only fortified, Solange gave Andi a smooch. "Andi is the most beautiful person I know—just like her father. She's pure love. All our babies are."

Cameras tracked them to the Dalmatian Building, which featured Solange's work-in-progress wall art.

"Tell me about this charming mural," Roberta said.

"It's called Flying Dogs," Solange said, briefly wondering if Daphne Isenberg was watching and was having second thoughts about her talent. Using her sable brush as a sweeping pointer, Solange highlighted a pack of winged dogs soaring through a starry violet sky. "These are dog angels," she said, then pointed to other dogs who were sitting in trees, lying paws-up and chasing each other in a lyrical meadow. "And these are Earth dogs. But all dogs are angels. Some are physical and some aren't."

"That's lovely," Roberta said. "Now, you revealed that Gary DiCaro is Andi's father after your former girlfriend gave an interview in which she claimed that Gary DiCaro had fathered Andi not by artificial insemination but in the traditional way...a fact you didn't deny."

Solange laughed, even though she had never regretted anything more than having confessed to Joie, who had betrayed her by giving detailed, tell-all interviews to anyone who would listen. After that, Solange felt she had no choice but to hide nothing. "I'm very proud that I knew Gary. He had the burstingest heart in the world."

"Did you love him?"

"I adore him. He's the father of my child."

"Your friend invited you to sleep with her husband on her wedding night."

"Lily wanted her to be conceived in the most loving way possible."

"That's quite a deep level of friendship," said Roberta.

"We love each other completely," Solange replied.

***

The interview continued against the backdrop of an interactive jamboree in which a group of disabled children was being instructed by dogs in the art of revelry. That much Lily understood. How they did it was a more complex issue; there seemed to be no line where the dogs ended and the children began but it was impossible to misread their wondrous fellowship. They informed and raised each other, and in that environment, even the most detached children responded. Tuning in to the joyous camaraderie constantly renewed Lily.

The women sat under a weeping willow on Davy's bent-cedar benches echoing the tree's graceful lines. When Roberta adjusted to a more upright position, Lily knew what would follow. "Lily, I must ask you about the stories and rumors about Gary: that he was a sexual predator, that he passed himself off as straight, that he had a bizarre sex life. What do you want to tell people? Was he gay? Was he bisexual? Did you convert him?"

"Gary is a beautiful comet who briefly lit on earth. The stories happened because no one knew what to make of him; people make up stories about things they don't understand. Gary continues to share his love. Everything else is unimportant."

"Do you believe he's here with you now?"

"Definitely," Lily said with a smile, as a blast of his scent whooshed in, a neat trick he performed for her often. "He's part of the dogs and part of the children." She inhaled deeply. "And he smells like heaven."

In the same moment, the dogs crowded into the area on the bench next to Roberta, tails whacking and whirling, noses power-sniffing.

"Can you smell him?" Lily asked.

"I do smell something," Roberta admitted, sniffing in and out of the space that a man of Gary's size might occupy. "And it does seem to be concentrated in this particular area..." Lily sensed Roberta's mind quietly blowing, making it hard for her to maintain a professional demeanor.

Leaping off their bench, Janey and Solange took in *eau de Gary.*

"That's him, all right," Solange declared.

"Couldn't resist one final interview with Roberta Landers," said Janey.

Just inside her consciousness, Lily heard Gary needing to go and she felt a sweet kiss on her cheek. "He left," she said.

"He left?" echoed Roberta, who seemed relieved.

"He felt it was a little too much for national television," Lily explained.

"But you speak to him?"

"All the time," Lily replied.

"Me too," said Solange.

"Dog House was Gary's idea," Janey said. "He's our guiding light and inspiration. None of this could have happened without him."

"Well," said Roberta, "this is all quite fantastic. How do you know it's not your imagination?"

"Imagination is as real a world as any other," Lily said. In her new multi-dimensional life, for example, she had a non-physical husband with whom she had frequent cosmic sex. Lacking the vocabulary to adequately describe that, Lily concentrated on projecting love while her brain grappled with the question. "It's hard to describe. But if you feel emotion when you 'imagine' something, that's a real feeling, and if imagination caused that, then imagination is real. That's the best I can do."

"So it's like the Eastern mystics say—life is an illusion?"

"And illusions are real," Lily said. "Just to make it more confusing." She laughed. "We can never figure it out with our minds so we think it's just best to enjoy it." She raised Giorgio in the air and he giggled on cue. "Babies and dogs have it right."

Roberta shifted her body, looking distinctly self-conscious. "Thank you. All right! We have one more person to hear from and you've all agreed that she would have the final word."

"That was her idea," said Janey. "We never argue with her. It's in our bylaws."

The camera followed the dogs and women to a large gazebo where Eleanor sat throne-like in a wicker peacock chair, cradling Bobbi Jean and waving.

"Are you waving to your fans?" Roberta asked as they approached.

"No, I'm waving to Johnny Carson. He can see me."

"He was a lovely man," Roberta said.

"He's not on TV anymore. But I am."

"Indeed you are." Roberta squeezed Eleanor's hand. "How old are you now?"

"One-o-four. And I can still dance."

In seconds, as if it was planned, which it was, Billy escorted Eleanor out of her chair and into his arms. Janey took the baby and grandmother and grandson took to the specially built dance floor and put merry twinkle toes to Guy Lombardo's sprightly ditty, "Enjoy Yourself."

Enjoy yourself, it's later than you think
Enjoy yourself, while you're still in the pink
The years go by, as quickly as a wink
Enjoy yourself, enjoy yourself, it's later than you think...

As Lily watched them dance, she divided her consciousness and sent a portion of it to Gary. In their special dimension he swept her up and they twirled across a bed of stars.

***

Watching her humans' lives bursting outward like rays of the sun, Rosalita's heart raged with love. As the humans danced they altered the prevailing smells and created happy fragrances.

The Human Training that Rosalita and her pack were conducting at Dog House was broadcast on dog frequencies all over the world. Until their project began, dogs had not realized the power of their unity.

Pioneer dogs Bean, Blossom, Fudgsicle, and Rosalita accompanied their people on dog adventures unknown to humans. They taught humans how to alter the molecules in their energy fields, to change their scent, to shift their frequencies. For the first time, humans entered canine dimensions and discovered what dogs really do all day when they appear to be so bored.

Their Human Master continued to be their intermediary, the first to cross the human-dog continuum and co-exist in both worlds. The dogs were thrilled when his scent-form appeared for their humans and delighted their guests. It was a scent that spread joy as far as hearts could imagine.

Using intervals between time so she didn't have to leave the party, Rosalita traveled to Dogstar. Her expanded self attracted loving energies from across the universe. Gathering wishes of peace and love offered her, she projected them back to her Earth family.

In the gazebo, while grandma and grandson danced and the rest of Rosalita's humans played with the babies, Fudgsicle led Bean, Blossom and Rosalita to a pile of twigs and trimmings they had collected. Marching to the melody, they laid the pieces around the humans, creating an enormous heart.

ACKNOWLEDGMENTS

My love and appreciation to my husband Thom, who makes my life possible; to the many reader-friends whose commentary helped guide this book to its birth, and to Uma and Ozzie, who taught me their deepest dog secrets.

Linda Segall Anable is a former TV writer, screenwriter, story analyst and script doctor who worked for all major Hollywood studios. Her credits include *Laverne & Shirley and Fernwood 2Night*. She is currently the editor of *The Horizon*, a Buddhist journal, and writes for numerous publications. She lives with her husband and two dogs in Portland, Oregon and has seen Bruce Springsteen in concert 57 times and counting. This is her first novel, except for the one she wrote when she was nine years old that never got published and can no longer be found.

To Uma...

1704479